The Dobie Paradox

The Dobie Paradox

Desmond Cory

St. Martin's Press
New York

Library of Congress Cataloging-in-Publication Data

Cory, Desmond.
    The Dobie paradox / Desmond Cory.
        p.   cm.
    ISBN 0-312-10969-5
    1. Mathematics teachers—Wales—Cardiff—Fiction.   2. Cardiff (Wales)—Fiction.   I. Title.
    PR6053.O774D63   1994
    823'.914—dc20   94-8219
                                                                          CIP

First published in Great Britain by Macmillan London Limited.

First U.S. Edition: August 1994
10 9 8 7 6 5 4 3 2 1

FOR DAVID
keep the fan mail coming

'I can't get out – I can't get out,' said the starling
Laurence Sterne

The Dobie Paradox

The second time around he hurt her with his hands in such a way that she knew he meant to hurt her but this was something she'd almost expected and she gasped a little but went right on doing it with him, screwing up her eyes tightly against the pain until they watered. Tonight she had for the first time come into contact – of the closest kind – with real violence, genuine violence, and in its way it was exciting, as if

all her life she'd been paddling about in a swimming pool and now here she was in the open sea, the sweeping rollers lifting her from side to side, the ship tilted over behind her on its beam ends, going down, going down, while she swam strongly towards a far-off shore, all round her other people struggling drowning in the foam-slashed waves,

'Mmmmmm-mmmmm,' she said, and then, 'Aaaaaaahhhh . . .'

and after a while the other people were gone and she was alone again as usual, beached and breathless on the shore

and a little later she rolled inelegantly off the hard and bumpy bed which was more of a couch, really, and had hurt her ribs and started to get dressed thinking, well, I made it again, it wasn't all that good but yes, exciting yes because of all that pent-up violence in him, a lot of other girls have probably found that out but they didn't matter because they were all gone now under the waves

looking down at her legs as she zipped up her short skirt and noticing the red fingermarks on her thighs that would soon be darkening into bruises, his grey slate-coloured eyes turned towards them also so for a moment she was afraid that he would want her and take her again.

'You didn't have to be so rough,' she said.

He didn't say anything. He didn't say much and when he spoke to her it was always in that flat gritty monotone which irritated her,

1

she didn't know why. He had a good body, though, for a man of his age; hard and muscular. All those press-ups and exercises he did. He'd hurt her all right.

She finished dressing quickly because she'd overstayed her time and because she wasn't wearing very much anyway. His grey eyes watched her all the time. 'So when do I see you again?'

'Better if we don't meet next week,' the man said. 'I'll phone you. Saturday.'

'You'll know by Saturday?'

Again, he didn't say anything. He reached down a hand to pick his discarded shirt up from the floor.

'You might at least talk,' she said. 'You were talking about five thousand before. That's something to talk about.'

'I'll call you. Soon as I've made the deal.'

'Five thirty. That's the best time.'

He swung his good white body off the bed, pushed back his tousled hair, using both hands. A strange gesture, that, but she'd noticed it before. 'Where do you fancy?'

'What?'

'For our holiday? Spain? Italy? Egypt? Or should we just stick a pin in a map?'

She didn't answer for a moment because the word Italy *had slipped into her now near vacant mind dripping like a golden honeycomb with the sun and the shadow of the mountains on the lake and the tup-tupping sound of a slow-moving motor-launch and once in her mind had expanded like a balloon, so fast that her mind couldn't absorb the sudden influx of images. And so in the end she didn't answer at all. She watched him pull up his trousers, buckle his snakeskin belt. He dressed very quickly, too. With him, it would be a matter of habit. She watched him open the metal cabinet that stood beside the couch. She watched him, she watched him. She found herself watching him all the time now, as he watched her, though not quite in the same way.*

'You'd better take this now,' he said.

'What?'

'The gun.'

'Oh. All right.'

It was heavier than she'd expected and when she took it from him she almost dropped it.

'Is it loaded?'

'Yes.'

But now at last his eyes had discarded her. There wasn't anything more to say or to do. The bed games were over and a new game could start. An even more violent game than the other. Oh yes, it was exciting.

She went out, hearing as she walked away the door close very softly behind her. Now she was swimming again, strongly, strongly, behind her the ship was going down

and she didn't care.

1

It had been, in Dobie's view, an unusually fine afternoon for the time of year – low-lying cloud, a little friendly drizzle, with cool pneumonia-provoking breezes drifting in from the north-east. By the early evening, however, normal climatic conditions for the Cardiff area had returned and the rain was coming down in torrents. The woods above Rhiwbina were heaving about in the grip of an Atlantic gale and the trees to either side of the road, already well in leaf, were barely visible through the blurred windscreen of Kate's battered Cortina, which chugged its way determinedly onwards with its headlights dipped against the prevailing all-enveloping fog. The roof was admitting a certain amount of freezing rainwater, much of which was dripping down on to the back of Dobie's neck, and Dobie was dispirited. He and Kate were arguing, as usual. He twiddled the volume control knob of the dashboard cassette-player to no noticeable effect; snafu, again as usual.

'He bellows, anyway.'

'He does not so.'

'Not a patch on Gigli, I assure you.'

'I don't care. He's sexy.'

On the tape the poor old Commendatore, defending his daughter's honour, was about to be run through and through by sneaky Don Giovanni. Dobie's favourite opera, but isn't it everybody's..? Except Kate's, of course. Kate preferred Verdi. Inexplicable. But they weren't arguing about that, anyway. 'He's not supposed to be sexy. He's supposed to be dying of something or other. You've got the wrong opera.'

'It's too loud anyway.'

'The knob thing won't work.'

'I *know* that. I've got to get it fixed. Look, why not switch the bloody thing off? This trip was *your* idea. Not mine.'

'It wasn't exactly *my* idea. This chap Train's, if anyone's. I don't know why he—'

'Oh, shut up, Dobie, I'm trying to *drive*.'

Staring fixedly through the smeared windscreen, where the wipers didn't seem to be working any too well, either. Instead of going flip-*flop*, flip-*flop*, they went flip-squeak. Flop. Flip-squeak. Flop. Disconcerting. Dobie turned the control knob again and he and Giovanni relapsed together into an injured silence. The argument wasn't really about Italian tenors or about car journeys undertaken in inclement weather. It was, Dobie knew full well, about his moustache, a recently acquired accoutrement to which Kate had taken totally unreasonable objection.

Everyone wore moustaches in Cyprus, the Island of Aphrodite, whence Dobie was but of late returned. At least, all the men did. The Turkish ladies there – and concretely Dobie's two honey-blonde and interminably legged assistants at the university there – had, as Dobie had discovered, a clear predilection for this unostentatious form of male adornment; the trouble was that Kate, of course, had discovered this as well and, since her feministic tendencies precluded her from admitting to an unbecoming jealousy, was now constantly making snide remarks about it. It was not true that, as she maintained, it made him look like a rat peering out from behind a lavatory brush; on the contrary, it lent a certain dignity and weight to his otherwise unremarkable features and anyway it was *his* blasted upper lip and he'd do what he liked with it. Really there were times when Kate . . .

'Whoops,' Kate said, steering into the ditch as near as dammit. Dobie removed his glasses and wiped them carefully.

'Where the hell are we, anyway?'

'*I* don't know,' Kate said. 'But if anything else breaks down we'll be up shit creek, that's where. Without a paddle. I can't see a bloody thing and what's more nor can anyone else. We haven't passed another car in ages.'

'It can't be much further,' Dobie said pacifically.

'There'll be a sign or something. Bound to be.'

Saying TONGWYNLAIS REHABILITATION CENTRE or words to that effect. Those, at any rate, had been the words heading the letter Dobie now carried in his inside coat pocket. But of course it wasn't in Tongwynlais. That would have been too easy. No, it was somewhere in that tangled confusion of narrow rutted roads crisscrossing the wilderness of woods beyond the Black Swan and leading you towards the Caerphilly mountains; only fifteen minutes out of Cardiff, yet you might as well have been out on the Brecon Beacons. The woods were two or three miles behind them now, down in the valley, and here on the bare exposed moorland the wind was tearing at them with a seemingly redoubled strength; the fog was getting thicker and the teeming rain was showing no sign of easing. Kate had slowed the speed of the car now to something like twenty miles an hour but the occasional angle of glistening grey granite walls still showed up in the tilted beam of the headlights with an alarming suddenness. 'We could go past it, just as easily. Maybe we should pull in somewhere till the rain stops.'

'I don't think it's going to. Pity we didn't start out a half-hour earlier.'

'Well, we didn't,' Kate said shortly. 'What's that light over there on the left?'

Dobie readjusted his glasses and peered out through the side window. 'Some kind of a farmhouse.'

'Ugh. Wuthering Heights, maybe.'

Kate, being a practising GP and out in all weathers, was presumably more used to this sort of thing than he was. It was almost unbelievably dark, bearing in mind that it wasn't all that late – not yet six o'clock, in fact. You could even say it was early for a social call, but then they weren't making a social call, or not exactly. On arrival, though, some kind of invigorating sustenance might well be provided for the inner man – or woman, in Kate's case – and couldn't come along too soon, as far as Dobie was concerned. This funny farm, or whatever it was, surely couldn't be very far away, always assuming they weren't on the wrong road completely, as had to be on the cards. Dobie leaned forwards in the passenger seat, gazing myopically through the swimming windscreen. Flip . . . Squeak . . . Flop. The headlights giving perhaps twenty feet of blurred visibility, the long dark streamers of rain swinging across their arc. Kate was right; you couldn't really see—

'What's that in the road?' Dobie shrilled abruptly. 'A head . . . ? I mean, ahead . . . ? Watch out you don't—'

Kate was already applying the brakes. The car, predictably, stalled. The object lying in the road a little way in front of it looked

7

more like a foot, in point of fact. They stared at it, perplexed.

'What is it?'

'Looks like a shoe,' Kate said.

'Well, what the hell of a place to leave a *shoe*. You'd think people'd have more sense than to—'

He stopped. Kate was getting out of the car. Dobie watched her run, shoulders hunched against the hurtling raindrops, to pick up the shoe and examine it for a few seconds by the light of the headlamps before returning to the car. 'It's a nice *new* shoe, Dobie. A running shoe, isn't it? A trainer?'

Dobie had seen that already. 'It's a very *wet* shoe.' It was, indeed. 'And just one shoe's not much use to anyone, is it . . . ? Even if it were your size. Which it isn't.'

'It's a pretty expensive shoe, what's more. It hasn't been thrown away, you know.' Kate was reaching into the glove compartment for her pocket torch. 'Hang on a mo.'

The car door admitted another brawling gust of wet air and a spatter of rain and Kate was gone again. Dobie, more perplexed than ever, saw the torch beam flick a pale half-moon of light along the side of the road clear of the wider pool cast by the car's headlamps, the upper part of Kate's body stooped a little and silhouetted against the semi-clarity. Surely she wasn't looking for the other one of the pair? With the rain coming down in buckets . . . ? A nice shoe maybe it was, but there have to be limits even to female rapacity. Dobie picked it up and looked at it but it didn't tell him anything. It was true that in Cyprus (and quite by accident) Dobie had discovered an important clue inside a lady's shoe, but there was nothing inside this one. Not even a foot. Indeed, but for its small size it could just as easily have been a man's; *all* the kids wore these things nowadays . . .

Kate had stopped by the side of the road, was stooping down even lower. She might even be kneeling. What *was* she up to . . . ? Dobie sighed and clambered out of the car, tugging the collar of his raincoat a little tighter around his neck. It didn't help much. He moved forwards a few paces and then saw what Kate was looking at.

'Oh my God,' he said.

'It's a nasty one.'

'Yes.'

'But she's still alive.'

She didn't look it. But that was probably an effect of the torch-light, of the open mouth and those widely staring eyes. 'Here, hold the torch for a minute, Dobie.'

'All right.'

He stood with his head lowered in the pouring rain, watching Kate's quick neat fingers moving over the bedraggled body, over the small dark-haired head. He saw that the other shoe was in place on her left foot, at the end of a straight and stiffened leg, a long bare leg, nicely shaped. 'Try and hold it steady. If you can.'

'Yes. Sorry.'

He moved a little nearer, but the torch beam went on trembling. After a few seconds Kate's hands withdrew but she stayed as she was, in a kneeling position, staring into the pale upturned face. 'Fractured skull. Could be some spinal trauma, too. There often is. We have to get her to hospital.'

'Hospital. Yes.' Well, you didn't have to be a doctor to see that. The kid looked ghastly, whoever she was.

'Think you can get her into the car? There must be *some* place near by where we can ring for an ambulance. Try not to move her head any more than you can help it.'

Dobie handed back the torch and Kate held it in her smaller but steadier hand as Dobie bent down to pick the girl up, feeling, as he lifted her, the impact of the heavy raindrops on his back and shoulders. It was really pelting down, but for the last sixty seconds or so he hadn't been aware of it. Carrying her over to the car wasn't so difficult. Dobie was a big man and the girl was small and light . . . and very, very cold. Dobie supported her head as he carried her, one hand at the nape of her neck, and the tendrils of hair that fell across his wrist felt like feathery icicles. The only tricky bit was manoeuvring her on to the back seat; Kate had pulled off her raincoat to serve as an improvised pillow and arranged the placing of the girl's head on it with some care. The dark hair was smeared with blood as well as damp with water, and two or three tiny green leaves were stuck to it; Kate flicked them away and directed the torch once again towards the ragged wound underneath. 'I'll stay in the back with her, Dobie. You drive.'

Dobie climbed obediently into the driver's seat, restarted the motor and engaged first gear, letting the car move cautiously forwards. 'Best if I go slowly, I suppose.'

'Yes. But don't waste any time about it, either. It looks pretty touch-and-goish to me. Just don't have any accidents is all.'

'Is that what this . . . was? An accident?'

'Hit and run, if so.'

'How did you know? I mean, what made you think . . . ?'

'It happens that way sometimes.' Coming from the back of the car, Kate's voice had a curious disembodied quality, as though she, also, had been pre-recorded on rather poor quality tape. 'Car swerves a bit too late, impact comes at an angle, shoe comes off and goes one way, body goes the other. Had a case rather like it up Roath way while you were in Cyprus, only that was an old geezer who'd had one too many at the local and this is just a . . .'

'Kid.'

'Yes. And unless we get her into intensive care pretty quick, the chances are she won't get to be much older.'

'Did the cops find the guy who did it? The other one? Who was on the case?'

'Jacko. No. They often don't. Hit and run capers are murder.'

'Yes,' Dobie said. 'I suppose they are. Or manslaughter, anyway.'

'Metaphorically, I meant. From Jacko's point of view. Unless there's a witness and a licence number, or part of one . . . it's pretty hopeless.'

No cars, no lights, no movement. Nothing. Only the wind and the rain and a glimpse in the reflected headlights of open moorland. Dobie had pushed the speed up to thirty-five, which was as fast a pace as he cared to risk; he was a professor of mathematics, not Nigel Whatsit, and his eyesight wasn't . . . Something over there on the left, another stone wall, maybe? But there didn't seem to be anything behind it, no buildings or anything like that. There did seem to be a small gap in the lowering clouds over there to the east, but the sky elsewhere was dark as pitch. The road was slippery but not too bumpy. No apparent end to it, though. It went on for ever, like a road in someone's nightmare. That was the trouble.

'Reminded you of something, did it, Dobie?'

'Well, yes. She . . . Sorry about that.'

'That's OK.' Kate's hand came over the back of the seat to rest lightly on Dobie's right shoulder. 'Look, with any luck we can save this one. We may be just in time. While if you hadn't seen that shoe on the road . . . It'll be a plus score for you, is what I'm getting at.'

'Bloody hell, *I'd* have driven on. I wouldn't have thought . . .' Dobie over-braked in sudden agitation, the car tyres skidding slightly on the wet tarmac. 'Hey. Here we go. A house. A light. This may do us.'

And a large sign saying, TONGWYNLAIS REHABILITATION CENTRE. They had arrived, at last. Dobie turned the car into the driveway with its bonnet nudging the heavy iron gates that barred the entrance, put his finger on the horn button and kept it there. It wasn't, as he now saw, a house but some kind of a porter's lodge. After some twenty seconds of ear-splitting blare the door was flung open and a thin young man in some kind of uniform emerged. If, that is, a peaked cap and a high-collared grey jacket constituted a uniform, as it might well, Dobie thought, nowadays. 'OK, OK, OK. Where's the fire?'

'No fire,' Dobie said. 'An accident. Girl's been hit by a car. We need some help.' Dobie, though innately prone to maunder, could be surprisingly cogent on occasions.

'Well, we got doctors here all right. But this ain't a hospital.'

'*I'm* a doctor.' Kate was out of the car already. 'What I need is a telephone.'

'Ah. Well, that we can manage. Come on in then, Doctor.'

In the absence of further precise instructions, Dobie decided he'd do best to stay in the car; Kate would of course know what numbers to ring and so forth. His arms felt curiously stiff and he took his hands off the steering-wheel to rest them on his knees, listening to the rather asthmatic turning-over of the motor and staring at the metal plaque affixed to the iron gates directly in front of him. It said, like the other and larger notice,

TONGWYNLAIS REHABILITATION CENTRE
Director: Morris J. Train

Dobie, as he quite well recalled, had an appointment with this guy Train. An appointment he was going to be late for. He recalled this, however, without any perception of its relevance to his present situation, which was that of a man sitting in the driving

11

seat of a stationary car in front of a closed iron gate – a man, moreover, whose hands for some reason wouldn't stop trembling. He wasn't, after all, the only occupant of the car.

Yes, Dobie had been reminded of something all right. That open mouth, those blindly staring eyes. And those loose tendrils of wet hair . . . Dobie's wife had looked very like that the last time he had ever seen her, and it's not only roads that people sometimes see in nightmares. Of course this kid was far younger than Jenny, there wasn't really any facial or physical resemblance, it was clever of Kate to have seen that he'd nevertheless been . . . But then for all her intense practicality, Kate had her feminine intuitions, which seemed, at least where Dobie was concerned, to verge at times on the telepathic. She might even have sensed that while carrying the girl to the car Dobie had become vaguely aware of certain things that in the circumstances a true British gentleman shouldn't, perhaps, have become aware of, the zip of her blue waterproof windcheater having slipped some five or six inches too far open. . . . She might be wearing something underneath but it hadn't seemed to be very much. Hadn't *felt* like very much. That had to be why the kid was so damned cold, the smooth skin like ice against the palms of his hands. How long had she been there? Strange no one had spotted her before. . . .

Dobie wriggled himself round in the seat to stare nervously at the slim figure slumped across the back seat. Touch-and-goish, Kate had said. He wished she'd hurry up. In the dimness of the car interior he couldn't be sure if the girl was breathing or not, but he could see her face fairly clearly in the light leaking through from the porch lamp and it seemed to be calm and relaxed; placid, almost. . . . *Much* younger than Jenny. Good Heavens, a schoolgirl, probably. Sixteen? Seventeen? No more, surely . . . ? Dobie turned back in the seat and looked instead towards the half-open door of the porter's lodge. Hurry *up*, Kate. . . .

She came out, walking quickly, and got into the car, this time beside him. As she did so the iron gates, obviously under electronic control, began to swing open. 'Couple of hundred yards up the drive there's a bungalow on the left. Should be a Duty Medical Officer there, someone like that. Porter's ringing him now. Come on, Dobie, what are we waiting for?'

Dobie grunted and edged the car forwards again. Here at least there were lampposts casting an orange glow, a reasonably well-lit driveway; the bungalow in question came into view as soon as they had passed through the gates. 'Did you get an ambulance?'

'Yes, but it may be twenty minutes before it gets here. The cops may get here quicker.'

'The cops?'

'I rang the CID Room direct. Foxy Boxy. He says they'll be right over.'

'But there hasn't been a *crime*, has there?'

Kate sighed. 'Be your age, Dobie. An unreported accident's a crime, of course it is. And in this case, a pretty serious one. That kid could be *dead*, you know, for all some bugger cares about it. There could be brain damage. . . . Anything. Of *course* it's a crime.'

'All right,' Dobie said. 'I was only—'

'Here on the left.'

'Yes, yes, *OK*.'

He pulled up just clear of the unlatched front gate, which was swinging to and fro in the wind, and Kate was out of the car before he had switched the ignition off. 'Bring her in then, Dobie.' *Tote* that barge. *Lift* that bale. 'Yessuh ma'am, Ah sho will, ma'am,' Dobie said. Scarlett O'Hara was already half-way up the gravel pathway and couldn't have heard him. Dobie, following her at a sedater pace and bearing his burden, saw the front door of the bungalow come open and a girlish figure appear as within a frame, silhouetted in the seemingly sharp light of the entrance hall. 'Daddy's on the telephone. But do come in.' Dobie did so and stood for a moment blinking on the doormat. 'Where should I . . . ?'

'Oh golly, yes, in Daddy's study, please. It's this way.'

His hostess of the moment, who might have been some two or three years younger than the girl he was carrying and hence might be accounted to have conducted matters so far with considerable aplomb, conducted them down a narrow pink-carpeted passageway and opened a door at the far end with a mildly theatrical flourish. Beyond the door was a small book-lined room with a desk, a swivel chair, and, in the far corner, a single bed with a blue coverlet and a thick spring mattress. 'Daddy said it's OK to use the bed and he'll be coming himself in just a minute, he's calling the dispensary just in case.' This, in a single breath and in a tone pitched slightly above the level of a whisper. In her clear, fresh teenager's voice, the end result was surprisingly audible.

'Fine,' Kate said. 'I'll need blankets, towels, hot water. Can you manage that?'

'Oh yes. No problem. You're the doctor?'

'I'm the doctor.'

'Dr Coyle, I think you said.' Someone bustling busily into the room from behind her. 'Right. That's the patient?'

'That's the victim.'

'Yes. She should be all right on that bed if you'll just . . . lower her . . . gently. . . . That's the way. Oh dear, yes. That *does* look rather nasty.'

The little room seemed to be suddenly full of people charging this way and that. Kate taking off her raincoat. The dark-haired child pulling open a squeaky chest of drawers, over in the corner. The new arrival, portly, balding, forty-fiveish, moving forwards to peer down at the victim's upturned face. Dobie, deprived of his role as a means of transport, stood still and did nothing. The girl on the bed did nothing, too.

'Severe cranial trauma, obviously.'

'And probable haemorrhage. Compound fracture of the ulna, quite a few minor contusions . . .'

'Pulse?'

'Weak. Very weak. Dobie? Outside, if you don't mind. We're going to get these wet clothes off her.' Kate, already removing the remaining shoe, stooping to chafe the small bare foot vigorously between her hands. 'Hypothermia's about to set in. If you could attend to that dressing while I—'

'Kate?'

Dobie, too, was staring down at the upturned face on the pillow. Arched eyebrows, the thin line of the nose, the suddenly prominent cheekbones. The face was the same as it had been a few moments before, but in another way it wasn't. Kate didn't seem to have heard him, either because her attention was riveted elsewhere or because Dobie, unlike the other girl, hadn't spoken very clearly or distinctly. He swallowed and tried again. 'What's happening your end, Kate?'

She didn't look up. 'Look, be a good chap, Dobie—'

'. . . Because I think mine's gone.'

'What . . . ?' She raised her head then, quite abruptly, to look first at Dobie and then towards the face of the victim. For a few seconds her hands went on rubbing, rubbing, rubbing, but then

14

her eyebrows lifted slightly and she straightened up and took her hands away and then stepped back. It was the portly chap who picked up the dead girl's wrist and, almost at once, dropped it again. He nodded slowly but didn't say anything.

Nobody said anything.

Dobie felt sad, on Kate's behalf. Of course it was as she'd said – a victim, not a patient. But it was one that she'd lost, all the same. He felt a little contrite on his own account, also. 'I'm sorry. I tried to be as careful as I could but—'

'No, no, no,' the portly fellow said. 'Nothing to do with the way you handled her. Or I shouldn't think so.' Since it wasn't this chap's reassurance but Kate's that Dobie required, he didn't find this altogether satisfying. But Kate still wasn't saying anything. The door opened and closed as the dark-haired girl left the room, probably in obedience to some unseen gesture by her father; not until then did Kate speak. To the portly chap, not to Dobie.

'The police'll be on their way here as well. So I'm afraid this is going to put you to some inconvenience.'

'That's all right. All right in the sense that it's only to be expected.' He was wearing at a somewhat corkscrew angle some kind of a regimental tie, the Buff Orpingtons or something like that, and this, looking at Kate, he now straightened. 'Didn't have time for the social niceties, did we? My name's Mighell. Robert Mighell. *Your* name's familiar to me but I don't think we ever met. Rather believe you're the police pathologist for the district, aren't you?'

'Paddy Oates is the full-time pathologist. But I help out.'

'Saw your name in the papers, I seem to remember, in connection with that extraordinary Dobie business. Frightful feller who killed his wife. I don't know if the police—'

'Yes, sorry, this by the way *is* Professor Dobie.'

'Oh. Pleased to meet you.' Mighell extended a hand towards Dobie without, as the saying has it, turning a hair. No doubt these minor social solecisms pass unregarded, Dobie thought, amongst people who work in a loony-bin, which was what, after all, this place was. Well, more or less. Having thus saluted Dobie, Mighell immediately returned his attention to Kate, which however unflattering was perfectly understandable. 'Well, I don't know if in the circumstances you'll want to carry out any further examination of the, ah . . . victim. . . .'

'Paddy'll be doing the PM in due course. Probably tomorrow.

But meantime,' Kate said, 'there *are* one or two points I'm curious about and which the police might like to know when they get here. They're going to be looking for a hit-and-run merchant, as seems to be reasonably certain, and I'm told that in these cases their chances of collaring the culprit disappear almost hour by hour. Of course, they'd find a second professional opinion very welcome, that's if you can spare a few more minutes of your time. . . .'

'Certainly. Pleased. Delighted. Though you'll realize that I haven't too much experience in this field.' Kate, however, was now restored to her customary business-as-usual attitude and seemed prepared to ignore this disclaimer; at any rate, she was now purposefully re-approaching the bed and the quietly recumbent corpse. '*You* still here, Dobie?'

'Well, yes, I am. Just going, though. Sorry.'

He realized that Kate's brusqueness arose in part from some kind of concern as to his reactions; Dobie wasn't at ease with corpses these days, especially young ladies' corpses. (Not, of course, that many people are.) But he wasn't about to throw a wingding or anything like that. He made his way back down the passageway to where a half-open door and the sound of some male pop vocalist, not loud but very hoarse and raspy, seemed to indicate the position of the sitting-room. Dobie went in. The dark-haired girl was, he saw, sitting in an armchair by the unlit gas fire and staring straight in front of her. She was quite a tall girl for her age, or for what Dobie assumed to be her age, but something about the posture she'd adopted made her seem smaller than she really was . . . if that made sense.

'May I come in?'

She looked up, not abruptly as had Kate but slowly and cautiously, as though adjusting her thoughts to some new and unexpected aspect of reality. 'Oh yes. Rather. I mean, please do. Come in and sit down.' And as Dobie was doing this, 'You see, I thought *you* were the doctor.'

'Oh no,' Dobie said. 'No. Nothing like that.'

'I suppose Bev – Beverley – I suppose she's . . . ?'

'Yes,' Dobie said. 'Yes, she's dead.'

Death could perhaps be called that, he thought. A new and unexpected aspect of. . . . Especially when you're fourteen years old, or thereabouts. But also when you're older. Much older. It shouldn't ever be unexpected, but it is, almost always, and whatever age you happen to be, it's not the sort of thing you tell pointless lies about. Because that's what it is. A part of reality. An aspect of it. Though not one that you can usefully say very much about to a teenaged girl, or to anyone else. Aware that his own reflections were becoming slightly unhinged, Dobie grabbed hurriedly for the only immediate conversational prop with which he'd conveniently been provided. 'You *know* her, then?'

'She goes to my school.'

'Really?'

'Yes, only she's a boarder and I'm a day-bug. And of course she's a Senior and I'm only Middle School.'

'I see.' Dobie nodded sagely. He guessed that this youthful creature found the use of the present tense in these circumstances to be comforting, if only because familiar; he felt rather the same way about it himself. 'And you're . . .'

'Five B.'

'No, I meant your . . . name. . . .'

'Oh. Sorry. Elspeth Mighell. How do you do.'

'How do you do. Yes. My name's Dobie.'

'But *her* name is Cole.'

'Coyle.'

'So you're not married.'

'No.'

'Oh, well, that's all right,' Elspeth Mighell said.

Dobie was relieved to hear this. The touch of formality that had entered the conversation, however, seemed to have reminded Elspeth of her duties as a hostess, such as she conceived of them. 'Can I offer you something, Dobie?'

'Eh?'

'Tea? Coffee? Lemonade? Or maybe a Coke?'

Dobie considered these tempting alternatives for a moment. 'You haven't anything a wee bit stronger? To keep the chill out?'

'Well. . . . We have to keep all that stuff locked up, you see, and Daddy's got the key. I could ask him for it if you like—'

'No, no, he's busy now, don't bother. Is it *fizzy* lemonade?'

'You bet. Burpy as anything.'

'Then I'd like a fizzy lemonade.'

'Right you are. I think,' Elspeth said grandly, 'I may join you.'

'That would be nice,' Dobie said.

He stretched out his legs and, while his hostess was fetching this filthy concoction, surveyed his surroundings, abandoning this pursuit a few moments later in favour of the less strenuous one of closing his eyes. A polite little girl, he thought. And nicely spoken, if a little over-conscientious in her enunciation. A fault in the right direction, anyway, given this modern tendency of the kids to mumble as though their mouths were filled with chewing-gum. Quite a number of them seemed to have their brains filled with chewing-gum as well, but that made a clear and correct form of diction all the more desirable. There didn't seem to be many schools nowadays where. . . .

School. Same school, she'd said. It must, Dobie reflected have been a bit of a shock for the kid, seeing a school pal brought into her house like that; even if you *are* a day-bug it can't be very nice. . . . But Mighell hadn't seemed to recognize her. Well, no real reason why he should have, schoolgirls tend to look pretty much alike and besides, if what's-her-name was a boarder she probably wouldn't have. . . . But the police would want an ID when they got here, wouldn't they? So that could be established right away, except that he'd already forgotten. . . . Some weird name suggestive of a canned fruit juice or effervescent liquid such as he was about to be offered . . . was *being* offered. . . .

'Sorry. Just closed my eyes for a moment. Warm in here. Er. . . . Thanks.'

Bev. That was it. Beverley something.

'I hope it's fizzy enough. The bottle popped all right when I opened it.'

Dobie tried a cautious sip and closed his eyes again, more briefly. 'Delicious,' he declared.

'Oh good. Sorry about the hard stuff but I'm sure Daddy'll give you a jolly good snifter when he's finished whatever it is he's . . .'

'Why d'you keep it locked up?'

'The booze, you mean . . . ? Oh, we have to. In case anyone breaks in and scoffs the lot or maybe makes off with it. We've got alcoholics here, you see, as well as drug addicts, and as they've all got criminal records already, well, Morris Train's very strict about that. We even had to get in special padlocks. No one's ever actually *done* it, though, that I'm aware of.'

Good Heavens. Morris Train. . . . Dobie looked at his wrist-watch. 'Oh, you know Mr Train, then?'

'Of course I know him. Very well. He's Daddy's boss. He lives in that big house just up the road and Daddy's screwing his wife.'

'*F'fffffff,*' Dobie said.

The fizzy lemonade had not been a good idea. He mopped with his handkerchief at his moustache, where the greater part of his last mouthful had arrived via his nostrils. 'I suppose,' he said eventually, 'your mother can't be any too pleased about that.'

'Oh, she couldn't care less. She lives in Canada now. They're divorced.'

'Ah. Then *that*'s all right, too.'

'No, it isn't, actually. I think there'll be trouble there before long. Mind you . . . she's very nice. I like her. She's what the French call *sympathique*.'

'I was never any good at French,' Dobie said. 'Not much good at English either, for that matter.'

'What *were* you good at, then?'

'Well. . . . Maths, mostly. I still am. I mean, I try to teach it.'

'I get pretty good marks at maths.'

'Do you really?'

'But I hate those . . . whatchacallum . . . differential equations. . . .'

'Ah yes. Nasty little things. But then there'd be no point in doing them if they weren't difficult.'

'What's the *most* difficult thing?'

'Paradox, probably.'

'What's that?'

'It's when two things that must be true can't *both* be true.'

'Come again?'

'Well,' Dobie said. 'Say you're given that God can do anything He likes . . . and you define the concept that way, just to be on the safe side . . . and then you ask yourself, "Can He create a stone that's too heavy for Him to lift?" . . . Well, then on the one hand—'

'He could create it all right but then He couldn't lift it.'

'No, that won't work because—'

'Right. Yes. So what's the answer?'

'There isn't one. Unless you can imagine Him creating it *at the same time* as He's lifting it. That's possible because *everything* happens at the same time as far as God's concerned. He exists *outside* time, so to speak. So you have to assign a new set of figures that'll take that into account and then incorporate that set into the other lot. Then you've established what's called a continuum and that's the object of the exercise.'

'What about God being supposed to be good and all that?'

Yes. Well. . . . 'You see, good and bad are *temporal* concepts, they have to do with cause and effect and things happening because of something else . . . and we've just gone and eliminated cause and effect, you see, from the equation. Unfortunately,' Dobie said, 'just about the whole of traditional physics is based on cause and effect, too, the laws of gravity and thermodynamics and everything. So we're out on a bit of a limb these days. Mathematicians are. Or *some* of us are, anyway.'

'But are you *doing* any good to anybody?'

'We can't tell that, can we? I suppose it should all make things like *that*' – Dobie nodded towards the other room – 'a bit easier to bear. Help you to see it in a wider perspective. And so on.'

'But does it?'

'No. Not really.'

He was aware that in the usual way he'd contrived to give the conversation a wrong turning, reminding the kid of exactly what he'd intended to divert her mind from. But she, too, seemed to have become aware of something, and almost with alarm. 'Oh gosh. . . .'

'What's the matter?'

'The music.'

The cassette-player was still emitting those weird noises, it was true. 'Why, what is it?'

'Michael Bolton. I should have turned it off, shouldn't I?'

'You mean because of . . .' Dobie considered the point. 'Oh, I don't know. *She*'d have liked it, would she?'

'Most of the kids like Michael Bolton.'

'Well, there you go.'

'Shall I leave it on, then?'

'Why not?'

'It's pretty near the end of the tape, anyway.'

Most ethical discussions, in Dobie's opinion, tended to take place near the end of the tape, when it's too late to matter much either way. In the present case, since Michael Bolton – whoever he was – wasn't, again in Dobie's opinion, a patch on Gigli either, or even on Pavarotti, the conclusion of these mournful caterwaulings should be regarded as a welcome event; really it was extraordinarily odd, though undoubtedly an empirically observable fact, that nowadays not only the kids but older and responsible people, such as Kate . . . *de gustibus*, yes, of course, but even so . . . though there couldn't be any point in moving the direction of the conversation towards such intractable issues or indeed any other now that the tape in fact had ended, enabling him to listen instead to the soporific tapping of raindrops on the curtained-off window panes, a sound that can best be appreciated, of course, with the eyelids gently lowered and the head . . . comfortably . . . resting . . . on the back of a well-cushioned armchair. . . .

'Mr Dobie?'

'Yum,' Dobie said.

'Mr *Dobie. . . .*'

'Yum?' Opening his eyes effortfully, Dobie perceived that the pop. of the sitting room had been recently increased by exactly fifty per cent, Dr Whatname having apparently effected an entry while he himself had been . . . doing what?. . . . Yes, listening to the raindrops. Of course. What else? But what was he . . . Ah yes. 'Yum?'

Dr Whoozit was, he thought, looking rather tired and puffy-eyed, though this could hardly be in consequence of over-indulgence in that form of activity to which his daughter had alluded in passing, it being surely too early in the evening for. . . . Though you never could tell with these bloody doctors. 'Sorry, sorry,' Dobie said, struggling ineffectively to sit upright. 'Just pursuing a rather complex train of thought and what with one thing and another—'

'Mr Dobie,' Elspeth said, nobly backing him up, 'knows all about differential equations, Daddy, and about a lot of other things I don't think I'm quite ready for yet but we've been having a most *illuminating* conversation.'

'I'm very pleased to hear it.' Tired, puffy-eyed, and a little flustered. He had, it seemed, just realized he was still wearing his surgical gloves and he was now stripping them off with well-practised but none the less obviously nervous jerks. 'But I'm afraid you'll have to continue it some other time because Dr Coyle tells me that Mr Dobie has an extremely important appointment with the Director, which he's now twenty minutes late for. I'm extremely sorry about that, Mr Dobie, but of course I had no idea. . . . Anyway I've just called him and advised him of the circumstances and he tells me he can still fit you in if you'd be good enough to make your way to his house as soon as possible. . . .'

'But shouldn't I wait till the police get here? In case they want to ask me any questions?'

'No, Dr Coyle says she can handle all that side of things perfectly well and in any case they'll know where to find you if they want you. It should be a routine enquiry, after all. Now if you'll excuse me once again, there are still just one or two details that we have to. . . . You'll have no trouble in finding the house. Elspeth will direct you.'

'I'll come with you, if you like.'

Dobie shook his head, listening now to the sound of the doctor's footsteps retreating down the passageway – a much less comforting sound, somehow, than that of the raindrops. 'No, no. I'll manage.' *A routine enquiry*, well, OK, but Kate had to have been in there for all of twenty minutes. Surely if you get knocked over by a car—

'It's no bother.'

'No, look.' Dobie was already on his feet. 'When the police get here, you should tell them you know who . . . who she is because they'll want to know that right away. Just tell them that her name's Beverley . . . Beverley. . . .'

'Sutro.'

'Yes, Beverley Sutro and she goes to school with you. They won't want to ask you any questions or I don't think so but if they do, I'm pretty sure you can handle them. Absolutely nothing to be *afraid* of, of course. It's been a pleasure meeting you, Beverley.'

'Elspeth.'

'I mean Elspeth, and having such an interesting talk. But it looks like I have to be running along.'

'Yes, but—'

'And I just may be seeing you again later. Ta-ta, then.'

'But Mr Dobie—'

Conscious of having handled his vital witness with a coolness and expertise that would surely have done credit to Marshall Hall, Dobie marched stoutly away towards the front door. Opening it, he perceived that it was still pissing down. No matter. The child's anxiety to detain him was flattering, of course, but business was business. He marched stoutly down the pathway to the parked car and then, after a moment's hesitation, turned and marched stoutly back again to the front door. He rang the doorbell. Elspeth opened the door almost immediately.

'Er,' Dobie said. 'Yes. Where am I—'

'Second left, first right, and it's straight in front of you.'

'Oh, right. Thanks.'

'You're welcome.'

Dobie was a little peeved as he drove off into the prevailing murk. He knew very well why Kate had wanted him out of the way before the boys in blue arrived and, though of course she meant well, he resented it. Just because on a previous occasion he had been, very understandably, a little confused and distrait when questioned by the police, she seemed to have formed the ridiculous impression that he was in some way an unsatisfactory witness. No idea could be more preposterous. If she. . . . If she really supposed. . . . He leaned forwards, peering through the windscreen. The weather conditions seemed if anything to have worsened since the time of their arrival; even with the overhead lamps it was really almost impossible. . . . Ah. The wipers. Dobie switched them on.

Flip. Squeak. Flop.

That was better. Here it was. Coming up. Second right. Dobie braked cautiously and effected the turning. This place was much larger than he had anticipated. Probably one of those old country estates, like Duffryn Gardens, converted to a rather different use. Another house there, but that wasn't the one. He had now to take the first turning on the left and the Director's residence would then appear directly in front of him, bang on schedule. Here we go, then. . . .

Oh.

That was funny. . . .

He braked again. No house to be seen. Those large iron gates, on the other hand, seemed to be somehow familiar. Dobie sighed heavily. Why even an apparently intelligent child couldn't nowadays give you a clear and simple set of directions was beyond him. No wonder she couldn't do differential equations. Indeed she probably couldn't even work out an elementary trigonometrically based vector analysis. The whole country's educational system was obviously going to pot. He'd often thought so.

However. . . .

Dobie executed a laborious U-turn in reverse gear (a manoeuvre he'd invented himself) and urged his steed forwards again. Five minutes later he brought it to a foaming halt outside Dr Mighell's house once more.

Somehow he didn't feel like marching stoutly up to the front door again. He'd done enough stout marching for the time being. Help from another source, in any case, appeared to be at hand, in the unlikely shape of a scantily clad jogger belting steadily along through the heavily falling sleet. Though the chances were obviously high that this gentleman would prove to be an inmate rather than a member of the staff of this establishment. Dobie felt desperate enough to wind down the window and hail him and the jogger slowed obligingly to a panting halt.

'Mr Train?'

'No, no. Just taking some exercise.'

Dobie, his suspicions confirmed, was about to turn regretfully away when he realized that his words had been given a different interpretation to that which he had intended. It was amazing how often . . . 'No, Mr *Train*, I mean I'm looking for Mr Train's *house*. Can you tell me where to find it?'

'Certainly. Take the second on the left, first right, and Bob's your uncle. Unless someone's gone and moved it since this morning.'

'But I've just *tried* that,' Dobie complained. 'And it wasn't—'

'I can show you if you don't mind your car seat getting a trifle damp. It's a little bit wetter out here than I'd thought. I like to get in a daily spin but I'd just as soon—'

'No, no, that's all right.' Dobie swung open the offside door and the jogger, still panting like an over-exerted dachshund, clambered in. His track suit was indeed so drenched that it squelched as he sat down and his dark hair was plastered so close to his skull that he looked like a seal emerging from an Atlantic roller, a resemblance which his long thin inquisitively twitching nose accentuated. 'Take it you haven't been here before. Believe it or not, there's a wonderful view from here on a clear evening. You can see to the Severn Bridge and well beyond.'

Dobie set the car in motion once again. Kate, he thought, would have to sit in the back when they returned, in view of the large puddle now forming on the front passenger seat. Well, serve her right. 'No,' he said. 'I haven't been here before.' Refraining from adding the obvious corollary.

'You're not. . . .' His passenger paused, clearly struck by a sudden and novel idea. 'You're not the chap who's come to see Adrian Seymour?'

'I'm supposed to see Mr Train *about* Adrian Seymour. I'm not a relative, though. Or anything like that.'

'But you knew him in Cyprus.'

'I *met* him in Cyprus. Seymour, that is. Not Mr Train.'

'And you teach at the University.'

'Yes, I do. Or did. Not right now. I mean I'm officially supposed to be still on secondment, you see, in Cyprus, only I'm not in Cyprus any more. I'm back here.'

'Ah. Horatio Carter.'

'Don't think I know him.'

'No, *I'm* Horatio Carter.'

'Ah. Dobie.'

'Sorry?'

'That's my name. John Dobie.'

'Right. We'll be releasing him soon, you see.'

No. Dobie didn't. 'Who will? Releasing whom? Why?'

'Adrian Seymour. On probation, of course.'

'I see,' Dobie said. But again, he didn't really. 'How long has he been here now?' There seemed to be trees over on his left, or something that *looked* like trees, but. . . . It was difficult, of course, to drive on a night like this and hold intelligent converse at the same time. If that was what he was doing.

'Six weeks. The minimum time, but they dried him out pretty well in the Dene before he came here and we reckon he's about as clean as he'll ever be. Possibly shouldn't have come here at all, because . . . Here's your turning. On the right. The *right*. That's it. . . . Because our people are in for drug-related offences, or supposed to be, and Adrian's a straightforward junkie, in so far as they're ever . . . Mind that lamppost! Whoooops . . . ! Well done. . . . In so far as they're ever straightforward, I was going to say. There was never anything to that other business. Adrian never murdered anyone. Absurd to suppose it.'

'The trouble was, he signed a confession.'

'Yes, I know, but that's quite usual in these cases of hallucinatory dementia. I don't suppose they have many such cases in Cyprus, but even so . . . Yes, now if you take this left-hand turn that's coming up you'll see the Director's house right in front of you. A cul-de-sac, you see.' Dobie, squinting through the windscreen, sighed with relief. Yes, there it was, sure enough. The tyres hissed noisily in the puddles as he brought the car to a halt. 'Not so difficult, was it?'

'No, indeed. It's these weather conditions, of course, which . . . But anyway, I'm much obliged to you. My name is Dobie, by the way.'

'I know.'

'Really? We've met before?'

'Don't think so. No, you just told me.'

'I did?'

'Yes. You did. And I'll be, ah, sprinting back to a hot bath now, if you don't mind.'

'Of course. Thanks very much, Doctor um er . . . Doctor. . . .'

Dobie watched Doctor um er's long hairy legs receding rhythmically in the light of the dimmed headlamps and then, reluctantly, got out of the car himself. He couldn't, after all, get much wetter than he was already.

He was also well aware that, apart from being wet, he was very far tonight from being on the ball (as Elspeth might have put it), the sad demise of her schoolmate Beverley Sutro having possibly shaken him up more than he'd realized. He was therefore considerably relieved to be at last offered, almost immediately after effecting his entry into the house, a sizeable snifter by the *sympathique* Mrs Train, who also relieved him of his hat and raincoat. She had, Dobie observed, the peculiar slanting eyes that he had always associated with Thai bar-girls (not that he had ever encountered a Thai bar-girl, other than in his wildest fancies), enabling her to cast sidelong glances from under her eyelashes while in a full-frontal position, evincing in Dobie a sudden desire to roll feebly over on to his back waving his paws in the air. Being, perhaps fortunately, seated in an armchair at the time he was able to resist the impulse and to focus his attention instead upon the words being at the moment uttered by the lady's husband. Far from casting sidelong glances at anything or anybody, Train apparently had the habit of fixing his eyes, as he spoke, on a point on the ceiling directly above the head of the person addressed (in this case, Dobie), either to indicate the profundity of his thought or, more probably, in order to evade the unpleasing spectacle of Dobie dripping rainwater over his expensively upholstered armchair.

26

In other respects he had the overall appearance of a retired Army officer of the old Imperial school and his voice had the fruity overtones suggestive of the regular consumption of innumerable post-prandial bottles of VSOP, ordered no doubt by the old Imperial gallon. Though in fact it was whisky that Dobie was currently sampling, and not at all a bad whisky at that. '. . . What a very unfortunate occurrence. Of course it's a dangerous road, as I've often pointed out, and on a night like this. . . . People drive too damned fast along it, that's another thing.'

Really a rather decent little whisky, and Train's was really rather a decent little study. More of an old-fashioned gentleman's den, in fact, and as such somewhat cluttered up with bric-à-brac, but Dobie – glancing around him – could perceive nothing that might be closely connected with anything so vulgar as your actual *work*. No portraits of Sigmund Freud hanging on the walls, or of Her Majesty the Queen. There was, it is true, a silver-framed portrait of Mrs Train on the highly polished desk in the far corner but that could hardly be connected with work, either, other than in the sense of doubtless being nice if you could get it. The original of the portrait, having fulfilled her wifely duties with the whisky decanter, was still hovering gracefully by the carved oak sideboard, concerned to see her guest comfortably settled in before beating a retreat or/and at the same time indulging her feminine curiosity.

'There's a school sign further up the road,' she said, 'but often people just don't see it.'

'That's right. That's right. Perhaps this incident will at least serve the purpose of drawing their attention. . . . But then it always seems to need some such disaster as this to wake the authorities up to reality, that's the devil of it.'

'It's a private school, of course. And a girls' school at that. I'll bet that if the County Council—'

'Well, but let's not bring politics into *everything*. The girl's dead, that's the point.'

'And you do have other matters to discuss,' Mrs Train said, pouting in her evident reluctance to withdraw from such stimulating company, 'so I'll leave you to discuss them. Perhaps Mr Dobie would like a little more whisky?'

'Well. . . . Thank you. . . . It *is* a little chilly out there.'

'Especially as you had such trouble in getting here. It's so lucky you managed to run over . . . run into Dr Carter, the place really is an absolute rabbit warren. Just a top-up for you, darling?'

'Eh . . . ? Oh well. I don't mind if I do.' Dobie had been *hoping* he'd say that. Grasping his own laden tumbler firmly in one hand, he rose politely as the lady of the house effected a sinuous exit; sat down again and lowered the tumbler's contents appreciably while Train went on staring morosely at the ceiling. 'Yes. Good feller, young Carter. And a promising clinical psychiatrist, or so they tell me. I'm not a doctor myself, of course. Should make that clear. I'm just an old-fashioned administrator trying to run a nice tight ship. Of course m'wife's right about the general set-up, I mean if you're given a great rambling place like this . . . but then between you 'n' me I don't think the local health authority has ever really decided whether it's a hospital or an open prison or a bloody Borstal, we've had a few dust-ups with *that* lot, I can tell you. And for the rest . . . under-staffed, over-worked, the usual story. Won't bore you with it. Of course it's the supervision that's the problem. *That*'s what they don't seem able to appreciate.'

'Supervising the prisoners, you mean?'

'In fact we don't call 'em that but yes, that's what it all boils down to. They think they can solve the problem with lots of damn pettifogging regulations. Reason I had to ask you to call in at this ridiculous hour is visitors ain't permitted here till six p.m. an' as the Director I have to set a good example to the troops, see what I mean? – an' one can't explain all these stupid details in a letter. Good of you to be so co-operative, though. Very public-spirited.'

Dobie sank another finger of whisky and felt his toes curl up in delighted response. He didn't know what the director of an establishment such as this might expect to pull in, but Train seemed to be doing very nicely at it. Some kind of a private income, perhaps, stocks and shares and bearer bonds and weird things like that. That would account for the quality of the whisky and, of course, also for Mrs Train. 'In fact you didn't explain very much. I was hoping—'

'Yes, yes. Quite. Brings us to this Seymour chap. We're not convinced he *belongs* here in any way an' so we propose to release him pretty soon. Soon as we can, in fact. Gather you know him pretty well and so I thought I should maybe consult you on the matter.'

'But I hardly know him at all. All that happened *was*, when I was out in Cyprus—'

'He's thinking of applying for a teaching job, you see, at some university or other. I'm a bit concerned about it.'

'So you should be.' You could hardly ask, Dobie thought, for more convincing evidence of advanced insanity. On the other hand, though, should he be accepted, most of his colleagues would certainly prove to be almost as loopy as he was, so that he might at least find himself working in congenial company. You had to look at both sides of the coin. 'Of course I understand he's a bright lad in his field, but it's not a field I'm well informed about. I mean, literature and all that pif—'

'But as to his overall suitability . . . ?'

'Oh, well, he's *qualified*, certainly.'

'You see, *we*'re not well informed about that kind of thing. Most of the lads here would probably pass out cold if anyone offered them a job and the idea of *asking* for one wouldn't cross their minds in a million years. So we don't have a Careers Advisory Officer or anyone like that. There again, we like to try to be helpful and you can see what I mean when I say that Seymour doesn't really *fit* in here. He had an addiction problem, yes, but we're satisfied that's been dealt with. And for the rest he actually seems to be *ambitious*, he wants to *make* something of himself. I mean, this is the Welfare State, damn it, we're just not geared to handle that sort of thing.'

Dobie found himself staring, to his mild surprise, at the photograph on the desk a little to his right. For a second there he had seen superimposed upon the pleasing features of Mrs Train the blank expression and glazed-over eyes of Beverley Sutro; an optical illusion, of course, but not an agreeable one. By now the fuzz would have arrived, of course. He wondered how Kate was getting on. '. . . No. I see. But what about his mental state? He got himself into an awful jam in Cyprus—'

'So he did, silly feller. Well, Carter and Ram reckon they've got to the bottom of that one and they regard it as totally drug-related, with an unhappy marriage as an overall inhibitory factor. Something about a Coleridgean guilt complex but even though I run this place I can't say I understand an awful lot of the jargon. I gather his wife was a university teacher, though. Worries me a little, that does. He might do better to stay clear of that atmosphere for a while. On the other hand, women can kick up their heels a bit in *any* sector of society, that's obvious. It's a situation one has to learn how to deal with as it arises, don't you feel?'

This, if Elspeth was right, was a matter upon which Train might well pontificate with some authority and which Dobie therefore thought it tactful to evade. 'In fact it won't arise, will it? – because she's dead.'

'Indeed. Indeed. Quite so. Yes, these apparently intractable problems often surrender to a very simple solution, haw-haw. Though in Seymour's case there *are* some signs of consequent mental trauma, I won't deny it. Not surprising. She was murdered, after all, and that can't be . . . But of course he didn't *do* it, as I believe was at one time suggested. No, no. The hypnotherapist's report is quite unequivocal as to that. And that's another point . . . Almost all the other lads here have got criminal records of one kind or another and Seymour hasn't. He's got an aggressive personality, certainly, and he often expresses it quite overtly but not in that *way*. No true sociopathic tendencies, none at all.'

'But then why was he sent here in the first place?'

'Well may you ask. Apparently his last registration with the NHS was when he was a student in Cardiff, so that put him under the Regional Health Authority when they sent him back from Cyprus. I've got about eight pages of computer printouts on file in my office and frankly. . . . You know, in this business you fight the ones you think you can win and the others you just let ride. Seymour was one of the others, very definitely. Answer is to get him back into circulation as soon as may be and out of everyone's hair. You'd like to have a chat with him, perhaps?'

'I would?' Dobie was startled.

'Because it'd certainly help if you would give him a reference.'

'What sort of a reference?'

'Well. . . . More or less suggesting that in your view he's capable of taking up a post in a university. Of being a useful member of the community. A reference from someone with your prestige would carry a lot of weight with the Committee, there's no doubt about it. And Seymour . . . I'm sure he'd feel greatly encouraged. Encouragement is what he needs right now. It'd make a considerable difference to his overall stability of mind, believe you me.'

'Yes,' Dobie said. 'There's one thing I'm not quite clear about, though.'

'I'll try to enlighten you, if I can.'

'Why is he . . . I mean, do you cater for criminals here? Or for outright nutters? Or both? Because to the best of my knowledge, Seymour is neither.'

Train hesitated for a few moments before replying, not, as it seemed, because he found the question embarrassing but because several possible answers had at once presented themselves to him. 'The truth of the matter,' he said, making his intention to skirt cautiously around it sufficiently obvious, 'is that we cater for such male miscreants as other institutions, in their wisdom, see fit to send on to us. In other words, a very mixed bunch. Under the old system, you see, the decision to release or to parole these characters was based on reports compiled over a period of time and often by not very well qualified personnel – social workers and such. What I have *here* is a small team of psychiatrists who are also qualified medical practitioners. . . . They carry out a series of interviews and tests and *they* submit the reports on which the decision is reached to release the patient or to send him elsewhere for further treatment. In the ordinary way I myself would make that decision, in consultation with Dr Mighell and the specialist concerned. In the case of Mr Seymour, our decision is very likely to be favourable. Does that clarify the position?'

'Partly. Are you, in effect, offering a guarantee of his future good behaviour?'

Dobie was being more than ordinarily cautious, but the Director seemed to find this readily understandable. 'Oh, no. No, we can hardly do that. All we can do is state that in any given case it's our opinion that the patient's future behaviour is unlikely to endanger the community . . . or in other words, that he may be eccentric or neurotic but that he isn't dangerous. In the present financial and economic climate, there's considerable pressure on us to relieve the charge upon the taxpayers' pockets as soon and as frequently as possible. We're all very much aware of that.'

'So you might be prepared to release Seymour even if he were nutty as a fruitcake?'

'Indeed. Or even nuttier. Provided we were satisfied, as indeed we are, that his eccentricities don't show any serious criminal tendencies. After all, the patients here are under constant close surveillance and restraint – they're not living under what you or

I would call normal conditions. Usually, they improve when they return to society. We have a few backsliders, I'll admit, but by and large we have a very satisfactory success rate.'

'I see,' Dobie said. 'If they're loopy when they get here, then the conditions here conduce to keeping them that way. Then when you let them go, they get better. Yes, I can follow that.'

'I'm not sure that I said that, exactly. But there's an element of . . . After all, there's always some mental strain occasioned by being kept prisoner, no matter how pleasant the surroundings.'

'And how does it affect them?'

'Well, that's exactly what my staff are required to observe. They can be affected in many different ways . . . often enough by memories of their childhood and of their childhood reading, or of . . . But basically they try to rationalize their imprisonment. Captain Scott, for instance, posed us a bit of a problem. He used to insist he was snowed up in an igloo in the Antarctic and sitting out the winter . . . which in view of the weather we've been having lately had to be accounted as little more than a slight misapprehension. But then he used to pass his recreation hours pushing a tea-trolley up and down the passageway shouting, "*Moosh! . . . Mooooosh!*" or something like that. . . . Nice fellow, of course, but when you shook hands with him he always looked you straight in the eye in a virile manly sort of way that got up the other fellows' noses. However . . . I mustn't waste your time with these idle reminiscences. You'll want to see young Seymour yourself and form your own conclusions.'

Dobie wasn't sure that he did, but he nodded politely. The form of conduct that Train had just described would of course have passed virtually without notice if adopted by any of his university colleagues, but . . . 'It takes,' he observed sagely, 'all sorts to make a world.'

'That's what *I* have to keep telling myself,' the Director said.

2

There was the world of the Centre, that he hadn't yet got used to and didn't much want to get used to since anyway they said he'd be out before too very long, and there was the world of the dream, which was well explored and familiar but which seemed to be receding further and further from him as the days went by. The world of the dream was familiar but deceptive and couldn't be trusted. There were colours in the dream, blue and red and yellow, blue of the sea, red and yellow of a million clustered flowers, blue again of the sky, but also there were mists, the mountain mists and the dust haze over the plain, and also there were people in the dream, people dimly seen and imperfectly recognized, men and women in the dream and therefore also sex though impersonal and shadowy, brown-bodied dark-haired figures jerking impassively in a swirl of dark foam-capped waves. Outside the dream there were perfectly clear and rational recollections of a place called Cyprus, of his wife and of his friends and acquaintances, but these recollections seemed to be unrelated to the dream and would in any case always be swiftly dissipated by the interminable ingressions of the present moment, of the routine of the Centre, of Reality, upon his thoughts.

As now. . . .

Pip pip *pop* of the ping-pong ball impinging on the table. The occasional rustle of Charlie Chan's newspaper as he leaned forwards in his chair, poring over the crossword. Now and again a high-pitched communal laugh, almost a giggle, from the brat pack over in the corner. This was the time of the teenagers, no doubt about it. They'd taken over Reality. Even closing your eyes, you couldn't keep them out. The laughter and the whispers and the mindless beat of their favoured music, if that's what you called it. Only a few older ones, he and Charlie and Harry the Horse

33

and maybe one or two others, nobody else to talk to except the doctors and you had to be careful what you said to *them*.

You had to be careful what you said to Harry, too. Harry had a nasty temper. Harry was going into snide on a GBH as soon as they got through with him here. Harry hadn't got much to look forward to, when you thought about it. Me, I'm different. By rights I shouldn't have been sent here at all. Everybody said so.

'Sporting effort,' Charlie said, 'by someone who can barely run. . . . Six letters. . . .'

'Got any of them?'

'Ends with a K.'

Easy. 'STREAK.'

'Oh yeah.' Seymour didn't open his eyes. He didn't have to. Charlie crouched over the plastic-topped table, ballpoint clutched in one ham-sized hand, chuckling to himself as he filled in the squares. . . . He'd seen it so often. They didn't allow you ballpoint pens here, not to start with. . . . Offensive weapons, you could take someone's eyes out with one. But Charlie was allowed a ballpoint and so was he, he even had a typewriter in his room so he could type out words words words whenever he liked, it was part of the therapy as he supposed. For a while he'd tried to find the words to fit the dream but none of them would and hadn't when he'd tried that once before so he'd given that up and now he was writing a novel, a new novel, about . . . about. . . . He'd remember that when he got back to his room. Meantime, this was Reality. Pip pip *pop* and a sudden blare of sound from the radio over in the corner where the kids were congregated, not all of them because some were just sitting around staring at the walls, the ones who were still on withdrawal and feeling the ache but me, I'm different, Seymour thought: I always said I could shake it if I really wanted to and now I've proved it. I'm older and I've got the dream and they haven't, I know they haven't. I've asked them. They don't seem to understand at all.

And *they* don't know about it, either. The doctors. I tried to tell them about it but the words wouldn't fit. All so confused, all those dead people and the flicker of the lamplight and on the edge of the lamplight those two great shapes, struggling, interlocked, the woman my wife and not my wife, the man me and not me, their legs sprawled out and kicking in the swirl of shallow waves racing up from the beach, and then of course I killed her but I know now it wasn't me but the other one, if it was me I wouldn't be here, all alone and facing up to Reality again. . . . Ping-pong and crossword puzzles and UB40 and Kingston Town. . . .

He opened his eyes and saw that Reality was a tweed-suited chap, sporting a truly weird moustache and wearing slightly too small a raincoat, plodding purposefully across the room towards him. Reality had got wet lately. Reality paused in front of the table and then drew up a chair and sat down, knocking over in the process an empty glass that had contained until recently something under half a pint of Coca-Cola. Reality was *real* all right but clearly a bit of a . . . Ah. 'Mr Dobie. . . .' Who else? It was the moustache, of course, that had fooled him. Briefly. 'Welcome to Toad Hall.'

'Is that what you call it?'

'It's what we call it and it's where I'm at. Thanks to you, I'm told. Instead of in that dump in Cyprus.'

Dobie blew out his moustache thing dismissively, causing it to rise and fall like a passing Pacific roller. 'I think you've been misinformed. I didn't have very much to do with it. And if it comes to that, these doctors here . . . Why do they all look like retired Army officers?'

'Could be that's what they are. Or cashiered, more like it.'

'How very odd.'

'Not really. They run this place like bloody Catterick. I mean, the nurses . . . Nurses they call 'em. NCOs to a man.'

'You had a Turkish Army guard last time I saw you.'

'So I did.'

'I expect you're better off here. But you'll be wanting to get out of it all the same.'

'That I am, sorr.'

Dobie was looking guardedly round him as he spoke, not, it seemed, finding his immediate surroundings altogether reassuring. 'Is it all right to talk here?' Though what he saw was a large and quite pleasantly appointed recreation room with oak-panelled walls upon which hung a number of tasteful nineteenth-century water-colours depicting benevolent aspects of the local scenery. These were without exception being studiously ignored by the room's inhabitants as was, for that matter, Dobie himself.

'Talk, walk, do anything you like between the hours of six

and nine. Anything, that is, that meets with the approval of the powers that be. As the weather's somewhat unseasonable this evening—'

'I meant talk in *here*. As opposed to somewhere a bit more private.'

'Privacy . . . ? Now, that's a little difficult to achieve. With television monitors everywhere and Big Brother forever on his guard. Now you mention it, I believe there *is* a Visitors' Room . . . but I haven't had many visitors. In fact, you're the first. Charlie Chan here doesn't get many, either. Right, Charlie?'

Charlie, hearing his name mentioned, nodded emphatically without raising his eyes from the newspaper on the table and while still chewing meditatively on the end of his ballpoint. 'Right. Lots and lots.'

'Gets a bit inscrutable at times, does Charlie.'

'I see,' Dobie said.

'Horse doesn't get many, either. That big old lad asleep over in the corner. . . . Horse, well, it's really Crazy Horse but people don't call him that, not to his face. Last chap to do it's still being scraped off a wall and that's why Harry's here. No, not many of us are receiving visitors, now I think about it.'

'Unlikely reaction of train-spotter to twenty-four across. Eleven letters, haven't got any of them.'

'What's twenty-four across then?'

'Haven't got that either.'

'. . . Doesn't get many visitors, Charlie doesn't.'

'Well,' Dobie said, a little desperately, 'how are *you* feeling?'

'Great. It's a great life. An elegant sufficiency,' Seymour said, 'content, retirement, rural quiet, friendship, books. . . . The eighteenth-century ideal, in fact. All our modest needs are catered for. Except booze and birds, of course, which anyway Thomson neglected to mention.'

Thomson . . . ? One of the doctors here, perhaps. 'But this isn't the eighteenth century.'

'You put your finger on the spot, Professor. Friendship's at a discount these days, and maybe it's just as well.' Seymour stared disparagingly towards the giggling group at the far end of the room. 'Idle shallow things, for the most part. I am not of their element. But it's better here than at Everdene, anyway, where I was before. They make you do deep-breathing exercises there.

And then they put you in a dark room and tell you to look at a candle.'

'How,' Dobie asked, 'can you see the candle if the room's dark?'

'The candle's lighted, of course.'

'But then the room isn't dark.'

Sharp as a nail this evening, was Professor Dobie.

'Be that as it may,' Seymour said, breathing deeply through his nose, 'it may be a useful exercise for Sufi mystics but it wasn't *my* kind of scene. I believe it's supposed to test your susceptibility to hypnosis but I'm not into that kick, either. Self-hypnosis, who needs it?'

'I thought you had to lie on a couch and talk about this and that. But I'm not very—'

'Oh, we do *that* here all right. And they give us hypnotherapy, if it comes to that, and do things with coloured lights – they could run a pretty good disco with the equipment they've got. But most of the time they leave you alone in your room to do your thing and that's OK,' Seymour said, 'because it's coming back.'

'What is?'

'The rise, the roll, the carol, the creation.'

'Eh?'

'I'm writing another book. Started one, anyway.'

In fact he did look a great deal healthier than he had in Cyprus some six months ago. Paler, of course, but fuller in the face than before and the ragged beard he had then affected was now neatly trimmed. No, he looked surprisingly fit, this in contradistinction to most of the other young people in the room who seemed, frankly, to be a weedy lot, with the possible exception of the fellow with the wavy blond hair who sat smoking over by the curtained window and who looked as though he might at any moment be going to bite his cigarette holder *right* through. He, and of course the formidable Mr Horse peacefully slumbering in the far corner.

'What sort of a book?'

'A novel.'

'Oh.'

A silly question, in that Dobie already knew Seymour to be a novelist and allegedly one of some promise – indeed he had actually read one of Seymour's fictional effusions, a minor opus entitled *The Mask of Zeus*, and had, he had subsequently decided, never before encountered such unadulterated guff. He quite saw, however, that it wouldn't do to say so.

'And,' Seymour said, 'I keep a journal. *Notes from Underground. Seymour in Loonyland.* It may be of interest in later years, to me if to no one else.'

'Well, I expect you'll have met some, er . . . interesting characters in here.'

'Not really. Just a crowd of teenage junkies, if you want to know the truth. With a few long-term nutters they couldn't find room for anywhere else.'

'You mean like Crazy—'

'*Don't* say it.'

'But he's fast asleep. . . .'

'Maybe he is and maybe he isn't. You never can tell with these screwballs.'

'So what's it about?'

'What?'

'The book.'

'Oh, the *book*. . . . Well, to begin with it was about the dream but now it's about something else.'

After a while Dobie said, 'What dream?' having in the interim taken off his glasses, polished them, and put them on again.

'I'm pretty sure it has to be a dream. Everybody tells me that it must be. But . . . the trouble is I've almost lost it. So I just can't be sure.'

'You know,' Dobie said, 'I had a remarkable dream myself the other night in which I imagined I was lecturing to a group of my students about a dream I'd had the night before . . . only to find that I couldn't remember it . . . and the peculiar thing is, that's exactly what happened in the dream as well. Most extraordinary.'

After a considerably longer pause Seymour said, 'No, it wasn't that sort of a dream at all.'

'What wasn't?'

'*My* dream.'

'Ah. Well, there you are, then.'

'It's a something wrong somewhere sort of a dream, you know what I mean?'

'Like, you're looking for something only you can't find it and you don't know what it is anyway?' Kate had once narrated to him a dream of this kind, though this was also in fact a fairly accurate description of Dobie's attempts at mathematical investigation. 'A friend of mine who once had roast pork for dinner—'

'There are dead bodies,' Seymour said. 'Everywhere.'

'Bodies?'

'Skeletons. Deep underground somewhere. And two of them are, *you* know, making love to each other and when the man looks up at me, it's me. And the woman's my wife. But when we speak, when *they* speak, I can't understand what they're saying. It doesn't sound very frightening. But it is.'

Dead bodies *are* frightening, Dobie thought. Though it's hard to say why.

'Did you have this dream when you were in Cyprus?'

'It *is* a dream?'

'*You* said it was. I don't see how it could be anything else, the way you tell it.'

'Well, that's right. Exactly. And yet . . . I don't remember ever having actually *had* the dream. But I must have. Else, how would I remember it at all?'

'Perhaps you should tell the shrinks . . . the doctors here about it. That's if it worries you.'

'Oh, I have. That's how we spend the time here, didn't you know . . . ? Thinking of things like that to tell the doctors about. I only just got through a session with Popeye, Dr Carter . . . He's all right but he doesn't . . . And the trouble is I'm starting to remember it *differently*. Like it wasn't Derya in the dream at all but somebody else.'

'Who?'

'*I* don't know. Some girl or other I've never seen before, or not to my knowledge. It's ridiculous. But her hair's all wet like Derya's was . . . and she has these big staring eyes. . . . There wasn't anyone like that in Cyprus that I can recall.'

Dobie's mildly interested expression didn't change. 'Then maybe it's someone you've seen here.'

'If so,' Seymour said, 'it's a something wrong *here* sort of dream and . . . Well, I'll be getting out of this place pretty soon and it's maybe just as well.'

*

39

He hoped so, anyway.

The typewriter was a few years old but in good working order. He slid a sheet of paper into the roller and, after the usual moment's pause for thought, began to type.

Saturday March 24th

D. duly appeared this evening, thereby rather confounding me. He didn't seem to be at all as I remembered him, though perhaps that isn't surprising. My memories of those last weeks in Cyprus are really very hazy. Unconscious suppression, Popeye claims. There may be something in it. If so, they can stay suppressed as far as I'm concerned. Sometimes I wonder if I wouldn't go back there one day, or to some other unsuspected isle in far-off seas. . . . But these are thoughts that have to occur to everyone at the fag-end of a long Welsh winter. The weather today was quite appalling; windy dark cold wet, the lot. I didn't venture out at all and I don't think anyone did. I may have eaten of the insane root that takes the reason prisoner but I know what I don't like and sheets of freezing rain come high on the agenda.

But I do remember thinking of myself (over-dramatically) in those days as living in a cage. A caged tiger. Now I really *am* in a cage I feel a good deal better, which is ironical. Or if not better, different. A tamed and shabby tiger, like all the others. I don't know if Professor D. can really do anything much to get me out of here – he really gave the impression of being more at home in this place than any of us, which again is ironical. I don't even know why he should want to help, unless it's because of Derya. Perhaps when I *am* out of here I'll be able to think about these things more clearly. Right now I don't choose to.

Change of subject.

A new neighbour for me today, as well as a visitor. The new boy got here this morning and they put him next door. Charlie's been moved further down the passageway. Only a glimpse of him so far but he's nearer my age than most of the others – maybe a bit older. A bad sign, I suppose, when you start assessing people in terms of their age-groups – it shows how difficult it is to *communicate* with anyone here. In fact the older ones are the worst, in terms of unpredictability – Horse, for example. The new one's a big guy, too, so they may be keeping a careful eye on him at the start.

He could be a real nutter, I suppose, like Chickenfeed was – I wouldn't care to have a next-door neighbour going round the place wringing the necks of imaginary chickens all the time. Perish the thought. 'Interesting people,' D. said. Well, that's one way of looking at it. All these little guys who're running scared here, they may be paranoiac or have persecution complexes like the quacks say but in point of fact they've got good *reason* to be scared. That fellow who thought he was Jack the Ripper was well before my time here, but they still tell stories about him. As far as I know he never actually did any harm to anyone but that's not the point. He *thought* that he had and that's enough. My own imaginings are weird enough, or D. seemed to think so, but they're not of *that* kind, not really.

Before my time. . . . I'm starting to use expressions like that quite naturally. It *is* like a boarding-school of the fiercer kind – Tom Brown's Rugby maybe – complete with bullies and cheats and beastly swots and sporting bloods oozing repressed homosexuality, not of course very notably repressed in some cases. . . . I'm Billy Bunter, of course, the fat Owl of the Remove, and they can't remove me quick enough as far as I'm concerned. Then I'll be an OB of the Rehabilitation Centre and I'll go to the annual reunions at Colney Hatch. Ladies and gentlemen . . . Her Majesty the Queen . . . Our former gracious hostess . . . And I'll invite Professor D. as Guest of Honour. Yes, *that*'ll be something for me to look forward to. . . .

These things always happened on a Saturday evening and of course it was Jacko who'd dipped stinking again. He absolutely loathed hit-and-runs and indeed all other forms of what he privately characterized as PPD (Piss-Poor Driving); this was partly because he couldn't remember the last time he'd got a conviction on a hit-and-run charge and doubted, moreover, whether he ever would until he found himself testifying before a jury composed entirely of confirmed pedestrians – a highly unlikely contingency in the civilized Britain of today. Being as cautious a driver as any other CID Detective Inspector standing in mortal fear of the uniformed branch, it had taken him the best part of forty minutes to get from the shop to the Rehabilitation Centre and, although he knew the location perfectly well, he had come within an ace of doing a Dobie and driving past it; if ever there was an evening when a spot of PPD might be excused, surely this was the one. But then he hadn't come here to find excuses for anyone. Far from it.

Jackson didn't look very much like a policeman. He looked like the man who comes round to fix the telly, and that was rather how he felt about the job these days. You unscrewed the panel, you took a bit of a shufti, you connected various loose wires, and then you went home to a nice cuppa tea. But in fact he was quite an old-fashioned cop with an old-fashioned black notebook in which he had recorded the essential facts of the case, as presented to him by Dr Mighell and Dr Coyle. Being an old-fashioned cop, he of course always called Kate 'Dr Coyle' in the presence of other parties, although he knew her very well and had in fact almost certainly saved her life a few months ago, in the course of an investigation to which nowadays neither of them ever referred. In his old-fashioned notebook he had duly recorded the name of the deceased BEVERLY SUTRO, Dr Mighell's name and address, and the address of deceased's last known residence DAME MARGARET SCHOOL FOR GIRLS nr TONGWYN-LAIS as supplied by his informant MISS ELSPETH MIGHELL (14).

His informant had also supplied him and Dr Coyle with the anticipated nice cuppa tea and they now sat together in the kitchen drinking it while Dr Coyle supplied him with further information on a more confidential and semi-informal basis; Detective Sergeant Box, who might otherwise also have been there, had nipped off smartly to inform the Headmistress, a MISS MIDWINTER, that one of her pupils the aforementioned BEVERLEY SUTRO might now be crossed off the list of potential A-level candidates – this in accordance with the broadly humanitarian policing policies emphasized by Jackson's superior officer, DETECTIVE SUPERINTENDENT PONTIN, whose name Jackson however hadn't entered in his notebook because it hadn't occurred to him to do so.

Now that he and Dr Coyle were alone in the kitchen, Jackson felt able to offer, on a confidential and semi-informal basis, his considered opinion of the case as so far outlined. 'Bit of a balls-up, this, if you ask me.'

'Aren't they all?'

'Yes, but I mean . . . A bit of a sod. How old do you reckon this kid was?'

'Seventeen. Eighteen.'

'All right. Better give me the rest of the medical. What you've got.'

'She died soon after we got here. Time of death, six ten p.m.'

'Cause?'

'Fractured skull with serious internal haemorrhage. Impending hypothermia a contributory factor.'

Jackson didn't even try to write *that* down. 'Not *that* cold, is it?'

'It is if you're lying out there in the rain with next to nothing on.'

'How long a time?'

'I don't know. I'd say at least twenty minutes.'

Outside the house the ambulance had just started up. It was a sound that they'd both heard many times before, but all the same neither of them spoke for a few moments. Jackson sipped at his tea mug and Kate rested her clasped hands on the surface of the kitchen table and then unclasped them again. They were both thinking the same thing.

'So the accident took place at some time before ten to six, on your reckoning. Not a hell of a lot of traffic goes down this road, you know. I'd say for once we've got a fair old chance of nabbing the bugger.'

'If there *was* an accident, yes.'

Jackson looked up from his notebook, pencil still raised. 'You're not suggesting someone ran over the kid on purpose?'

The noise of the motor outside rose and then faded as the ambulance drove slowly away.

'Look,' Kate said. 'I'm puzzled. Paddy'll do the PM for you tomorrow and that'll maybe clarify the picture. Meantime I ought to stick to the obvious medical facts. There's a fractured skull, like I said, and a compound fracture of the right forearm and there's a whole list of minor injuries and contusions that aren't in any way consistent with her having been hit by a motor-car and which therefore we have to attribute to some other cause, right . . .? And my provisional conclusion is that the girl was beaten up. Or else got herself into some kind of a fight. Dr Mighell agrees. In fact he'll go a stage further. He thinks she was raped.'

'But you don't?'

'I think it very likely, too, but I wouldn't commit myself on that until Paddy finds some harder evidence of it than what we've got. You'll want to get the clothes she was wearing off to the Heath, of course, but . . . some of the normal items appear to be missing. No panties. No underclothes of any kind. No stockings. And of course only the one shoe, though we found the other lying on the road . . . as I told you. . . .'

'What had she got on under that anorak thing?'

'White cotton blouse. Short blue skirt. Nothing else.'

'The tabloids'll like it,' Jackson said. 'But I don't.'

'I don't, either, but I wouldn't call it evidence of rape. There's some very characteristic bruising but you sometimes get that in normal intercourse, and whatever happened, *if* it happened, it wasn't her first sexual experience. In any case, the cause of death was that blow to the head and *that* wasn't done in a fit of over-enthusiasm, you can take that as read.'

'Hard blunt object?'

'A hard blunt-*edged* object, yes.'

'A brick, maybe? Or a rock by the side of the road? Something like that?'

'Or the edge of a wall. Only there wasn't one. Not where she was lying.'

'Yes,' Jackson said, putting away his notebook. 'That's going to be a problem – finding the exact spot. . . . Of course you did the right thing, picking her up, but on a night like this—'

'Do us a favour, Jacko. I left a marker.'

'You *did*?' Jackson was delighted. 'Good on yer. We won't be able to do much more than rope it off tonight but the scene-of-crime boys will be there first thing tomorrow morning, don't you worry. You didn't notice any skid marks on the road, I don't suppose?'

'Cars don't leave tyre tracks in puddles. The road was damned nearly under water.'

'So all you noticed at first was that shoe?'

'At the side of the road, yes. In fact I didn't see it. Dobie did.'

Jackson's expression became somewhat apprehensive. 'Yes. Where *is* Mr Dobie?'

'Over at the Director's place, wherever that is. He had an appointment with the Director this evening – that's why we're here. We can go round and pick him up if you want to have a word with him, but frankly I don't think—'

'I know what you mean,' Jackson said, and sighed heavily. 'Yes, better leave *him* out of it as long as we can. I know he *means* well, but the Super still froths at the mouth whenever he hears Mr Dobie's name mentioned. Which isn't often. We make sure of that.'

He finished off the remains of his cuppa, his expression clearing slightly. After all, Kate was right. There wasn't any reason for Dobie to be involved in *this* one, not that he could see, and every policeman learns to count his blessings, such as they are. Yes, stay out of this, Dobie, Jackson said to himself. Stay out of it and Make My Day.

'The point is that when the reports come in . . . you may find that this is a nasty one.'

'Know what I'm thinking?' Jackson pushed his empty cup away and leaned an elbow confidentially on the table. 'Maybe not a hit-and-run at all. Maybe one of those back-of-the-car snogs that goes wrong. *Badly* wrong. So Charley just shoves her out of the car door and drives off. He'd have to have lost his chump completely but it's been known to happen. Four years ago out at Newnham, to give you an instance.'

'But the girl wasn't dead.'

'He might have thought she was. If he panicked.'

'But she wouldn't have got herself bruised all over like that in the back of a car. A car with seat cushions, anyway. That's not a medical opinion. That's my personal experience.'

'And in any case, only a hypotenuse.'

'Some pretty acute angles are involved, certainly.'

'Have to come up with *facts*, Kate, not fragments of your imagination. Still less with trips down Memory Lane of however flagrant recall.'

'Fragrant.'

'That's what I said.'

All the time the rain was whispering at the windows, running down from the roof gutters; as yet, no sign of a let-up. Against that sound, the louder grumble and creak of another car coming to a halt outside. Jackson went over to the window and drew back the curtain. 'Foxy's back. Couldn't have had too far to go.'

'Elspeth says the school's only half a mile up the road.'

'Well, there you go.' Jackson was buttoning his raincoat, his shoulders hunched a little in anticipation of the coming drenching. 'Could only happen in this country, of course.'

'What?'

'Putting a posh girls' school right next door to a remand home full of junkies and juvenile delinquents. Some kind of a genius for organization, that took.'

'I know which of the two I'd rather be in,' Kate said, 'if *my* school was anything to go by.'

'Best days of your life. Not for *her* they weren't.' Jackson turned round sombrely. 'We'll go and pick up your Mr Dobie and then we'll take a look-see where she ended up.'

No way Dobie was going to take a look-see.

From his damp roosting-perch on the passenger seat he watched the dark raincoated figures sploshing up and down the side of the road, shadows leaping across the ground in the light of their waving torches. The squad car had been drawn up some little way ahead and from its roof a sharper, more powerful beam of light was directed downwards towards the neatly roped-off area where the formulaic printed sign said:

POLICE
SCENE OF ACCIDENT

—swinging to and fro in the gusty wind. The rain was coming down as hard as ever but the clouds to the south and east seemed to have lifted a little; peering through the closed and spattered side-window, Dobie could make out the distant lights of the M4 motorway and beyond them the paler glow emanating from good old Tin City, Cardiff itself. Leaning back then and pressing the back of his unfractured cranium against the head-rest, he thought of the sparkling lights of Iskele seen in the afterglow of a Mediterranean twilight against the crouching outline of the Karpaz mountains, only a little brighter than the millionfold sparkle of the stars in the darkening sky beyond; he sighed to himself, as Jackson had done. Cyprus hadn't been *all* bad, by any means.

Kate, sitting beside him, wasn't saying anything. She was watching the activities of Jackson and the other two officers, holding in her hands the sodden handkerchief that, knotted round a stone, she had left as a marker for them and now and again twisting it between her fingers as though to wring the water from it. Something was up, Dobie thought. *Something wrong here, too.* But she wasn't saying anything and he thought it best for the time being to respect her silence. In the end, sure enough, it was Kate who broke it. Casually enough.

'Did you get to see your friend?'

'Yes. But he's not a friend, exactly. Just someone who . . . you *know* about all that.'

'So how's he doing?'

'Well, it seems they're proposing to release him. Actually, the place isn't at all what I'd expected. Everyone there seemed perfectly normal to me.'

'Well, they would, wouldn't they . . . ? But what did this Train character *want*, exactly?'

'He wants me to recommend Seymour for some kind of a teaching job. So that *he* can get shot of him, I suppose.'

'And will you?'

'I don't see why not. But I have to see one of the other shrinks there first. To discuss Seymour's case history, as they call it.'

'Mighell?'

'No. Not Mighell. Why?'

'Didn't strike me as a man of biting intellect. That's all.'

'Oh. He's having an affair with this chap Train's wife, according to Elspeth.'

'Very likely. It's a favourite occupation with psychiatrists. Screwing each other's wives and then psychoanalysing themselves to find out how they feel about it. Research activity, they call it.'

'What *do* they feel about it?'

'They usually feel they haven't yet collected enough material so they have to try it again with someone else's. What's with this Train geezer then?'

47

'He isn't a man of biting intellect, either. But his wife's a bit of a hum— a strikingly attractive woman. If,' Dobie added hurriedly, 'you like the type.'

'Not altogether a wasted evening, then.'

'Not altogether, no, I wouldn't say that.'

'H'mmmmmm,' Kate said.

At which juncture, perhaps opportunely, Jackson's face appeared at the driver's window, which Kate wound down.

'Won't be needing you any more, Dr Coyle, so there's no point in keeping you hanging around. In fact we'll try not to trouble you again until the inquest.' A sizeable dollop of rainwater decanted itself from the car roof and landed splashily at the back of his neck. 'Lumme, *what* a night,' Jackson said.

'Have you found anything?'

'Hell, no. Nothing here but mud. We'll have to take another look come daylight.'

'Policeman's lot,' Kate said, rather more cheerfully than might have been expected. When, after all, one has got wet oneself, some satisfaction is to be derived from the prospect of other people getting a great deal wetter, especially when a steaming hot bath awaits one at home. Though Dobie would be needing one, too. He didn't seem to have realized yet that he had his backside parked in the middle of a puddle. . . . Yes, how had all that water got on to the passenger seat, anyway?

When they got back to Ludlow Road they took a hot bath together, in order to save hot water, and subsequently went to bed (Kate's bed). After this equivalent of a Special Birthday Treat Dobie should have gone to sleep like a lamb, but he didn't. Kate knew why not.

'Want to take a pill, Dobie?'

'Good Lord, I thought *you*'d taken it.'

'Not *that* one, you fool.'

'Oh,' Dobie said. 'Am I being restive again?'

'Yes, and for the wrong reasons.' Kate switched on the bedside lamp and stared at him somewhat grumpily. She couldn't help but feel that Dobie's inability to relapse into post-coital coma reflected somewhat adversely upon her own recent spirited performance or, to be exact, performances. Though on the other hand . . . 'Dobie, it's what I *do*, you may think it an unsuitable job for a woman but that's not my fault.'

'I don't think that for a moment.'

'Yes, you do.'

'She wasn't hit by a car, though. Was she?'

After a pause, during which Kate fumbled for a cigarette and lit it. . . .

'No, probably not,' Kate said.

'But she was hit by *somebody*.'

'Yes. It could still have been an accident, though. In the sense that maybe no one meant it to happen. She could have hit her head against the side of a wall or the edge of a table, that sort of injury's . . .' She stopped. No, this wasn't a good idea. 'Look, I gave the kid a once-over because I was *there* but it's Paddy's pigeon now and Jacko's, there's nothing in it for me any more and God knows there's nothing in it for *you*. You want to know what I think. . . . ? I think she had a spat with the boyfriend and he got a bit too rough with her. Maybe she'd let him go ahead a few times before but today for some reason she wouldn't and this other kid got over-excited and went ahead anyway and while she was thrashing about . . . *that* happened somehow. . . . And so within a couple of days or so Jacko's going to pull in some shit-scared little yobbo and send him down for a stretch because that's what *he* does for a living, like he's a cop, but it's not my sort of scene and it's not yours, either, so . . . stop *thinking* about it, will you, Dobie? If you'd be so kind. . . .'

It wasn't like Kate to get so worked up and Dobie was a little puzzled by her vehemence. 'Well, I'll try. It's just that she looked . . .'

'I *know* how she looked. I may be a doctor but that doesn't mean I haven't got any human feelings.'

'Indeed no,' Dobie said.

Kate smoked most of the rest of her cigarette and then said, 'What made you think she hadn't been hit by a car? It looked that way to *me*. At first.'

'I don't know,' Dobie said. 'There just seemed to be something wrong. Somewhere.'

3

By the morning it had rained itself out and although the sky was laden with fast-scudding clouds, these parted every so often to let a weak and wintry sunlight filter through. Dobie, having golloped down a nourishing breakfast, put on his raincoat (well, not *his* raincoat, in fact, but one that he had mistakenly acquired when leaving a late-night party at the house of a friend of his – now an ex-friend, in all probability, although, as Dobie pointed out to Kate, the raincoat fitted him perfectly well, at least when left unbuttoned, and certainly no worse than Colombo's), and climbed into his battered blue Fiesta (which really was his own, it having been some time since Dobie had driven home in someone else's car) and set off, waving nonchalantly, to keep (it was hoped) his appointment with Dr Carter. Kate had intended to spend a quiet Sunday morning answering some extremely important letters but the day (thanks to Dobie) had got off to such a parenthetical start that she found herself instead pottering about the house in an unusually aimless sort of way, doing things that needed to be done and thinking about this and that. She was telling herself severely that this wouldn't do when Jackson rang, providing yet another interruption, certainly, but a welcome one. And it wasn't long before Jacko, never a cop to bush for very long about the beat, raised the matter of their mutual concern.

'I don't understand what it *is* about Mr Dobie. He just seems to have some sort of natural infinity with the criminal mind.'

'Bollocks, Jacko. He has nothing of the kind.'

'Well, but take that other business. I know he *says* he worked it all out on his little computer but he's the one who *sets* the computer, isn't he? Or pogroms it or whatever it's called.'

This was undeniable. 'I suppose that when he's being a math-ematician he inhabits a totally amoral universe, and on that

50

occasion he turned out to be dealing with a totally amoral criminal. But not many criminals are like that. In other words, that time he fluked out. Chances are he never will again.'

'Well, I dunno,' Jackson said. 'He could probably tell you exactly what the chances *are*, of that or of anything else. That's the trouble.'

'No. That's not the trouble. The trouble is that people *talk* to him. They *tell* him things and they don't even know they're doing it. Because he's such a dumb cluck on the face of it that . . . I mean, I find *myself* doing it, damn it. I wasn't going to tell him a bloody thing about that girl and next thing you know there I am, spilling it out, and it's all sheer *speculation*, I mean what do *I* know about it? He really is the most *aggravating* man.'

'The Super would agree with you on that one,' Jackson said. He produced a sinister rumbling sound from the inner depths of his stomach. This was not the product of indigestion. It was a laugh. The special one he used when he found himself having to work on Sunday mornings. Hollow, you might call it. Though Kate, in fact, ignored it.

'But there again – he has a sweet nature, though you mightn't think so. He's kind and considerate. In fact he's a kind, considerate psychopath and you've got to admit *that's* rather unusual.'

Jackson repeated the sound, occasioning a crackling sound in the telephone receiver. 'We all know you're *keen* on him, Kate, but what's wrong with that? Why bring it all to me on a damp spring morning?'

'Because I want you to keep him out of this business with the Sutro girl, if you possibly can. And anyway *you* raised the subject. I didn't.'

'He's not *in* it, is he? Except as a witness to the finding of the body. And at that time it wasn't even properly speaking a body, the way you tell it.'

'Exactly. But if there's any way he can get sucked further into it he's bound to find it, because he's . . . Well, I don't know why, but I'm sure that he will.'

'Look,' Jackson said. 'OK. There are suspicious circumstances, yes, I'll grant you that. But we're very far from sure as yet that we're talking about a murder. If we are, I repeat *if* we are, then the last thing I'll want is to have Mr Dobie running in and out between my feet again and you needn't have any fears on *that* score. Whenever I think of . . . Hey. Just a minute. Where *is* he this morning, anyway?'

'He's gone up to that Rehabilitation Centre place again. In fact he's only seeing one of those doctors about one of the nut cases there but . . . you see what I mean?'

'Yes, I do,' Jackson said. 'Or I think I do. Oh dear. Oh lumme.'

By ten o'clock the clouds had lifted considerably; it was difficult, Dobie thought, to relate this morning's panorama of sweeping moorland to the gloomy rainswept darkness of the previous night. The scenery was rather too bare to be thought in any way hospitable, but with the weak sunlight gleaming on the pools of water retained by the rock furrows and off the drops still clinging to the heath and furze it wasn't without a certain beauty, either. Certainly Dobie wasn't driving across an almost uninhabited patch of desert, as last night he might have suspected. There were slate-roofed farmhouses dotted about the fields in the lower valley; in the distance to the right he could see the sun blinking on the metal roofs of cars scurrying like files of ants along the Caerphilly Road, and the rear-view mirror gave him occasional glimpses of the high-rise blocks of Cardiff itself, of the grey sea beyond, and of the low dark hills on the far side of the Severn estuary. It wasn't, as Carter had said, a bad view; not a bad view at all. And the Centre itself was clearly visible beyond the left-hand curve directly in front – perhaps not clearly, because of the twelve-foot stone wall topped with glittering jags of glass surrounding it; this hid from view most of the small staff houses but not the main building itself, red-roofed and three storeys high, rising from the clusters of tall trees, well into leaf, that shadowed the parkland around it. Dobie slowed down. Braked more sharply. Stopped the car. Got out. It was indeed still a fresh and windy morning and the air felt damp against his face.

The police signs were still there, otherwise he wouldn't have recognized the spot at all. Nothing seemed to distinguish it from any other point along the last couple of miles of road. Seen by daylight, it seemed to be quite extraordinarily *open* for any such sexual shenannigans as Kate had hypothesized, a totally inapt site for a spot of slap-and-tickle, let alone a . . . Nothing but open moorland for at least half a mile all around, though a few gorse bushes over to the left might have . . . But no, not *gorse* bushes, surely. Even Dobie, inexpert in these matters, would have known better than to elect upon a clump of *gorse* bushes; the prickles aren't just on the branches, they get *everywhere*. With embarrassing and extremely painful results . . . However. What he had failed to notice last night was that the girl had in fact been lying at the bottom of a slight declivity at the side of the road, not nearly deep enough to be called a ditch but deep enough, certainly, to account for her clothes and hair having been so extremely wet. The rainwater would have drained into it. It might even be deep enough to account for the failure of the drivers of any other passing cars to have spotted her rather earlier . . . especially if you considered the miserable driving conditions prevailing at that time. . . .

Dobie frowned. There was something *odd* about that part of it, something that he'd noticed but couldn't now seem to remember. He moved a few paces to his left, staring moodily down into the declivity. Yes, it was odd that if it had happened the way Kate thought . . . not the slightest attempt had been made to hide the body, you'd have thought that would be a fairly obvious. . . . But no, *that* wasn't it, there was some at least equally obvious *fact* that he was missing out on. . . .

'I'm afraid I'll have to ask you to move along, sir, as you can see this is a . . . Oh my God. It's Mr Dobie.'

'Oh hullo, Foxy. Sorry about that, I didn't hear you coming.'

Dobie's leap of startled surprise had carried him some three feet up into the air and terminated in a particularly splashy puddle. Box stooped patiently to brush at the dollops of wet mud now decorating the legs of his neatly creased grey trousers and then, recognizing this procedure to be ineffective, straightened up again. 'Oh well. It doesn't much matter. The boys'll be coming back in a few minutes' time to clear this lot away so I reckon there's no harm in your having a bit of a shufti, if that's what you want.'

'Everything's completely *different* to last night,' Dobie complained.

'It's stopped raining, you see. Quite nice and dry here. Until *you* arrived.'

'I just wanted to make quite sure there was nothing here.'

'Nothing here?'

'Nothing that she could have hit her head on.'

'Ah,' Foxy Boxy said. 'I think I can say that painstaking police procedures have established that as a fact. Might have broke her arm all right, being hit by a car or falling out of one. But a split head like that one had, no.'

'Unless it was the car hit her on the head.'

'Wasn't an Irish dog, was she?'

'Eh?'

'Irish dogs,' Box explained, 'have all got bumps on their heads from chasing parked cars.' His Sunday-morning laugh was quite different to Jackson's, rather resembling a soda-water syphon abruptly exploding. 'Sorry, sir. Joke in bad taste, really. But it's a possibility, of course. Fell and hit her head on the bumper or something when the car was stationary. Well, we have to pursue every avenue, so to speak, but I don't say it's *likely*.'

'You saw the Headmistress last night, didn't you? What do they say about it all at the school?'

'What you'd expect. Surprised 'n' horrified. The usual thing. But I reckon they were at that. In fact I didn't get to see the Headbeak 'cos she was incapacitated with toothache, or so they said and I got no reason to doubt it. Saw the School Secretary instead. May be a bit of a problem notifying the parents but I was able to ease her mind on that one. Our job as much as theirs an' we have our methods.'

'What's the problem?'

'Divorced and living abroad, the both of them. Mother remarried and in Italy some place, father gone to Canada. Managerial consultant, whatever that means. Sounds a bit niffy. What's *your* concern in all this, Mr Dobie?'

'Well, I've . . . certain information I should give the police.'

'You have?' Box delved in his inside pocket and whipped out a notebook. He, too, was an old-fashioned cop; otherwise he would have sent Dobie packing long before. 'Yes?'

'Yes?'

'Well, what is it?'

'I don't know,' Dobie said. 'I mean . . . I've sort of forgotten.'

Jackson, habituated like all policemen to the solitary boredom of endless hours on the beat, was never averse to edifying conversation and Kate had some minutes earlier drawn up a chair up to the telephone in recognition of the fact that whatever it was she hadn't been doing that morning wasn't going to get done anyway.

54

God knows (she thought) why women are notoriously supposed to over-indulge in idle gossip; men are far worse than we are, and policemen are the worst of the lot. Though Jacko did seem to be a little off-colour this morning, lacking in his usual verve and brio. His account of a recent run-in with (of all people) Dr Emrys Williams Williams, the police MO, who had wrongly diagnosed a disagreeable stiffness of his (Jackson's) triceps muscles as being due to a niggling attack of arthritis rather than to a serious flesh wound which, having been incurred in the line of duty, might reflect beneficially upon an eventual pension award was, though superficially moving, notably deficient in fervour and zip, especially when you took into account the disagreeable nature of the said Dr Williams Williams, a blight (in Kate's opinion) on the medical profession and a crumb of the first water. 'You *do* sound a bit under the weather, Jacko. But you don't want to let these things get on top of you.'

'I know, I know.' Jackson seemed to be slightly mollified by this sympathetic comment but still very much less than gratified. 'It's been a troublifying week, though, apart from all that nonsense, and now this hit-and-run thing . . . if that's what it *is* . . . Still, at least we went and won a case for a change. Warms the cockles, it does, when that happens. Of course,' returning to the elegiac mode, 'it doesn't happen very often.'

'A big one?'

'About as big as they come round here. Dai Dymond. Gone down for a good old stretch at last.'

'*That* bastard? About time, too.'

'That's just what he'll be doing. Time. Seven years of it. Went down heavy and not many people are shedding tears about it, I'll tell you that. Didn't you read about it in the papers?'

Kate rarely read the newspapers and when she did, invariably later wished that she hadn't. Good news of this kind, however, might have come as a welcome variant. 'No, I didn't.'

'They gave us a pretty good spread. Pontin had his photo in an' all.'

'He'll be pleased, then.'

'Chirpy as a poodle with two tails. We had a bit of luck, though, no question of it.'

'Someone grassed?'

'Spilt it all over the shop. Haining, it was. Just who you'd have least expected. Funny how it happens that way sometimes.'

'Who's Haining?'

'Chartered accountant bloke. Used to keep old Dai's books and fudge up his tax returns.'

'You're not telling me you sent him down for income tax evasion?'

'No, no, no. We got him on possession of something like half a ton of crack in one of his warehouses and the Customs and Excise boys nabbed the blokes on the other end. All went like a dream. On information received, of course. No names, no pack drill.'

'But how did you get Haining to—'

'Ironies of life, Kate, ironies of life. One of the uniformed branch brought in Haining's son on a breaking-and-entering charge, pharma-suiticle store, usual story – kid was dying for a fix. Haining had no idea the boy was into drugs, apparently, and when he found out he'd been getting his fixes through one of Dai Dymond's pushers he went bananas. Walked straight into the CID room with a whole load of papers and talked Dai straight into Strangeways, just about. See what I mean when I say it's ironical, right?'

'Biter bit.'

'Exactly.'

'What sort of a deal did you give him?'

'Best we could. Indemnity for himself and a spell on probation for the kid, subsequent on proper medical treatment. Protection, no. He didn't ask for it. I imagine he'll have dug himself a nice deep hole and buried himself in it by now, because there'll be quite a few very nasty customers who have to be very cross with him.'

'And maybe quite a few kids who won't be trying to break into my clinic over the next few years.'

'I wouldn't rely too much on that, if I were you. Like a hydrant, those people are.'

'Like *what*?'

'*You* know. Cut off one head and they grow another.'

'Ah. Right. I'm with you. Mind you, we do a better job of it in the medical profession.'

'Stay dead, do they, when you've finished with 'em? I suppose they do.' Jackson rumbled obscenely again. 'Well, I reckon I'd best get off the line and give Paddy Oates a ring. See how he's getting on.'

'You know Paddy. Slow but sure. You can always drive round to the mortuary and check on his progress, if you want to.'

'A nice quiet Sunday morning I was looking forward to, Kate, till this happened.'

'So was I.'

The porter replaced the telephone and with his other hand pushed the clipboard across the desk towards Dobie. 'That's all in order, sir, if you'll be good enough to sign in. . . .'

Dobie did so. He then observed that he had incorrectly entered *Time of Arrival* as 1145 instead of 1045; it was indeed extraordinary, when you thought about it, that a Professor of Mathematics . . . He shook his head sadly, crossed out the offending entry and tried again, getting it right this time.

'Main building, sir, main entry, and you'll find Dr Carter's office second door on the right.' The porter had clearly summed him up as a stray lamb in need of all possible assistance, if not indeed as a likely future inmate. 'I take it you're carrying no offensive weppings nor nothing that could be used as such.'

'Me? Offensive weapons? Good Heavens, no.' Dobie was alarmed. 'Surely I'm not likely to be—'

'Oh no, sir, no, no chance of *that*, we don't allow 'em to wander around the place just as they like – this *is* Her Majesty's property after all. We take all the proper security precautions, you can be sure.'

'Does *everybody* have to fill in that form?' Dobie stared down resentfully at the clipboard before handing it back.

'All visitors do, yes sir. Certainly.'

'I didn't last night.'

'Ah well, that was an emergency now, wasn't it? But I made a note of the number of your car, don't you worry about *that*.' The porter nodded towards the television monitor on the right-hand side of his desk, which indeed showed a full-frontal black and white view of Dobie's mud-splashed Fiesta parked before the closed iron gates of the Centre. 'No, the people here never give us any trouble but that's because we make sure that they don't. They've put in these monitor camera things all over the main building so the staff can keep an eye on them. And some of the things they get up to . . . Well, you wouldn't believe me if I was to tell you. Real screwballs, some of 'em. But harmless enough.'

'Can you get any other programmes?'

'Eh?'

'*Watch with Mother*? Anything like that? They used to have a really rather amusing programme in which this small animal, I rather think it was a hamster or possibly a gerbil—'

'I don't think that's on any more, sir, and anyway no, we couldn't get it, that's not the idea at all. It's just a tool of the trade, so to speak. By the way, those look like your car keys on the desk. Don't go off without 'em.'

'Right. Yes. So they are.' Dobie picked them up and put them away in his pocket, where presumably they'd be safer than anywhere else. 'Splendid. And thanks for your help.'

'Main building, sir. Main entry. Second office—'

'Yes, I've got that. I *think*. But I really meant to say, for your help last night.'

'Did what I could, sir, and I'm sure Dr Mighell did. Sorry things didn't work out any better. I'm told the young lady didn't make it.'

'No. She didn't. It's a police matter now.'

'And so it should be. Had the boys round earlier this morning, in fact, and having been a cop myself I'd've liked to be of help but what could I tell 'em? Had I seen any girls walking down the road yesterday afternoon? You have to be joking, I told 'em, with a girls' school just round the corner from here they're going up and down the road all the time. Nice little bits, too, some of 'em, but that's by the way. But I don't know any of them to reckernize, how would I? Except young Elspeth, of course. She's running in and out of here all the time, specially on a Saturday afternoon. As for *your* young lady, sir, I got no more'n a glimpse of her sitting in the back of your car but from what I saw I didn't know her from Adam, or Eve rather, and even if they brought me a photograph of her I doubt if I could say if I'd ever seen her before or not. I mean, these kids are much of a muchness when you think about it, some are older than the others is all you can say. And when they're all in school uniforms or else in them blue jean things, it doesn't make it any easier.'

All this garrulity, Dobie decided, had to be attributed to the extreme boredom inherent in the other's occupation rather than to any desire to communicate information. As this was true of himself also in his role of university lecturer, he was able to sympathize. 'You know,' he said, 'some of my students nowadays. . . . I can't always tell if they're girls or boys. It's embarrassing, sometimes.'

'*They* seem to know all right.'

'I suppose they do, but they don't always seem to care.'

'Well, you got to live and let live,' the porter said broad-mindedly, 'where these kids are concerned. As long as they don't end up *here* . . . but a damned sight too many of them do. Ninety per cent of the blokes that get sent here are under twenty-five, and more than half of *them* are teenagers. Take it from me. Because it's a fact.'

Dobie wasn't surprised at this second intimation that Jackson and his cohorts were in action, because it was clear that action of one kind or another was likely in any case to be forced on them. Dobie, like Kate, wasn't a great peruser of the daily press, but he was well enough aware of that broad journalistic dictum which insists that while the violent death of an eighty-year-old grand-mother who gets kicked on the head by a group of yobbos after picking up her pension at the Post Office merits three or four lines of comment on page five, the murder of a seventeen-year-old schoolgirl by a (hypothetical) sex fiend deserves very different treatment and invariably gets it and the police will be wise, in such circumstances, to make sure that their own tracks, if not those of the sex fiend in question, are very well covered and can be seen to be so. There was, after all, an element of mystery in this affair.

To put it mildly.

As indeed there was about the edifice that now rose up in front of him as he drove sedately in through the entry gate. Toad Hall, viewed at this distance in sombre Welsh daylight, did indeed resemble, nay *was*, one of those huge castellated monstrosities wherein the local mine owners had, in Victorian times, been wont to incarcerate their families and whole armies of obsequious servants, all forelock-touching and curtsying away like billy-oh. From that point of view, you could say it had been obviously readily adaptable to its present purpose, especially when you considered the twelve-foot stone wall that surrounded the entire establishment and which had been no doubt originally designed to hold at bay footpads, gentlemen of the high toby, and others of *hoi polloi*; their contemporary equivalents could now with similar ease and efficiency be kept inside, an interesting example (Dobie thought) of the concept of the reversional equation.

However, in response to the demands of all those inky-pinky libs in the Welsh Office the premises had been livened up considerably by a group of youthful architects whose chief aim might well have been to give the Prince of Wales a severe attack of the heebie-jeebies, a great deal of plate-glass, ceramic tile, and cracking concrete having been superimposed upon the original structure to create an effect that grew ever more weird and wonderful as one approached near enough to observe the shiny metal bars that obstructed egress from all those trendy picture windows and the red-brick facings that irresistibly suggested the street perspective of the Odeon Cinema, Clapham, as recalled by Dobie, constructed in 1932 and mercifully pulled down by property developers some twenty years later. Dobie parked his car outside the main entrance and entered the foyer, blinking round him instinctively in search of the box office. There wasn't one, though there was a sort of reception desk by the far wall with nobody there. Instead, then, Dobie made his way down the well-lit passage opening to his right where a sign said REGISTRY and where other doors to either side of the passage, like that of the registry itself, remained inimically closed. The door immediately beyond the registry bore a plastic plaque that said DR HORATIO CARTER, white lettering on a navy-blue background. Dobie stared at it in mild surprise. He seemed to have lucked out the first time round. He knocked on the door. 'Come,' someone – presumably Dr Carter – said. Obediently, Dobie came.

'Ah, hullo again,' Dr Carter said. 'Take a chair.'

Dobie compiled with this instruction also. 'I suppose,' he said, 'it's after Nelson.'

'Sorry?'

'The Horatio bit.'

'Oh, that. After the footballer, actually. My old grandad was a fanatical admirer of his – named his son after him – my father, that was – and my father just followed the trend, you might say. Great player, of course.'

'Your father?'

'No, no. Horatio Carter.'

'But you said your father *was* Horatio Carter.'

'Yes. So am I, if it comes to that.'

'What I don't quite see is how your grandfather comes into it in the first place.'

Dr Carter began to look rather worried.

'This *is* a friendly visit, Mr Dobie? I mean, you haven't come in search of any kind of *treatment*?'

'Of course not. No. Naturally not. It's in connection with my friend Mr . . .' Dobie paused. The name seemed to have escaped him – only momentarily, of course. Annoying, all the same. 'Bloke with the ginger beard. *You* must know him.'

'Adrian Seymour.'

'*That*'s the one.'

'Of course I know Adrian,' Carter said. 'It'd be surprising if I didn't.'

'Why?'

'Why what?'

'Why would it be —'

'All right, don't tell me, I've got it,' Carter said, speaking with great rapidity and ejecting a very small globule of spittle from the side of his mouth. 'I know him because he *has* been coming to me for psychiatric treatment – three times a week – for, let's see, something like six weeks now. Ever since he came here, in fact. *That*'s why I think I can claim to know him – if anyone does.'

'What do you mean, if anyone does? *I* do. For instance.'

'Yes, I'm aware of that. A figure of speech, merely.'

'A what?'

'Never mind. Can we get to the nitty-gritty, Mr Dobie?'

'Oh, certainly.'

There followed rather a long silence, at the end of which Carter cleared his throat. 'Perhaps, Mr Dobie, you'd feel a little more comfortable if we went into the inner office. There's a comfortable couch there where you can lie down and perhaps feel a little more at ease. Sometimes people here encounter a little initial difficulty in giving their ideas free expression —'

'No, no,' Dobie said. 'I'm perfectly comfortable in this chair. No, I was waiting. That's all.'

'Waiting?'

'For you to get to the nitty-gritty. Like you said.'

'Oh. I see. A little misunderstanding. I was waiting for *you* to get to the nitty-gritty. Whatever that is.'

'Ah. I thought . . . Silly of me. Ho ho ho.'

'No, no. Ho ho ho. Silly of *me*.'

'Ho ho ho ho.'

'Ho ho.'

Another long silence.

Dobie had stopped laughing but, in order to show that this implied no dimunition in the general amicability of his intentions, had continued to display almost the entire register of his lower mandibles in a quizzically macho grin, rather in the manner of Michael Douglas. But not *altogether* like Michael Douglas. More like Christopher Lee, really, in one of his spirited impersonations of Count Dracula. Carter, disconcerted either by this or by the sudden alarming fixity of Dobie's gaze, allowed his hand to stray in the direction of that small button at the side of his desk which, on being depressed —

'*Ha!*' Dobie said explosively. 'Got you now.'

'Wock?' Carter said, sucking his knuckles.

'Got you placed now. You're the jigger.'

'I am?'

'I mean the jogger. Chap who kindly showed me the way last night.'

'That's right. I remember the occasion distinctly. I'm a little surprised —'

'Showed me the way to whatname's house. Extremely kind of you. Well, it just goes to show. It's a small world.'

'Perhaps it would help,' Carter said, though frankly he was now beginning to doubt that *anything* would, 'if I were to describe to you the situation as I presently see it. A brief *recap*, so to speak. Now then. As a result of your last night's conversation with Morris Train, some parts of which it's possible you may recall, Morris asked me to make myself available to you this morning at ten o'clock' – he glanced at his wristwatch – 'so that we could discuss the position of Adrian Seymour, who is my patient here and as I understand it a personal friend of yours. Morris also said that you might be prepared to recommend Adrian to certain prospective employers upon his release from the Centre and that therefore I should seek to satisfy you, not of course as to his professional capacities but as to the overall stability and reliability of his personality, bearing in mind the drug-addiction problem to which, as we know, he's been subject, and certain other psychological traumas arising, we believe, from his exposure to a very difficult and trying domestic situation. And that assurance I believe I can give you. With every confidence.'

'Yes, but—'

'In my opinion, Adrian's reliance upon drugs is to be attributed to his inability to deal with the personal problem that I mentioned and which I've discussed with him at considerable length on many occasions. Although in one sense the problem has now disappeared – the woman being dead – the resultant guilt complex, I'll admit, required a fair amount of detailed investigation and in-depth therapy. The suggestion that he himself killed his wife can be dismissed as ridiculous. There's nothing in it, nothing whatsoever.'

Dobie's attention had not unnaturally begun to wander. Or more exactly, become focused on his immediate surroundings. Carter's office appeared to be rather smaller than he had originally supposed, and the inner office even smaller, being virtually filled by the couch to which Carter had made allusion – which looked in fact more like a hospital bed, with various ominous-looking metal projections jutting from its base – and by a no less ominous-looking metal machine on a table with wires looped around its frame and by a black swivel chair with a tilted headrest. It could indeed only be called an inner office by courtesy, being screened off from the room where they now sat only by a gunmetal-grey curtain. All quite different from Kate's cheerfully old-fashioned consulting room. 'Yes, quite,' Dobie said. 'But—'

'And that's not a mere opinion. It's been firmly established through hypnotherapy. Despite a certain surface show of aggressiveness, Adrian really possesses a remarkably mild and pacific personality. Indeed one might almost say that there lies the root of the whole matter. The inability to take positive steps when steps of such a kind are called for. The Hamlet syndrome, in fact.'

'It's odd you should say—'

'I expect you'd like to know what forms of mental therapy are practised here. Well, I think I may safely say our methods are highly non-eclectic. We've found gestalt therapy to work very well where the root problem can be ascribed to acquired rather than to hereditary characteristics, which is the case with Adrian. And of course the drug addiction responds best to chemotherapic treatment, in other words a phased withdrawal. If you wish, our secretary will let you have the printout which gives you his whole medical history since his return to this country and a more general picture of his social and personal background. Needless to say, it's a confidential document, but in view of Morris Train's express instructions—'

Dobie was beginning to feel a little desperate. The porter's garrulity had been as nothing in comparison with this seemingly interminable flow of garbage. 'What I'd like to know,' he said, 'is about the dreams.'

'The dreams?'

'Yes. The dreams.'

'Ah. The *dreams*. Well, you know – all that Freudian-interpretation stuff is regarded as a little old hat these days. If that's what you . . . We have a number of EEG recordings, however, which may interest you. He's certainly a highly imaginative feller but clinically speaking one's always wise to dismiss—'

'He said he'd talked to you about them.'

'So he has, so he has. So many patients seem to think . . . But we don't practise psychoanalysis here, not really. Of course everything's recorded on tape but quite honestly that's something of a placebo. . . . As long as the patient sees that the spools are turning he seems to be satisfied that we're taking his problems seriously. And indeed we are. I've never discouraged him or anyone else from talking absolutely freely, quite the contrary. And some of his ideas have struck me as being quite . . . I've even suggested that he commit them to paper as he clearly has some sort of literary aptitude. In fact I don't mind betting . . . Well, let's see. . . .'

He moved the television monitor on the side-table round on its swivel, flicked a practised finger towards one switch on the console and then another. The blank screen turned misty in a quite familiar way, then cleared to show a less familiar image; Dobie, craning his neck a little, could see Adrian Seymour sitting at a small folding table and staring gloomily at a portable typewriter, from the roller of which a sheet of paper protruded. 'There you go,' Carter said. 'Scribble, scribble, scribble, eh, Mr Gibbon? I don't know if creative work has any *real* value but it has a valuable therapeutic effect, no one disputes it. And music, of course.'

'Music?'

'*Good* music. Classical music. Not Beethoven, of course, he's a bit too . . . disruptive. . . . But lots of Bach and Handel and . . .

and so forth. The kids take to it after a while, you know, even the ones who've never heard anything but pop.' Carter pressed another switch and Seymour disappeared in a puff of smoke, like Mephistopheles or an Arabian djinn. Dobie blinked.

'There's one of those at the main gate. I mean, the porter chap has one.'

'There's one in every consulting room if it comes to that. Any time we want to run a spot check on any of the lads . . . We're really quite proud of our surveillance system. Time- and energy-conserving, you see. Far better than the old judas window.'

Dobie was looking around the room. Books on a shelf, a cassette-recorder and microphone tucked away underneath, a green filing cabinet, a built-in clothes locker, everything almost offensively neat and tidy. 'Very clever how you conceal the camera, too. I really wouldn't have thought—'

'Oh, there's no camera in *here*. Here you're on the other end of the line, so to speak, we wouldn't want anyone eavesdropping on our consultancy sessions even by accident. They're highly confidential, as you can imagine. There are cameras damned near everywhere else, though. I can tell you, we had the security inspectors round only a month ago and they were greatly impressed. *Very* greatly impressed.'

'But just now you said something about tapes. . . .'

'Tapes?'

'Yes, you said you recorded the—'

'Oh yes, so we do, so we do, and they're all tabbed and dated and stashed away in my little filing cabinet but they're not a hell of a lot of practical *use*, I mean with the best will in the world no one's got the time to listen to *playbacks* all day long. I've got all I ever need in my little notebook, thank you very much, and any of the other consultants will tell you the same.'

A somewhat querulous tone seemed to have entered his voice, giving an edge to the flatness of his northern accent. 'I suppose,' Dobie said, 'it must get a little boring here at times. You're rather far removed, aren't you, from the bright lights and that sort of thing?'

'True. But I'm not much of a one for that sort of thing anyway. And now that I've taken up jogging—'

'And female companionship. It's pretty much of an all-male community here, isn't it?'

'Ah well, for that we've always got our Miss Daly right next door. We'll step round there now,' Carter said, rising from his desk with some alacrity, 'and see if she can't let you take a quick look through Adrian's records. She won't let you take away the printout, I'm afraid, that's not permitted, but you can make a note of any information you may need and . . . It's all a matter of public record after all.'

'So it is,' Miss Daly said, 'in the sense that it all comes through to us from the Central Records Office. But I can't believe that the CRO would approve of my handing out printouts to all and sundry.'

Even while staring severely at Dobie she found herself relenting. Well, slightly. There was something inexplicably appealing about the way he was wrinkling his forehead at her, like a basset hound. Even his ears appeared to be drooping mournfully.

'But just this once I'll see what I can do.'

Dobie, in fact, often wore just this expression when in the process of succumbing to feminine charm. Perhaps something a little more *secretarial* in the way of kimono-style silk blouses might have . . . And there again, it mightn't. 'Here you go,' Miss Daly observed. 'Seymour, Adrian. That's your boy.' She flipped a folder from the filing cabinet and returned to hand it to Dobie. 'I can't allow you to take it away, of course. It's highly confidential information. In fact I don't remember ever—'

'I can take notes?'

'I suppose so. Sit down here if you like.'

'But surely this is your desk?'

'That's all right. I'm working at the computer right now.'

Dobie, thus reassured, sat down at the desk and opened the folder in what he hoped to be a businesslike manner. He didn't imagine for a moment that taking notes would serve any useful purpose but that, again, had seemed to him a businesslike sort of thing to say at the time; accordingly, he drew a felt-tip pen from his inner pocket with an executive-style flick of the wrist, suggestive of King Arthur whipping Excalibur from the rock, and pulled a notepad (presumably Miss Daly's) towards him. It was rather a posh notepad with headed paper:

66

Registrar's Office

Under this heading Dobie wrote purposefully:

Adrian Seymour

pausing then to regard his handiwork. There. He'd made a note. So far so good, it had to be supposed.

He opened the folder.

It contained exactly what he'd expected. Several sheets of printed medical gibberish. Far more in Kate's line than in his, but in all probability Kate wouldn't have made very much of it, either. Interspersed with all that impenetrable jargon, however, were a certain number of comments recorded in normal English and a certain number of dates. Seymour, it seemed, had been transferred from the Eljit Mental Hospital, Nicosia, to the Everdene Institute, Gloucester, in October last year; had undergone an approved course of treatment for drug and alcohol addiction; and had, on completion of this course, been sent to the Tongwylais Rehabilitation Centre on February 12th last, his release being now, it seemed, dependent upon the production of satisfactory reports as to his psychic condition and overall health by his personal Case Officer. In other words, Dr Horatio Carter. Everything, in short, appeared to be very much as Dobie had supposed.

Miss Daly had retired to some kind of inner sanctum or Holy of Holies behind a plywood partition – her office was virtually identical to Carter's but was even more crowded with filing cabinets and other less easily identifiable items of equipment, these necessitating the sinuous and hip-wiggly mode of progress that Dobie had earlier observed – and appeared to be there telephoning someone, or at any rate trying to do so without meeting with much success. The fault, Dobie reflected, probably lay not so much with the system as with the fact that it was a Sunday morning. 'I know, I *know*,' Miss Daly was saying petulantly, 'but even so. . . .' Dobie tore off the sheet of notepaper upon which he had seemingly scrawled something and stared at it. *Adrian Seymour. . . .* Strange. That was Adrian Seymour's name. Oh well. He put it in his pocket along with his pen and closed the folder and picked it up and, circumnavigating the filing cabinets, found himself at once staring lugubriously down into the V-neck

67

of Miss Daly's blouse. She had abandoned the telephone and was now staring equally lugubriously down at the monitor screen of a somewhat antiquated computer. 'Shit, shit, shit,' Miss Daly said. Then, becoming aware of Dobie's insignificant presence, raised her eyes to direct at him the malignant gaze of a basilisk disturbed at its breakfast. 'What is it *now*?'

'Nothing,' Dobie said. 'I mean, I've finished.'

'Lucky you,' Miss Daly said, taking the folder from him and tossing it contemptuously on to a wire tray standing on a side table. 'Did you find what you wanted?'

'Well, not really. But then I'm not quite sure what it was I wanted to find in the first place. Do you *always* work Sundays?'

'When I'm running behind schedule I do. In other words, yes, I always work Sundays. But no one else seems to, that's for sure. So sometimes I don't know why I bother.'

'There's a problem?'

'There is indeed. So if you're quite *sure* you've finished doing whatever—'

'Oh yes. I have. But if I can be of use to you in your hour of need—'

'I regard that as highly unlikely,' Miss Daly said. 'Unless you know something about computers.'

'I know everything that there is to know,' Dobie said, 'about computers. What you do is, you press that little button at the side and then when the doodah thing lights up—'

Miss Daly sighed deeply, causing interesting convulsions in the inner configurations of the blouse. 'The computer, as such, is working perfectly. But the link doesn't seem to be operating properly. Or, in fact, at all.'

'The link?'

'To the main computer in the Records Office.'

'Ah.' Dobie considered the problem for a moment. 'Well, I can see where the trouble lies. It's all buggered up.'

'You put it in a nutshell.'

'Have you tried reprogramming the access code?'

'Have I *what*?'

'That should do it.'

'I'm sure it should, if you say so. But I haven't the least idea how to set about it.'

'Well, would you like me to try?'

Dobie, anxious to impress, sat down beside her and tried. It took him a little less than three minutes. 'There you are,' he said.

Miss Daly stared at him in disbelief. 'But that's *miraculous*.'

'No, no. All these government offices use very simple access acronyms, I mean they *have* to, you see, or this sort of thing would be happening all the time and no one could put it right. Or not very easily. If you like, we'll run a printout to check but you've got your linkage all right.' Dobie stood up, his eyes still fixed on the lines of outwardly impenetrable jargon running across the monitor screen. 'It's quite an efficient system in the ordinary way. I take it they transmit the medical history sheets to you direct and you update them every so often – is that how it goes?'

'Once a week,' Miss Daly said. 'The staff hand in their report sheets and I record them. So the CRO have access to up-to-date information on the progress of all our clients and can advise the Parole Board accordingly. That's how it goes in theory, anyway.' She appeared to have melted considerably. Dobie for once had clearly scored some useful Brownie points. Splendid.

'And in practice?'

'All I do is record and file the information. It's no business of mine who acts on it.'

'Have you had any hiccups before?'

'Not since I've been here. Just on a year now.'

'And you like the job?'

'I dunno. It's interesting. Sometimes. I mean, some of the people here . . . They're a bit bizarre. . . .'

'The inmates? Or the staff?'

The faintest flicker of a smile momentarily disturbed the smooth impassivity of Miss Daly's countenance. 'I don't get to file reports on the staff. Maybe it's just as well.'

'It's rather a male-orientated community, isn't it? Are you the *only* woman in the place?'

'Apart from the kitchen staff, yes. But I don't mind that particularly. Why should I?'

Paddy Oates had been cutting up other people's bodies for some thirty years now, though not, of course, all the time; he had, unlike Miss Daly, the weekends off and sometimes when the supply of corpses ran regrettably short he was even able to take a short holiday, usually in Majorca. Having very recently returned from just such a jaunt he was looking brown and healthy, if a little bleary-eyed, and this did something, Jackson thought, to relieve the overall cheesed-offness of his expression. If he had on this occasion to relieve the monotony of a Sunday morning by dissecting a cadaver he didn't, his expression suggested, have to like it.

'I know what you're going to say,' Jackson said tiredly. 'But as you're going to say it anyway, you may as well go ahead.'

'Ah, what's the point of it all if you're not prepared to listen?'

'I didn't say I wouldn't *listen*. What I said was—'

'You'll get my report tomorrow morning without fail, Jacko. That's my usual custom and I see no reason to diverge from it because it happens to be *Sunday morning*.'

Paddy took his lab jacket off and stabbed it into the waiting laundry basket. It *did* seem to have got a bit . . . Yes. Not a nice job, Jackson thought, even on a weekday, though some kind of satisfaction might be derived from being extremely good at it, as Paddy Oates was. 'The trouble is,' he said, 'this is one of those bastards where I need something to go on if I'm to take the appropriate action. Otherwise I wouldn't push you. Hell, you should know that by now.'

'And *you* should know that I won't commit myself to any definite statements until I'm sure of the medical facts. What was it exactly that you wished to know?'

'Oh, come *on*, Paddy.'

'The girl was *killed*, no question of natural causes. Severe cranial trauma and contributory hypothermia. As to *how* she was killed . . .' Paddy drew a cigarette from its shoulder holster with notably tremorless fingers and, seemingly with the same movement, lit it and exhaled an enormous streamer of smoke across the preparations room. 'That's what at the present stage I'm not prepared to say. But I agree with Kate that the hit-and-run theory can be discarded – unless she was trying to butt a moving motorcar like a goat, which is hardly credible behaviour by any standards. The minor contusions – which aren't so *very* minor, by the way – aren't consistent with that theory, either. What *they* suggest is that she got beaten up, and very badly. The fractured ulna, now . . . She might have been holding up her arm to ward off a blow. That kind of an injury very often occurs in just such a way. But of course there are alternative explanations.'

Jackson nodded. 'Right. That gives me a GBH charge to work on, at least. With a strong premonition, wouldn't you say, of an eventual committal for murder?'

'*I* would say a strong *presumption*, but that's all. There's no indication of considerable blood loss, but that's not very significant either way.' Jackson crossed something out in his black notebook and made a hurried correction. 'The girl was struck repeatedly and with vicious intent. I can't say what she was struck *with*, but it wasn't a cutting instrument. An edge, but a blunt edge. You say Kate suggested a brick, or something like that. . . . OK, but it could as easily have been a mallet or a heavy spanner. Swinging blows, anyway. Not thrusts.'

Jackson continued to scribble busily. 'She got bashed about, then. Was she raped?'

Paddy made a clicking noise with his tongue, indicative of irritation and impatience. 'You know as well as I do that I can't say yes or no to *that* one. She had intercourse, certainly, shortly before she died – maybe immediately before, maybe an hour or so previously. Not more. But rape, I mean, what are you *asking* me? The girl says yes and it isn't. The girl says no and it is. I can't tell you what the girl *said*, for God's sake. What I *can* tell you is that she bit her fingernails – as you probably noticed for yourself. Right down to the quick. Therefore, no skin tissue caught up in them. Not that it would of itself be completely convincing, even if there were.'

'It'd indicate some kind of a struggle, wouldn't it? It'd show that she put up a bit of a fight.'

'Yes, but perfectly ordinary acts of intercourse can be pretty violent, you know. There are quite a few bite marks on the shoulders and breasts, if it comes to that, and they show up pretty well on the photographs. But the contusions are too ragged to be useful. I know Simpson once got a conviction on the strength of a bite mark, but that was in the old days. Juries aren't impressed by odontological forensics and judges aren't, either – as you very well know.'

'But isn't it indicative of sado-whatsit? I mean—'

'Not even that. Not really. Especially not when girls are as young as this one was and there's a certain amount of purely nominal resistance.'

'She'd have been a bit tight, you reckon?'

'You put it cogently for once, Jacko.'

'But Kate seemed to think it wasn't her first time out.'

'Oh no. It wasn't. Definitely not. And the answer to the next question is negative. She wasn't pregnant. No.'

'Even so.' Jackson closed his notebook. 'It looks as though the next step is chair-shay le boyfriend. As usual.'

'Maybe. Though if you chair-shay les girlfriends first, they'll probably be able to tell you who the boyfriend was. You may well get a better line from them than you'll get from the forensics. She had to have been lying in the rain for quite a while.' Paddy shook his head sadly. 'Might as well have been lying in a cold bath from *their* point of view. And her clothes, such as they were . . . just about washed clean. Don't hope for too much from the lab on this one, Jacko.'

'Hope springs internal,' Jackson said, 'as my old Dadda used to say.'

'Still at school, wasn't she?' Paddy was at the washbasin now, completing his scrubbing-up. 'Well, we've had a good few of 'em in the past, haven't we, one way or another. . . ? But it still makes you think. If you've got kids of your own, that is. Like we have.'

'I'm going to put this boyo away,' Jackson said. 'Don't you worry.'

'Sure you will. But your Charley's going to be another stupid little kid like *she* was, had one drink too many or sniffed up something he shouldn't have. . . . That's the trouble. But talking about liquid refreshment, they should be open by now if you'd fancy a pint.'

'Ah, well,' Jackson said. Sunday morning. *He* wasn't officially on duty, either. 'Why not?'

Dobie wasn't a highly imaginative and certainly not a superstitious man but the sight of the figure seated at the side of the road gave him a considerable shock. He distinctly felt his hair stand on end, a feat of levitation he had previously imagined only to be attainable in works of fiction of the triter sort; his moustache might also conceivably have stood on end, if most of it hadn't been in that condition already. He was able, however, a moment later completely to recover his aplomb and to brake the car, get out of it, and approach the seated figure at an appropriately calm, sedate, and professorial gait. 'Oh hullo, hi, hi,' Elspeth said.

From a distance her posture had seemed to be somewhat disconsolate but the smile with which she greeted him was cheerful enough. Indeed, almost radiant. Really, Dobie thought, an attractive child; the navy-blue parka and short sports skirt she was wearing didn't reflect in any way adequately her personality. 'You gave me a bit of a turn, sitting there,' Dobie said.

'I did? Why?'

'Because you're wearing the same things as—'

Dobie stopped short. Not quickly enough, but the girl had sensed his meaning at once and didn't seem to be at all perturbed. 'As Bev was? We've *all* got these things. It's the school uniform, sort of. They don't give us *clothes* nowadays. Just clobber.'

'Oh, I see. May I . . . ?' Sitting down beside her. 'How very odd.'

'No, it isn't. It's progressive and democratic and all that jazz. Unless you meant it's the clobber that's odd.' She looked down doubtfully at the long, slightly skinny legs protruding from her skirt. 'Yum. Maybe. But at least it's practical. Been visiting the old folks at home?'

'Someone called Carter.'

'Oh. Popeye. He's a bit of a nerd but he's all right really. Always tearing round in his underpants and flexing his muscles generally. I wish he wouldn't.'

'And what have *you* been doing?'

'Oh, just out for a walk. My Sunday morning stroll. I usually walk best sitting down, as you've noticed. Anything to get out of that horrible dump, really. I mean, *school*'s better. I don't mind *school*. But weekends . . . They're pretty awful.'

Dobie could see what she meant. Literally, since the high stone walls of the Centre were clearly visible a half-mile or so down the road, distance in this case failing to lend any kind of enchantment to the view. The barren sweep of moorland to either side of them might well have excited the poet Wordsworth, who would doubtless have sallied immediately forth in search of leech gatherers and such, but held no comparable appeal to Professor Dobie, while Elspeth and her companions in exile would certainly have exchanged the whole bang shoot for a decently appointed bowling alley or even, if it came to the crunch, for the Odeon Cinema, Clapham. 'No, it can't be very nice living in a place like that. I'd hate it.'

'Yes, but it's the *house* I meant. I really wish I could be a boarder but Dad says there's no way he can afford it. He probably can't. Not now. With his alimony payments and all.'

'It seemed like quite a pleasant house to me.'

'The trouble is I'm an inconvenience.'

'Yes.' Dobie, having considered the matter further, nodded. 'I can see how you might be.'

'It's great to meet someone who doesn't just pat me on the shoulder and say something consoling. I *know* Dad loves me and all that but it doesn't help.'

'When I was your age,' Dobie said, 'that's what I used to think about God. As a matter of fact, I sometimes still do.'

'Oh, well, I wouldn't bring *Him* into the argument. Or *Her*, as the case may be. I really *loathe* all this stupid feminist stuff, don't you? But I'll tell you something else that *is* consoling. About ninety per cent of the kids at the school think just as I do about it. I don't know what girls' schools were like all those years ago when *you* were a boy,' Elspeth said deflatingly, 'but nowadays they're repositories for unwanted female children, *that*'s what they are. Girls like me who're *inconveniences*. And I think it's a bloody awful state of affairs, I really do.'

'The education can't be all that bad, though,' Dobie said. 'You've got a remarkable range of vocabulary for a girl your age.'

'That's what Dad said the other day when I went and caught my toe under the door. Absolutely shocking, he said it was. I told him a doctor shouldn't be shocked by references to a perfectly natural human function but that only seemed to make matters worse. Men of his age are so *peculiar*.'

'I expect he does his best,' Dobie said.

'Yes, he does. But all this crap they give you about single-parent families being just as good as the other kind, it really is a lot of . . .'

'Balls?'

'Yes. Thanks. I mean, how can it *be* a family if there's only one of you? It's like one of those para-things you were talking about.'

'A contradiction in terms. Like multi-cultural society.'

'Oh, we got that, too. At school, I mean. Girls from all over. E.g., Bev. She came from Italy, you know. She could speak Italian, or said she could. It must be really glam, living in Italy, gosh.'

Dobie stared again at the wild Welsh countryside surrounding him and at the skies which once again were clouding over fast. He'd been wise, he thought, to take his raincoat, whoever's it was. It would certainly be a bit of a change, he thought, for a girl accustomed to the tropical delights of a Mediterranean country to land up in a dismal dump like this. 'She couldn't,' he said, voicing his thought, 'have fancied the school all that rotten, then.'

'No. Of course, she wasn't an Italian, I mean she was born in Wales. In Cardiff, I think. But last year her mother married an Italian or something like that . . . and I suppose Bev got to be an inconvenience like the rest of us. So they sent her back here. I don't know the whole story, mind.'

'She hadn't been at the school very long, then?'

'No, she only came this term. That's why no one knows her very well. Except maybe Midge. Midge shared a room with her, you see. And so she's quite cut up about . . . what happened.'

'Is Midge another inconvenience?'

'Very probably. It seems to be becoming a pretty common cultural phemonnymum.'

'Phenomenon. One of these days,' Dobie said, 'I'll introduce you to my friend Detective Inspector Jackson. You two should get on like a house on fire, improving each other's vocabulary.'

'I think I've met him already. If he's the one who came round last night asking us questions.'

'Yes, that was probably him. What did he ask you?'

'Just if I'd seen Bev at all that afternoon.'

'And had you?'

'Nope. Couldn't have. Saturday afternoons I play hockey. I'm in the First Eleven, you see.'

'Really?' Dobie's experience of the sport was virtually limited to a single occasion upon which a scratch college team of which he was an (unwilling) member had rashly undertaken to engage one of the women's colleges on the field of battle; three of his team-mates, he well remembered, had been carried off (groaning) on improvised stretchers and he himself had carried the imprint of a small spiked boot on his tummy for most of the remainder of the term. 'You must be a good player.'

'Not really. I'm just big for my age and I can run quite fast. When I have to.'

'Ah. A useful accomplishment,' Dobie said. 'Nowadays.'

She was appropriately dressed for it, too, he noticed, in a pair of rather flamboyant Nike trainers, though these didn't seem to have any spikes and hence could be regarded as defensive rather than offensive weapons. Of course the kids wore those things all the time at the University, all day and every day; they probably went to sleep in them, for all he knew. Plimsolls, they'd once been called. Why?

'So Beverley didn't play hockey?'

'No. She was sadly lacking in team spirit, according to Miss Midwinter. The Head. Sort of a . . . loner.'

'Isn't that a difficult thing to be? In a girls' boarding school?'

'It's difficult to get any privacy. But that's not the same thing at all.'

'I suppose not.'

Dobie turned his head, looking now across the moorland and the shaded hills towards the distant shapes of the Caerphilly mountains. Beyond those mountains, the Rhondda, the mining valleys; he'd been working in Cardiff for twenty years now but the Rhondda was another world again, as different to his own as that of a girls' school or of the Rehabilitation Centre. Somewhere over there was Aberfan. . . . Of course you had to see things in perspective. Things like the death of a schoolgirl. You had to keep a sense of proportion. But even so. . . .

They usually feel they'd like to try it again, Kate had said. Talking about the usual middle-class adultery rituals, things of no interest to anyone except the persons concerned and sometimes not very interesting even to them. But it wasn't so long since Dobie had heard Jackson say very much the same thing about murderers. They like to do it again, too. And that wasn't a very nice thought. Especially when you thought also of likely future targets and then thought of your present companion, trudging up and down this lonely road every weekday on her way to and from school. Right now they were sitting not very far from the spot where he'd picked up Beverley Sutro on the point of death, though of course Elspeth couldn't have known that; that was why her presence there in her blue skirt and parka had given him something of a shock.

And thinking about her blue parka, Dobie remembered what it was he'd meant to tell Foxy Boxy about but had at that moment forgotten about. It might not, after all, be very important. Just two or three small blood-stained leaves that Kate had brushed from the girl's blood-clotted hair-roots and which had now to be lying on the back seat of her car. Probably not important, no. But certainly odd. . . .

'Not so bad for me,' Elspeth said, breaking abruptly into Dobie's train of thought. 'I live at home, if you call. . . . Otherwise I wouldn't really get any time off at all. Saturday afternoons and that'd be it. Still, we'll be breaking up in two weeks' time. Easter holidays. Big fat deal. Not a lot to choose, when you think about it, between a boarding school and. . . .'

She nodded towards the high wall on the far side of the road and the buildings beyond. 'Funny,' Dobie said. 'Kate said very much the same thing. But I don't remember my own school as having been all that bad. Maybe it's more fun for boys.'

'You betcha. Is Kate the doctor lady?'

'Yes.'

'She's awfully attractive, isn't she? I couldn't believe she *was* a doctor at first. Perhaps not *pretty*, exactly. But very sexy.'

Dobie blinked. 'Well, there's really no reason why a doctor shouldn't be sexy. They nearly always are on the TV.'

'The ones here certainly aren't. Popeye is about the best of the bunch but of course he's terribly *old*. He must be at least thirty if he's a day. And Ram, well, he's *exotic* all right but I don't care for beardies.'

Dobie wondered what her attitude might be to extremely bushy moustaches. 'Who's Ram?'

'Ram Singh? He's an Indian. Sikh.'

'Why, what's the matter with him?'

'Not *sick*. A Sikh. He wears a turban all the time and he's not allowed to shave. You know?'

'You mean he's a Sikh-iatrist?'

Elspeth laughed a good deal at this witty rejoinder. Dobie was also pleased with it. He didn't make many amusing remarks as a rule, or at any rate, not on purpose. 'That's *very* good, Dobie. I'll try it on Dad.'

'I'm glad to hear it. What about the whatchamaycallum? The inmates? Most of them are nearer your age group, as far as I can see.'

'*What* about them?'

'No one there you fancy?'

'There might be if I ever got to see any of them. But I don't.

No way. They're supposed to be prisoners, after all, and I know they call it an open prison but it isn't really. Anyway, I don't want to give you the impression that I'm thinking about sex *all* the time. I mean, there are other things in life.'

'Yes. Like hockey.'

Elspeth's gaze grew distant. 'I hope sex is *better* than hockey, that's all. Else I'll probably want to shoot myself.'

'Not so much better,' Dobie said, 'as different.'

'I expect I'll find out soon enough. Of course everyone *talks* about it at school, but it's nearly always stories about what other girls have been up to, I mean *gossip* really. Not a lot of real hot tips from the horse's mouth.'

'Do they tell stories like that about Beverley?'

'They won't any more,' Elspeth said, almost absently. Then looked up sharply. 'Sorry. I didn't mean that the way it sounded.'

'I know,' Dobie said.

Jackson, back at the ranch. And Box also.

'We've got a case, then,' Foxy said.

'Let's say that foul play is suspected.'

'May as well call it murder and have done with it.'

'You know Paddy,' Jackson said. 'He'll never do *that*. Death was brought about by violent means and that's as far as he'll ever go.'

'And Dr Coyle?'

'She didn't think it was a hit-and-run, either.'

'Might have been made to look like one.'

'Maybe. Hard to tell, as we never got to see the body in sitchoo. Pity it was moved, in a way . . . not that she could've done anything else. After all, the kid was still alive at that stage.'

'And then,' Foxy said, 'there's the rape issue.'

'Doesn't fit in, does it? But whether it was an H-and-R or not, Charley had a car. Gives us something to work on.'

'I suppose it stands to reason.'

'Course it does. Nasty cold rainy afternoon like that, where else could they have gone? I mean, you've *seen* the place. Open country for miles around. Nowhere he could have taken her for a spot of hoo-ha. Not even any buildings or barns or anything like that. No, he had a car all right. All we got to do is find it.'

'Question is, did they meet somewhere? Or was it just a pick-up?'

'Maybe some of her school friends can tell us that. Or at least tell us if she was dating anyone regular or not. You'd think kids nowadays have too much sense to get themselves picked up by strangers, but . . .' Jackson took out his notebook and opened it; stared at it for a few moments unseeingly. 'I'll go round to the school tomorrow morning and see if I can pick up a few bits and pieces. We'll have to have *something* to show Pontin when he gets back.'

Box frowned and shook his head, regretting the intrusion of this discordant element into what, up to then, had been an amicable discussion between colleagues. 'Pity this should come along right now. The old fart's been in a good mood lately.'

'Because we got Dai Dymond put to rights is why. Well, maybe we all need bringing back to earth. The tabloids ought to do the trick when they get hold of *this* one.'

Box nodded glumly. Detective Superintendent Pontin was a man who appreciated the value of media coverage and liked nothing better than seeing his name favourably mentioned in the organs of the popular press. There could be little doubt that the said organs would be immensely stimulated by certain features of the Beverley Sutro case and Pontin, on his return from the Smoke, would unquestionably be taking the case under his personal wing, issuing handouts, holding press conferences, giving interviews on *Crimewatch*, and generally making life difficult for his underlings and for Jackson and Box in particular. It was widely known that Pontin had achieved promotion largely in consequence of a sudden flurry of activity amongst his immediate superiors some five years back, when several CID high-ups had resigned, pending enquiries into charges of corruption. Pontin had emerged with his reputation unblemished. Nobody had ever for a moment supposed Pontin to be corrupt. He was far too stupid.

'He could have made a clear ten thousand on that bit of non-sense, y'know,' Jackson said. 'That's what DD's shyster offered him, under the table, to get the charges dropped. But he thought it was some kind of a racing tip. Wasn't about to tell him, now, was I? So he went out and put his shirt on Money For Nothing at fifteen to one and lost the bloody lot.' Both men snickered uncharitably for some little while. 'All the same, some of these lawyer blokes are going a whole lot too far. I wouldn't at all mind putting *that* one away, for a start.'

'Micky Mannering, was it?'

'Who else?'

Box clicked his tongue. 'Too fly, that boyo.'

'I know. But I still say Pontin's being too eupeptic these days. A nasty bugger, is Dymond. Just because he didn't sit there in the dock singing "We'll Meet Again", it don't mean he hasn't got plans. There'll be a kickback coming along soon or I miss my guess.'

'Big Ivor's out of town, they tell me.'

'Never any shortage of villains these days,' Jackson said. 'At least the geezer who did that girl in won't be a professional. We'll wrap him up quick and pop him in the post. No point in waiting for the lab reports. You get out there and find that car, Foxy. There'll be blood on the seat cushions as like as not. Do us nicely, a few old blood stains would.'

4

If Jacko was in a somewhat nervous state in consequence of recent events, then so was Dobie.

Dobie was, as the saying goes, at a loose end, and had been for some little time now. It wasn't his fault. He had returned to Cardiff after an enlivening stint on a secondment in Cyprus to find that no specific teaching duties had been timetabled for him and that his presence at the Department of Mathematics wasn't – his HoD assured him – required. This was partly because someone else in the Department of Mathematics had calculated (in consequence of a minor and altogether excusable slip in his Hoolean algebra) that an academic year lasts for eighteen months, but more importantly because Bill Traynor, the HoD in question, had decided that Dobie could do with a nice long holiday away from the Department, or more precisely that the Department could do with a nice long holiday away from Professor Dobie.

This wasn't because, or only because, Dobie's name (and worse, his photograph – in *academic dress*) had last summer been largely featured in the tabloid press in near-libellous connection with the murder of the young lady to whom he had been married at the time. Traynor, unlike Detective Superintendent Pontin, had no great relish for newspaper publicity of the lurid kind, nor for that matter had the Rector of the University, but *that* wasn't it. Since then, matters had gone from bad to worse.

While lurking in his Cypriot backwater, Dobie had in a cowardly and underhand manner committed a *publication*. The evidence was incontrovertible. In black and white, so to speak. It lay on Traynor's desk at this very moment. Not only a publication, but a *joint* publication. With an *American*. The offence, as one of Traynor's literary colleagues assured him, was rank; it smelled to heaven; and other people thought so, too. Indeed, for a fort-

81

night it seemed that Traynor's telephone would never stop ringing. All manner of influential and academically distinguished personalities appeared to be taking a polite interest in the matter. The Maclennan Professor of Theoretical Physics at Cambridge University, for instance. 'What in fuck's name,' the Maclennan Professor etc. had courteously enquired, 'does this bloody Dobie of yours think he's *up* to? He's making a right sodding charley of himself with all this cock about the Lorenz effect, look, I've been *into* that these past fifteen years, mate, and believe me he doesn't seem to know the first thing about it. Bringing your place into disrepute, that's what he's doing.'

'Oh come now,' Traynor said. 'I'll admit that certain of the paper's conclusions are a little far-reaching—'

'Sheer bloody fantasy, in my opinion. Balls from start to finish. Give the bastard the push if I were you.'

'I think you're as well aware as I am that University regulations don't permit—'

But the Maclennan Professor etc. had rung off. Traynor picked up the *publication* for the umpteenth time and stared at it hopelessly. Part of the trouble was that he didn't really understand it – not *any* of it – and he suspected darkly that the Maclennan Professor didn't, either.

And Kate, of course. . . . Not a clue. She could see that Dobie was worried about it, though. 'But what exactly is it that you've *said*? I realize it has to be all very technical—'

'All the paper does,' Dobie said tiredly, 'is establish the various sets of conditions under which the twin propositions compounding a mathematical paradox can themselves be maintained to be paradoxical.' He spoke tiredly because he'd just got back from Cyprus and he'd found the flight more than a little fatiguing. 'And all *I* did was set out the theoretical basis. George Campbell did the computations, and no one's going to refute them because they're irrefutable. That's the trouble.'

'So why all the fuss?'

'Well, it's bad news and good news. On the one hand, if George is right, as he obviously is, conventional quantum mechanics theory will have to go back to square one. On the other hand, using the new equations we can go a whole lot further towards developing an integrated field theory – perhaps *all* the way, though we don't make that claim. Or not yet.'

'I thought as much,' Kate said. 'You've been mucking up other people's nice tidy arrangements and then leaving them to sort out the mess. Yes, I might have known.'

'It's not *my* fault,' Dobie said.

'Whose fault is it, then?'

'God's, I suppose.'

'Well, there you go. He's another of you male chauvinists.'

'But you see, He's been misrepresented. There wasn't a Big Bang after all, and the universe *isn't* expanding. Or blowing up like a balloon. The Doppler—'

'I never thought it was.'

'No, but a lot of people did, and do, and they won't be any too chuffed to find out that it isn't. All the Friedmann solutions will have to be thrown out. . . . At least, I suppose you can still argue that the universe is in fact expanding *inwards*, but they won't like that, either.'

'No. I can see why they wouldn't.' Kate shook her head sadly. Some kind of *royal* weird was what she'd got herself landed with, somehow . . . How had *that* happened? She couldn't understand that part of it, either. 'They'd say that in that case it was contracting. And so would I.'

'Oh certainly. Yes. Contracting outwards, yes, why not?'

'Why *not*? Because—'

'Of course, some of the Russians have been saying it for years. That's what the USSR's been doing lately, you see. Expanding inwards or contracting outwards, depending on how you look at it.'

'What what what what Russians?'

'Oh, the Kiev crowd. And Platanov in Moscow. Oh, there's been quite a lot of back-up coming through from Russia, one way or another.'

'My God, Dobie, now it's *Communist* beastly male chauvinism already.'

Et tu, Kate. No, Dobie couldn't help but feel a trifle nervous, as a man well might who had (metaphorically speaking) removed the pin from an academic hand grenade and was now holding it neatly tucked away inside his trousers. His paper had, after all, been out for almost four months now and the resultant silence was itself becoming explosive. Apart from the irate telephone calls that Bill Traynor had fielded, there'd been no comment at all. Dobie couldn't doubt but that in universities and research establishments all over the States and throughout Europe thousands of hands had been raised not in mere dissent but to swat him like a buzzing mosquito . . . but as yet none had descended. It was odd. The computations employed in his paper were indeed irrefutable, unless the Mack IV computer at MIT could be shown to be at fault; the theoretical basis was another matter. 'The Dobie Paradox, they call it. Very flattering. In fact it isn't. It's just the opposite.'

'What's the opposite of a paradox?'

'Exactly. Well, that's what it *is*.'

Nothing in the mail that morning, either. Only a couple of circulars and a threatening letter from the council about community charges. Yet Dobie, returning to the kitchen clutching these missives and the daily delivery of milk bottles, wasn't wearing his usual frown of concern. 'I forgot to tell you. Jackson rang last night.'

'Jacko? What about?'

'He's asking for the inquest to be postponed. Pending police enquiries. He says he doesn't think you'll be called until next week.'

'I could have told *him* that,' Kate said, expertly snatching at a slice of toast as it leaped away from the pop-up toaster. 'Paddy's good but he's awfully slow. That's probably *why* he's good. No one's ever caught him out yet in a mistake – or not to my knowledge, anyway. What's the time? Nine o'clock? Good Heavens.'

'What it does,' Dobie said, cautiously adding milk to the powerful brew already in his tea cup, 'is give you a sense of perspective. Know what I mean?'

'Frankly, no.'

'It's something I was thinking about yesterday. Seventeen-year-old kids getting raped and murdered next door to some weird kind of institute catering for drug addicts who're apparently most of them under twenty. I mean, that's what's going *on* in the world today, whether you like it or not. There's no denying it.'

Kate sighed. 'I could have told *you* that, Dobie-oh.'

'So why am I getting worked up about an exercise in theoretical mathematics? I don't say it isn't important because it is. But someone else would have put it forward if I hadn't. Sooner or later. Platanov or some other of the Russians. Or maybe Mancini.

These ideas just sit there, you know, waiting to happen. They're *bound* to happen. Murder isn't. Murder *shouldn't* happen. Least of all to a schoolgirl. Things like that. . . . They matter in a different way. *That*'s what I think.'

Kate stared at him, her hand still clutching a butter-laden knife. 'That's what I think, too. But I'm a doctor. You're supposed to be different. For God's sake don't start going *human* on me, Dobie, I don't think I could stand it.'

'You don't see me as the little friend of all the world?'

'Frankly—'

'No. Well, you're wrong. Right now the world needs all the friends that it can get, and you don't have to be a mathematician to see that. It's obvious.'

'But you *are* a mathematician. It's what you *do*. And from what people tell me, you're a bloody good one. What they probably mean is that you do less damage being a mathematician than you would working in any other capacity, but that's beside the point. Dobie . . .'

'Yes?'

'Say after me, "I'm a mathematician." '

Dobie shrugged. 'All right. "I'm a mathematician." '

' "I am not, repeat *not*, engaged in the practice of criminal investigation." '

'Kate, be *reasonable*. Why should you think—'

' "I am in *no* way to be confused with Sexton Blake or even with bloody Batman and my good friend Kate Coyle, who is familiar with my foibles, is prepared to sign an affidavit to that effect. She is also prepared to shoot me dead with a double-barreled shot-gun if I start sticking my nose *again* into matters which are best left to our hard-working and efficient police force, under whatever pretext, including that of a misguided and muddle-headed philanthropy." I hope the message is coming through loud and clear, Dobie bach, because—'

'Kate, you haven't *got* a double-barreled shot-gun.'

'No. But I know someone who has.'

Some little time after this rather one-sided conversation had been thus brought to a crushing conclusion, the hard-working and efficient cohorts of which Kate had made mention tiredly converged, all three of them, on Detective Superintendent Pontin's office. Jackson, Box, and Detective Constable Wallace, a recent and bewildered recruit from the uniformed branch, had spent an exhausting morning at the Dame Margaret School for Girls way out in the back of beyond; Pontin, on the other hand, was fresh from a hearty and satisfying lunch at the Rotary Club and from a point of vantage behind his desk was hence enabled to inject his team with a touch of his own unquestioned dynamism and energy, to say nothing of his intimate and hard-earned knowledge of the criminal world. 'First of all, Jackson, what you do *is*, you round up all the wogs and nignogs and see what they've got to say for themselves. Standard interrogation procedures, of course. Stamp 'em into the floor if you have to but no *rough* stuff, mind, I'm prepared to be very strict on that point. Just make sure you swab up afterwards and don't let the buggers see their lawyers whatever you do.'

'Sir, we can't do *that*, sir.'

'And why the hell not?'

'They're aren't any wogs or nignogs, sir, in the middle of Glamorgan. Hardly any Welshmen, if it comes to that. And besides you shouldn't call them that, sir, on account of its being racial incrimination.'

'Who says so?'

'The Chief Constable, sir.'

'Well, it's about time someone took a firm line on the matter because I for one have had about enough of it. We're in the Common Market now and don't you forget it.'

'Yes sir. That's clearly understood, sir.'

'It'd better be. Now then. Who've you got lined up to take the chop?'

Jackson cleared his throat. 'It's early days yet, sir, but we're pursuing some very promising lines of enquiry.' Most of the Sixth Form at Dame Margaret's might, he thought, be held to fall into that category, and not a few of the Upper Fifth, for that matter. 'I think I can say we've established a fairly definite *terminus ad quim*.'

'Excellent. Splendid. A what?'

'Let me expatuate, sir.'

Pontin listened with barely concealed impatience while Jackson expatuated and Detective Constable Wallace wiggled his finger about inside his nose. Pontin gathered that his A-team had covered a good deal of ground, had explored a considerable number of fruitful avenues, and that at the present moment in time it could safely be said that several likely suspects had been subliminated from future judicious enquiries. 'Don't,' Pontin said, 'come the old soldier with me, Jackson.'

'No, sir.'

'What have you got to *report*, man?'

'Well, sir, bugger all, really.'

. . . Except, of course, for the *terminus ad quim* which seemingly had nothing to do with bus stops but merely established that moment (in time) when the deceased person to wit Miss Beverley Sutro had last been seen alive and in robust health and ingesting, in fact, a sizeable portion of roast lamb and potatoes with treacle pudding to follow. 'Do themselves all right, they do,' Detective Constable Wallace interjected. 'Cor.'

'In short, sir, she partook of lunch with the rest of the chicks, ah, young ladies, and no one claims to have seen her since. Seems that Saturday afternoons a lot of the girls play hockey and the rest mess around. Go out for invigorating walks and such. They're supposed to tell the duty mistress where they're going and then to go there in couples but the senior girls sometimes don't bother and go out by themselves as often as not. Beverley Sutro did, anyway.'

'But no one saw her leave? Bit odd, that.'

'No one *remembers* having seen her leave. But there'd have been a lot of toing and froing going on at that time, from all accounts. It's the only free afternoon the kids get and everyone's anxious to make the most of it. They all have to be back for six o'clock roll-call, you see. Six o'clock they all have sort of a high tea. With currant buns.'

Detective Constable Wallace sighed windily. Pontin had enjoyed an excellent lunch but the A-team hadn't. In fact they hadn't had lunch at all. Even an old currant bun, Wallace thought, would have gone down very nicely. On the edge of bloody starvation he was, boyo. Wallace sighed for his former cosy beat on the Hayes with its friendly coffee stall on the Island. Not all beer and skittles, Mum, working in the CID.

'We can't complain,' Jackson said, 'at any lack of copperation on the part of the public. Or the school authorities, like. No fuss about a search warrant, nothing like that. They let us take a good look at the girl's personal belongings but I can't say we came up with very much. No diaries, nothing useful like that. Except it seems she was on the pill and they weren't too happy about that. They didn't *say* anything, though.'

'Who didn't? Who's *they*? Try to be more *explicit*, Jackson.'

'The School Secretary, sir. Name of Bramble. Not too prickly, though, was she? Haw haw. Made the school records available to us,' Jackson continued hurriedly, 'and we've got photostats of them for what they're worth, which at first glance isn't very much. I couldn't get to see the Headmistress. She was feeling poorly. But I don't think the answer—'

'Prostrate with shock, no doubt.'

'No, sir. Toothache.'

'*Toothache?*'

'Terrible toothache, Miss Bramble told us. But anyway, I don't think the answer to this little problem lies at the school, unless any of the kid's friends can give us a lead on where she was that afternoon or who it was she was seeing. Because that's what we've got to find out. What she was doing between the hours of two and six pip emma – *that*'s the mystery.'

'Having it off,' Box said. 'According to Paddy Oates.'

'And getting herself beaten up. But where and who by? We have to assume that the feller who did it had a car. Whether he had a meeting arranged with her or whether it was a casual pick-up, he'd have to have wheels. No other theory makes sense.'

'A sordid encounter, by the sound of it.' Pontin seemed to be noticeably cheered. 'We'll get the Press Officer on to it at once. Might even make the nationals if we act promptly. Got a photograph we can use, I hope?'

'Yes, sir. Several. Of course if she was taking the pill the inference is she was getting . . . or was seeing someone on a pretty regular basis, so maybe we ought to proceed on that presumption. And Saturday afternoons is just about the only free time she'd have for that sort of thing, so that could give us a useful starting-point. Unless she sneaked out at night, which of course is a possibility. Miss Bramble didn't think it was very likely, though. They do their best at the school to stop that sort of behaviour, she says. Any girl doing that would be instantly repelled.'

'And so I should damn well hope,' Pontin said. 'That's the trouble with the younger generation these days. No discipline.

Satan finds work for idle hands to do. Bring back the cat is what *I* say.'

'I wouldn't say the girl seems to have been *idle*, exactly.'

'You miss my point, Jackson. As usual. Bit of a trouble-maker, was she? In other respects?'

'No, sir. A well-behaved girl, they say. And the school records seem to bear it out. Intelligent, too. Down for her A-levels this year and expected to do very well in them. A model pupil, you might say.'

'A *model*? What sort of photographs have you *got* of her, Jackson, for God's sake?'

'Not *that* sort of model, sir. At least, nothing like that has been suggested to me. Mind you, it's quite a respectable career for a girl these days, or so I'm given to understand. Not that my wife would be very happy if our Winifred—'

'Can I prevail upon you, Jackson, to leave your Winifred out of it? Unless she can make material contribution to this enquiry?'

'I've no reason to suppose so, sir, but if you wish me to pursue the matter with her when I get back home—'

'I don't wish for anything of the kind, I'm only suggesting, I'm only putting forward the tentative *suggestion*, Jackson, that you stick to the bloody point at issue, else we won't get anywhere. Will we now? Will we, Campdown?'

'Wallace, sir. Gwynfor Wallace, my name is. Well, in fact my friends call me Edgar, but that's not my real name, see? They only call me that because—'

'Never you mind all that, Wallace. Most interesting, but never mind that now. What, in your opinion, Wallace, is the most promising lead you've so far turned up in this enquiry? What course of action do you feel should be undertaken in this matter? I think you must agree that I've shown a remarkable degree of *patience* in listening to all this guff but sooner or later, Wallace, when push comes to shove—'

'Well, sir, I reckon as we ought to find out who done this girl in.'

Pontin's pent-up breath emerged from his nose with a loud hissing noise like an overloaded electric kettle. 'I must admit I've been slowly coming round to that same conclusion. So why don't you all get out of here and do exactly that? This bloody girl's been raped and murdered, damn it, you're looking for a rapist and a murderer, not someone who's pinched a couple of quid from a pinball machine, and I want the bugger collared by this time yesterday. So get things *moving*, Jackson. I don't want reports, I want *results*.'

Outside the office, Wallace cast longing eyes down the passageway in the general direction of the cafeteria. 'Does he *always* go on like that?'

'Often enough,' Box said. 'This sort of thing, you see, it upsets the apple cart. *That*'s why he's sounding off.'

'Upsets it how?'

'You ought to *know* how, Edgar. Blokes who go out and rape girls . . . It usually isn't very long before they're trying to do the same thing again. And *this* one could have had a bit more fun than he expected, stomping her as well. Could be a nasty business. Very nasty.'

'Ah,' Wallace said. 'Well, I'll just nip round the corner and get us some packets of crisps.'

'That's good thinking, Edgar,' Jackson said.

Dobie, in abstracted mood, had driven past the main entry to the crematorium but, realizing his mistake, had lit before he could turn back on an unobtrusive back entry leading to a small and unobtrusive car park shadowed by an appropriate growth of cypress trees. Walking from there towards the main buildings, he was mildly surprised to find the pathway running through a substantial acreage of assiduously laid-out graves with marble fenders, gravel, and all the doings; apparently you could also be buried here, if you so desired, in what people conservative in their tastes (such as himself) would take to be a right and proper way. The tended lines of graves stretched out to left, to right, from where he now stood, all in formal order, revealing an impersonal symmetry of the kind that laymen usually call mathematical – being ignorant, as the laity by definition are, of the jungle-like confusion, disorder, and chaos upon which the logical constructions of the physical sciences are totteringly based. Dobie sat for a while on a convenient bench, leaning forwards into the sunlight which hurled an unimaginable jumble of cosmic particles at his no less inconceivably elaborate physical form and feeling a certain melancholy awareness of the difference now existent between his own vaguely contemplative brain and that of Mrs Jennifer Dobie, now deceased, reduced to ashes and incarcerated underground somewhere not very far away. Or very far away indeed, according to how you looked at it. Dobie felt sad.

He had, of course, the minor consolation of having made what is called a *contribution*; he had made, that is to say, the unimaginable jumble of cosmic particles now bombarding him a little more unimaginable than it had been before. Only a little more, perhaps . . . but the effects of even so tiny an adjustment to the balance of so inherently rickety a structure could, as he well knew, prove catastrophic. The walls of Jericho, about to crumble. . . . Those who suppose that what is already unimaginable can hardly be made *more* unimaginable are clearly unfamiliar with what is conveniently referred to in the textbooks (or in *some* of the textbooks) as the Dobie Paradox, the exposition of which had originally occupied some fifteen pages of closely written foolscap and some six thousand five hundred hours of Dobie's own personal space–time continuum. In the seventeen years that had passed since its publication, fourteen people (to Dobie's knowledge) had read it and three (as far as he could tell) had understood it; the important thing was that no one had undermined or otherwise exploded it, so that as a mathematical theory of unusually long standing it had perforce now to be regarded with some respect.

What George Campbell and his aides had done with it . . . That was something else. For a long time now Dobie had politely co-operated with the MIT research team, had answered their queries, had checked their computations. . . . But the truth was it had all passed out of his hands; Dobie thought these days very little about his Paradox, and when he did, it was with a kind of sad wonder – the same kind of sad wonder with which he thought of the late Mrs Dobie's lively little brain and of what had happened to it, shattered by metal, invalidated by fire in the crematorium furnace. When he thought about it, his thoughts were almost always the reflection of a mood. And that, too, was a curious fate to befall fifteen meticulously argued pages of cold and unimpassioned logic. Mathematicians, though, had moods. The same as anyone else. That was what Kate didn't seem to understand.

Dobie stood up, clutching his bouquet of early roses, and walked on.

This was where he'd met Kate for the first time. Here among

the gravestones, sitting on a bench. Not quite a year ago. He had been in rather a strange mood then, too, from which she had rescued him – that didn't seem to be an inappropriate word. But that didn't mean that he needed to be rescued from *all* his moods, to be constantly protected from himself, as Kate now appeared to think. Far from it. Perhaps, Dobie thought, I'm a little worried at what I've done, or at what has been in effect done in my name. But I'm not alarmed and I'm not afraid. Here, so to speak, I stand, like Martin Luther. I can do no other. *Après moi le deluge* – that, too, perhaps. But soon Ararat will poke through the waters again. Life's like that.

Here, anyway, was a small patch of dry land at his feet. A small rectangle of grey granite, lettered by a stonecutter's chisel. The letters said

JENNIFER DOBIE
1962 – 1989

Dobie stooped and dropped the roses on to the granite block, where they obliterated his wife's name from view. Then he turned away and marched back to his car.

When he got back to Ludlow Road Kate was still out but the telephone was ringing. She'd switched it through from the clinic reception desk downstairs but she'd forgotten for once to connect it to the answering machine so Dobie picked up the receiver. He was practically an answering machine himself these days, at any rate in so far as the telephone was concerned.

'Dr Coyle isn't in right now this is a human being speaking but if you wish to leave a message I'll connect you at once to the recorder if you'll wait one moment —'

'Is that Mr Dobie?'

Eh?

'Yes,' Dobie said. 'Dobie speaking.'

A call for *Dobie*? Unheard of. Unprecedented. Best to proceed with caution. These indeed were deep and uncharted waters.

'I thought I recognized your voice. This is Elspeth.'

'Oh yes?'

'Yes, *you* know. . . . *Elspeth*. . . .'

'Oh, *Elspeth*, of course, how nice to hear from you. How's everything at school?'

'Perfectly bloody, thanks. That's what I'm ringing you up about.'

'Well, I don't quite know if I—'

'The *police* have been round here, you see. Asking people questions and . . . looking for things, they were poking round the school all the morning.'

'I'm afraid that's only to be expected,' Dobie said. 'They're just doing their job. No need to *worry* about it, no need at all.'

'Oh, but there is. Some of the girls have been saying the most *awful* things.'

'To the police?'

'No, no. Or . . . Well, I don't think so. But I . . . We feel we need some advice, I mean really *intelligent* advice. Right away.'

'Oh, I see. Then it *is* Kate you want. Look, as soon as she gets back in—'

'No, I want *your* advice. So does Midge.'

'Midge?'

'She was Bev's best friend. You see, it's all very confidential.'

'Well, but . . . Honestly, Elspeth. . . . Don't you have a student counsellor or someone like that? I mean, if it's a problem of a personal nature—'

'We'd be most awfully grateful,' Elspeth said, ignoring all this dithering and adopting a stridently hectoring tone rather reminiscent of Mrs Thatcher addressing a group of Young Conservatives, 'if you could . . . Well, if you could manage to come round after school, Midge can't get away, you see, she'd never get permission unless . . . There's quite a good cafeteria here, you know. We'd be delighted to sock you to tea and a rock cake. Or even two, if you're feeling peckish.'

Victory in the next election campaign was clearly just round the corner. 'Oh, wow,' Dobie said. 'Well, if you're sure your finances will stretch to it. . . .'

'Just about. Does that mean you'll come? Today?'

'*Today*, that may be a bit difficult, in fact, because—'

'It's going to be far more difficult after today 'cos Midge reckons that once the newspaper reporters and people start clustering round the place old Midders won't let any visitors in at all.'

Midge, whoever she was, clearly had a point there. 'Just tell me one thing, though.'

'Yes?'

'Why *me*?'

'Because you're clever.'

'Oh dear,' Dobie said. 'Not always.'

'But you'll come?'

'I suppose so.'

'Oh, brilliant! I'll tell the porter to expect you. Four o'clock, right after school. And I'll meet you at the main gate. So don't be late.'

'You *did* say rock cakes?'

Monday March 26th

I wish to God that Dobie would come and see me again. If I could get a message to him somehow. There it is in the newspaper, there's no mistake, I have to talk to *someone* about it. So I just have to see Dobie and tell him. Popeye's useless.

Besides you worry about these things, of course you do. With all these screwballs around, you start to wonder. And I don't want to give Popeye any wrong ideas now I'm so near to

They could keep me here longer if they wanted to, or even send me back I suppose to that other dump. It's as easy to go back as to go forwards, they're always saying that. Up the ladder and all of a sudden there's a bloody great boa constrictor sprawled across the passage and down you go. For more ping-pong and crossword puzzles and games of chess with Horse. Horse can't even *play* chess. I'm always having to show him how the knight's move goes.

Pressing lidless eyes. And there she is all the time in the newspaper, by the barbarous king so rudely forced, poor kid. I never know what you are thinking, Popeye, except that you think you know what *I'm* thinking but you don't. It's all like that. It's all a game. We all have different moves, one square forwards and one diagonal, up the ladder and down the snakes, another barbarous king for a royal flush, shake the dice and try again. We have ours and the shrinks have theirs, men make certain moves and women make others, up and down in and out fucking they call it but it's all the same, it's all a game, our favourite indoor sport. I know the moves all right but not since Derya

94

Outside they play at making money but you need different moves for that, it seems I don't know them. A teaching job I suppose would have a fair screw, my wife didn't do too

and Dobie must do all right, a professor and all. They ought to teach you *all* the moves at school, that'd stop all those buggers out there from inventing their own. Those girls' schools, they can't teach you anything, no wonder the kids have to pick it all up as they go along. *One across*: Someone who's picked it up too late. *Answer*: FEMINIST. See how *that* fits into the squares, Charley.

Training them for their future role in society. That's what they're supposed to be doing to *us*, isn't it? But are they kidding us or are we kidding them? *We*'re society and this *is* the future. *We*'re the post-industrial world. Popeye and all the other middle-aged freaks, they've been left behind. *And* they know it. Or if they don't, they should by now. That kid in the newspaper, *she*'s the future, that's what she's doing in the dream. *She*'s been showing them the moves. Fear, that's what. In a handful of dust? Bloody hell, no. Eliot, you might as well say Aristotle. All that stuff's gone for ever, and a good job, too. All that punk *school* stuff.

I don't think I'll write any more today. And I don't think I'll ever be a teacher. I've learnt too much in here for that. Thanks a lot, Dobie, now fuck off. And don't bother to wave as you turn the corner.

No, no more today.

That's enough.

Midge's real name, it appeared, was Annabelle Midgley-Johnson but Dobie appreciated that in those circumstances abbreviation might well be a matter of convenience. 'How do you do,' he said. Midge was not a notably attractive girl, bearing in fact a marked general resemblance to a very thin Ojibway Indian totem pole with a tangled mop of red hair on top and an all but expressionless mask directly underneath; her eyes, however, were attentive and intelligent and Dobie imagined that her apparent expressionlessness was due to an initial and no doubt very proper caution. 'One lump or two, Mr Dobie?' She sounded not at all like Mrs Thatcher but, on the other hand, almost exactly like Hermione Gingold, whom she couldn't, on the other hand again, possibly be old enough to remember.

'Three please,' Dobie said.

'Oh, splendid. I do so admire *immoderate* men.'

Older than Elspeth, though. Probably about the same age as . . . Well, yes, if indeed she were Beverley Sutro's best friend, a similarity in their age-groups was to be expected. Seventeen, then, or thereabouts. Dobie swirled his teaspoon around in the cup, liberally splashing tea into the saucer.

'And it's extremely good of you to come, Mr Dobie. I expect you're veddy veddy busy, being a university teacher and . . . and all that. It must be such a *wearing* profession.'

She was, Dobie thought, overdoing it a bit. Nobody could possibly be as posh as Annabelle Midgley-Johnson sounded to be. 'No, not really, or at least . . . not right now. I'm not actually teaching at the moment, you see.'

'But there again, it must broaden the mind. Dealing with your students, I mean. And all their problems.'

'There's always room,' Dobie said, 'for a little further mind-expansion. You want to tell me something and you're afraid I'll be shocked. . . . Is that it?'

'I was really hoping you'd tell *us* something first. It's really true, is it, that Bev was . . . ? Someone killed her?'

'Yes. That's why you don't have to worry. You can't tell me anything much more shocking than that.'

'I see what you mean. But . . . even so. . . .'

She looked down at the tablecloth. There were tablecloths all right, nice clean white ones, and the cafeteria itself was nice and clean and white with a well-scrubbed highly polished parquet floor and with reproductions of Impressionist paintings hanging in whitewood frames on the shiny walls; it was quite different from the comfortably slummy kitchen where Kate and Dobie usually enjoyed their meals and totally unlike the University cafeteria, where Dobie now and again consumed a greasy lamb chop with watery greens. It was more like a very up-market tea room in one of those Olde English villages frequently featured in the pages of *Country Life*. But then, Dobie thought, the whole damned school seemed to be like that. He hadn't expected to feel at home here and he didn't.

'You *wanted* to tell him,' Elspeth said suddenly. Not to him, of course, but to Midge. 'He's come here, hasn't he? No point in changing your mind about it now.'

'I haven't changed my mind, silly. What I don't quite see is how to . . . how to put it. Other than quite bluntly. So, well, bluntly then . . .' She turned back to Dobie. 'Bev was a *tart*. I mean, she really was. The policeman asked me this morning if I knew who she'd been seeing and I said no, because I didn't. I really don't. But whoever it was, I know she took money from him for . . . *you* know. Doing it. She told me so.'

Dobie could do the expressionless bit, too. 'You think it was true? She wasn't having you on?'

'No, I thought it was true and now I *know* it's true. I mean, it's awful, but I've got to tell *someone* because it could have something to do with her being killed. . . . Couldn't it?'

'I suppose it could,' Dobie said. 'You should certainly have told the police about it. It's not really—'

'I just didn't *dare*. There'd be such a terrible scandal. I know Miss Midwinter is always going on about us girls showing enterprise and initiative, but she doesn't mean in *that* particular direction.'

'No, probably not. And besides, you couldn't really prove anything, could you?'

'Except I've got the money.'

'*You* have?'

'Yes. When the cops were looking through her things this morning, I thought maybe that was what they were looking for, I thought maybe they *knew* something. . . . But they didn't find it because they didn't know where to look for it. And I did. Lots of us have got hidey-holes, you see, where we put . . . And I knew where Bev's was. I've got the money but I don't know what to *do* with it. I can't possibly keep it and if I give it to the police *now*, I suppose I'll get into trouble, even if I tell them I don't know where it came from. That's the problem.'

She had, Dobie noticed, lost all her earlier aplomb. And he himself, if it came to that, was a little puzzled. . . . Puzzled that he wasn't feeling particularly surprised. 'I think,' he said, 'we can find a way round it. Between us. Apart from anything else, the policeman in charge of the case is a friend of mine. I think if we explain the situation to him, he'll be ready to keep it all under his hat. In fact, he'll *want* to. Even if it should lead to an arrest,

I can't see why he should need to bring *you* into it. He'll act on information received, as the saying has it. It happens all the time.'

'Yes, that's what Elspeth said, but—'

'How much money did you find?'

'Two hundred quid. All in twenties. Yes, but that's not all. She said she was going to get a whole lot more.'

'Perhaps she was getting greedy,' Dobie said.

'And perhaps the man she was seeing didn't like it. *Exactly*. I think she was planning to run away from school and go off on a holiday with him and she was asking him for two thousand pounds. At least, that's what I—'

'Tooth . . . ?' Dobie was staring at her. 'She must have been kidding you.' He couldn't believe it. They didn't make that much even on the Gulf Air flights. No, Jackson wouldn't wear *that* one. Unless, of course. . . . He shook his head. 'It's just not on. Not just for *sex*.'

'But that was for starters. Look, she didn't exactly *tell* me about it, but . . . there was this bit of paper rolled up with all those banknotes. It's her handwriting all right. What do *you* make of it?'

Dobie, normally – to put it mildly – somewhat distrait, retained enough presence of mind at that juncture not to touch the thing. 'Just put it down on the table, will you, so I can . . . That's it.' Craning his neck, he found he could read it without too much difficulty, though it looked to have been written very hurriedly and possibly on an uneven surface. It said: *Holiday March 24th £2000. £3000 to follow*

'What's it mean?'

'I don't know. But it would have to be somewhere abroad, wouldn't it? Maybe it's what she thought the tickets would cost him but . . . you could fly to Australia on that, surely? So it can't mean that after all.'

'March 24th. That was Saturday. The day she was killed.'

'Yes. So she didn't go.'

Dobie took a paper napkin from the holder on the table, used his knife to fold the note inside the napkin, and put it in his inside pocket. 'You haven't showed that to anyone else?'

'No, I haven't. Here. You'd better take the money as well.'

'I'll give you a receipt.'

'I don't want a receipt. All I want is to get shot of it and to know that . . . that something'll be done about it. If anything can.'

'Yes, something will be done about it all right. She didn't tell you anything else?'

'Not really.'

It was remarkably quiet, Dobie thought, in the cafeteria. Somehow he had expected a girls' school to be a great deal noisier. There didn't even seem to be very many girls about the place; through the windows, opened to invigorating currents of healthy Welsh air, he could see only the grey stone walls and red-brick facings of other buildings, a damp-looking slate roof and, a little further beyond, the almost startling green gloss of a well-tended playing field. 'She didn't ever say *why*? I mean, this is a pretty expensive school, isn't it? She couldn't have needed the money all that badly.'

'She wanted to get away from here, I think. She didn't like it.'

Looking out the window again, Dobie could see why. All right for South Walians, maybe. But Italy it wasn't. He asked the question anyway. 'Why?'

'None of us do. Very much. This is hell, nor are we out of it.'

'It's as bad as that?'

'Maybe I'm exaggerating. But only slightly. And anyway I'm quoting. *Doctor Faustus.*'

Dobie hadn't met him, but he could, he thought, always ask Kate about that later. And it probably didn't matter. 'Not many of us run away, though,' Midge was saying. 'Not much point in it. But if someone offered me two thousand quid to do it, I don't say I might not be tempted. As yet nobody has, needless to say.'

'The note doesn't say that, exactly. It could be about something altogether different. Are you sure she never told you anything else which might . . . ?'

'Well. . . .' The damned girl had gone all hesitant again. Dobie waited patiently, fingering the remnants of his rock cake and reducing them to crumbs. 'Except she once said her mother started off as a call girl . . . and always wished she'd stayed that way because her marriage hadn't worked out all that well. . . . *So*,' Midge said, with sudden emphasis, 'she said she didn't see why she shouldn't. . . . Oh, it was all very vague and I'm not sure if *that* part of it was true. Though I wouldn't be surprised if it were. And *I'm* not throwing any stones, I don't know that my own

99

bloody parents are very much better. But that's by the way.'

Dobie wasn't throwing any stones, either, or even picking up the bill, so they left the cafeteria together, Dobie standing politely aside to allow the ladies priority of egress – a gesture which, he noticed, seemed to occasion some private amusement on their part. Extraordinary creatures, girls, when you thought about them. Perhaps the trouble was that he didn't, or not very much. He still couldn't feel that he had learnt anything of very much value about the object of his present concern, except that her family background appeared to be slightly unusual – though perhaps no more unusual than most. 'What,' he asked, blinking vaguely upwards towards the upper storeys of the school buildings, 'was she *like*? You shared a room with her, after all. You must have got to know her quite well.'

'That depends. Some people you do. Some people you don't. She only came this term, you know . . . but even if she'd been around for years I don't think I'd have got to know her very much better. Bev was one of the don'ts, you see.'

'But did you like her? As a person?'

'I think I admired her. For that reason. She never seemed to want to weep on your shoulder like lots of the other kids do. I suppose she was a bit of a tough, really. Especially about the sex thing. Somehow I never got the impression that she, *you* know . . . *enjoyed* it. She didn't talk about it hardly at all. Maybe that was *it*. With all those other nincompoops sounding off all the time about how terrific it was the last time round . . . some of them never seem to talk about anything else. Bev was different. You felt she really did know the ropes. I hope,' Midge said, after a pause, 'I'm not giving you the wrong impression. The girls here aren't such a bad lot, really.'

'Of course, Bev, as you call her . . . I suppose she was prettier than most.'

'Actually, no. It was odd. She looked quite ordinary with her clothes on. But when she wasn't wearing any . . . she was gorgeous. She looked . . . *alive*, you know what I mean? I used to think, well, if that's what sex does for you . . . but it wasn't that – or I don't think so. It was just the way she was. Sort of natural. I'm not explaining it very well, but perhaps you're getting the picture.'

'I'm trying very hard not to,' Dobie said.

100

His car was parked just round the corner. He shook hands courteously with his informant and with Elspeth (a mistake in the latter case, since he'd promised to give Elspeth a lift back home) and was opening the car door when Midge, who had fallen rather silent, spoke to him again.

'There *is* one other thing she said.'

'Yes?' Dobie paused attentively.

'Only it sounds so awful I really . . . don't like to tell you.'

Dobie continued to pause attentively. This not through any profound insight into schoolgirl psychology; it was just the way he was. Sort of natural. In fact he was thinking about something else.

'But I suppose the police are trying to find out who it was she was seeing on Saturday afternoons. . . .'

Dobie stopped thinking about something else. 'Yes?' he said again.

'Well. . . . She once said there were two of them.'

'*Two* of them?'

'Two men. Yes. Only there was something *funny* about it. Like it was some kind of private joke she was keeping to herself. I couldn't understand it, really. But that's what she said.'

'Do you think she meant there were two men who were—'

'I think that's what she *wanted* me to think. But that wouldn't have been very funny, would it? Just rather . . . sordid. And disgusting. No, there was something about the set-up that *amused* her. That's all I can say.'

5

Elspeth had been rather silent, Dobie thought, throughout that interview and she was silent now, staring out through the side window of the car at acres of inauspicious moorland as they drove through the school gateway and out on to the road. In a way, that was understandable. 'Are *all* the girls at your school so confiding?'

'You mean like Bev?'

'No, no, no. I meant like your friend Midge. She doesn't really *know* me at all.'

'Perhaps you inspire confidence,' Elspeth said.

'I don't know why I should.'

'It's like I said. You're clever. And . . . people *like* you.'

The Maclennan Professor of Theoretical Physics didn't, to name but one. But for once that gentleman's fulminations seemed to be of relatively little importance; it was Annabelle Midgley-Johnson who had now given Dobie food for serious thought. 'Do *you* like me?'

'Yes, I do.'

'That's good, because I want to ask you a favour.'

'*Me?* Sure thing. But what can *I* do?'

'When we get back to the Centre, do you think you can get me inside again? Invite me in or something?'

'I think so. You have to fill in a form thing at the gate and then you can just drive in. No problem.'

'*You* don't have to fill in a form?'

'Oh no. I *live* there. No, Bill just checks me in and out, same like with the staff. It's a lot of nonsense really. But . . . why do you want to . . . ?'

'I just want to take a look at some trees.'

'*Trees?* Well, we got plenty of *those*. . . .'

*

102

'It used to be called an arbor-something.'

'An arboretum, perhaps.'

'Just a posh name for a wood, I suppose. Though it's not exactly that. More of an avenue, wouldn't you say? Of course, the main buildings here used to be some kind of a country house, I forget what it was called but it must have been a nobby sort of place. And there was a path going through the trees up to the side door. Only it's all grassed over now.'

'I thought there might be.'

'Mind you, that's only what I've been told. Dad won't let me go over there because the inmates are allowed to walk there sometimes. Take exercise and so forth. I s'pose it's all right for *you* to go there, though. As you're a friend of Mr Train's.'

'I'm not exactly a friend,' Dobie said, 'but I might take a look around all the same. I'm, er . . . interested in trees. I'll leave the car parked here, though, if I may.'

Here was directly outside Elspeth's house, which for once he had been able to find without any difficulty. Elspeth had been right about the porter, or guard, or whatever he was. No problem at all. On the other hand. . . .

'That's OK. Dad won't be back till eight and he wouldn't mind, anyway. But he likes a bite to eat when he gets in so I'd better go and see what's in the fridge.' She glanced back over her shoulder towards the house, a little uneasily, Dobie thought. 'There wasn't too much there last time I looked.'

'You do the cooking?'

'Nights, yes. Well, *somebody* has to.'

After a long day at school, that had to be a rather tiring chore. And then there'd be homework to do. . . . This small creature, Dobie thought, seemed to have taken rather a lot on to her shoulders. Girls seemed to *know* so much more than they used to, nowadays. Beverley Sutro had certainly seemed to know plenty. 'Well, thank you,' Dobie said. 'I'll run along, then, if I may. Ta-ra for now.'

'*Ciao*, baby,' Elspeth said. Unexpectedly. Dobie turned away.

The trees extended in a long unbroken line from the far side of the road towards the main building. They did indeed rather resemble an avenue. Entering their shade (not of course at a run but at an appropriately sedate mathematical pace), Dobie found himself in a sudden near darkness, though patches of a greyish-greenish light showed here and there through the overhanging leaves. It was indeed an arboretum, whatever it looked liked; Dobie knew next to nothing about trees, but even he could see at once that the trees around him were of many different varieties. He walked slowly, his footsteps tracing a wandering course to and fro; now and again he paused to reach up and pluck a leaf to examine it more closely. The trouble was that of course unless you were an expert, leaves tend to look pretty much alike.

But then towards the end of the avenue, 'Ah,' Dobie said. '*There* you are.'

He snapped off the end of a branch and examined his find cautiously. 'Eureka,' Dobie said. '*Tilia platyphyllos*, if I mistake not, Watson. *Quia impossibile est.*' But he was almost sure he'd found what he was looking for. Outside those high walls, of course, there was nothing but empty moorland. Plenty of bracken, fern, gorse. . . . But no trees. And this really seemed to be exactly the right shape of leaf, not quite triangular because with rounded edges, a little like the blade of some ancient Iron Age spear or maybe an assegai. . . . Yes, Dobie thought. Most interesting. . . .

At this point his meditations were disturbed by two large gentlemen in white jackets, who bore down upon him purposefully.

'Nah then, nah then. 'Oo's that 'idin' 'imself away be'ind that there moustache? Joe Stalin, are we? Come along then, Comrade Commissar, time for beddy-byes.'

Dobie, briefly flabbergasted, found himself being seized in a firm grip by both elbows and conducted towards the Centre buildings at a rate of knots. 'No, wait,' he protested feebly. 'I think there's some mistake. I'm not a . . . an *inmate.*'

'Course you're not, Comrade. Ruler of the Rushun Empire, yus, we know all about that and I can see you've 'ad a long tiring day.'

'No, no. You don't understand. I'm conducting a criminal investigation.'

'Oh I *see*. So 'ow are all the boys in the KGB? We'll be 'avin' a bit of a purge there pretty soon, I shouldn't wonder. *That*'ll be nice, won't it? Now just step through 'ere into the Kremlin if you'll be so kind.'

'This isn't the Krem—'

The door closed with a significant-sounding click. Dobie looked around. No, it certainly wasn't the Kremlin. It looked more like a padded cell. It *was* a padded cell. Dobie banged his head exper-

104

imentally against the wall once or twice to see what would happen and when nothing did sat down on the floor. It seemed that what his colleagues at the University had so often sadly presaged had at last occurred. How very extraordinary.

But he realized now that his so-called investigations had been carried out somewhat indiscreetly. He had been, in a word, incautious. Glumly, he regarded the small glass eye of the camera lens that from a point high up on the far wall regarded him back. It was placed, obviously as of design, too high to be reached unless you stood on a table or a chair, and there weren't any tables or chairs. That was why he was sitting on the floor. And anyway, he didn't want to reach it. If the surveillance here was as effective as was claimed, someone before long would be peering at a monitor screen and wondering, *Who dat down dere?* Dobie hoped so, anyway. All this *Man in the Iron Mask* stuff wasn't really in his line.

Meanwhile, while awaiting the arrival of the Romney Marsh Mountain Rescue team or its local equivalent, he could conveniently contemplate the recent course of events. This was, at any rate, preferable to thinking about what Kate would say when she got to hear about all this. Possibly, as would almost certainly be the case with young Midgley-Johnson, a certain amount of hush-up and sweep-under-the-carpet might prove to be advisable. Certainly, Dobie thought, *I'm not going to tell her.* After all, I'm not in this because of Kate. I'm in this, if anything, because of Jenny.

Or because another and even younger woman has been similarly bashed on the boko, and badly beaten up into the bargain. So there has to be a very nasty fellow somewhere about. So it's no good Kate telling me to mind my own business. It seemed to be the case that Beverley Sutro hadn't been a very *nice* girl, but then Jenny hadn't been very nice, either, if in a different way. Dobie shook his head sadly, pondering once again on the difference.

Two thousand pounds was quite a substantial difference. It could even have been the difference between staying alive and getting dead, if someone hadn't wanted to pay up. Two thousand, and three thousand to follow. It had to be blackmail, of course. What else?

That's the difficulty with a permissive democracy. All people are permissive, but some are more permissive than others. Dobie could think of several of his colleagues who had, on occasion, had it off with students who hadn't been very much older than this Beverley girl, but a very few years can again make a very big difference. Technically, well, all right, she hadn't been a minor, but undeniably she'd been a schoolgirl and screwing schoolgirls has still to be a little bit *off* in the minds of many, unless you're very, very young yourself . . . but then you wouldn't be paying two hundred pounds for the dubious privilege, much less two thousand pounds with three more to follow. To follow what? To follow when? Dobie took the folded napkin from his pocket and once again spread out the enclosed sheet of paper. A half sheet, really, hurriedly torn off from a parent notepad; hurriedly torn off and hurriedly scribbled on. . . .

Holiday March 24th £2000. £3000 to follow. . . .

One thing about it was certainly very curious. Dobie took another sheet of notepaper from his pocket and compared the two. A university teacher and a student, he thought, is one thing; a doctor and a schoolgirl is another. An old-fashioned and very restrictive profession. You could get yourself struck off the register for that sort of thing, or at the very least dismissed from your post. And right here there were quite a few members of the medical profession conveniently available. Elspeth's father, for one. Carter, for another. . . .

Or even Morris Train. . . .

Not a doctor, but none the less in a responsible and therefore vulnerable position. Of course, one might be vulnerable for other reasons. A married man, for instance, might have excellent reasons for . . . *hush-up and sweep-under-the-carpet.* . . . Dobie sighed. Kate, he thought, she'd *kill* me. And we're not even married. This isn't logic, this is sheer idle speculation. Start out on a list like this one and the list becomes endless. All the same, you have to start *somewhere*. So why not here?

Really his rescue was being unconscionably delayed. Perhaps he should shout for help or something. What manner of use is it – Dobie wondered crossly – having all these state of the art technowhatsits if they don't help to rectify these silly little mistakes when they occur? They had to have spent a bomb on them, too. Taxpayer's money. This was one of the most up-to-the-minute institutes of its kind in the Principality, according to Kate, who after all knew a bit about these things. Yet here he was, stashed away like a kopek or whatever they called them in the bloody

Lubianka. Joe Stalin, indeed. There wasn't the slightest resemblance. And besides . . .

Ah.

At long last the door was coming open. Dobie rose to his feet. The geezer in the white jacket entered and stepped smartly to one side, permitting the further entrance of Morris Train, who seemed somewhat perturbed.

'What in Heaven's name are you doing in *here*, Professor Dobie?'

'I think,' Dobie said, 'the gentleman to your right has been labouring under a misapprehension as to my true identity. It's true that I may have inadvertantly contributed—'

'Chattin' away to a tree 'e woz. I 'eard 'im distink.'

'I may have unintentionally conveyed an impression—'

'Nutty I sez to meself. Bleedin' bonkers.'

'Possibly open to misinterpretation—'

'An' talkin' in Rushun wot's more. To someone called Yurika. Well, I *arsk* you.'

'*Russian?* I can't speak a word of Russian. No, I deny it categorically.'

'There 'e goes again.'

'All right, all right, all *right*,' Train said, hopping up and down like a boxing referee urging the contestants to abandon a hopelessly non-productive clinch. 'We'll go into the rights and wrongs of this matter later, Whyburn. Professor Dobie is known to me personally. If you'd care to step round to my office, Dobie, I think I'll be able to arrange for you to be spared any further inconvenience.'

'Obviously a touch of over-zealousness. I hope you'll feel able to excuse it.'

'In fact,' Dobie said, 'I'm probably to blame. I didn't realize that I was wandering out of bounds, so to speak.'

'This whole area, strictly speaking, is out of bounds. You know, our whole external security system is designed to prevent visitors from coming in and not, as you might suppose, to stop people from getting out. That does cause problems. I like to think we have them licked but these occasional little contretemps do occur.'

'It wasn't in any way Elspeth's fault. I ought to make that clear.'

'No, no. The staff and their dependants are permitted free

access, naturally. It'd be difficult to keep them here otherwise, we're so . . . isolated, so to speak . . . but really it's essential to keep casual visitors well away from the people undergoing treatment here, or else the patients might well be able to supply themselves with dangerous habit-forming drugs, such as the one you're now holding in your hand, or others a good deal easier to smuggle in. . . . You take my meaning?'

The addictive drug in the glass in Dobie's hand had indeed done something to mollify his ruffled feelings and he mollified them further before nodding comprehendingly. 'Yes. And do they in fact?'

'No, they don't. On the whole, we find them very co-operative. It's a matter of not putting temptation in their way. After all, they know that if they keep their noses clean they'll be out of here within a month – or two at the outside. It *is* a prison in a sense, but we don't really have to worry about anyone *escaping*. There'd be very little point to it. And of course, a certain number of them are here of their own choice. Indeed I'm happy to say that the percentage of voluntary patients has increased very notably of late, thanks to some good work by the local police.'

'You mean the police persuade them to volunteer?'

'Oh no.' Train, unlike Dobie, hadn't taken a seat but instead was stumping steadily to and fro across the office carpet, his hands folded behind his back in approved military style. Behind the desk, Dobie had observed, a small group of Army officers were indeed glaring at him from a framed regimental photograph, a peak-capped Morris Train being one of their number. 'Though that may sometimes be the case. No – but they seem to have run a very effective crackdown recently on the local dealers, indeed to have put several of them where they belong. In jail.'

'So you may expect to see them here in due course.'

'Well, that's possible. But,' Train said, executing a sharp right about-turn, 'the point is that right now addictive drugs are in very short supply in the Cardiff area. People who're in any way dependent on them have either to pay prohibitive prices or kick the habit. Well, for quite a few of them the latter is the only viable alternative. One way or another, this Centre is likely to be running just about to capacity over the next few months. Unfortunately it doesn't look as though the Welsh Office will be granting us any additional financial allocation, but that's by the way.'

'But you have quite a few people here who've committed criminal offences.'

'Drug-related offences, yes. That's so.'

'Rape?'

'Rape,' Train said, 'is a serious crime, whether committed under the influence of drugs or not. I suppose you're thinking of that unfortunate girl who . . . ?'

'Yes.'

'You know, I had a call from the CID office in Cardiff on that matter this morning, and I felt able to assure the officer concerned that there's no possibility of any of the patients here being in any way involved. We're talking about *internal* security now, you see. And I gather we may also be talking about murder. Well, we haven't any murderers here, thank goodness. They'd go to a maximum security prison as a matter of course – as the Cardiff police know very well.'

'You've got someone here who has been *accused* of murder.'

'We have? Ah.' After a pause for reflection, Train nodded pontifically. '*That's* what's worrying you, is it? Our young friend Adrian. But surely it's been established that those particular charges were brought in another country and in any case have since been dropped. Otherwise, he'd hardly be here.'

'They've been dropped but they're mentioned on the medical record sheet. To which you very kindly gave me access the other day. And I have to presume the police have access also. In which case they might—'

'My dear chap, these people are under constant surveillance, they're *prisoners* after all. And indeed I seem to recollect that in Adrian's case . . . But we can easily check on this. It may indeed be wise for me to do so. Let's step round to the Registry, shallers? It's only just round the corner.'

'Here we are,' Miss Daly said. 'On Dr Carter's schedule. Last Saturday, March 24th . . . 1600 to 1800 hours, Mr Adrian Seymour. Just the usual consultancy period. Wednesdays and Saturdays. That *is* what you wanted to know?'

Yes, it was. 'He was with Dr Carter then?'

'Exactly,' Train said. 'Not merely under surveillance, but in Carter's physical presence. If you wanted an alibi for him, you've got it. I take it, Miss Daly, there was no departure from the normal programme that afternoon? Adrian was indeed at that time in Dr Carter's office?'

'Oh yes. It's right next door. I saw them arrive together. And if anything out of the ordinary had taken place, Dr Carter would certainly have reported it.'

Dobie fingered his upper lip with a certain circumspection. 'Do *all* the doctors have consultations at that time of day?'

'Indeed they do,' Train said. 'Two o'clock to six o'clock every day. Plus a certain number of group therapy sessions in the mornings. We all work to a very crowded schedule, Professor Dobie, and indeed it's often difficult to fit everything in. Luckily we have Miss Daly here in charge of the organization of it all. *I*'m the merest figurehead, I assure you.'

Miss Daly smiled bleakly and slid the timetable sheet back into its protective plastic folder. Dobie was far from sure that he was still in her good graces, if indeed he ever had been. 'Where would Adrian be now?'

Train glanced at his wristwatch. 'Twenty past six, isn't it? He may very well be in the recreation rooms, or possibly . . . Can you check on it, Miss Daly?'

'Of course.' Miss Daly smiled even more bleakly than before and retired to her inner sanctum behind the filing cabinets, where a succession of rapid clicking sounds indicated various manoeuvrings of the television monitors. Meanwhile Train glanced again, and this time more pointedly, at his wristwatch. 'I'm afraid I really must be running along. You'll excuse me, won't you? I've no objection at all to your having another little chat with Adrian, if that's what you had in mind. As soon as Miss Daly has located him —'

'In the Common Room,' Miss Daly said frostily, reappearing and plumping herself down at her desk. 'Playing a game of chess with Harry the Horse, I mean with . . . Mr Douglas.'

'Harry Douglas, eh? One of our rough diamonds, but sound enough at bottom, wouldn't you say? Well, it's more or less on my way. Let me take you there.'

'I think in fact I can remember —'

'It's no trouble at all,' Train said firmly.

'You got your name in the papers, you know that?'

No, Dobie didn't. He hardly ever read the newspapers.

'This morning's *Echo*. Front page at that.'

It was lying folded on the table in front of him. Dobie picked it up and glanced at it. The photograph ran across three newsprint columns but his name, he saw, was only mentioned at the end of the report and was moreover wrongly spelled. The photograph, of course, was of Beverley Sutro or more precisely of Beverley Sutro's head and shoulders; staring wide eyed into the camera lens, she looked about twelve years old, younger even than Elspeth. Possibly it was an old photograph. Given the choice of doing something quickly and doing it right, there was never any doubt as to what the sub-editors of the local press would plump for. Of course they'd have deadlines to meet and so on. Dobie folded the paper again and tossed it back on to the table. 'Spelled it wrong,' he said. 'They usually do.'

'You've seen that photograph?'

'Yes.'

'That's the girl.'

'Oh yes, that's the girl all right. What they *say* is true enough. I and my friend Kate Coyle, we found her. Kate's a doctor, you see, she did what she could but it wasn't . . . She didn't . . .' Dobie realized from the expression on Seymour's face that he had somehow gone off the track again. Or in some way had contrived to miss the point. 'Sorry. What do you mean – that's the girl?'

'The one I told you about.'

'You've *seen* her somewhere?'

'No. I don't think so. She's the girl in that . . . dark place. . . . The one in the dream.'

'Ah,' Dobie said.

Today Seymour really didn't look very well. Though he didn't look exactly ill, either. Chiefly, he looked tired. Worn round the edges. 'You remember?'

'I remember your telling me about it, yes. But I thought that dream had to do with that time in Cyprus. With . . . your wife and all that. This girl couldn't possibly have come into it. Could she?'

'I don't know. They've got me back on sedatives again. I haven't been sleeping well lately. It's Valium, I think. Works all right, in that either I don't dream or I don't remember my dreams when I wake up. She's still *there*, though. She hasn't gone away.'

'Have you told the doctors about it?'

'I tried to. But Popeye's not interested, he says all that Freudian stuff is too old-fashioned and no one goes in for interpreting dreams any more. I don't care if it's old-fashioned or not, that damned girl's *there*, I mean . . . it's as though she's *waiting* for me, for when I go to sleep . . . Her and that other fellow. . . .'

'What other fellow?'

'I can't see *him*. That is, I can never see his face. He's wearing a mask.'

Dobie inhaled deeply but managed not to sigh. 'Tell me about it again. What do you see, exactly?'

'I don't see anything *exactly* because it's dark, it's somewhere deep underground but there are sort of pools of light here and there and colours, blue mostly and black and . . . the whole thing's somehow *static*, like a painting. . . . It's hard to explain.'

'You say you've tried. OK. Try again.'

'Well, this chap's doing it to the girl and that's all there is to it, really. Except that it's frightening. It makes me feel scared. I want to run away and I find I can't.'

'And you can't see the man?'

'Because he's on top and his face is turned down. But the girl's on her back and I can see *her* face all right. And,' Seymour said, tapping the folded newspaper, 'that's her. That's the face. I can't understand it.'

'How do you know the man's wearing a mask? If you can't see his face?'

'I just *know* he is. That's all.'

Dobie shook his head, not in negation but as though to dispel a certain unwanted mental image. 'Maybe you've got that story thing you wrote at the back of your mind. *The Mask of Zeus* or whatever you called it. And I imagine it has to be some little while since you had a girl yourself. I wouldn't be surprised if it hasn't all got something to do with sexual repression, I mean your being a perfectly healthy young—'

'*Everything*'s got something to do with sexual repression, if you're into Freud.'

'But you say that Carter isn't.'

'No, he isn't. And anyway it isn't the dream that worries me. It's the *girl*. It didn't worry me much before because I thought she didn't exist, except as a figment of my imagination. But she does. Or *did*. Maybe it's . . . Do you think I'm *psychic*? Or something?'

If he weren't *something* he wouldn't have been put where he now was, but Dobie tactfully refrained from pointing this out. 'Well, as a mathematician I wouldn't be any too happy with that explanation, because of course it doesn't explain anything, not really. But on the other hand I wouldn't be prepared to discount it altogether. You've had this dream a number of times?'

'Since I got here, yes. I don't know how many times. At least a dozen.'

'And it's always the same?'

'Yes. Except sometimes I'm standing still looking at it and sometimes I'm moving. . . . Not walking. More like floating. You know? Moving, anyway. Unless it's the shadows moving about. I can't be sure.'

'But the girl's always the same? Can you see what sort of expression she has on her face? I mean, you say you're frightened – is *she* frightened?'

'She doesn't have any expression at all. I don't know. . . . Perhaps it's more like a statue than a painting. I know it sounds weird when you try to describe it, but it doesn't seem at all weird in the dream, it's just *scary*.'

'I don't quite see what's scary about it.'

'Well, that's right, and that's what's scary.'

After a while Dobie said, 'Perhaps you'd better not tell anyone else about it, at least until they've let you out of here. They say they plan to release you pretty soon and maybe when you've got a job lined up . . . or anyway when you start work somewhere. . . . I don't know if my recommendations will be of much good to you but I've filed a reference, for what it's worth.'

'Yes. Well, thanks. Yes, you may be right. I don't much *like* it here, you know . . . but then nobody does.'

'It has its advantages. For instance, you seem to be completely in the clear on this one. And that, I suppose, has to be a pleasant change.'

'In the clear?'

'Whoever killed the girl, it wasn't you.'

Seymour stared at him. 'Good God, of course it wasn't. Why the hell would I want to kill a girl I've never even met? Except in —'

'It's been known to happen.'

'I said I might be psychic, not a psycho. And anyway, I wasn't serious.'

'That's just the sort of distinction,' Dobie said, 'that Detective

113

Inspector Jackson gets all mixed up. But at least he won't get confused over a good sound alibi.'

'And I've got one?'

'You were with Dr Carter at the operative time. Or so it appears.'

'Saturday afternoon? Yes, I was.'

'Four to six p.m.'

'Right. My usual straightening-out session. Excising my alleged guilt fixation. I suppose he's done a good job on me, as far as it goes. I'm certainly not about to confess to anything ever again, whether I happen to be guilty of it or not. It's a great mistake. He's convinced me of it.'

Dobie felt a little relieved that the conversation had taken slightly more light-hearted a turn. He picked up one of the discarded chess pieces from the table and looked at it. Judging from the appearance of the board, Harry the Horse hadn't proved to be too redoubtable an opponent; his skills would no doubt be better displayed in a boxing ring. 'Perhaps *I* should book in for a session. I'm feeling more than a little guilty these days.'

'Really? What of?'

'Blowing up the universe.'

'Oh. Is *that* all? No, it wasn't you. Must have been some other bloke.'

'Perhaps this Indian chap,' Dobie said, 'they mention in the newspaper. Professor Dhobi.'

'A very likely culprit.'

They'd got the girl's name right, though. Which should have sufficed to put Professor Dobie and his delusions of grandeur in his proper place. He hadn't, after all, admitted to the true reason why he was indeed feeling a little guilty.

He was himself, properly speaking, a criminal. He had just stolen something.

His reaction, therefore, when Detective Inspector Jackson clapped one hand on his shoulder in the classic gesture was to bound once more up into the air like a demented wallaby (always assuming that the said wallaby were to be found initially seated on a white plastic chair with a foam-rubber cushion, a sufficiently unlikely supposition, though if the animal were indeed demented, that might account for it). Lost in the ramifications of this after all quite casual similitude, Dobie was slow to recognize that his assailant on this occasion was not, in fact, Jackson but (as was logical to suppose) someone else; to wit, Dr Carter. 'Hullo there,' Carter said jollily. 'I hope I didn't startle you.'

'Not at all,' Dobie said, startled. 'I thought you wolla wozzaby, I mean *were* a . . . worraby . . . or anyway, someone else.'

'A *wallaby*?'

'No, no. A linguistic confusion arising from . . . Never mind the wallaby. Forget the wallaby. Wallabies,' Dobie said, becoming more and more anxious, 'have got nothing to do with it, I assure you.'

'To do with what?'

'With what we were talking about.'

'We weren't talking about anything. I only just got here.'

'I meant my friend here and myself.'

'Ah.' Carter had already acknowledged Seymour's presence with a smile and a courteous nod. 'So what *were* you talking about?'

Dobie had in fact forgotten; it was therefore Seymour who replied. 'We were telling sad stories,' he said, 'of the death of kings.' If you call *that* a reply. Carter was clearly nonplussed. So was Dobie. To the best of his knowledge, they hadn't been doing anything of the kind. 'Kings? What kings?'

'And queens. By implication.'

Dobie looked round him nervously, his anxiety now bordering on agitation. 'There aren't any of *those* here, are there?'

Seymour sighed. 'Ah no John, no John, no. Only sad kings and princes all. Mourning for la belle dame sans merci.'

At last, Dobie dug. 'Poetry again, is it? That's all right, then. Just for a moment I thought—'

'*If*,' Carter said rather loudly, 'you've in any case now concluded your conversation, my colleagues and I were wondering if you would care to join us in the Staff Common Room. Not as commodious as this place, of course, but we do have certain amenities on tap that aren't available here. And we'd all be interested to hear your version of a somewhat singular incident that, as rumour has it—'

'Oh, *that*, yes, an amusing misapprehension. . . . But all very easily explained.'

*

115

In fact, of course, it wasn't.

'What I can't make out is why he took me to be a *Russian*. You haven't been made subject to Communist infiltration, I hope? It's surely a little late in the day for that.'

'Not as far as we know,' Carter said. 'Though of course Tigger here is a bit of a radical.'

'Ha ha,' Dr Ram said. 'Ha ha ha.'

'Thick as a brick, that Whybrow fellow,' Mighell said. 'Mind you, you have to be, to deal with some of the blokes we've got in here. Or anyway, it helps. He can talk to them on their own level, so to speak.'

'*Those* are rather radical sentiments, Robert.'

'Don't quote me on 'em,' Mighell said glumly.

Dobie, the centre of present attention, beamed at everyone through his glasses with vague benevolence. He was finding the atmosphere and general ethos of the Staff Common Room very much more relaxing and convivial than that of the Recreation Hall, and after all, why shouldn't he? It was one with which he was extremely familiar, not at all unlike that of the Senior Common Room at his university. The promised amenities, in the shape of a bottle of cream sherry, had indeed been provided and his companions of the moment were partaking of its content freely and in a spirit of general bonhomie – Dr Mighell's air of somewhat cynical gloom excepted. In this ambience, Dobie's enthralling narration had, he thought, gone down rather well. 'There's something faintly Chaucerian about it,' the tall thin one said. Hopkinson? Hodgson? *Hudson*, that was it. ' "The Professor's Tale" . . .'

'Though lacking something in the element of ribaldry.'

'Possibly our Miss Daly . . .'

'There are certain roles in which one might readily imagine her.' Hudson, yes. The thin one. Why, Dobie thought, am I so *bad* with names? And why, if it came to that, didn't people have numbers instead? So very much more convenient and practical. And the inmates here *did* have numbers, come to think of it. 1248758 Seymour, A. . . . There you go. Nobody could possibly have any difficulty in remembering *that*. Dobie's fingers encountered the slip of folded paper in his jacket pocket and closed over it possessively. 'Though, wishful thinking apart,' Hudson continued, 'I suppose one would have to cast her as the Lady Prioress. Within these walls, anyway.'

'I wouldn't say she was remarkable for her tender heart,' Carter said. 'Though in that same general physical region, of course . . . some rather remarkable . . . I don't know . . . The Merchant's wife, perhaps? Or even the Wife of Bath?'

'Ha ha ha. Ha ha.'

'Did she get around to sorting out that problem . . . ?'

'Yes, everything's back to normal,' Mighell said. 'Or so the Director tells me. In fact, I understand the Professor here was instrumental in ironing out the difficulty – whatever it was. Really, there should be some technician available on the premises—'

The conversation was now becoming general as well as largely incomprehensible, at any rate to the Professor here; Dobie, however, was content enough to take refuge in his glass of sherry – metaphorically speaking – and let all this obscure stuff about the Brides in the Bath wash – speaking more metaphorically yet – over his head. It was bad enough, really, getting all that poetry crap from Seymour – quoting poetry is after all a safe and recognized method of convincing other people that one's *mentis* is appropriately *non compos* – but it was disturbing to find the members of staff here also affected, presumably by contagion, with the malady but not after all *very* disturbing, not when one had other and more pressing matters to think about. . . . Ah, but Mighell, apprised perhaps through telepathic means that his guest's mind was beginning to wander, was leaning forwards now in his armchair to address Dobie confidentially, though in sufficiently stentorian tones for the others to hear his question and to break off their own conversation in consequence. 'My daughter tells me you take an interest in criminology, Mr Dobie, or in criminal cases as such. And in this business of Beverley Sutro in particular. Is this true?'

'Oh no. Not exactly. It's just that, as you know, Kate and I, Dr Coyle and I . . . Well, we saw her lying there. Beside the road. As you know. But I've no interest in criminal cases, no, not in general. Not at all.'

'How very unusual. Most people are fascinated by them. You know, of course, the girl was almost certainly raped? The police seem to be acting on that assumption, anyway. Or seemed to be when they interviewed me this morning.'

'Inspector Jackson?'

'The same fellow who questioned me on the Saturday night.

Yes, I believe the name was Jackson. He's something of a friend of yours?'

'Something, yes.'

'But you're not in any way privy to his thoughts on the matter? Or to his conduct of the case?'

'Oh no. No, indeed.'

'Ah.' Mighell's air of studied melancholy seemed, if anything, to deepen slightly at this intelligence. 'Well, I hope it's not developing on the usual readily predictable lines. We *do* have two or three convicted rapists here, but they most certainly couldn't have been involved in *this* tragic affair and I trust the Director was able to convince your, er . . . Inspector Jackson of that.'

'Rapists, yes,' Hudson said cheerfully. 'Murderers, no. No Hannibal the Cannibals here, ha ha.'

'Ha ha. Ha ha ha.'

'In fact we pay a great deal of attention to dietary considerations. That,' Hudson explained to Dobie, 'is why the food's so bloody awful.'

'He he he he he.'

Schoolboy humour, Dobie decided, invariably finding in the bearded and otherwise solemn Dr Ram a ready market. *Tigger*, indeed. *Snigger* would be more like it. Ram's explosive and often curiously timed chuckles seemed to be the only contribution he had so far made to the discussion. But then in some ways the atmosphere here resembled that of a public school rather than a university common room, with Mighell in the admonitory role of senior housemaster. 'That,' Mighell was now saying, 'is not to the present point. It's been clearly established, I hope, that the patients here have all been committed for drug-related cases only. If that little . . . if the girl was indeed murdered, the crime clearly must fall into a totally different category. This, apart from the sheer physical impossibility of any of our patients being responsible. We don't *call* this a prison, but that's what it is, and an exceptionally well supervised prison at that. I refuse to believe—'

'But what about that chap of yours, Raich?'

'What chap?'

'The one they sent back here for murdering his wife out in the boondocks somewhere. Malta, wasn't it?'

'Seymour.' Carter snorted. 'Absolute piffle. All based on a

drug-related *confession*, if you'll credit it, which wouldn't have passed muster in . . . Ask the Professor about it, if you like. *He* knows a great deal about the case.'

There was a brief silence. Tigger opened his mouth as though about to interject yet another chortle, but then didn't. 'Professor Dobie,' Mighell said, 'seems to know a good deal about a great many things with a criminal connection, despite his disclaimer.'

Dobie felt more than a little uncomfortable. 'Not really. Only through pure chance that led to our finding . . . You see, the Director wanted to ask me if I'd be prepared to recommend—'

'We know all about *that*,' Mighell said, somewhat brusquely. 'But we've all learnt to be sceptical when we hear of events being attributed to the workings of chance. Unconscious motivations – that's what we look for. Not only in criminals, but in all those connected in any way with the crime. The victims, even. No, the victims *especially*. There are very powerful arguments which suggest that murder victims are often drawn towards their own deaths and indeed often unconsciously but actively work to bring their own deaths about. I don't know if you've read—'

'I don't think the girl could have wanted to die,' Dobie said, 'if that's what you're saying. She was only seventeen, after all.'

'The age is irrelevant, and in any case the sixteen-to-twenty age group is demonstrably more prone to suicide than most others. But that *isn't* exactly what I'm saying. You've just put forward the classical layman's misinterpretation, in fact. You see, it's been statistically established that children of divided families, children whose parents are divorced or otherwise separated—'

'Like Elspeth?'

'Yes and no. I'm putting forward a generalization to which you might cite any number of individual—'

'What sort of generalizations would you make about the person who killed that girl?'

'Oh, I think a fairly normal and easily recognizable type.'

'So you'd say – generalizing, of course – that in murder cases it's usually the victim who's a bit weird and not the murderer?'

'Oh, yes. I think that modern psychiatric research has established *that* pretty firmly.'

'Ha ha ha ha. Ha ha.'

Jackson, Dobie thought, should at once be informed that he was barking up the wrong tree. But then he hadn't been told about the *right* tree, not as yet. All the same, if, as it appeared, it was the murder *victim* who ought to be arrested, then some substantial revision of normal police procedures would certainly be necessary. Maybe if he . . . Oh. 'Sorry?'

'I was only saying that if you'd care to read my recent paper on the psychopathology of the violent criminal, I'd be happy to lend you a copy.' This was the tall thin one. Hudson. 'I think it'll bring you up to date on the latest thinking on the matter. Recent research, you see, has suggested that many preconceptions of the general public—'

'Does that chap you mentioned come into it?'

'Seymour? Oh no. But that's a case in point. The citing of actual case histories is decidedly *vieux jeu* these days, indeed it's an unfortunate survival—'

'I meant that cannibal chap.'

Hudson regarded him curiously. 'You haven't seen the film?'

'The film? No, I rarely go—'

'Ah. That explains it. My allusion was to a fictional character, you see, who was in the habit of murdering people and storing various parts of their anatomies in the fridge, this against the contingency of unexpected guests having to be entertained to dinner. The same unexpected guests, in their turn—'

'I see.' Dobie thought that for once he did, but it was obviously prudent to be cautious. 'He'd be some kind of a pervert, to your way of thinking?'

'Well, we shouldn't jump to over-rash conclusions. Cannibalism has a long and respectable history and is after all regarded with approval in many cultures. In the context of our own culture, of course . . . but then that's what clinical psychiatry is all about. Taking the broader view.'

'I suppose,' Dobie said, 'it helps you to stay sane.'

'Well, that's one way of putting it.'

'Kate?'

'What?'

'Killing people *is* wrong, isn't it?'

'Yes. Very wrong. Unless, of course, you're a doctor. Why do you ask?'

'I just wanted to be reassured on the point,' Dobie said. 'I was afraid I might be indulging myself in outmoded preconceptions.'

'Well, what's wrong with that?'

'It seems one has to take the broader view. But there again, they're a very strange lot up at that place.'

'They have a remarkably high success rate, though, in dealing with these social misfits. A model institute, in fact, of its kind.'

'I'm not surprised,' Dobie said. 'If *I* thought I were a social misfit, a brief chat with any of those fellows would do a great deal to restore my confidence.'

'You *are* a social misfit.'

'I am? Well, there you are, then. That accounts for it.'

Kate sighed. 'Accounts for what?'

'For . . . I don't know. For my feeling a good deal better about things in general.'

'You mean your paradox?'

'I suppose so. With all these other advances in the frontiers of knowledge that are being made day by day, I don't really see how my little effort is going to make things any worse than they are already. By the way, you threw four then. Not five.'

'Oh yes.' Kate said. Since the dice still lay face upwards on the board, the evidence was incontrovertible. Gloomily, she made the required adjustment. 'Sorry.'

'You're *always* cheating, Kate.'

'Only when I'm going bankrupt.'

'You're *always* going bankrupt.'

This being also incontrovertible, Kate took refuge in bluster. 'It's a silly game, anyway.' Though the source of the whole trouble lay in over-investment, as she knew very well. It was so much *nicer* to have a little red hotel sitting snugly on the corner of the square rather than on all those nasty little green things that got knocked over when you threw the dice. Or more exactly, when Dobie did. 'All games are silly, when you think about it.'

'That's why people play them,' Dobie said. 'The silliness is the only common factor. At any rate, that's what Wittgenstein decided. Come on, hand over.'

'Don't *rush* me.' Kate passed across the table an enormous bundle of funny money, hoping he wouldn't count it. Ruin now stared her in the face. It was a pity, she thought, Dobie couldn't be persuaded to bring his undoubted mathematical talent to bear of the *real* world of high finance and make a killing on the market. Or there again, perhaps it wasn't. 'There must,' Kate said, 'be something else we could do to while away the evening.'

'Yes, but we usually do that later.' Dobie rattled the dice, threw them, reached across for the Community Chest cards. 'Oh dear.'

'What is it?'

'I have to go to a Rehabilitation Centre.'

'Serve you right. Your sins were bound to find you out.'

Dobie placed the small plastic motor-car he was driving round the board on the appropriate corner square and sat back, moodily surveying his considerable gains. 'Do you have any dealings with that lot, Kate?'

'With the psychs, you mean? No. When I was at Guy's I once had to give forensic evidence against the Professor of Criminal Psychiatry and it wasn't a very pleasant experience . . . but hell, he was nice about it afterwards and I haven't any hard feelings. I mean, they have their methods and we have ours.'

'But what *are* their methods? I mean that lot up at the Centre?'

Kate also sat back, leaving the dice on the table. At this stage of the game, a few moments' respite was welcome. Not that she had much hope of . . . 'I don't know much about them at all. The place used to be a straightforward remand home but under the new dispensation I don't think anyone knows what they do, exactly. Well, they rehabilitate people. Obviously.'

Dobie shook his head, unsatisfied. 'What they do is, *they* play games. If you ask me.' He reached across for his borrowed copy of Hudson on *The Psychopathology of the Violent Criminal* and riffled through the pages. 'The people they're treating play games with them and so they play games right back. Only thing is, they're all writing books of rules . . . like this one . . . and all the rulebooks seem to be different. I'm going to have a chat with Jacko tomorrow, in any case.'

'I don't think Jacko's very interested in psychopathology or in anything else that he can't spell.'

'He wouldn't mind catching a murderer, though.'

'Listen, Dobie, you are *not* going to—'

'Someone's playing games,' Dobie said. 'There's a games player around somewhere. I'm sure of it. Like Wendy. I've been through this before. That's *how* I'm sure.'

For a moment Kate didn't say anything. Dobie had just mentioned a name that hadn't been mentioned by either of them for quite a time, and Kate didn't know if that was a good sign or not. In the end she said, 'But of course you don't know who.'

'Not yet. But I've got some evidence. And it's *evidence* I'm talking about. Not theories.'

'Well, Jacko might be interested in that. Not an awful lot of evidence had come his way, as far as I can make out.'

'It said in the paper that Pontin expects an arrest at any moment.'

'A cardiac one, if so. He's overdue for it.' Kate reached absent-mindedly for the box and started to put the pieces away. Commencing, naturally, with Dobie's hotels.

'Anyway,' Dobie said, 'even if he doesn't want the evidence, I still have to give him the money.'

'Money? *What* money?'

'Yes, I was going to tell you about that.'

So he did.

6

Miss Bramble's office was pleasant enough, Dobie decided, if you could rid yourself of the illusion that you were in some Red Army outpost in the wilds of Kazakhstan, with a wide-open window giving out on to versts and versts and versts of the frozen tundra. A closer examination might have revealed that the view was in fact of muddy and water-logged playing fields, their monotony relieved by the occasional set of drab grey goalposts, but Dobie preferred not to examine the view at all, regaling himself with the more agreeable spectacle of pair after pair of nicely rounded and well-scrubbed schoolgirls' knees, emerging from neat blue skirts in the frieze of colour photographs that ran almost the whole way round the room and which immortalized the outward aspect, if not the achievements, of the Dame Margaret's First XI over the past twelve years or so. Dobie searched in vain for Elspeth's pleasing features among those displayed in these assemblies, but couldn't find it . . . one face among so many . . . and found himself shuddering retrospectively at the raw determination with which these charming young ladies grasped their hockeysticks. How did hockey ever become a game for *girls*, Dobie wondered. Loosely organized mayhem. That was what it was.

No doubt it all went back to the Greeks and the bloody Olympic games and so to the public school tradition, Thomas Arnold and all that. The Greeks had a lot to answer for, when you thought about it. And not least, of course, for their bloody language. God, Dobie had *loathed* Greek at school, and still did. . . .

A fine training for the mind, they'd always told him. Then when he'd got to Oxford they'd told him mind was an outdated concept and anyway didn't exist, the double-crossing bastards. Luckily, there was always mathematics. No outdated concepts there. Everything exists in mathematics, quite independently of mind.

You know where you are with mathematics. While outside the field of the integer . . . Well. Yes. Room for confusion. And plenty of it.

Miss Bramble's office was pleasant enough, if you didn't mind the Spartan atmosphere. Not much in the way of refinements. A formica-topped desk, a swivel chair (standing forlornly empty in its owner's absence), a white telephone set, an electric typewriter on a side-table, a couple of filing cabinets, and underneath it all, bare floorboards. Highly polished, certainly, but bare. So were the walls, except for all those team photographs. Beverley, from all accounts, had lacked the team spirit. She hadn't gone a bundle on the Spartan way of life. The cold showers and fresh air ethos. All those dank and dismal playing fields, stretching away out into infinity. Not after Italy, and life with a rich new poppa. Dobie found it rather hard to blame her.

He looked round as the door opened.

'The Headmistress will see you now,' Miss Bramble said.

Not all that formidable a lady, Dobie decided. Fortyish and bespectacled, certainly, but to all outward appearance amiable enough. Amiable, but definitely displeased. 'I trusht,' she said severely, 'thish shcurrilous shtory will not be refeated outshide thish room. It sheemsh to me thatsh not too much to ashk.'

'Only to the pleesh, I mean the pleeth, of coursh.'

'I musht inshisht that nothing be shed to the presh in the present shercumshtanshish.'

'Oh, indeed no,' Dobie reassured her. It was apparent to anyone gifted with Dobie's acute powers of observation that some considerable part of Miss Midwinter's testiness had to be attributed to the after-effects of a substantial injection of novocaine, which had swelled up the left side of an already impressive jawline to balloon-like dimensions and which, of course, fully explained Miss Bramble's initial extreme reluctance to admit him to the Headmistressly presence. 'It's just that . . . there's all this *money*, you see, that apparently belonged to . . . And you can't account for her possession of it in any other way?'

'I cad dot.'

The Headmistress's office appeared to be almost as conspicuously lacking in creature comforts as that of her secretary. Indeed, Dobie couldn't even console himself with the contemplation of all those rows of delectably girlish knees and things, the only aesthetic indulgence here permitted being that which might be (improbably) derived from the large oil painting on the wall directly behind Miss Midwinter's desk, where her visitors had to look at it but she needn't – a fact confirming Dobie's impression that no flies were likely to settle on Midders. The portrait in question was of a fearsome grey-haired harridan in full academic dress and steel-rimmed glasses – no doubt Dame Margaret herself – and faced with this unfortunate reminder of the quintessence of Somervilleanism Dobie could not but shrink, quivering, back into the recesses of his armchair. *Non sum qualis eram*, he said to himself. But out loud – though not *very* loud—

'Could she have left school premises at any time, I mean without the proper authorization? Maybe at night?'

'Thatsh imposhible. Our rulesh are mosht shtringent. *All* our girlsh have been fucked in bed by nine o'clock, without eschepchon.'

'Good Heavens.' This was the last thing that Dobie had expected. He was aware, of course, that girls' boarding schools nowadays offered all manner of popular extra-curricular activities, but this seemed to be somewhat out of the ordinary. 'Isn't that rather difficult to organize?'

'Fucked *up* in bed, I should've shed. And the shchool gatesh are alwaysh closhed at sheven. We escherchishe conshtant vigilansh in that reshpect.' Miss Midwinter took a white linen handkerchief from what, Dobie thought, could only be a reticule and pressed it to her cheek. Once the sense of numbness had departed it would, no doubt, hurt like billy-oh. He sympathized but none the less persevered.

'Have you been able to contact Beverley's parents?'

'Her padents? Imboshable. I hab always been obriged to deal with her buvver's shallishiter.'

'Her *brother*'s?'

'I shtinkly shed, her *buvver*'s, dibben I?'

'Ah. Yes. Where *is* her mother, then?'

'In the shoush of Iddly, ash I bereave. Her turd husbin I bereave ish an Iddalian.'

'Her *third* husband? Really?'

'Yesh.' The Headmistress lowered her head in sorrow. 'Marridge bows are not reshpected as wunsh they were, Perfessor. In my own shchooldays, a gel would eshpect to ged married for bugger or worsh, bud it shtifferent now.'

'I'm sure it must be. So I take it this solicitor chap you mentioned will be, ah, responsible for the funeral expenses and so on? How can I get in touch with him?'

'Hish dame ish Maddening. Of Maddening, Maddening, and Polecat. Offisesh in Wesh Shtreet.'

Dobie had a feeling that he had pushed his luck about as far as it would go. Not that luck had anything to do with it. The obscure form of blackmail that he was currently practising, then. 'I'm sure,' he said, 'that he, too, will be anxious to avoid any untoward publicity that might reflect unfavourably upon the school in general. And I'll certainly do all that I can to prosecute that end.'

'Bed barden?'

Dobie didn't feel like going through all *that* again so he shook his head sadly, instead. 'Of course it's all very tragic. She was quite a promising student, I believe.' And would seem to have fulfilled her promise in certain directions, but he didn't much want to go into *that* again, either. 'Did you in fact teach her? That's to say . . . personally?'

'Id deed I did. I dook her for eddycushion.'

'Education? What particular form—'

'I shed eddy-*kew*-shun. Our padents inshist that our gelsh be nishely shpoken. Soddem.'

'Ah,' Dobie said. She *couldn't* have meant that. 'Of course. Of course.' Elocution. What else? He couldn't help wondering, though, how Jackson had fared in his interview with Miss Midwinter. It was difficult to imagine, somehow.

The mind boddled.

In fact Jackson had confined his investigative techniques to the interrogation of the blue-eyed Miss Bramble and the information he had gained from that source was now bearing fruit. The blackberries in question were neither abundant in growth nor particularly juicy but he had at least *something* to show for his horticultural efforts, while the reports from the uniformed branch now accumulating on his desk seemed to reveal, in contrast, nothing at all. Unless (as was the usual practice with the uniformed branch) you assumed negative evidence to be useful. No murderers had, to Jackson's knowledge, been so far convicted on negative evidence only – though the advent of so desirable a development couldn't surely now be very long delayed. Meanwhile he leafed through the typewritten reports with increasing despondency.

Usually with hit-and-run cases, either the vehicle responsible can be identified and located within thirty-six hours or it can't be identified at all. This, it would appear, wasn't in fact a hit-and-run case but the same general principle clearly applied and no leads to the vehicle or to its owner had as yet appeared. What the reports *did* make clear was that recent heavy rains sweeping up the valleys had earlier last week converted what was in any case a notably lonely and desolate stretch of moorland road into what was effectively a *cul-de-sac*; some five miles beyond that damned school and half a mile short of its conjunction with the main Cardiff–Caerphilly route, a fifty-yard length of the road had been flooded to a depth of three feet, preventing the passage of all vehicles save (conceivably) farm tractors and the like. According to report, the road was still impassable, Saturday's heavy rains having added a thick wash of muddy slime to the already slithery banks of the dip.

Since even under normal conditions the road served only the occasional needs of car trippers bent on a country picnic and of people travelling to the school, to the Rehabilitation Centre, or to three small farms at the bottom end of the moorland slope, and since there was in any case shorter and easier access to Cardiff driving down to Tongwynlais in the other direction, nobody (for once) was making much of a fuss and the Traffic Section (as usual) were therefore not too concerned about the obstruction, which seemed anyway to be pretty well of yearly occurrence. All of which helped to explain why the road last Saturday afternoon should have been virtually unused by traffic and completely unpoliced, and the weather conditions probably accounted for the apparent additional total absence of observant (or otherwise) pedestrians. Not only did the flimsies offer no report on the presence on the road of Kate Coyle's car; they offered no report on the presence on the road of any car *at all*.

Which for a Cardiff City cop was a bit of a facer.

'Tell you what, Foxy,' Jackson said. 'We're going to have to go back to that school again. With a new line of enquiries.'

'Trying for the car?'

'Right. A hundred schoolkids with a Saturday afternoon off. . . . Yes, I know, crummy weather, a lot of them playing games and so forth, but *some* of them have to have been swanning round the place, maybe some of the teachers, too. . . . I can't credit there was *nobody* on the road that evening. Well, we know for a fact there was. Dr Coyle and Mr Dobie. And our Charley, too. He *must* have been. Deliminate the impossible—'

'You know what those kids are like,' Box said glumly. 'Tell you anything that comes into their heads, some of 'em will.'

'Maybe, but it's no good taking a futilistic attitude about it. We'll question every damned one of them if we have to. Tell you something else.'

'What's that?'

'You're not going to believe it.'

'Try me.'

'Know who that Beverley kid's mother is?'

'Her *mother*? Lives somewhere away abroad, doesn't she?'

'She does now. But she didn't always. One of our locals, she is. They had her maiden name on the school records. Jones.'

'Big help, that is.'

'Ah but . . . *Irene* Jones. Remember?'

'Irene Jones? Can't say as I—'

'Little blonde bit of crumpet. Used to work the Casino and then went to the Flamingo Club when Mike O'Neill was running it. She was on Big Ivor Halliday's string for a while but she kept her nose clean enough, right? Till we had to pull her in on a—'

'Oh.' Box nodded slowly, thoughtfully. '*That* Irene Jones. Yes, the memory lingers on all right, but . . . Got married, didn't she?'

'That's what I'm *saying*. Sutro, he was the guy with that chain of betting shops over in London. Did all right for herself there, Irene did. Done even better for herself since, from all accounts. Well, she can afford to send her kid home to a posh boarding school, you can draw your own conclusions. But then she was always a tough little bundle.'

'You reckon like mother, like daughter?'

'I'm not drawing any infrrences in that respect.'

Foxy wasn't drawing any, either. Rather was he effortfully

dredging up distant memories of his early days on the East Bute Street beat. Little blonde bits of crumpet. . . . There'd been so many of them. And all of them tough little bundles, as Jackson had put it. They'd had to be. 'Irene was always high class, in her way.' The Jane Fonda type, you might have said. Except that in those days they'd *all* been trying to look like Jane Fonda. Most of them, unfortunately, hadn't succeeded. But quite a few had done all right for themselves, all the same. Mary Williams, now. Or Marty, as she'd called herself. Married to a football club director and rolling in pelf. It made you think. . . .

'Pool de lux,' Jackson said. 'That's what they call it in Italy, where she is now. I don't doubt she's put all that behind her.' He paused, wondering for a moment if he hadn't hit upon an unfortunate choice of idiom. 'Local girl makes good, that's the story – as the Super would say. But she's on the books for all that.'

'Twenty years back.' Box shrugged. 'What was she shopped for?'

'She wasn't. She got off.'

'She would have done.'

'Ancient history, though. It's the daughter we're interested in now. Wheel's gone full circle, so to speak. You know, it all makes me feel a bit too damned *old*, Foxy? Or let's say, advanced in years.' Jackson sighed windily. 'A tempus fuggit sort of feeling. That's Italian, too.'

'It's not fuggit. It's foo-git.'

'Maybe. But the other way expresses my feelings better. Nothing from Forensic yet, I don't suppose.'

'No.' Foxy reluctantly abandoned his journeyings down Memory Lane and reached across his desk for another orange-coloured file. 'Wouldn't hope for too much, either. That kid was so wet, they said her clothes might as well've been through the laundry.'

'Yes, but the shoes . . . Funny about the shoes,' Jackson said thoughtfully. 'I don't figure them shoes, somehow.'

'*Those* shoes. It ain't right to say—'

'Don't you come the pederast with me, Foxy bach. You know what a pederast is? One of them clever dicks, that's what. Comes from the Greek, it does. *Pedo*, meaning a pedal, and *erasto*, something what gets up your nose. I hope I know how to speak proper when the occlusion arises.'

'Talking about clever dicks, Duty Desk had Mr Dobie on the phone.'

'They did? Well, you're right there. *He's* a pederast if ever I met one. All the same, he . . . What did he want?'

'Wanted to speak to you.'

'Why didn't they put him through?'

''Cause you weren't in.'

'Oh.'

'He still wants to talk to you, though. Said, could you come round and see him this afternoon, Dr Coyle's place.'

'I know where he lives. I ought to.' Jackson had in fact sustained a nasty flesh wound at Kate's clinic not so very long ago, endeavouring to apprehend a dangerous criminal. Although Kate had treated it quickly and effectively, the damaged tissue still gave him jiminy in the cold weather. Arthuritis, hell. 'Did he say what it was about?'

'Just said he'd got something he wants to show you.'

'Oh well. Maybe I'd better go round, then. He may have a funny way of speaking but just now and again it's worth while listening to what he's got to say. But for God's sake . . . don't tell the Super.'

'Me? When did we ever tell the Super anything?'

Dobie, who – being deep in thought at the time – had turned in the wrong direction on leaving the school, was at that very moment discovering for himself the precise position of the watersplash barring the road and would probably have vanished for ever into its muddy depths had not the car very intelligently stalled while still only axle-deep. 'T'ck t'ck,' Dobie said to himself. 'How provoking.' Extrication, however, proved to be no very serious problem; having worked out on the back of an envelope the exact figures relating to reverse engine torque, inertia, centrifugal force, gravitational factors, et cetera, and having established a directional vector integer correct to five decimal places, Dobie was able to reverse successfully out of his present predicament and end up on dry land again, having taken in the process only five or six minutes more than a non-pederast would have done. Panting slightly from his exertions, he effected a neat three-point turn and drove the car up to the top of the slope, stopping there and alighting (with a wet squelchy noise) to inspect the vehicle for signs of imminent deterioration.

Apart from being thickly sploshed with mud to door-handle level, the Fiesta seemed to have survived the ordeal well enough. Dobie walked around it once (squelch, squelch, squelch) and then resumed his seat. He was relieved. His relief, however, was immediately tempered by the realization that he had inadvertantly taken the passenger seat instead of the driver's. T'ck t'ck. He got out and wearily plodded round the car again, like something out of an Elegy in a Country Churchyard; he was beginning to feel that way, too.

Certainly all the world had seemingly been left to darkness and to him; or if not to darkness, then to the prevailing cloud-streaked gloom of a Welsh spring morning. The weather forecast had hinted strongly at more rain to come and at deep depressions marching steadily in from the mid-Atlantic trough, whatever that was. In other words, more of the usual. Dobie paused before re-entering the car to look around him. *Take me home*, he thought, *country roads*. This had to be one of the *loneliest* country roads he'd ever seen. The moorland stretching out all around him, bleak and bare; the road a narrow grey ribbon, shiny with moisture, running downhill across it. In the distance and beside it, the grey slate roofs of the school; further yet, the trees and high stone walls of the Rehabilitation Centre. Looking down upon them from this height, they might have been a scatter of historic ruins, centred around the broken statue of Ozymandias, King of Kings.

In fact, of course, they weren't. He was looking at an expensive private boarding school and at a luxuriously equipped and high-tech correctional establishment, a model institute (as he was assured) of its kind. The first, dedicated to the outmoded nineteenth-century principles established by Dr Arnold and taken up with so much enthusiasm by the suffragettes a half-century later, concerned with the efficient production of nicely spoken (and naturally well heeled) young ladies for eventual consumption by ravening yuppies; the other, concerned at least ostensibly with the recuperation of all those varied, yet basically similar, dropouts from the organizational world of the 1990s, all the refinements of modern technology being there called in to repair what the refineries of modern technology and their ingenious chemical products had come more or less close to destroying. It was odd, Dobie thought, that from a distance it was almost impossible to tell the difference between them.

132

Of course the brick walls surrounding the school didn't constitute a very effective barrier. Any reasonably athletic seventeen-year-old bent on nocturnal perambulation would be over them in a trice and on her way. But Beverley Sutro hadn't done that, or he didn't think so. There wasn't any way she could have nipped out during the night without her friends knowing about it, that Midge girl and the others; you didn't have to be a Rehabilitation Centre trick-cyclist to realize *that*. OK, so life in a girls' school isn't worth living if you don't have secrets, but murder is a serious matter – serious, and even terrifying at that age; if Midge or Elspeth had known of anything like that, they'd have told him about it when they'd had the chance to do so. If the Beverley girl had had assignments outside the school, sexual or otherwise, it hadn't been at night.

Not much point, though, in telling Jackson *that*. Jackson had to have seen that for himself already, and might therefore be a little more easily convinced of the value of Dobie's evidence. Or, well . . . of Midge's evidence, really. Of course it would be a great deal better if Dobie could put up some explanation of what that damned note *meant*, but he wasn't in a position to do that – or not yet, anyway. It was all very difficult, Dobie thought, engaging the car gears and urging the Fiesta once again forwards. And he wasn't looking forward to his imminent interview with Jacko.

Or not particularly.

Because Jackson, on occasion, could show a nasty sceptical streak.

'So what's it mean, then?'

'I was afraid you'd ask me that,' Dobie said sadly. 'I don't know. And the girl who gave it to me doesn't know, either. But it's Beverley Sutro's handwriting – she's sure about *that*.'

'Bloody awful handwriting, too.' Jackson leaned forwards to study it. 'Don't seem to worry about that sort of thing in the schools nowadays, do they? It's all computers and calculators and such. You can hardly read a word of my daughter's handwriting, if it comes to that. No wonder they say illiteracy is wrife.'

'It *is* the girl's handwriting, though. That's the point.'

'Mebbe it is.' Jackson leaned back again. 'So what? Could be something she scribbled down weeks ago. Or months. I can't see what it's got to do with the present case.'

'March 24th. That's the day she was killed.'

'Grant you that but it's hardly the same as going on a holiday, is it? If that's what the note means to say. It's hard to be sure.'

'Anyway,' Dobie said, 'it's not so much the note I wanted to show you. It's the paper.'

'The paper?' Jackson leaned forwards once more. 'What's so odd about the paper?'

'It's the same as *this*.' Dobie produced with a dramatic flourish his own annotations of the recent medical history of Adrian Seymour and pushed them across the table. 'And this comes from the Registrar's Office at the Rehabilitation Centre. As you can see by the heading.'

'Oh, come *on*, Mr Dobie.' Jackson leaned back again; his movements, Dobie thought, were beginning to resemble those of the brightly plumaged toy birds that, constantly dipping their beaks into glasses of water, had enjoyed an inexplicable popularity and substantial sales in the days of Dobie's childhood. Not, of course, that you could describe Jackson as brightly plumaged, exactly, and glasses of Brain's Best Bitter would be more in his line. 'There's got to be thousands of scraps of paper like that one lying about the place. I've got a notebook that same size in my own office. I'll betcha we could find—'

'You haven't got a notebook like *this* one,' Dobie said, taking the notepad from his jacket pocket and placing it on the table, beside the other items of what his fevered brain imagined to be evidence. 'Now look. Here we go.' He used an illegally acquired set of Kate's forceps to slide the Beverley Sutro note on to the notebook and then to align the roughly torn top edge with one of the notepad stubs. 'See? A perfect topographical consistency.'

'A what?' But Jackson had taken the point and was beginning to show faint signs of interest, though not to the extent of inclining his body forwards yet again. He was a policeman, not a bloody oil derrick. 'It *fits* all right, I can see that. Where'd you get that pad from?'

'I told you. The Registrar's Office at the Centre. I, er . . . whipped it.'

This was an excellent opportunity for Jackson to administer the classic reproof. 'You didn't ought to have dunnit.'

'I know.'

'I see what you mean, though. It's rum.'

'Very rum.'

'And what you're really trying to tell me is that the girl must've been . . .'

'There. Yes. In the office. Physically *there*. How else could she have got to tear that sheet of paper out of the pad?'

A tricky one, that was. Jackson considered the matter. In the end he said, 'She couldn't've been.'

'That,' Dobie said, 'is exactly why it's rum.'

'*Very* rum.'

'Yes.'

'That place is a . . . It's supposed to be a *prison*, damn it. Not the ordinary sort of a slammer, I'll admit. All the same, people don't just stroll in and out.'

'And in fact they don't. There's a guard on the gate, as I'm sure you know.'

'Tell you one thing, though,' Jackson said. 'If she *was* there, if she managed to get in somehow . . . it might explain why no one seems to have seen hide nor hair of her all that afternoon. We haven't turned up a single sighting of her so far, nor of the car, neither.'

Alongside the accumulated evidence on the table the coffee was bubbling cheerfully in the percolator. Dobie reached across to the kitchen shelf to take down two large mugs, each decorated with colourful representatives of very small elephants wearing short red trousers. 'She was there all right on Saturday,' he said, making with the milk and sugar. 'But that wasn't when she wrote that note, of course. Quite a few sheets have been torn out of the pad since then – you can tell that by looking at the stubs. Thirty-four, by my reckoning. I don't know how often Miss Daly *uses* that notepad, but she couldn't have used up thirty-four sheets in a couple of days. More like a couple of weeks – but of course I'm guessing.'

Jackson wasn't prepared to dispute Dobie's figures; he was supposed to be good at counting, after all. Instead, he stirred the contents of his mug, using the fork with which Dobie had kindly provided him – no doubt under the impression that it was a coffee spoon – and said, 'Who's Miss Daly?'

'The Registrar. She's a sort of . . . *you* know . . . well-developed young lady. More to the point,' Dobie said, returning to it with a visible effort, 'she kept this notepad on her desk. In full view, I mean. Anyone could have taken a sheet or two from it, with her permission. Or without it, for that matter, if she wasn't there.'

Jackson sipped at his coffee thoughtfully and looked around him, extending the aura of his approval to Kate's tastefully appointed kitchen. 'Nice cosy little kitchen, this.'

'Yes. I think so, too. But—'

'Warm,' Jackson said, 'and quiet. And peaceful.'

A blood-curdling shriek expressive of unutterable misery and anguish rent the air. Jackson leapt to his feet, his normally rubicund features turned on the instant to a whiter shade of pale. 'What was *that*?'

'One of Kate's patients, I rather think.'

'Ah,' Jackson said.

He sat down again.

He drank more coffee.

'Fact of the matter is,' he said, his jaded nerves having in the interim calmed down somewhat, 'it doesn't *prove* that the kid was there last Saturday afternoon. It doesn't even prove she was there a couple of weeks ago, like you said. All it does is establish what's called an infrarence, like. Having said that—'

'But look at this.'

Dobie produced an envelope from his pocket. The contents of the envelope, when shaken out on to the table, Jackson thought to be deeply disappointing; in his schooldays he had been able to perform much better conjuring tricks than that, notably one where you tied a knot in a handkerchief . . . 'What's this, then? A *leaf*?'

Three small leaves, in fact, attached to their parent twig. 'I found it on the back seat,' Dobie said proudly, 'of my car.'

'A leaf. Yes. Very nice. Well, Mr Dobie—'

'Kate's car, really. But anyway . . . where I put the girl. That's where she was lying. On top of it, in fact, that's why it's got . . . sort of crumpled. It was sticking to the wound on top of her head – I noticed it when I picked her up but I didn't think anything of it at the time.'

'Don't know that I think anything of it now. A piece of paper is one thing but a *leaf*—'

'With blood on it.'

'Blood?'

'Can't be anything else. That's why it stuck to her, you see.'

Jackson poked at the leaf-stem cautiously with the tip of one finger. 'Well, it would have done, wouldn't it?' But his expression had become very thoughtful. He could, on occasion, be sceptical, but he wasn't stupid. 'Leaves,' he said. '*Trees.* There's aren't any, not where it happened. Not on that stretch of the road. Just open moorland, right? No trees until you get right down into the valley. Plenty there, of course.'

'And quite a number in the grounds of the Centre. There's an arboretum, in fact. Going back to the days when the place was a country house, or so I'd imagine.' Dobie replenished the coffee mugs. 'I mean, trees take a long time to grow, don't they? Anyway, the thing you're at this moment attempting to dismember is in fact a linden leaf. *Tilia platyphyllos.* The large-leafed lime. I'm sure of that because I looked it up. Besides . . . there's a whole avenue of them at Trinity College, Cambridge, and at one time I used to walk down that avenue at least twice every day. That's how come I'm able to recognize the thing, you see. They're quite famous, the lime trees at Trinity.'

'Yes. Very beautiful, I'm sure. But—'

'But it isn't all that common a tree in *this* part of the world. I doubt if you'd find another for miles around. . . . Oh, maybe at Dyffryn or in some other of the botanical gardens. But not in the woods at Tongwynlais.'

Jackson was now staring at the elephant on his mug as though it had just done something that it shouldn't. Red trousers and all. 'But there's one in the grounds at the Centre. Is that what you're trying to tell me?'

'I *am* telling you. In fact, there are two.'

'Are there now.' Jackson shook his head slowly. 'Well, yes, I can see the imprecations of your testimony. And I'll have it checked out first thing.'

'Professor Goatcher would be your man. A colleague of mine.'

'You wouldn't by any chance have contacted him already?'

'Of course. I'm a mathematician, Jacko. I try to avoid putting forward propositions that haven't been properly tested, and you can take it from me that Jim Goatcher knows his onions. He knows about trees as well, of course. That's why he's a consultant to the Welsh Forestry Commission.'

A smug old bastard at times, Jackson thought. But at least he made a decent cup of coffee. 'Well, you've been getting around a bit, Mr Dobie. And you do seem to be putting it all together very neatly . . . as far as it goes. Only trouble is, I just don't see myself arguing it out in front of the Super like you just did, I don't have your gift for succulent expedition. Look, Pontin doesn't go much of a bundle on the sort of evidence you're coming up with, it's all a bit too Doctor Dickhead for us, see what I mean? You try going into the Criminal Court waving a bit of paper in one hand and a treeleaf in the other, you'll have some smartass defence lawyer like Micky Mannering tearing your whole case to shreds in no time at all. We got to have a whole lot more than *this* to work with.'

'Yes, yes,' Dobie said, a little testily. 'But at least we know now where to look for it. Besides . . . there *is* another item . . .'

'Ah yes.' Jackson looked at the small pile of banknotes neatly secured with an elastic band and stacked up on the far side of the table. '*That*'s evidence right enough. No doubt about it. I'll give you my receipt for it and I'll have to ask you to make me a brief written statement explaining how you came by it – *and* the girl's note, for what it's worth. If we can find out where all that lolly came from, well, that could turn out to be quite a long nail in some Charley's coffin. As for all those other concussions you've been drawing, p'raps you won't mind keeping them under your hat for the time being. Give me a chance to look into all your instigations. You've given me quite a lot to think about,' Jackson handsomely admitted, 'and that's the truth of the matter.'

All very well, Jackson thought, for Professor Dobie to leap from crag to crag of ingenious speculation, like a chamois – or was it a chameleon? – all right if you were one of them intellectual geezers, but not (I'll repeat that) *not* if you were a police officer and doing your best to be a practical cop. Of course the lindum-leaf things would go to Forensic and it was always possible that they'd come up with something. The great Ted Greeno (Jackson seemed to remember) had once got a conviction on the strength of a blood-stained ear of corn and the case had been in some ways similar to this one: another battered teenager – Daphne Bacon, wasn't it? – found on the edge of a field of corn, not yet dead but dying. Way back, though, some time in the early '50s. Things, Jackson thought, had to have been easier in those days, when murderers had been regarded as evil people and not as the unfortunate victims of social circumstance. Now it was one hell of a job putting them away, even on the hardest of evidence.

Even the villains that everyone knew about, Dai Dymond and Big Ivor and Joe McKenna. . . . Well, we slipped DD the dropsy all right, but only through a fluke. And you couldn't blame it *all* on the lawyers. The juries played their part, too. Giving geezers the benefit of the doubt is fair enough, but not when there isn't any. On the whole, you had to say that nowadays the public got the crime rate it deserved.

And as for the police, well. . . . Routine was still the key to all good police work. Routine was what got things done. Routine was what you stuck to. It was coincidental, in view of Jackson's present line of thought, that the next visit on his planned itinerary should be to the West Street offices of Mannering, Mannering, and Polegate, Solicitors and Commissioners for Oaths. That, Jackson reflected sourly as he stumped up a lengthy flight of sumptuously carpeted stairs, had to be why he'd inadvertantly and maybe somewhat tactlessly brought Mannering's name into his conversation with Dobie. Not that it mattered, but . . . well, *smartass lawyer* . . . It wasn't the kind of remark that a policeman, practical or otherwise, would much care to have quoted back at him. Dobie wouldn't do that, of course. The greater part of what you said to Dobie went in one ear, as the saying goes, and out the other. Yes, but it was always best to be careful.

Jackson knew Micky Mannering pretty well – rather better than he knew Dobie, in fact. He didn't think that in the ordinary sense of the word he really *knew* Dobie at all. And Mannering he'd certainly known a great deal longer. But there again . . . in a different way he didn't *know* Mannering, either. Policemen never really get to *know* lawyers, no matter how many times they assist or oppose each other in court. It's better that they don't, for obvious reasons. Especially obvious, you might say, in Mannering's case, since there were those who maintained him to be a criminal lawyer in both senses of the expression. If not bent, then pretty damned near it.

Always polite, though – you had to give him that. Any time you had an appointment with Micky, you could be sure he wouldn't keep you waiting just because you were a cop. And once you were within his office, you'd find him to be affability itself. The manly handshake, the disarming smile. 'Haven't seen you in a goodish while, Inspector. So how are you? And how's the family?'

'Fair to middling, thanks,' Jackson said. 'We've no complaints.'

'I should think not. I should rather think not.' Maintaining an amicable clasp on Jackson's elbow, Micky escorted him to the sort of plush-upholstered armchair in which you sink out of sight rather than sit down, then returned to his own more stoically cushioned swivel-chair behind an impressive assortment of heavily laden correspondence trays. 'Be getting your promotion this year, is it, when that silly old buffer Pontin moves on to Hereford? In line to be Assistant Chief Constable there, so they tell me. But of course you'll know all about that already.'

Jackson nodded thoughtfully. This, in fact, was the first he'd heard of it but he allowed no shadow of surprise or of joy to cross his placid countenance. Joy, not so much at the possibilities of forthcoming promotion (which he considered to be slim) but at the idea of at last getting shot of that bloody Pontin for once and for all. 'Well, sir, it may never happen. They move in a mysterious way, the powers that be.'

'They do. They do.' Micky placed his elbows on the desk and interlaced his fingers in a vaguely judicial pose. 'The case you're currently engaged on goes far to prove the point. I need hardly say I'm even more than ordinarily anxious to be of assistance to you in your enquiries, since the victim chances to be the daughter of one of my oldest clients. But then you know that, or you wouldn't be here. A shocking business altogether. Tea or coffee?'

'I've just had some, thanks. To be honest I thought the girl herself was one of your clients.'

'Oh no. I never met her. No, I'm simply enabled under power of attorney to pay her school fees and other incidental expenses, within reason. The present situation is frankly rather . . . I've been trying to contact the girl's mother by telephone, but without success. Firstly, of course, to notify her of her daughter's death, but also to take instructions. I take it that the police haven't . . .? No. I see. Well, it's all very difficult. As you know, it's not the kind of work I normally undertake . . . but as Mrs Feltrenelli is a client of very long standing . . .'

'From when she was Irene Jones, I suppose.'

'Ah.' Micky wrinkled up the corners of his eyes engagingly. 'You remember.'

'I do indeed. Standing wasn't exactly her speciality in those days.'

Micky allowed a spontaneous gleam of carefully rehearsed humour to appear in the murky depths of his still engagingly screwed-up eyes. He had read somewhere about the charm of the Irish. A pity, he sometimes thought, that he couldn't do the accent very convincingly. 'Yes, I suppose you'll have had a look through your files. I've had a quick glance through my own, I may as well admit.'

'I remember the Jones girl well enough, anyway,' Jackson said. 'A memorable young lady, in her way. And I gather since then she's done rather well for herself.'

'Financially, yes.' The gleam taking on for a moment or two something like a genuine lambency. 'There's no secret about *that*. But I understand her latest marriage is running into certain difficulties. She was never really the uxorious type.'

'Really? I thought she always fancied a bit of high life, as we used to call it. All the creature comforts and indemnities.'

'I said, *uxorious*, Inspector. Not *luxurious*. Domestic happiness, in other words, seems so far to have eluded her.'

'That's maybe why she got rid of the kid? Sent her back here?'

'No, I didn't say that. Nor did I mean to imply it.'

Oh yes you did, Jackson thought. Lawyers always seem to leave this almost frightening gap between their words and their meanings. Even so, after half an hour of Dobie . . . 'Do you pay her an allowance?'

'A small dress allowance, yes.'

'How small?'

'Ten pounds a month. Ridiculous, really, for a teenage girl nowadays. And paid, moreover, to the Headmistress, though Beverley naturally knows . . . knew that she could draw on it.'

'Did she have any other source of income?'

'Not to my knowledge. But I suppose she could always have appealed to her mother directly, by telephone or through the post.'

'Because,' Jackson said, 'she seems to have died possessed of around two hundred pounds.'

'In cash?'

'In cash.'

Micky shook his head firmly. 'She wouldn't have received a sum like that, or anywhere near it, on *my* authority.'

'And didn't?'

'And didn't.'

'I see. Well, we'd very much like to know where she got all that oscar from and we'll be trying to trace the notes, though that probably won't be easy. Naturally,' Jackson said, 'the money will be treated as part of the girl's estate and our legal officer will be handing it on to you in due course. You'll be getting a formal whatchamaycallit to that effect. Very shortly.'

'Ta very much,' Micky said, rather surprisingly. 'Appreciate the courtesy. It's a substantial sum, no doubt, to a schoolgirl, but I don't think our Irene will be greatly concerned. However, that's by the way. What *is* strange is that the school secretary made no mention of the matter when she phoned me.'

'Could well be she doesn't know about it.'

'Ah. A secret cache, maybe? Well, I know I'll get nowhere trying to press you on *that* one. So I don't intend to.' The telephone on the desk rang sharply and he picked up the receiver, tucking it with professional ease under the second of his chins. 'Yes? . . . No. . . . Yes, yes, give me just a couple of minutes,' he said, cradling it again. Jackson watched this performance admiringly, doubting not that the telephone had sounded in response to the small button under the carpet that Micky was wont to press with his foot when it seemed desirable to end a consultancy. We all have our little tricks of the trade, Jackson thought, and Micky Mannering had more than most.

'Irene . . . Would you say she was now *extremely* rich?'

'It depends on what your standards are. But yes, I think you might. Why do you ask?'

'Because we have to consider the possibility that we might be dealing with a kidnap attempt. Only one that went badly wrong, of course.'

'I imagine the police have to consider *every* possibility. But I don't think I can offer any comment . . . and obviously I shouldn't.'

'Irene made a few enemies, you know, when she was working the casinos.'

'Yes. That's *why* I shouldn't comment. But of course *everyone* has enemies . . . You, me . . . Everyone.'

Jackson reached for his briefcase in preparation for his departure. 'You wouldn't happen to know who the girl's father was?'

'Oh, come now, Inspector.'

'Off the record?'

Micky shook his head regretfully. 'Well, she was shacking up with Big Ivor at the time, as you'll recall, so not many people would have cared to attribute paternity elsewhere. . . . Not the gentlest fellow around, was he, when he got his dander up? And it can hardly be claimed that he's aged gracefully.' He went on shaking his head, as one amazed at the infinite depths of human turpitude. 'On the other hand, if you're indeed considering every possibility, you'll have a pretty wide field of candidates to choose from. As for our Ivor . . . that's one laddybucks you really *should* have managed to finger by now. No one would weep salt tears if you did – least of all Irene.'

Jackson shrugged, not very elegantly. 'He's had good protection. Up to now. But one of these days we'll grab his collar, see if we don't.'

'And while we're on that subject,' Micky said, rising courteously, 'I heard an interesting whisper about Dai Dymond the other day. That's all it was, mind. A whisper. But I pass it on to you for what it's worth. A whisper to the effect that a certain ginger-haired friend of ours had best look out.'

'A contract out on him? That doesn't surprise me.'

'Where *do* you pick up these regrettable Americanisms, I wonder? From the TV, I suppose. Don't we all? But, well . . . yes . . . *Something* like that. So the gentlemen who now have him in protective custody might appreciate the warning. Dai's a vindictive bastard, too.'

'A warning from an undisclosed source.'

'Naturally.'

'Maybe this once,' Jackson said, extending his hand towards another vigorous shake, 'we'll be able to frustrate the workings of Amnesia. I'll pass on the word.'

'Always happy to be of help, Inspector.'

Humping his briefcase, Jackson turned away towards the door. The briefcase contained, of course, Dobie's assorted *corpus delicti*; Dobie was always happy to be of help, too, but he wasn't, not really; the tried and trusted methods (Jackson thought) are what you should rely on. He wouldn't mind betting that the fifteen minutes he'd just spent with Micky Mannering would ultimately prove to be of more value to the investigation than the thirty minutes he'd spent in the kitchen at Ludlow Road, even throwing in all those pieces of papers and those bits of London leaf or whatever he'd called it. Mannering, after all . . .

'Oh, by the way . . .' Micky said.

Jackson turned back, one hand on the doorknob. 'Yes, sir?'

'You don't know a man called Dobie, do you?'

'Yes. Dobie? Yes. I do. Why?'

'Because he was round here this morning asking me pretty much the same kind of questions that you've been putting to me. And I was faintly curious.'

The same kind of . . . 'You didn't *tell* him anything, did you?'

'I saw no reason to reveal any privileged information.'

'Good. Good,' Jackson said, making his exit.

In fact he wasn't mollified. In fact he was wondering what Mannering had *meant* by that. No doubt there's a distinction to be made between leaving a convenient gap between words and meaning and being a bloody liar . . . but it's not a distinction, Jackson felt, that many lawyers are prepared to recognize. And least of all Micky Mannering . . .

Kate came in from the bathroom lightly parboiled and pink-flushed and slid herself with an interesting undulatory motion into the bed. The mattress, which was old and had been through a lot lately, creaked comfortably. Dobie, the ever observant, noted that she was wearing, if only just, one of her more stimulating nighties, the one whose use was normally reserved for their occasional weekend visits to country hotels. OK, Dobie thought, it's Tuesday, but who's counting?

Not Professor Dobie.

For once.

She was, he further noted, looking down at him solicitously while undoing the buttons of his pyjama jacket. (The green one with the trendy purple stripes.) 'Not too tired?'

'No, no, oh no.'

It was warm in the bedroom and Kate almost at once decided that she didn't really need the nightie after all. Half an hour or so later she began to make occasional puffing noises instead of near-continuous yowly ones and said, 'No. You weren't.'

'Nor were you.'

'It behoves a doctor to stay fit and get lots of healthy exercise. Indeed, as many lots as possible. You can be quite effective in your methods sometimes, Dobie, *outré* though they may be.'

'We like to think so,' Dobie said complacently.

'*All* men like to think so,' Kate said. Deflating him.

Fortunately at this stage a little deflation might pass as being natural and even inevitable; Dobie was well enough aware that, in general terms, the bed thing was going rather well these days – bearing in mind, as you had to, that the vestigial remnants of Kate's Irish Catholic conscience hadn't yet quite disappeared down the plughole and no doubt added, in her case, a distinctive sinful savour to the proceedings. . . . He himself had been prone on occasion to self-recriminatory moods of rather more idiosyncratic a nature; these had arisen when he had first realized that theirs was not, after all, to be a short-term relationship (of the kind that he, and probably Kate, had originally envisaged) but more of what you might call a long haul – a prospect which almost invariably arouses certain misgivings in the male partner, especially those who happen to be pushing fifty and who hope to be able in due course to push sixty with an equal confidence.

Nowadays, though, they seemed both to have returned to that earlier pristine state of innocence in which the whole thing had seemed to be perfectly natural and extremely nice and they didn't even have to be anxious any more as to whether such a desirable state of affairs could be indefinitely maintained; it certainly could, Kate assured him, always provided (she added severely) he was able to keep his mind on the job, at any rate while he was actually doing it – something the other blokes of whom she had had carnal experience (well, two, in point of fact, including her husband, not very impressive statistically or physically, either, come to think of it) had seemed to have no difficulty in doing but which Dobie . . . Dobie . . . Oh, *fuck* Dobie. Yes, why ever not? . . . A certain amount of wool-gathering and whatnot had after all to be expected if you chose to shack up with an acknowledged world-class berk, and absence of mind could always be compensated for by a sufficiently emphatic presence of body. Thought control isn't everything, indeed no. Better to let the whole bang shoot go haywire, as quite frequently now it appeared to.

Indeed yes.

'I didn't *hurt* you, did I?' Dobie enquired. Hopefully.

'No, but keep right on trying, by all means. Well. . . . Perhaps not by *all* means. But don't feel you have to impose strict limits on your range of expression.'

'I'm afraid I must for the moment.'

145

'Well, get off, then.'

Dobie did so and lay on his back, snorting quietly. After a while Kate said, 'I know what you're thinking about.'

'Hmmmm-*mffff*.'

'I'm telepathic. Or getting to be. It's funny how it always happens after . . . Maybe you should ask your new psychiatrist friends about it. Bedepathy. A fascinating topic.'

'An interesting field for experiment, certainly.'

'Forget it, Dobie. You've got all the lab equipment you need right here.'

'So what *was* I thinking about?'

'Sex.'

'Good God. That's *amazing*.'

'And violence.'

'Violence. Yes. I suppose I was. I was sort of wondering what . . . brings it out.'

'*I* don't know,' Kate said. 'It's inherent in the act, isn't it? Or ought to be. But of course there are . . .'

'Limits. Like you said. But nobody *likes* limits. So if the violence thing gets really brought out . . . That girl must have brought it out somehow. In someone.'

Dobie reached for and lit a cigarette. Kate disapproved of his smoking in bed, but tonight with any luck she might feel that he deserved a self-congratulatory whiff. Anyway, she didn't say anything. She just went on staring up towards the ceiling. But after a while she turned her head towards him and said, 'Dobie, there isn't any point in going into all that. Not really.'

'I suppose it could be argued that she asked for it.'

This suggestion stung her up a little, as he'd expected it would. 'That's a pretty typical male-chauvinist-pig sort of comment, isn't it? Coming from *you*.'

'I didn't mean asking for sex. I meant asking to be. . . .'

'Murdered?'

'Yes.'

Kate, having turned her head, shook it, returning it in the process to its original position. 'I'm familiar with the theory. I don't believe it.'

'All the same,' Dobie said, 'there *was* something about her. Something I can't quite . . . Maybe you didn't sense it, but *I* did. I felt it quite strongly when I had to carry her over to the car . . .

I don't know how to describe it, but it was almost like feeling scared. Not of *her*, of course. Of myself. That girl was *dangerous*. Really, she was.'

Kate went on looking at him out of her large moist greenish-grey eyes. She seemed at least to be taking him seriously. 'You have hidden depths, Dobie. You know that?'

'So have lots of other men and it probably isn't a good idea to stir them up.'

'You think that's what she did?'

'Well, don't you? She didn't have anything on, did she? I mean underneath. No knickers or bra or anything like that.'

'But that doesn't mean what you want to make it mean. Maybe she wouldn't . . . I never used to wear a bra myself. Not until I was twenty.'

'Why not?'

'Because I didn't need one.'

'What about knickers?'

'Mind your own business,' Kate said.

'I'm not, of course, doubting your word—'

'I should hope not. Girls don't *like* wearing bras, you know. Not necessarily. Finicky things. You're usually much more comfortable without them. Besides, it's a nice feeling when you haven't got one on and you're running downstairs. Not, of course, as nice . . . But I digress.'

Dobie sensed that his attention was being distracted from the main point at issue, possibly deliberately but in any case very successfully. 'All the same, there was something very unusual about that girl. Something . . . *sly*. . . .'

Kate snorted contemptuously. 'How can you be sly when you're unconscious? Don't talk such rubbish. And use the bloody ashtray – not the carpet.'

'Maybe you can't *be* sly but you can *look* sly. She looked as though she liked playing games – and I don't mean hockey or basketball or anything like that. I mean games with people. Games with *men*.'

'Sex games?'

'Yes, but sex games she thought she could win. If that makes any sense.'

'It does, in a way. But, Dobie, the kid was only seventeen.'

'You get to play that kind of game early if you play it at all.'

147

She was silent for a moment. 'Yes. That's true.'

'After all, it makes the world go round.'

'Sometimes it makes it *seem* to. Just now, for instance. And I can see what you're getting at all right. Games of the kind you mean can be pretty dangerous.'

'That's their attraction,' Dobie said. 'For that kind of a girl.'

'The fact remains that someone raped her and killed her and you ought to be thinking more about what kind of a man . . . That's if you have to think about it at all. And I wish you wouldn't.'

'I can't help it. Because there's a paradox there somewhere and paradoxes are what attract *me*. Rape and murder are crimes all right but there's nothing paradoxical about them. So they don't interest me, much. But that girl does.'

'Dobie, she was a *girl*, not a bloody theorem.'

True enough, Dobie thought. And what do *I* know about girls? All I really know about Beverley Sutro is that she's dead. And death embarrasses people. So at once they try to turn you into some kind of an abstraction, and the living person that once was there gets left by the wayside. I'm like everyone else in that respect, but I'm very much more used to dealing with abstractions than most people are. Perhaps I'm *too* used to dealing with abstractions, as Kate's suggesting. But she knows me better than anyone else does, and she knows that in bed or out of bed it's all part of the same thing which isn't just physical and isn't just mental but either way has very little *abstract* about it. Dobie could also well enough recall, though, the surprisingly slight weight of the Sutro girl's body against his arms as he'd picked her up, its youthful flexibility, the suggestion of an almost feverish warmth under the cold damp skin; nothing very abstract there, either. No more than a reminder, perhaps, of sexuality, of a potential for sexual violence, but if you're *too* used to dealing with abstractions – as many men are nowadays – then maybe that kind of a reminder can come as a bit of a shock. . . .

'Jacko,' Dobie said, 'knows her mother.'

'The Italian woman?'

'She isn't Italian. She *married* an Italian. But her maiden name was apparently Irene Jones. Jacko *used* to know her, I should have said. Professionally.'

'Why, what *was* her profession?'

'*His* profession, I meant, not hers. She had a few brushes with the law in days gone by, or so I gather.'

'What sort of brushes?'

'Well, I'm not quite sure. The usual, I suppose. Ripping off the mugs in the casino where she worked. Drugs, maybe. This, that, and the other. As far as I can see, she started off as what they used to call a good-time girl, though in her case that's a bit of a misnomer. Anyway she borrowed too much money from the wrong people and couldn't pay them back . . . so as she was a looker they gave her a job on the tables. Then she went on the game for a bit and in the end she got shacked up with some night-club manager or someone like that. Well, not the end, exactly, but—'

'Dobie . . .'

'Yes?'

'Your methods are effective but you have some pretty weird ideas about pillow talk. What's *with* you tonight?'

'No, listen. That's when Jacko put the arm on her, see? But she had a smart goby called Micky Mannering and he got her off. Then she met some rich character from London who got off with *her* and went and married her. But then two or three years ago she ditched *him*, in favour of the Eyetie. I like a story that has a happy ending,' Dobie said. 'Don't you?'

Kate by now was regarding him with deep suspicion. 'You didn't get all this stuff from Jacko.'

'Well, no. Not all of it, no. Most of it I got from this Mannering bloke, in fact, after the school headmistress had very kindly—'

'You've been talking to Micky *Mannering*?'

'Yes. And in return for a modest consultation fee—'

'How much?'

'Fifty nicker. Very reasonable. I mean, even the vocabulary I've picked up is cheap at the price.'

'*Dobie*,' Kate wailed. 'You are some kind of a *freak*, did you know that? Micky Mannering—'

'You see, the kid's name isn't really Sutro at all.'

'Micky Mannering—'

'It's her *adopted* name. From the guy who married her mother. But that was only about ten years ago, she'd have been . . . seven, eight years old at the time. No, her real father's reckoned to be this night-club bruiser bloke her mother was living with at the time. Who's a bit of a villain. A complex picture, isn't it? And a somewhat chequered childhood, wouldn't you say?'

Kate gave up. 'You want to take a look at my relatives in Ireland if you're into complex pictures. God knows how many of them there are. I lose track myself. As for a chequered childhood, you should hear poor old Jacko go on about *his* . . . and his own man whaling into him with a carpet slipper.'

'Set him on the straight and narrow, though.'

'He's a straight cop as they go, certainly. I *like* Jacko.'

'So do I. But this Beverley kid may well have learnt her lessons in a different way. Had a schooling in the university of life, so to speak.'

'One might think so. Yes. Yes, I suppose so.'

'So she'd have been something of a fish out of water in that school which in fact they sent her to. I know they say she was bright in class and all that. But that isn't the point.'

'Where did she come from anyway? The mother?'

'You mean originally?'

'Yes.'

'Monmouth, I think. I'm not sure. Why?'

'*Monmouth?* That's interesting.'

'In what way?'

'The Duke of Monmouth. He caused an uprising.'

'So did she, apparently. On any number of occasions. And you're doing very nicely yourself in that respect.'

'Ah.' Kate brightened. 'Going for the record, are we?'

'Well . . .'

'That's the trouble with you,' Kate said, nuzzling his neck. 'You lack ambition.'

'I'll tell you one thing for free,' Kate said later. A good deal later. 'I get to see a lot of dead bodies in my profession. And live ones are better.'

Dobie didn't feel like offering any cogent reply but on the whole he thought that Kate was right. As usual.

7

The following morning he had some good news. The good news arrived, as Kate observed, in an envelope carrying an Austrian stamp and a Vienna postmark and after listening for the best part of a minute to his self-satisfied grunts, 'Who's it from?' she asked.

'Otto Bodenheimer.'

'Is he offering you the lead in his next biblical epic?'

'No, no. He's the Director of the Heisenberg Institute.'

'Oh well,' Kate said consolingly. 'Never mind.'

'But it's all most encouraging.' Dobie waved a slice of buttered toast vehemently in the air, dripping Oxford marmalade over the tablecloth. 'Listen to this. He says . . . Where is it? Ah yes. he says, "It is with the most profound reluctance that we have concluded that the paradox as propounded, in the absence of any of-a-decisive-nature refutation and subject to an in-all-parts-effectively-demonstrable confirmation, must stand." There you are. He couldn't put it more clearly than that, now could he?'

'In German, probably not.'

'*This* should make those berks sit up in Cambridge,' Dobie said, chortling. 'It's going to be like Eddington, all over again.' He looked in some surprise at his marmaladeless slice of toast and reached for the butter knife.

'Who's Eddington?'

'He didn't like black holes.'

'Nor do I,' Kate said. 'They breed mice.'

'Anyway, he wants me to give a lecture.'

'Eddington?'

'No. He's dead. Bodenheimer.'

'And will you?'

'He'll pay me two thousand dollars and expenses.'

151

'I'll pack your bag right now.'

'No, don't do that. The conference isn't till next September. That'll give you time to pack your own bag as well.'

'I can come, too?'

'Of course.'

'*Wünderbar.*'

'Provided,' Dobie said morosely, 'Bicknell and the All Souls crowd haven't shot me down before then.'

'They won't.'

'What makes you so sure?'

'Because *you* 'ave the little grey cells, 'Astings, an' *zey* 'aven't.'

'*C'est vrai,*' Dobie said, brightening. And then, on reflection, 'No, it isn't. You've got that the wrong way round, somehow.'

'Ah, forget about it, 'Olmes, gizza kiss, Vienna, huh? *Vienna . . . ! Oh wow!*'

Dobie, too, was reasonably chuffed and even sang to himself in a weird guttural soprano as he washed up the breakfast things. '*Drunt' in der Lobau,*' he carolled erratically, '*hab' ich ein Madl gekusst . . .*' His German was extremely wonky these days but so vot, he liked Vienna and moreover knew from past experience that the various amatory exercises in which he had of late been over-indulging might also be pleasantly performed amongst the trees of the Wienerwald, which would be at their best in September. So that was something he could look forward to . . . unless of course Kate and the past experience got together and compared notes, a contingency sufficiently remote to preoccupy him very little. Yes, Kate would enjoy the trip and they might even take a boat up the Danube as far as Melk and then . . . Plenty of linden trees there, of course, and there were songs about *them*, too, which right now he couldn't remember. He stooped to recover the shards of a breakfast plate which had just come to pieces in his hands and placed them in the refuse bin, where with any luck at all Kate wouldn't spot them. He was pretty sure she wouldn't. This was his lucky day.

Kate, who was at that moment causing temporary inconvenience to one of her more elderly patients with an expertly wielded spatula, was wondering if she mightn't indeed have made a mistake with Dobie . . . an error of judgement, anyway, or maybe

152

of tact. The guy was pushing fifty, after all, he was a fully grown human being, and it had to be supposed that he knew what he was doing . . . even if he was hardly likely to be doing it *right*. And perhaps, Kate thought, I'm wrong to try and discourage him from doing it, because this inexplicable and far from commendable urge of his to undertake criminal investigations, or in other words to stick his nose into other people's business . . . perhaps in some way this peculiar penchant offers him some kind of distraction from the problems that – being some kind of loony – he probably regards as more important and pressing. She had only the vaguest of notions as to what the Dobie Paradox was and even less of an idea what its implications in the world of physical science might be, but Dobie did – at least, she was prepared to take his word for it, even though this knowledge had to make him virtually unique in the human race. And being unique, or nearly, he had to be aware of certain rather unusual forms of responsibility; she could quite see that. Responsibilities that might weigh on him, even worry him. Well, he *was* worried. It was obvious. So perhaps it would be a thoughtful and considerate thing to do some worrying on his behalf, for a change. It needn't be any very serious worrying, after all. Murder is a serious business, yes, but Dobie's futile attempts at research could hardly be anything but harmless. Completely innocuous. Surely . . . ?

'Hhhhrrrrffffffffgh,' the elderly patient remarked.

'Nasty sore throat you got there, Mr Prothero. I'll prescribe you something for it.'

'Hrrrrrrch you,' the patient said. Patiently.

Jackson was also concerned about Dobie, though for quite other reasons. These reasons were chiefly related to his interview with Micky Mannering and to Micky's intimation that bloody Dobie had been chatting him up already. This wasn't a development of which Jackson could approve. There are some very undesirable elements in the Cardiff social swim and Micky, as was notorious, knew most of them.

All right then (Jackson thought) for Dobie to go Boy Scouting round the place turning up various items of material evidence, even if he did his *Boy's Own Paper* funky stuff in places where he had no business, on the face of it, to be. He had at least handed his evidence over, such as it was, and in view of the

153

rather startling interpretation that apparently had to be granted it, Jackson was prepared to act on it. Forthwith. That very morning. Even though to do that he'd have to stick his neck out rather further than was his normal custom. But that was also what Dobie would be doing, if he wasn't careful. Indeed, it was what Dobie had done already.

The silly bugger.

What he obviously hadn't realized was that with Micky Mannering, money talked louder than anyone else. Micky could be a right old chatterbox and telltale tit when it paid him to be so, and information could often be a valuable commodity to Micky's little chums. Some of them might be interested to know that Dobie had been asking questions about little Beverley and – more importantly – Irene Jones, and some of them might very well wonder why he was asking them. Since Micky wouldn't be able to tell them why, they might take it into their pretty little heads to seek the needed information from Dobie himself, and that wasn't a prospect that Jackson could relish. Not in view of the character of some of the boys who might be concerned. Naughty boys like Ivor (the Terrible) Halliday, who when all was said and done might well be – and probably considered himself to be – the kid's father. Not that he could ever have played convincingly a paternal role; that wasn't Ivor's scene. Nor, for that matter, could any child under any conceivable circumstances have *fancied* Big Ivor as a Dadda. Dobie clearly had no idea of the kind of villain his enquiries might for one reason or another be annoying. Dobie had never seen any examples of Ivor's handiwork. Jackson, who on the other hand had viewed over the years some of his victims when they'd been pulled out of the river, was quite well informed on the subject.

No, Dobie would do well to confine his investigations to the botanical field – and preferably to those trees he'd talked about at that Cambridge college, which would have the advantage of being at a considerable geographical remove from Micky and Ivor and Irene Jones' numerous other gentleman friends. The further, the better. Jackson thought he might well have a word with Kate Coyle about it. Kate would make him see sense.

After all . . . these academic geezers may know all about *things*, facts and figures and so forth. . . . But people, now – that's another matter. That's where the dumb old copper comes into his own – in dealing with people. Human beings. That's if you could count Big Ivor as a human being.

Perhaps you couldn't. . . .

Though the real trouble with the Beverley Sutro business (Dobie decided) was that it didn't seem to have any kind of a shape to it, any readily discernible pattern. He and Kate had stumbled upon a body that hadn't become a body until a little later and everything else had been like that, somehow. All manner of rather bizarre detail, any number of probably misleading impressions, but no *shape*. And Dobie found that a little disturbing.

Apart from anything else, he couldn't clearly picture in his mind the girl herself. Her physical appearance, yes. But her mentality, no. Girls in their late teens are always a puzzle, because you don't know whether to treat them as girls or as women. Often enough they're not sure about this themselves. At least in one obvious sense you had to count Beverley Sutro as a woman . . . but also as enough of a child for childhood influences to be still affecting her personality and her behaviour. And according to Micky Mannering, those influences couldn't have been altogether . . . well, let's say propitious.

The girl couldn't have had a very high opinion of men, anyway.

It was odd, perhaps, that Dobie should feel convinced of this, in view of the evidence of her precocious, if not all *that* precocious, sexual activities. It just stood to reason, given her family background – or lack of it. She'd have learnt, no doubt, to recognize her mother's various lovers and husbands as powerful and authoritarian beings, exerting an inexplicable influence on the behaviour of her mother and – ultimately – of herself. Beat it, Bev. Get lost, Bev. Keep out of the way for a while, darling, Mummy's busy. So busy that apparently she can't even be found, when she's needed. OK, so what's left but rebellion? Against the unwarranted male assumption of domestic authority, and by implication against established authority in general?

Of course that didn't make her anything out of the ordinary. Quite the contrary. Every other teenager you met these days seemed to be rebelling against established authority and to be almost painfully self-conscious about it. Those kids were the new Puritans, if only they realized it. All established authority demands a reasonable degree of tolerance and they weren't, as far as Dobie could see, prepared to extend it. They'd concede you nothing. They preferred the alternative culture, as they called it, meaning plenty of teenage sex and drugs, and that was how they ended up in the Rehabilitation Centre. And that indeed was the paradox . . . or an aspect of it. Beverley belonged *there*, by rights. If she was instead enjoying the comforts of privilege in the Dame Margaret School for Girls just round the corner, that was because she was protected by the material benefits arising from her mother's financially advantageous second (or third) marriage . . . which obviously had enabled her to get the kid out of the way for quite a long while, darling, and at just the right age, too, rich Italians being notoriously prone to poking the odd stepdaughter or two, at least if all those films about the Mafia were to be believed. . . . Dobie was rather vague on this point since he'd slept through most of them but anyway he was involving himself in a digression. The damned woman had sent the kid to a posh girls' school, that was the point, run if anything on even more authoritarian lines than the Centre itself. She wouldn't have been happy there, as went without saying. And so . . .

'Would you say that doctors are symbols of authority, Kate? I mean, do people often see them as such?'

'*Wouldn't* it be nice to think so. I could derive a good deal of satisfaction from that idea, especially when I'm down on my hands and knees scrubbing the kitchen. But . . . oh, if you're serious, yes, I suppose they do. My dad certainly was one. Ruled his patients with a rod of iron, the old sod. And us, too.'

'More so than school teachers, perhaps?'

'That would depend. It cuts both ways. School teachers hardly ever get blamed when they make a mistake, but doctors *always* are. So it's just as well we bury most of them.'

Dobie thought about this for a while. 'You're respected, but you're also resented.'

'Sometimes, yes. Nearly always by men . . . who think I shouldn't be doing the job and can't be doing it right, anyway. Not many of *them* left around, though, thank goodness.'

'And conversely, a woman might sometimes resent a male doctor?'

'A certain type of woman might. A very young woman or a girl, probably, who . . . But then he'd be resented as a *man* more than as a doctor, or so I'd imagine. I certainly resented Dad that way but then a lot of kids resent the activities of their parents, whatever it is they're doing. What—'

'Sexual activities, too?'

Kate stared at him. 'What's all this *about*, Dobie? You're talking in riddles. And it worries me.'

'I'm delving into female psychology.'

'Well, don't do *that*. Just keep on delving into more material parts and I'll be perfectly satisfied. Or if I'm not, I'll let you know.'

'Oh. OK,' Dobie said. 'Thanks.'

Tuesday March 27th

Some weird interruptions to normal routine this morning. Comings and goings by sad-looking men in regrettable suits. I take them to be plain-clothes (*le mot juste*) police officers. The Horse says they are and he should know.

I'm confined to my room until further notice. We all are. Recreation period later, they say. It's raining in any case, so I don't mind. I got the draft of my novel out an hour ago, but yet again I don't feel in the mood for any kind of serious endeavour. I don't think I'll ever recapture the mood until I get clear of this place.

I don't need any recreation periods – all I seem able to do is re-create, which is the opposite of create. It's almost like it was in Cyprus. Nothing comes but clichés. *I can't get her out of my mind. That* kind of thing. And after all it's only a face. Or no, that's not true. 'When her loose gown did from her shoulders fall' – I know now how he felt, poor old Wyatt. Cooped up in there. In Cyprus, too. In the cage. But it's not like it was with Derya, not even remotely. I'm distressingly sane these days; I feel I'd just be saner yet if I could get out of this dump. Popeye says it won't be long now but he's such a liar. They all are. Only of course it's not ordinary lying, it's psychotherapy. That's supposed to make a difference. They don't explain why.

Too many kids here still on withdrawal, that's why. Yes, you can see why they have to tell us all these lies – the truth's what most of us are trying to escape from. Even the nuts and addlebrains who'll be let out in the end because they're harmless and because they can't go on getting treatment here for ever. That's all the doctors try to do, really – make sure we're harmless. Not all of us are. The Horse most certainly isn't. But he's trying to escape from the truth all the same. That's what I always feel about the girl whenever I see her. She's trying to escape. From what? From my dream? Where's the truth in dreams? It makes no sense. That's the trouble.

At least I don't feel scared, not any more, like a lot of us are. Like the guy in the next room when he starts screaming at night. Says he sees spiders. There aren't any spiders, I wish there were. They'd keep me company. And the dark-haired one who reckons they're out to get him, except he doesn't know who 'they' are. A crackpot. Always looking out the window and ducking back. He's scared of Horse but then a lot of us are. That's natural. And that other little white-faced chap, maybe seventeen or eighteen, who always looks scared half out of his wits or would if he wasn't that way already. Another persecution complex. A real twitcher. *Quelle galère*. I'd write a book about the people in this place if I thought anyone would believe it.

Instead, just notes. Always notes. Where's the point?

Sometimes I think I'd sooner be a doctor than a writer. Or even a mathematician, like Derya was. Or John Dobie. Someone anyway who's trying to *find* the truth, not run away from it. But if you drop your doorkey in the dark, it's no good going over to the nearest lamppost to look for it, which is what I reckon all the shrinks here are doing. Dobie seems to have the right idea. Moving over the lamppost. At any rate I *think* that's what he's trying to do. Sometimes I wish Derya were still alive so she could explain it all to me, the mathematical bit, but mostly I don't. I'm not *glad* she's dead, I just feel that things are getting better now she's gone. Yes, I know – but it's the truth, that's where I dropped the key and it's no good looking somewhere else for it.

They're all looking in the wrong place, the psychs. I know it and they don't. The same with all those bastards in the tatty suits. They wouldn't say they were searching for the truth, they'd say they were investigating a crime. It's all *wrong*. A crime isn't something you *do*, it's something that you *are*. I know because I've been one. I've been a crime, I know what it feels like. Someone killed that girl, I know that, just as someone else killed Derya, and maybe they'll find out who it was and maybe they won't but if they do, then what?

In here. In some place like this. With us. Re-creation, correction, rehabilitation, whatever you call it. It can't be done. I know because *I*'m in here. They've tried it on *me*. They've told me all the right lies but the lies get in my way, all I can do is re-create, I can't create any more. Not while I'm here. I suppose that's a paradox, the sort of thing that Dobie goes in for. I hope he can move the lamppost. I hope *someone* can.

'Of course computers tell lies if *they*'re told lies in the first place. They're just like human beings in that respect . . . though I don't know why I'm telling *you* this, of all people.'

'That's all right,' Dobie said. 'It doesn't do to forget the obvious. Besides, I rather think that's what's been happening.'

'Human error.' Merrick shook his head. 'That's difficult to trace.'

'And sometimes even more difficult to correct.'

'Naturally.'

The human being, female in gender, standing beside them seemed to be a little perturbed at the direction the conversation was taking. 'If we have any erroneous information on file, Dr Merrick, I can assure you that the Director will wish the matter to be rectified as quickly as possible. But I really don't think it very likely—'

'Oh, we didn't mean to imply any criticism, Miss . . .'

'Mgono.'

'Miss MacGonogh, no criticism at all of your procedures. Or of your infrastructure. Nothing like that. We just wanted to . . . see what there is to be seen of it, so to speak.'

'Better call me Maggie. Everyone does.'

Not very much of the Main Computer Room's infrastructure was, in fact, visible, most of it inevitably consisting of microcircuitry effectively concealed from the human eye. The same was broadly true of Miss Mgono's infrastructure, though the principal screening agent in her case was a voluminous cotton lab jacket, the gleaming whiteness of which afforded a startling contrast to the equally gleaming blackness of her face and hands and also conduced to an overall impression of almost minatory efficiency. Miss Mgono – Maggie – was indeed a good deal more impressive in outward appearance than the electronic machinery of which was the present custodian, being – even in her flat-heeled lace-up sneakers – six foot three, at least, in height and of correspondingly substantial bodily proportions; she might, Dobie thought, easily be able to secure alternative employment as the chucker-out at a night club, should Ol' Man Redundancy cast a beady eye in her direction. (Though not the night club in which Irene Jones had at one time made her own admirable bodily proportions available to a discriminating public, that particular den of vice having long since, as Dobie had discovered, been closed down.) With some effort, he diverted his attention from Miss Mgono's – or Maggie's – mighty thews to their immediate surroundings, which mainly consisted, of course, of computer consoles and monitor screens.

The days of wildly spinning tape spools and of clicking digitals being now as long since past as those of the Flamingo Night Club, the display here didn't seem very much more complex than that which a mere couple of years ago Dobie had observed in the travel agency his then wife had worked for. 'It's all simple enough,' Merrick said, confirming this impression, 'as you can see for yourself. Reciprocal units on modems feeding the central memory bank, cross-filing on the reciprocal computers on various rather elementary access acronyms, simultaneous feedback to the Welsh Office files . . . All quite primitive, I know, but adequate to the purposes it was set up to serve. And just about problem free, wouldn't you agree, ah . . . Maggie?'

'There was a problem last Saturday, though,' Dobie said. 'That's really what I've come about.'

Miss Mgono looked perplexed. 'There *was* a little trouble on the Tongwynlais relay, yes. It doesn't happen very often but when it does it *always* happens over the weekend. The Director of the Centre was rather annoyed about it.'

'Morris Train?'

'Mr Train, yes. He sent Kathleen Daly in right away to check

160

with us – she runs the shop for him as best she can but she's only trained as a programmer and *I'm* not really a comp technician either – so there wasn't much we could do about it. It looked as if one of the digits in the access code had been accidentally erased but as my boss wasn't here I couldn't get at the coding lists. . . . But anyway I'm told they've re-established the relay now so probably my diagnosis was wrong in the first place . . .' Under the folds of the lab jacket, her shoulders heaved mountainously in a colossal shrug; Dobie wasn't sure what it signified. Probably indifference. 'It's happened before. Glitches, the boss calls them. They don't amount to *errors*. Errors, they're more . . . serious. Obviously.'

'Why wasn't your boss here then?'

'Because he leaves at five o'clock on Saturdays. So do I, when I'm not on evening duty. But that night I was. Miss Daly must have looked in at around . . . six o'clock, I suppose. Of course Mr Train was on the phone a good deal earlier, but he spoke to Mr Lacey. To *my* Director. Not to me.'

Merrick was showing some signs of impatience, 'What's all this *about*, Dobie?'

'No, no.' Dobie gestured ineffectually. 'It's all very much as I'd supposed. There *was* an erasure in the access code. I know because I re-set it. On the Monday.'

'*You* did? How did you manage that?'

'I hacked it in. Worked the usual combinations until one of them clicked. . . . It wasn't so difficult. As you say, the set-up's rather primitive. But the point is, there *was* an erasure. And accidental erasures . . .' Dobie turned towards Miss Mgono again. 'You don't get many of them, do you? As a rule?'

'No. Hardly ever.' Miss Mgono might have blushed becomingly, had her coloration permitted it. Instead she shuffled her size ten plimsolls about uneasily. 'It's an expression we use, though, or let's say it *has* been used . . . to save someone or other his job when there's been a goof-up. In other departments, that is. Not in this one.'

'Suppose,' Dobie said, 'that some item on the file were intentionally erased . . . then a digit of the access code might have been accidentally caught up in the erasure. Right?'

'That *could* happen,' Merrick agreed. 'If you had an inexperienced operator and a . . . It's a weakness in the system, certainly, but not one you can very well guard against. Not without going back to square one and designing a virus-proof signal pattern. Of course, we're now able to build in a trip acronym that'll stop people from hacking in the way *you* did, but once they *are* in it's hard to see how you can check them from making unauthorized erasures and addenda without at the same time preventing—'

'Exactly, exactly,' Dobie said. As he knew from past experience, it was also difficult on these occasions to prevent Merrick from dropping into his accustomed lecture-hall stride and droning on for ever. 'But what we have to do now, you see, is *find* the erasure and see what's been entered in its place, if anything has. That, so to speak, is the object of the present exercise.'

Merrick stared at him. 'I say, that's a tall order, Dobie.'

'Well, let's look on it as a challenge,' Dobie said.

Kate, meantime, was having a tiring morning. She was well aware that the waiting room of her clinic, being warm and cosy, served as a convenient gossip-retailing centre for a goodish many of her female clientele (and not a few of the male) who seemed indeed to be on her panel for no other reason, their overall state of health being uniformly excellent. Today that ethos seemed even to have percolated through to the consulting-room, where patient after patient – their morbid appetites whetted, no doubt, by the reports now appearing not only in the local but also in several organs of the national press – clearly didn't want attention paid to their chilblains and tummyaches but rather detailed information about

TEENAGE GIRL'S NAKED BODY
Found By Lady Doctor

—from, so to speak, the horse's mouth. 'It's strange,' Kate said, 'that the older people get, the more ghoulish their interest becomes in that sort of thing. It casts a rather disconcerting light on human nature.'

'You certainly look whacked out,' Dobie said.

'I expect I do.' She was demolishing a plateful of lasagna, however, with her usual exuberant appetite. Today they were lunching together, as was frequently their wont, at Luigi's Trattoria on the City Road, a noisy, convivial, and reasonably priced establishment much in favour with the local car dealers and others of that ilk. The Italian cuisine was in fact prepared by a Bangladeshi from Rhiwbina but was none the worse, Dobie considered, for that. 'And how,' Kate asked, 'was *your* morning?'

'Fairly active. I was looking at a computer installation with Gwyn Merrick. He's not the liveliest guy in the world but he does know a lot about computer systems, especially the ones he helped set up himself.'

'I see.' Kate was rather relieved to hear this. It would appear that Dobie was reverting to his normal sphere of arcane and incomprehensible activities, instead of unduly concerning himself with TEENAGE GIRL'S et cetera. Maybe that letter from Frankenstein or whatever his name was had done the trick. Kate would have appreciated some such diversion herself earlier that morning, after the first fifteen minutes of Eileen Lewis's monologue. Or harangue. 'On top of all the others, along comes Eileen Lewis. You remember her?'

'The chatty one?'

'That's her. The others only wanted to *hear* about it. Eileen, she wanted to tell *me* about it. *All* about it.'

'Really?'

'From A to Z. Anything Jacko doesn't have on file, he's only got to ask our Eileen. *She*'ll tell him. She's got it all worked out. Wages of sin, in her opinion. Sins of the father visited on the children. Though principally of the mother, in this case. Preached me a sermon she did. John Knox has nothing on Eileen when she has the bit between her teeth, I can tell you.'

John Knox? Another of her patients, Dobie supposed. 'D'you think there's anything in it?'

'Of course not. Poisonous rubbish, as usual. And a lot of racism mixed up in it because the woman went and married an *Italian*. Eileen Lewis disapproves of Italians. They all go round with stilettos and mandarins, as she calls them, and they have unhygienic habits. So of course the kid . . . Look, I don't know how I *got* into all this. I'm still steamed up about it, that's why.'

Dobie was now peering cautiously downwards at the tomato-soaked inside of his pasta. 'That sort of crude racism really annoys me, too. And he's only the stepfather, anyway. I mean the wop.'

'Eileen Lewis,' Kate said vehemently, 'is the voice of the *people*, you realize that? The voice of the popular press – as they call it. You don't want to get mixed up with all *that* again, do you?'

Dobie considered the matter. The truth was that he really didn't give too much of a damn about that side of things, not any more . . . but then it isn't always politic to tell the truth, least of all to the woman you're living with. Unfortunately, he wasn't a very politic sort of person. 'Kate,' he said. What was that outdated but expressive military phrase? Ah yes, 'I couldn't care less.'

'You mean that?'

'Yes. I'm not too highly regarded by the University Senate these days, anyway, because . . . Oh, they have their reasons. But they can't actually give me the boot. Though I wouldn't, mind you, be specially worried if they did.'

'This business could be the last straw, Dobie.'

'I never liked camels, anyhow. And maybe I've been one for a bit too long already.'

'A *camel*?'

'Sticking my head in the sand.'

'That's what ostriches do, you git. Not camels. You're sure about this?'

'I'm sure.'

'OK.' Kate sighed. 'Then you'd better tell me what you've *really* been up to this morning.'

8

Detective Superintendent Pontin came into the Investigations Room like the Flying Scotsman entering Euston Station, his arms working vigorously away like pistons, his eyes flashing irascible warning signals from side to side. It couldn't be said that the scene they now detected was one of indescribable confusion since, apart from the considerable bulk of Detective Constable Wallace (sprawled out across, rather than on, a wooden chair directly behind the telephone console), the room was empty. 'What's,' Pontin wanted to know, 'going on in here?'

'Nothing, sir,' Wallace informed him, raising smartly to his feet.

'What do you mean, *nothing*? Where the hell has Jackson got to?'

'He's in his office, sir. Co-ordinating the enquiry.'

'And what the hell's *that* object?'

Pontin gestured towards what might have passed for the station's arrivals-and-departures indicator, had such a device been designed by a raving lunatic and its schedules arranged by a one-eyed Mesopotamian mule-driver. It occupied most of the space on the far wall normally taken up by the departmental notice-board, which had been taken down and stacked in a far corner.

'That's where we're collating the results of our enquiries, sir. Looks a bit of a mess with all them squiggles on it an' all, but that's—'

'We? We? *We?*' Pontin cried, in involuntary emulation of the fifth little piggy of his childhood days. 'Who's *we*, may I make so bold as to ask?'

'Me an' the Inspector, sir. He's the collator an' I'm the chalker-upper. A bit of organized teamwork, you might call it.'

'No, I mightn't. A bit of a bloody fuck-up is what *I*'d call it, I've never seen such a shambles in all my life.' Crimson sparks glowed in the depths of Pontin's otherwise somewhat murky pupils. 'I think I'll be having a short natter with Detective Inspector Jackson, that's if he can manage to spare the time.'

In fact Jackson couldn't, but then neither could he very well say so. Not with Pontin in one of his President Kennedy moods. 'Well, sir, the present phase of the investigation seems to be just about finished, or will be as soon as we've simulated the results.' Desimulated? Assimulated? 'Got them all worked out, so to speak. We've got an investigations board in the Operations Room with the details all filled in, like, all in discord with contemporary recommended practice.'

'I know. I've seen it. And where do you get this Operations Room twaddle? This is a police station, I've been given to understand, not Guy's bloody Hospital. It's always been the I Room since I've been here and that's how it's going to remain while I'm in charge. Get that clear in your mind by way of starters, Jackson.'

'Yes, sir.'

'Which brings me to the gravamen of the case or the gritty nitty. I've allowed you a considerable latitude in the conducting of this investigation, a *great* deal of latitude, and what do I find you've been and gone and done? No, don't tell *me*, Jackson. I'll tell *you*. You've pulled in no less than six detective constables from Central, no less than *six* of Cardiff's best, I say, and you've set them off on as ridiculous a wild-horse chase as I've ever come across. Any damned fool can see —'

'Goose, sir.'

'What?'

'People chase wild gooses, sir, I mean geese. Not wild horses. I don't know why.'

'But policemen chase *criminals*, Jackson, wild horses and geeses don't come into it.' Pontin had become dangerously suave, as though about to order the invasion of the Bay of Pigs and the destruction of umpteen Russian missile sites. 'What I want to know is why you've seen fit to go and chase criminals in one of Her Majesty's open prisons. I'll grant you that in one sense it's a logical place to look for them, but generally we wait for them to come out before we start stomping them again. I would have thought that by now you'd have grasped that elementary principle of policing practice.'

'The boys have only been conducting interviews, sir, and I'm sure that fact has been depreciated.'

'To what end, Jackson? To what practical purpose?'

'To see how many people in the place you're talking about can come up with hard and fast alibis, sir.'

'I see. And how many interviews have the boys, as you call them, conducted?'

'Eighty-seven, sir. They've interviewed everybody there, without exception.'

'And how many hard and fast alibis have they established?'

'You're not going to believe this, sir.'

'Oh, yes, I am.'

'Well, er, eighty-seven. To be exact.'

Pontin breathed slowly and heavily, as though recently emerged from a strenuous encounter with Marilyn Monroe. 'Are you saying that they've *all* got alibis?'

'So it would appear.'

'Well, perhaps that's not so very surprising, Jackson, in view of the fact that they're all supposed to be doing porridge.'

'Not all of them, sir. There's the doctors and the kitchen staff and the, er . . . male nurses . . .'

'Jackson, you're wasting *my* time as well as that of all those other buggers, to say nothing of untold sums of the taxpayers' money. What got you *off* on this bloody ridiculous caper? The girl was killed *outside* the Goddam institute, all those guys are *inside* and dam' well supposed to be that way. What kind of a bee have you got stuck in that bonnet of yours *this* time?'

Oh God, Jackson thought, let him not find out about Dobie. Don't let him ever even *suspect* that it was Dobie. 'It's just a matter, sir, of deliminating the impossible, so that you're left with . . .' Something or other. Oh God, just don't let him ever find out. . . . 'In other words, once you've explored every avenue, so to speak . . .'

'Jackson.' Pontin's voice was rising now to a vibrant falsetto. 'Do you realize I've had *four* telephone calls from the Director of the Centre complaining of what he calls an unwarrantable intrusion upon the privacy of the inmates? And a *very* irate call from someone called Dr Ram who considers himself to be a victim of racial discrimination and who intends, he says, to take the matter up with his member of Parliament, whoever that is? Are you aware that the CDI at Central has received a similar number of calls from interested persons, some of them of a frankly abusive nature? How do you think it *looks*, Jackson, to the general public when the press get hold of incidents of this kind? I fully intend to get to the bottom of this matter, oh, ho, I promise you I *will*, and when I do. . . .'

'Will you 'ark,' the Duty Sergeant said gloomily, 'at them two in there soundin' off. Argue argue argue. No wonder bugger-all *work* gets done round yurr.'

'Don't reckon as they're like to come to blows, do you, Sarge?' Wallace, ecstatic at the prospect.

'Duw, boy, no such luck,' the Sergeant said. 'Just the usual thrust an' parry of intellectual rapier-work, same like in the House of Commons.'

'I'll tell you what we *have* got, sir. We got a preliminary report in from Forensic and it seems there are clear indications the girl was struck on the kipper with some sort of a kind of a wooden implement. Leastways, they say that under microscopical examination they found a lickle prickle of wood on the edge of the head wound. A saliva, they call it.'

'A saliva of wood? What kind of a lead is *that*?'

'It enables us to deliminate certain other possibilities, sir. We know she wasn't hit on the bonce with a flatiron, for a start.'

Pontin tried for a moment to visualize a wooden flatiron, but failed in the attempt. No, Jackson probably had a good point there. 'Or, for that matter, a cavalry sabre.'

'That's right, sir. You take my point. It means we needn't go round looking for someone carrying a cavalry sabre around with him. Or, for that matter, a flatiron.'

'That's true. That's very true. Yes, I'd say you were on to an altogether more profitable line of enquiry there. You push ahead on *that* one, Jackson, never mind all these Indian doctors and junkies they've got stashed away in that loony bin. Just find some nignog or other who's got a car *and* a wooden implement and pull the bugger in. Well, don't just *stand* there. Get creaking.'

'Don't you mean crackling, sir?'

'What?'

'A wooden implement? Well, *I* could have told him that.'

Dobie, being insufferable again.

'Then why didn't you?'

'Because I couldn't prove it. The way I proved the other thing.'

'Dobie, you haven't proved *anything*. In fact, if I were you I'd keep out of Jacko's way for a bit. He's hopping mad at you as it is.'

'He is? Why?'

'Because he and a whole lot of other cops wasted something like the whole morning . . . It's *obvious* that she wasn't beaten up like that at the Centre. When everyone there was either locked up in their rooms or doing something with somebody else or else just wasn't *there* . . .' Kate's voice was growing squeaky with exasperation. 'Apart from the fact that the girl couldn't have got *in* there in the first place. Which I'd've thought made the whole thing what you'd call academic anyway.'

'Oh, well,' Dobie said airily. 'I worked *that* part of it out all right. That's where the wooden implement comes into it, you see.'

But *really* insufferable. 'Not the original wooden whistle that wooden whistle? Look, Dobie, it's all very well your developing these theories—'

'Not a wooden whistle, no. But in a way you're not far off. There's certainly a connection.'

A pity, Kate thought, I don't have a wooden implement to hand right now. Or indeed an implement of any suitable material. Hard and bumpy.

'On the other hand,' Dobie said, blithely unconscious of his lady friend's homicidal inclinations, 'it can't be true that *everyone* at the Centre has a whatdyacallum . . . an alibi. No, I take that to be an incidental difficulty of the kind one often runs into when one tries to match mathematically established certainties against heuristic evidence. Schrödinger ran into that problem back in the '30s, you know, when he propounded the so-called Dead Cat paradox and hybrid-state theory. I think George Campbell and I have managed to demolish that one between us, but of course the *difficulty* persists and always will. I think Jackson will find that as the evidence he has accumulated is empirical, merely—'

'He isn't dealing with a dead cat. It's a dead *girl* he's worried about. It's different.'

'Yes, but the principle is very much the same. You just have to shake the evidence around until something falls out and then everything'll fit together again.'

He made, Kate thought, his much-vaunted mathematical

method seem pretty much tantamount to hitting a malfunctioning television set a few smart blows with a heavy hammer. But then her thoughts had already been inclined in that direction. Just a few smart blows on top of that smart-alec skull of his . . . Just a few . . . *bang! BANG! BANG!* There, she felt better already. 'You want to know what I think? I think you're crackers. Completely meshuggah.'

'Be that as it may,' Dobie said, looking at his wristwatch, 'I can't sit here nattering away with you all day. It's time I was running along.'

'Why? Where are you going?'

'I'm entertaining another lady to tea and cakes. At David Lumley's.'

'Are you, by God,' Kate said.

No. Not a hammer. A Colt .45 would be infinitely preferable. With expanding bullets. You'd push it up his earhole, press the trigger, and *KERR-RAASSHHHH!* Oh yes! *He he he!*

That *would* be nice . . .

In the Cathays Park shop, the A-team had been called to panic stations. At least, that wasn't what it said on the invitation cards, but Foxy and Edgar Wallace weren't deceived. There were long faces in the I Room under the masks of professional aplomb and looking at the arrivals and departures board on the far wall didn't do much to alleviate the air of general concern. But Jackson was doing that, anyway. 'We got to account,' he said, 'for the girl's movements. *Somehow.* That's obvious. Maybe it doesn't take long to kill a girl. And maybe it doesn't take very much longer to screw her first – with or without consent. But then nobody seems to have set eyes on her from the time she must have left the school'—Jacko rapped the arrivals board authoritatively with bony knuckles – 'until the time Kate Coyle and Mr Dobie picked her up from the roadside. Three to six o'clock. Something like three hours. So it don't make sense to suppose that she was walking along and someone jumped her. No. Chances are she was *with* someone. Somewhere. Number one question of course is *who?* We don't know. No one's telling. That's significant. So that brings us to number two question. *Where?*'

'We don't know that, either,' Box said. 'That's significant, too.'

'An' if we could find out where she was,' Wallace said thoughtfully, 'that might give us a clue as to who she was with. Like.'

'In any case you've followed my reasoning closely.' Which in itself might be taken to show there was something pretty seriously wrong with it, Jackson thought. 'And as certain items of evidence seemed to indickitate that the girl might somehow have got herself *inside* that Centre place during the period in question, we've just carried out a highly intensive enquiry in which Foxy here and some of the boys from Central have been through the joint with a . . . What *is* that thing you go through places with, Foxy?'

'A fine-toothed comb, you mean?'

'That's it. A fine-toothed comb. With results that we now see clearly . . . that we now see demonstrated on this here board, not counting that bit in the bottom corner which seems to be last month's lunch menu. With results that . . . Well. Frankly. Disappointing. Or in a word . . . Napoo.' He gave the arrivals indickitator a much more vindictive (and possibly significant) wallop. 'Eighty-seven interviews. All aimed at finding out who could have been even briefly with Beverley Sutro at any times between four and six o'clock. Answer is apparently that *nobody* could've. Which isn't exactly the answer we expected or wanted.'

'It *is* a prison, after all. Maybe a funny kind of a—'

'Just what the Super said. And I'll admit it looks like we got to strike out the dickies right away, though first off I thought that was the most likely. . . . However, I shouldn't prejudice the issue. Turns out in any case they're all tucked up in their cosy little cells and under television surveillance, whatever that means . . . except for five of 'em who're undergoing – what's this word . . . ?'

Wallace peered at it hazily. 'Yeah, what the geezer said was *therapy* but I wasn't too sure how to spell it.'

'Who're undergoing what the geezer said and are all in the consultation rooms with the doctors. So *that* lot are all in the clear and so for that matter are the medical staff, except for this doctor – Hodson, is it? – who says he left his room around three o'clock for a jimmy riddle, took him about three minutes he says so we can hardly clap the handcuffs on him without a bit more than *that* to go on. Picture's no better with the male nurses, warders, whatever you call 'em. Eight on duty at that time, none of 'em saw or heard anything suspicious and as they always work in couples, same like with bobbies on the beat, they can all vouch for each other, so to speak. And do. Kitchen and laundry staff –

all off duty, it seems. Gone into Cardiff or anyway, not on the premises. Same with Mrs Train. The Director's wife. She got back about half-past six, right?'

'Porter checked the car in and out,' Foxy said. 'Same with the other one. The Datsun.'

'Eh?' Jackson studied the board once again. 'Oh yes. That Miss Daly. Went out at five thirty, which is really almost. . . . And up to then she was with the Director, right? Trying to sort out some trouble with one of the computers. . . . And then it wouldn't do to forget the gate porter himself, would it? Seems *he* had someone with him all the afternoon, though I'm not sure if he was supposed to. No, it's all very . . . Like I said. Disappointing. But at least we know where it leaves us.'

'In the shit.'

'I wouldn't put it that way myself but yes, that about sums it up. After all, interviewing people is all very well but we can't discount the possibility of deliberate collision between them of one kind or another. Say, two of the warders covering up for each other. But Foxy did the verbals with them and he seems to be pretty satisfied there was nothing like that going on. . . . Right, Foxy?'

'Ye-es.' Box sounded dubious. 'But what they all *said* was that there wasn't any way the girl could have got into the Centre in the first place and if I found any way of smuggling in a bit of fluff I was to be sure to let them know. And I can't say as I have. We thought maybe over the wall somewhere, in view of the trainers she was wearing, but Crawford walked the whole way round and he says it isn't on. Not because the walls aren't climbable but because what you've got all round them now is a sea of mud. She couldn't've done it without leaving tracks. No one could've. And there aren't any.'

A short silence, broken by an unpleasant gurgling noise. This was Wallace, giving notice of his desire to speak. 'Bit like Puzzle Corner, innit? Like they used to have in the kiddy magazines. There was one where you had to get a fox and a goose and a bag of corn across a river but I misremember—'

But Jackson had had enough of geese, wild or otherwise, for the time being and this intervention, too, went unregarded. 'All right, but are you sure your boys got to see *everyone*, Foxy? Nobody got missed out?'

'We talked to everyone who was there between four and six p.m., yes, and to quite a few who weren't. Everyone except that other kid, the nice one.'

'Elspeth.'

'Elspeth, 'cos she was at school while the boys were doing the rounds . . . and anyway I'd talked to her already, the day before, and *she* wasn't there, either. She was playing hockey and she didn't get back home till six o'clock. Mind you—'

'She isn't a suspect, anyway. Given the nature of the case.'

'No, but all the same . . . Maybe we should give the kids at that school a bit more of a going over. The teachers, too.'

'Yes.' Pontin would just *love* that idea, Jackson thought.

'Why?'

''Cos I reckon that's where the girl must have been all that time. Hidden away somewhere. *That*'s why no one saw her. Be much easier, surely, for her to meet a boyfriend in the school than to go lolloping off to the Centre, of all places. There'd be empty classrooms on a Saturday, that sort of thing. Makes much better sense—'

'Where'd he put the car?'

'Maybe round back of the school somewhere. I agree it's a bit odd no one seems to have seen it, but we know for a fact at least two cars went down that road after five o'clock that day because the porter checked them out. Mrs Train's and Miss Daly's. And of course Dr Coyle and Mr Dobie. . . . But so far we've had no reports of any cars being sighted on the road, none at all. That's not unusual, of course. On a night like that one was . . .'

Jackson was studying the squiggles on the board once again. 'Mrs Train left at three o'clock, I see. Well before the . . . But the Daly woman, she left at five thirty. I suppose she can't confirm . . . ?'

'No. She can't. That was when it was getting dark and the rain was starting to come down like. . . . She's pretty sure she'd have seen the girl if she'd been lying *on* the road, but as according to Dr Coyle she wasn't . . .'

'It's *all* like that, isn't it?' Jackson said despondently.

Puzzle Corner. Dobie might be into solving these elaborate conundrums, but Jackson wasn't. That isn't what policemen are *for*. On the one hand an enormous indicator board covered in negative evidence, backed up by Heaven knows how many scrib-

173

bled notebooks the contents of which were even now being translated by the police secretariat into Heaven knew how many sheaves of typewritten flimsies. . . . On the other, two or three battered and bloodied leaves on a fresh-cut twig and one single sheet of torn-off notepaper. No contest, really. Unless of course Dobie . . .

'I've been thinking about Big Ivor,' Foxy said abruptly. 'No one seems to have seen *him* around lately, either. And in the ordinary way . . . if you was to show me a nice girl with a broken arm and a few front teeth missing, well, my thoughts would just wander naturally in that direction.'

'So would mine,' Jackson said. 'And my feet would just wander naturally in the other.' This was a joke, but not altogether. 'But you can't be . . . No way the girl could have been seeing *Ivor*. Micky Mannering reckons she's really his daughter and so do most of the grasses I've talked to. Or if she did . . . he wouldn't have . . . Surely . . . ?'

'Wouldn't put it past him,' Foxy said glumly.

'And then have . . . beaten her up like that?'

'Might not have meant to do her in. It's second nature to him. And he *has* gone missing. I saw Bronwen Bates the other day and *she* was asking after him. Odd, that.'

Wallace cleared his throat again, with similarly revolting results. 'Heard he'd got another bit of tail on the books since some while back. Maybe nothin' in it, though. It's been pretty quiet down at the docks of late.'

'Bronwen'd probably like to be sure he isn't coming back. And wouldn't we all? No, he's probably drifted up to the Smoke with the rest of Dai Dymond's crowd, maybe looking for an in with the Stainers. . . . We could put out a query to Central, though. Maybe we should. Yes,' Jackson said thoughtfully. 'Maybe we should. Rather than stand round here gossiping like a lot of old charwomen.'

'There's unkind,' Wallace said reproachfully.

'Well, we're not going to take matters much further tonight. That's plain as a . . . one of them whatsits.'

'Pikestaff,' Foxy said.

'Oh, belt *up*. And close the door behind you. Meeting concluded.'

That didn't mean, however, that the day's work was over. Far from it. Jackson took his own little notebook from his inside pocket and stumped over to the armchair in the corner to sit down and have a bit of a think. Something it isn't easy to do when you've got a high-powered team of trained investigators sounding off all around you. Making disgusting *kkhhhrrr'hhhh'cch* noises and things like that. Now everything – for the moment – was quiet and peaceful Jackson reckoned he could turn things over in his mind and maybe even get a spot of kip-time in without anyone noticing.

In the shit, though, Foxy had said. That was putting it pretty crudely, of course. But that was all right. *That*'s what policemen are for. *That*'s where they're supposed to be. Up to their oxters in the doodlums, stirring it about. Puzzle Corner, indeed. Lindum trees, forsooth. All it took was a good sniff at Ivor the 'Orrible to bring you up against reality – the policeman's lot. Not that Ivor had done young Beverley in; Jackson didn't think that for a moment. Since interviewing Micky Mannering he'd done a bit more homework with some of his old oppos, including Inspector Price of the old Vice Squad who had cause to know Ivor (and Irene Jones) better than most.

'Believe it or not, he was quite fond of the kid. No doubt about it. That's why he wasn't so chuffed when Irene lit out with that London character, but as he wasn't in so good with the Mac-Manuses at the time there wasn't much he could do about it. Then he got in with Dai and the Bristol boys and I suppose he felt he'd best let bygones be bygones. Oh, he'd have roughed up Irene if he could have got hold of her, no doubt about it, but he'd never have touched the girl. Soft spot he had for her, from all accounts.'

'What I'm wondering,' Jackson said, 'is if he knew Irene had sent her back. To that school. In which case —'

'Don't see how he could have known, unless she wrote and told him, which – to put it mildly – isn't likely. Of course he knows *now*. If he reads the papers.'

'And then he'll be even less chuffed than he was before.'

'So you might suppose. Yes, he'll be mad all right.'

'How mad?'

'*I* dunno, Jacko. Killing mad, maybe. You never can tell with duddos like that. He's half-way to a psycho, anyway, if you ask me.'

Old Pricey, he'd been shovelling it for years. Fifteen years on the Vice Squad, which is where the money normally is, only he'd never made any because he'd never been on the take. He still knew a damned sight more about psychos than any of those half-arsed shrinks whose views on the present case Foxy and Crawford had been canvassing, he knew more about Ivor and Irene Jones than Micky Mannering did, he might even know more about girls like Beverley Sutro than any of the school teachers even though he lived and worked in a very different world. And yet, Jackson thought, he hadn't really *helped*.

Dobie hadn't any business at all in Eddie Price's world. In Dai Dymond's various rackets, in Ivor Halliday's brutal little bylines. He just didn't know what he was meddling with. Coming into even the most casual of contacts with Ivor or, say, Tiny Goodman, or any other of the red-haze merchants in one of their *killing mad* moods, doing or saying – as he almost invariably did – the wrong thing. . . . It wasn't a nice thought to take home to bed with you. Not if you *liked* Dobie. And Jackson did.

Killing is very simple, for some people. That's why murder rarely presents you with any serious problem: means and motive are usually transparently obvious. Proving your case is, of course, another matter. Pricey knew as well as Jackson did that Big Ivor had three big scores on the sheet, together with any amount of GBH, but the only time they'd ever got him inside had been on a breaking-and-entering charge he hadn't even bothered to get himself cover for. . . . Eighteen months, with remission. It'd make a cat laugh. Yes, but that didn't alter the fact that murder is about the simplest crime there is. Say, nineteen times out of twenty. It's the twentieth time that gives you the sleepless nights. The rest are business as usual.

The twentieth time, Jackson thought, it's like dropping a stone into a pond. The ripples circle outwards and you go where the ripples take you, further and further afield. . . . From Dame Margaret to the Rehabilitation Centre, from there to Micky Mannering's West Street office, from there to Irene Jones and Ivor Halliday . . . not just to the Cardiff of today but to the Cardiff of twenty years back, the days of Aberfan and Vietnam. . . . All right, but usually as the ripples move outwards a clear patch forms in the middle, where the stone went in, and in that clear patch some kind of a picture takes shape. A picture of the deader. That's the whole point of the exercise. And that was just what wasn't happening in the present instance. After chasing moving ripples for nearly a week, Jackson could say that he had some idea of what the damned girl had looked like . . . and that was all. Even the readers of the *Echo* and the *Daily Spook* knew *that* much. That smooth clear patch of water was as smooth and clear as ever . . . but reflecting nothing. No image. No picture. *Niente.* It was odd.

Nobody seemed to have *known* the kid, that was the trouble. Not even her schoolmates. She'd only been with them a few weeks, after all. She'd only been in the *country* a few weeks. Before that, Italy. Before that, London. Or someplace else. She might as well have been a foreigner. No relatives around. . . . Her mother wasn't around. Or Sutro. Or anyone. Even Big Ivor – assuming he *was* her dad – seemed to have disappeared. Flown the coop. Wherever you turned, you found that blank space staring at you.

Of course, kids of that age don't always have very clearly defined personalities. But *something* had to have been there, inside that slim and shapely little body. Irene Jones' daughter, after all. . . . Well, Irene had never been lacking in personality, even if her purely physical attributes had been more evident. And the kid had to have been a tough little package, in her way. To be a loner in a girls' boarding school. . . . It isn't easy. . . .

And even if you hated to admit it, Pontin was right. There was nothing to go on and nothing coming up. A blank all along the line. The A-team, blocked and baffled; no apparent way through the impasse. Some new idea or piece of information had to come along from somewhere, some sort of a . . . breakthrough . . . and Jackson had a funny feeling about that. A tutorial sort of feeling. No, not tutorial, a tuition . . . Intuition. *That* was it. Dobie had to come up with something else, something a bit more . . . well, with something that no one else had thought of. Because when all was said and done, no one else was likely to.

Not until another girl got killed. Jackson liked Dobie, but he had a daughter at school himself and he disapproved strongly of murders anyway. So it all came down to what you might call a calculated risk . . . except that you couldn't really calculate it. Probably not even Dobie could, not even with his goddam computers. So if he really wanted to take that kind of a chance . . .

Jackson put away his notebook, which he hadn't opened, and got up from the armchair and walked out of the I Room towards his office. The paperwork would be coming in from Central at any moment. . . . And he had an idea at the back of his mind that some time tonight the telephone on his desk would ring. . . .

Wednesday March 28th
. . . . All kinds of fun and games today, with the fuzz descending on us like a swarm of locusts seeking whom they may devour and in the process disorganizing all our normal schedules to sometimes amusing effect. What's it all about, one wonders? . . . Or no, one doesn't. It's obvious. Anyway instead of seeing Popeye today I was taken for an interview with the transcendentalist of Uttar Pradesh, Dr Ram Singh. A change of venue and a very notable change of attitude, but all variety in this damned place is welcome. I got the message quickly enough – Popeye is into guilt complexes/anal retention while Ram (as you might expect with a name like that) is into sexual hangups, though of what kind it's difficult to determine. I was able to oblige him with quite a few.

Started off by asking me if I'm not a little uptight at the prospect of returning to the big wide world in the near future, getting a little nervous about it, maybe? Oh yes indeed, I tell him, the uptightfulness is terrific. Then he asks me a few rather personal questions about Derya and seems quite interested in the cave dream, which I relate to him without any imaginary embellishments – not that it needs them. Shares my puzzlement, or seems to, at the intrusion of Beverley whatname into the picture, makes copious notes, suggests a source in sexual repressions etc. Yarooo, my lord, there was no such stuff in my thoughts. And yet at the same time . . .

What it all boils down to is that like everyone else I want out of here, soonest. I wrote another job application this afternoon, tap tap tap on the typewriter, all a waste of time as I suspect. This address is going to put any prospective employer off for a start. Maybe Dobie would let me use his address for that purpose only, at least till I shake the dust, c/o Professor John Dobie would certainly make a better impression than c/o the Headshrinkers, the Nutcase Centre, though (from what they tell me) only marginally. At least he's well intentioned. But then I suppose they all are, really. That's the trouble.

Funnily enough the cop who came round to see me knows Dobie, or says he does. Big bloke with the traditional enormous feet and a very soft voice. Fox, I think the name was. I told him all about Dobie and he said, Yes, but what about earlier in the day? – so that has to be the time they're interested in. Asked me why we call Raich Carter 'Popeye' and I had to admit I didn't know, unless it's something to do with all that bicep-building he does; his eyes don't pop very noticeably. A bit surprising, too, that I couldn't remember very clearly what it was we were talking *about* that afternoon – that's the trouble with these chat-sessions, one seems to merge with another as time goes by and it all becomes a sort of introspective blur, it was just the same at the other place. I suppose it's because there's no real contact with reality, with the world outside, to give it a proper context. I tried to explain it that way to the cop but he didn't write anything down in his notebook so he couldn't have been very interested. So now *I'm* writing it down in my notebook though I don't know that I find it very interesting, either.

The world outside. . . . It worries me more than a little. Yes, I want out, but what am I going to do once I *get* out, other than start pushing my overloaded cart through the sand again, straining and puffing away just like before? Who wants to read books? Who wants to write them? What can I do? It's strange that nobody here seems ever to ask himself that question. We're all lilies of the field, I suppose, all is provided for us, all our wants supplied from the cradle to the grave, but in that sleep of death what dreams, etc., yes, I know, I know. . . .

more about dreams of death than Shakespeare ever did but what's the use? He never had to ask himself *that* question, surely?

'What question is that?'
'Well, not exactly a *question*,' Dobie said. 'I wouldn't call it a question, or not precisely. It's really more of. . . . Owwww.'

179

'I think you'll find that if you pick the teapot up by the handle —'

'I know, but when I do that the handle usually comes off. I don't know why it is, but . . . It's the same with milk jugs. Something to do with static electricity, or so I've been told.'

'Then perhaps you'd better let me be mother.'

Certainly, Dobie thought, Mrs Train's maternal attributes were once again well in evidence this evening, even more notably so when she reached across the table to reach for the teapot. In this and in certain other respects he found himself reminded whenever he looked at her (or them) of those buxom and begartered chorus-girls of the Naughty Nineties, who supposedly invariably married sprigs of the minor nobility and ended up as pillars of respectability and sturdy devotees of the Anglican Church. Mrs Train, however, would definitely represent the pre-pillar or possibly cater-pillar stage of this process of metamorphosis, in which her male company of the moment would also as of necessity become involved; Dobie, for instance, was finding it difficult in her presence to restrain himself from twirling his moustaches like an accomplished masher, or even a downright knut (Kate, no doubt, would have spelt the word differently), behaviour that seemed from whatever viewpoint to be scarcely appropriate to the plebeian, if comfortable, surroundings of the Tea Gardens at David Lumley's, that well-established refuge of better-heeled middle-class shoppers fatigued from the never-ending battle at the neighbouring department stores.

'In fact,' Mrs Train said, with a bohemian flash of her bright blue eyes, 'it's very gallant of you to allow me to do the honours. So much more fun, don't you think, to be *doing* something? That's why men are always so chivalrous about driving the car when you're going shopping. On the way in, that is. They're not nearly so nice about it on the way back, I can't think why.'

'Well, Mrs Train, I can only suppose —'

'Jack.'

'Er, pardon?'

'Please call me Jack. I *hate* unnecessary formalities.'

'Oh yes. Well. Yes, er . . . Jack. . . . That would be Jacqueline, I take it? You see, I was wondering if —'

'In actual fact my first name is Olwen but my friends always call me Jack. It's a long story that I think I'd do well to save for later.'

The implication that this was to be the start of a beautiful friendship was not altogether lost on Dobie, who saw, however, no immediate or tactful means of disabusing her on this account. He sipped tea, slowly and thoughtfully, instead. His mind, naturally inimical to all illogicality, continued perversely to prey upon the matter. Why *Jack*? Jack the Stripper? Jack and the Beanstalk? Certainly there was something about her husband's emaciated and somewhat careworn appearance that might suggest . . . Though that was probably an unprofitable, and indeed hardly proper, field for speculation. 'In fact,' Mrs Train – or Jack – was saying, 'I drove myself in to town today. Quite an unexpected treat this is, I promise you.'

'You don't come to Cardiff very often?'

'I'm not *invited* very often.'

'Ah. But for shopping, you said? And things like that?'

'Oh, things like *that*, yes.'

Difficult, one might have thought, to invest her last two utterances with innuendo of any kind, but Mrs Train had managed it somehow. But then it was also difficult to determine what *kind* of innuendo. 'Because,' Dobie said, floundering rather badly in his attempt to pour more sugar into a bowl that (*a*) was already full, (*b*) had a lid on it, 'I imagine that out there, where you live I mean, it must get rather, well . . . Boring. Sometimes.'

'You imagine quite correctly.' She rolled her eyeballs skywards, like a startled horse. 'Extremely boring. *Painfully* boring. Though I shouldn't say so, of course. Things have got a bit more lively lately, with the police descending upon us like a swarm of ants, though I suppose I shouldn't say *that*, either, in the circumstances. In some ways annoying, of course – Morris was quite put out by it but at least they're *men*, I mean, goodness me.'

'The police are?'

'Well, aren't they?'

'Not all of them. They have policewomen, too.'

'Oh, we didn't have any of *those* this morning.' Mrs Train made a sweeping motion of her wrist, rejecting an obviously inferior article from the bargain counter. '*I* had a very charming young man. A Sergeant Box. Or Cox.'

'Box. They call him Foxy Boxy.'

'Really? What a *very* inappropriate nickname. He seemed to me completely without guile.'

'I think maybe some kind of ironic intention—'

'But of course you *know* all these people, don't you? That's why I was so excited by your invitation. *Now*, I thought, I'll be able to get all the latest news from the horse's mouth, er . . . so to speak. Sergeant Box, I'm afraid, was dumb as an oyster in that respect.'

'But he wouldn't have got very much out of *you* either.'

'Indeed no. I wasn't even *there* that afternoon. And I'd never met the girl or anyone who . . . No, I was useless. Quite useless.'

'All the same,' Dobie said, brushing away unobtrusively (he hoped) at the tablecloth with a folded napkin, 'I can't help feeling that in more general terms . . . I mean, the observer sees most of the game, don't you think? – and that's what you *are*, in a sense. I mean, you're the only person living at the Centre who doesn't actually *work* there, so maybe you can see the wood where the others can only see the trees, and again you're a woman and almost all the other people there are men, and women are usually better than men at noticing the sort of things I'm talking about.'

Mrs Train stared at him, for the first time with no discernible accompanying sweep of the eyelashes. 'I don't quite know what you *are* talking about. I don't have anything to do with the boys *in* the prison, you know. I'd like to, but Morris won't allow it. Maybe life would be a little less boring if I could . . . but I'm not allowed to, Morris says, as I'm not trained in social work or anything like that. Morris can be a little *fubsy* about these things, I don't mind telling you. What they call a stickler for regulations.'

'But you meet the members of the staff. The doctors and so on.'

'And a pretty dull lot they are. All they ever talk about are their patients, as they call them. Well, you've *met* them, haven't you? So you'll know why that darling Sergeant Boxy came as a pleasant change.'

Box would be pleased to learn, Dobie thought, that he'd made such a hit. 'And of course there's Elspeth.'

'Oh, Elspeth, yes. She's a sweetie. With such refreshing ideas about life in general and maybe me in particular.' Mrs Train sighed heavily. 'She doesn't like it, of course, being cooped up in that. . . . But there I go again. And it isn't all *that* bad. Once you've got used to it.'

Dobie retrieved the napkin from beside his left foot, where he had inadvertantly dropped it. Mrs Train, familiar no doubt with the subterfuge and conscious that her own neat ankles would bear any amount of even more detailed examination, smiled at him sweetly. 'In fact I'm a little concerned,' Dobie said, 'about her reaction to this Beverley Sutro business.'

'Her father thinks she's reacted very well. But then . . . They went to school together, I know, but they weren't close friends or even enemies, as far as I can make out.'

'No. But the girl died in her house, she saw me bring the kid's body in and . . . what I'm getting at, it has to be very *alarming* for her, wouldn't you say? A girl she knew being raped and murdered on a road *she* has to walk down twice a day, whoever did it still at large, she *ought* to be scared, surely? And yet she doesn't seem to be. Not very much.'

Mrs Train pouted thoughtfully, considering the point. 'She's a very self-possessed young lady, that one. And of course her father's a doctor, she's perhaps a little more accustomed at least to the *idea* of illness and death than some other children might be.' She retrieved a teacup and saucer that, propelled by a careless flirt of Dobie's retrieved napkin, were on the point of disappearing over the edge of the table. 'I don't think you need be too concerned about her, I don't really. In one way, yes, she misses her mother, certainly, but in another way she's adapted to the situation very well. Not that it's easy for her. It isn't. But in any case, it's good of you to take an interest.'

In fact, Dobie's interest was at that moment centred on the cake tray. Gluttonously, he helped himself to a second slice of chocolate-coated sponge and popped it into his mouth, where it was instantly assailed by hordes of ravening enzymes. This was indeed the second time this week that Dobie had partaken sumptuously of tea and sugary refreshments in female company and if the company on this occasion was distinctively different then so after all were his surroundings. He felt that he was learning, if nothing else, the arts of social adaptability. 'She said one thing that puzzled me,' he remarked, showering a spray of saliva-sodden cake crumbs over the tea-tray. 'Something I wanted to ask you about. In the course of—'

'Well, now,' Mrs Train said, rather hurriedly. 'In other respects you might call her an over-imaginative child. I really don't think you should attach too much weight—'

'She said her father once ticked her off for playing in the wood.'

An absurdly incongruous rhyme entered Dobie's head seemingly out of nowhere, only to be at once and impatiently dismissed as a total irrelevance. Which it was. *My mother said I never should Play with the gypsies in the wood* . . . 'Or at least, it's not a wood, or not exactly. An arboretum, I believe it's called. Those trees in front of the main building. . . .'

Mrs Train seemed for once to have been slightly taken aback. 'Yes. That's right. It's quite true. She's not allowed to play there. The boys in the Centre go there sometimes to take exercise and . . . Oh, it's silly, of course they wouldn't *harm* her in any way. It's just another of those stupid regulations I told you about.'

'But you see, I wondered how her father knew about it. You can't really see the wood from their house, or from the offices in the main building, either. Really the only house with a clear view of the arboretum *and* the avenue is the Director's. In other words, yours. So there again, I was wondering if—'

'If *I* told him about it?'

'Exactly.'

'Yes. I did. Good Heavens, there's no *mystery* about it. Except that I didn't mention it to Morris, I didn't see any need to do that because he might have been—'

'Fubsy?'

'Yes. Fubsy. You know what I mean.'

'But you did see Elspeth playing there?'

'Not exactly playing, I never said *playing*. No, just walking through the trees. So all I did was tell . . . Dr Mighell to have a word with her about it, I mean, the matter didn't have any *importance*, none at all.'

'He wasn't there at the time?'

'Her father, you mean? No, he wasn't. In *my* house? Whatever can have given you *that* idea?'

'Well,' Dobie said. 'Something else she said. If we're to be frank.'

Mrs Train sighed profoundly. 'I thought so. That's the trouble with children. They draw the wrong conclusions. *That* matter didn't have any importance, either, though I can understand why she may have thought so.'

'Perhaps,' Dobie said, 'she was being over-imaginative. Like you said.'

'Well, no. Not over-imaginative, no. Just over-early, if anything, in getting back from school, though I suppose we were at least equally to blame, we just didn't notice the time. You know how it is . . . or at least . . . but the point is it just wasn't *important*, is what I'm saying, in the way she may have thought. If I happen to kick over the traces once or twice, as the saying goes, or maybe a little more often, it doesn't mean. . . . Well, what it *means* is that I get so bored in that damned place that if I didn't let off a little surplus steam once in a blue moon I'd probably go stark raving bonkers. *That*'s what it means. I'm sure,' Mrs Train said, bringing the eyelashes into play once more and so forcefully as almost to create a refreshing breeze, 'you can understand that. As a man of the world.'

This had to be almost the first time in which Dobie had been so regarded and he checked the automatic movement of his hand towards his moustache. It couldn't, he reflected, after all be very effectively twirled until it had first been disentangled. And possibly disinfected. Comrade Commissar, indeed. Play with the raggle-taggle gypsies O. . . . Anyone might have supposed Dobie's thoughts at that moment to be also a raggle-taggle, in dire need of disentanglement, and anyone would in that case have supposed correctly. But then Dobie's brain always worked that way. Mathematicians don't deal with order. Some kind of order is what they end up with, if they're lucky. What they *deal* with is total chaos. 'We all have to let off steam,' Dobie said, 'when we're under pressure. We just do it in different ways, that's all.'

'And your way is to invite middle-aged ladies to tea and cakes at Lumley's?'

'As part of what you might call a wider picture, yes.'

'It usually is. But yours is at least a *different* wider picture, just as you say. I suppose that's why I'm talking to you like this. It's certainly why I accepted your invitation in the first place.' The blue, blue eyes had become cloudy and even introspective. 'It makes for a change. Quite a pleasant one, really.'

'You mean . . . ?'

'I mean I'll accept all men's motives as being ulterior but some are more ulterior than others. And yours are very ulterior indeed. Morris said he thought you were an interesting man and I agree, I agree with him in most things, really. *That*'s what's important in marriage – in the long run.'

'I wouldn't say my motives are more ulterior than Sergeant Box's. Or the Elephant's Child's, for that matter.'

'Satiable curiosity?'

'Yes.'

Mrs Train shook her head. 'Your questions, as you call them, aren't at all like Mr Boxy's. They're hardly questions at all. You're not curious about the same things.'

'Well, no,' Dobie admitted. 'I'm not a policeman. *I'm* just letting off steam, that's all. Just trying to—'

'Because you're under pressure?'

'Yes.'

'I know. I can tell. Maybe that's what *makes* you seem so interesting. All the men at the Centre, even Morris . . . They're not like that at all. Everything's routine and they go along with it, all of them. I dare say they're clever but they're oh so *dull*. They're never under any kind of pressure at all. That's why I don't think . . . You have to be under pressure to commit a murder, don't you?'

'You also have to be physically able to do it. And it seems that nobody at the Centre was. Everyone's got some kind of an alibi. At least in so far as the police have been able to discover.'

'Really? *Really?* Morris will be greatly relieved, I can tell you. Of course it wasn't the staff he was worried about. It was the inmates. Because some of them, well, some of them are . . .'

'Under pressure.'

'I was going to say, maybe a little unstable.'

'Well,' Dobie said. 'They're all in the clear. Everyone is, on the face of it. That's why this little chat with you has been so enlightening.'

'It has? Well, good Heavens. I can't think how.'

Dobie, having paid the bill like a little gentleman, was about to turn away counting his change when someone tapped him belligerently on the right shoulder. Not Jackson. Not, this time, Carter. But another chap. 'I'd like the chance of a word with you,' Mighell said, 'Professor.' He invested the last word with far more sibilants than it could decently be expected to contain, so that the overall aural effect was that of an overloaded kettle boiling over, or possibly that of an irritated black mamba, poised and about to strike. The darkened colour of his visage indeed suggested these unlikely images to be more appropriate to his mood than one might have supposed. 'Er, well,' Dobie said, ever ready with a witty comeback.

'*If* you can spare the time. . . .'

'No problem. Of course. Yes. No hurry at all.' Dobie glanced towards the welcoming covert of the adjacent saloon bar. He wasn't fond of Earl Grey tea, not really; a short snifter, he thought, might help to take the taste away. Besides, after forty-five minutes of Mrs Train . . . 'I thought maybe a quick one. . . .'

'If you insssissst,' Mighell said, doing it again. 'But what I have to sssay I can sssay quite briefly. I sss-suggessst that the business you may imagine you have with the ss-staff at our Centre, whatever it is, is frankly none of yours, and you have no right to bother Mrs Train with it. Or anyone else. It's improper behaviour by any sss-standards and,' advancing his face to within six inches of Dobie's, 'I *trusssst* I make myself clear.'

'Not altogether,' Dobie said, fumbling for his handkerchief. 'Let's talk it over, though, man to psychiatrist.'

A further forty-five minutes later Dobie was (more or less) securely ensconced at the bar counter, one leg curled around the bar stool and the other straightened out and perpendicular to the floor (which appeared to have receded from him slightly during the past ten minutes, though this was strange). This posture caused him somewhat to resemble a more than slightly inebriated marabou stork about to launch off from a chimney-pot, although Dobie had, in point of fact, no such eccentric plan of action in mind. His companion of the moment, however, appeared to be quite seriously considering the advisability of such a gesture, or of some other less spectacular form of suicide, such as heaving himself in front of a bus, Mighell's former mood of extreme irateness having slowly subsided into one of profound dejection, possibly similar to those celebrated in verse by the poets Coleridge, Wordsworth, and Shelley, *inter alia*. 'Yes, I suppose you're right,' he was saying, not very distinctly. 'But psychiatrists are subject to these fits of jealousy in just the same way as everybody else. Doctors, after all, aren't immune from smallpox. We're all human beings, after all. And besides, jealousy isn't *always* irrational. It's a great mistake to imagine that it is.'

His clarity of utterance wasn't notably impeded by the quantity of whisky and ginger he'd recently imbibed but by the head-in-hands and generally mopey posture he was currently adopting. Dobie, who had failed to catch most of the foregoing, was relieved – although only slightly – to see him raise his chin in order to stare sadly at his own reflection in the angled bar mirror. 'All the same,' he, Dobie, ventured, 'being surrounded as you are by professional advisers—'

'I wouldn't dream of taking my troubles to any of *that* lot,' Mighell said scathingly. He seemed almost to be alarmed at this suggestion. 'My God, no. They'd be useless. Besides, my position precludes . . . I'm the Senior Consultant, after all.' He continued for a while to survey himself from this position of lonely eminence. 'They're supposed to come to *me* if they have problems.'

'And do they?'

'Do they what? Have problems? Or talk to me about them?'

Dobie wasn't sure, either. 'I suppose I meant, do they ever ask you for—'

'Do they hell. No. They don't. Of course, I haven't *been* there very long. But even if I had . . .' Mighell at last withdrew his gaze from the mirror in order to study the contents of his tumbler, which would soon stand in urgent need of replenishment. 'I don't see eye to eye with them on any number of issues. That's not unusual, mind. Psychiatrists hardly ever agree about *anything*. You see, there are so many different . . . different. . . .'

'Approaches?'

'Yes. Or methods of evasion, more like it. It's like being a bloody *schoolmaster* sometimes . . . in a public school at that . . . All that breezy superficial optimism on the surface and underneath . . . Oh my God. . . .'

'It's odd you should say that.'

'Why?'

'It's what I felt myself when I was there. I was reminded in some ways of that school your daughter goes to. . . . It struck me as being almost equally repressive, in its way.'

'We don't try to be repressive. Just the opposite. We try to offer, offer. . . But of course we're dealing with delinquents. There has to be a severe underlying discipline.'

'I was thinking more of the staff.'

'I see what you're getting at. Yes.' Mighell considered the idea in silence for a moment. A morose silence, but one seemingly indicative of serious thought. Serious thought, however, clearly required a little more material sustenance. He summoned the barman. 'I see what you mean. Yes, you have a point there.'

'The school has a discipline, too. Naturally. But—'

'And I approve of it. Certainly. Otherwise, I wouldn't send my daughter there. But it's an *established* discipline, the place has been run like that for years and years and so have lots of other private schools . . . and *our* place hasn't. Every damned thing's been changed. We've got all these blasted hi-tech devices, we get all the backing we need from those fools at the Ministry for any proposal we make that strikes them as being in some way *new*, everyone's into the latest theories of psychotherapy and what have you . . . but if you ask me whether we really know what we're *doing*, then I'd be hard put to it to give you an honest answer. The old Remand Home system had its faults, Heaven knows, but at least everyone knew where they *were*. While now . . .'

'Kate says it's the same with doctors. *She* doesn't know what she's doing half the time, but of course the patients can't be allowed to guess that. Because you can't do anything at all if you haven't got their confidence.'

'*Exactly*. But,' Mighell said, 'a doctor can assume he has the patient's trust to begin with. Otherwise the patient wouldn't have come at all. But a psychotherapist can't work from that kind of a premise. Far from it. Ingrained distrust of us – that's the usual attitude.' He surveyed his freshly loaded tumbler with affection and tested its contents briefly. Ah. Yes. Excellent. He tested it some more.

'It must be fatiguing work. Trying to overcome it.'

'You had better,' Mighell said, rather surprisingly, 'believe it. Normally, a patient *wants* to be cured. Our lot very often don't. Not really. They don't want to be coerced into taking up a useful role in society. They're social misfits and they *like* it that way. Sometimes it's difficult to blame them. Sometimes you may even start to think that they may be *right*.'

'And that way madness lies?'

'That's the trouble. Some of them *are* mad. Quite a few of them, in fact. Mind you, that's layman's language. Any time you want to define what madness *is* . . . well, you can go crazy *that* way, too. The inside of the brain might as well be filled with blotting-paper, for all we really know about it. But I'm being much more frank than I really should.'

Dobie shook his head. Nothing actually rattled about in there, so presumably all was well for the moment. 'Isn't that the Director's job, though? To give direction?'

'That's easy to say. Morris is an admirable chap and he does his best, but . . . he lacks sensitivity. That's the root of the problem with Ja . . . He's basically a very insensitive man. *My* tragedy is that I'm extremely sensitive. . . . But I don't look it. I know I don't. I have deep feelings but when I give them external expression, people laugh at me. Which makes me more sensitive than ever. *You* didn't, of course. Just now. I'm grateful to you for that.'

It can't be very nice, Dobie thought, to be possessed of a totally humourless personality. It has to make you prone to all kinds of untoward emotions . . . such indeed as jealousy . . . while at the same time disabling other people from taking you seriously. One might normally expect Morris Train, rather than Mighell, to be anxiously treading in Mrs Train's footsteps; Dobie had tactfully refrained, however, from pointing this out. Instead, he had indeed taken Mighell's initial and rather incoherent complaints quite seriously; it would be an exaggeration to say that he now had Jack's outraged suitor eating (metaphorically) out of his hand, but the central issue was now being circumlocuted, as usual, on a reasonably friendly basis. Psychiatrists, Dobie had decided, are unhappy men.

'My ex-wife,' Mighell said, 'never really understood me. I don't know that Elspeth does, either. Now that she's at an age when . . . That's where Jack was so helpful to me, to begin with. The teachers at the school are all very well but . . . it's not the same. And Jack is a thoroughly nice woman, you know, despite appearances. And despite these, er . . . complications that have arisen. . . .'

'*She* doesn't seem to regard them as such.'

'I know. That's because she . . .' Mitchell heaved the anguished sigh of a shattered soul lacerated by the thorns of life and leaking blood over what Jackson would have called the lickle prickles. 'She seems to regard me as in need of some kind of *sex* therapy or, or . . . some purely temporary release from frustration. . . .'

'Aren't we all? According to you lot?'

'No, no. Or, yes, in a way, but that's *another* misunderstanding. Perhaps she's spent too much time in the company of psychiatric specialists – a little learning is a dangerous thing, in whatsoever field of specialization. And I wouldn't say that many of my present colleagues have progressed very far beyond that stage, for that matter. As for—'

'It may just be that that's how *she* looks at things.'

'It is. That's what I'm *saying*. The problem is to persuade her that things are otherwise, when everyone else is . . . or is trying to relieve their inner tensions in different ways. And distressingly old-fashioned ways at that. Look at Carter and Hudson . . . all those cold baths and vigorous physical exercises, rushing round and round in little white shorts. . . . It's positively nineteenth century, the way they behave.'

I arise from dreams of thee, And my little shorts I get in, And I do some foul P.T., And I feel a perfect cretin. . . . It was very curious how these ludicrous rhymes seemed to be entering Dobie's head, totally unbidden. 'Sex is quite old-fashioned, too, surely. Although some of my students seem to think they've just discovered it. As indeed they have,' Dobie said genially, 'from their point of view. One has to be – what's the word? – tolerant.'

'Indeed one has. We are. We try to be. And I for one,' Mighell said, 'am getting pretty sick of it. Bring back the birch, I say. Why not?'

'For juvenile misdemeanours?'

'For everything. Not just for other people, either. I see nothing wrong with self-flagellation, in principle. They may have had sound ideas about that in the Middle Ages, though steel-tipped whips would perhaps be a little extreme. Again, the old-fashioned schoolmaster's cane. . . . They should never have abolished corporal punishment in the schools. *I* had many a thrashing in my time. Six, eight, of the best, as we used to call it. And I don't believe I'm a penny the worse for it.'

Dobie's gaze, long since somewhat distrait, became positively distant. A curious idea had at that moment occurred to him. An idea that was . . . well, really a little *outré*, even by Dobieian standards. But then it would be even more curious if his first real insight into the Beverley Sutro killing should indeed be derived from this obviously unbalanced and half-way sozzled egomaniac and through an encounter brought about by chance and which, until that moment, he'd on the whole have wished to avoid. 'Yes,' he said vaguely. 'An integral part of our British culture, after all.

Naval tradition and all that. Rum, sodomy, and the lash. All helped to make us what we are today.'

In a right mess.

And that indeed summarized the situation, if only (Dobie later thought sadly), in the sense of a *reductio ad absurdum*. The more pieces of the jigsaw you pushed into place, the more ridiculous the final picture became. You could say that in that way it closely resembled the Dobie Paradox – a theoretical formulation that had been created under pressure and had served ultimately only to subject its unfortunate begetter to even greater pressure. Or a vicious circle, in vulgar parlance.

He wondered if it was really true that people only murder when under pressure. It certainly seemed a reasonable assumption, but one from which false conclusions could too easily be drawn. Look for someone who's obviously under pressure and there's your murderer . . . but *that* wasn't logical at all. All the same, the police often seemed to think that way. He himself had been under tremendous pressure at the time when his wife had been murdered, and that in itself had apparently made him an object of immediate suspicion. Much the same thing with Adrian Seymour. No, it's all a matter of the kind of pressure and of who happens to be exerting it. In Beverley Sutro's case, that second question was easy to answer. Beverley herself had been exerting it and that was why she was dead. In his own case, well. . .

A much less tangible pressure. You could say that his whole professional career was at stake but it wasn't lying at the mercy of any one person; murdering the Maclennon Professor of Theoretical Physics at Cambridge, however desirable and even laudable an aim in itself, wouldn't affect his position in the slightest. Nor, of course, would his jumping into bed with a seventeen-year-old girl – or with Mrs Train, for that matter. Were he not a professor of mathematics but a psychiatric consultant at the Centre, however, the wider picture would be – as Mrs Train had said – different. He'd be guilty of unprofessional conduct in the one case and of unethical behaviour in the other. And open, surely, to attempted blackmail on either count. Yes, but, but, but. . .

It all came down to one thing, one thing that had been obvious from the first. Somebody was playing games.

He picked up the telephone.

*

'The sports mistress at the school. Ask her if anything's gone missing lately. Or maybe been stolen.'

'Stolen? Look, Mr Dobie, that's a matter for the uniformed branch, I can't spare the time for that sort of thing right now, especially not after the bollocking I've just had from the bloody . . . from Superintendent Pontin. I'll tell you the trouble with these ideas of yours, they *sound* all right but—'

'Jacko.'

Dobie breathed heavily over the telephone, misting the receiver.

'—but then when push comes to shunt—'

'Jacko,' Dobie said. '*Do* it.'

A pause. Jackson appeared to be breathing heavily, too.

'Oh duw,' Jackson said. 'All right, then. But this is positively the last—'

'And then ring me back,' Dobie said.

Fifteen minutes later, Jackson did so.

'A hockey stick,' he said. 'Gone missing, stolen, or strayed. As of last Saturday. So what's that got—'

'There you are, then,' Dobie said. 'That's it.'

'What do you mean, that's *it*? How can I—'

'That's your blunt wooden implement. A nasty weapon. Fine for beating someone up, but difficult to *kill* someone with it. You'll have to look for it, of course. It may not be easy to find, but it's well worth trying.'

'A hockey stick,' Jackson said. He considered the matter for a while. 'A hockey stick,' he said again. Then, in more thoughtful and measured tones, 'A hockey stick. . . .' This seemed likely to go on for ever.

'She was carrying it, you see,' Dobie added, with a view to introducing an element of variety into the conversation.

'She was carrying it. A hockey stick. Yes. *Who* was?'

'Beverley was.'

'Why?'

'She had to. Look, never mind all that, Jacko, unless you can *find* the thing or some part of it you'll never be able to prove anything. But that's what she was struck with. Take my word for it.'

'A hockey stick. Yes. No. Look, in all my professional experience I've never heard of anyone being murdered with a *hockey stick*. It's . . .'

'Don't say it, Jacko. *Look* for the thing.'

'In the Centre?'

'Yes. Because if it isn't there, you'll never find it.'

'You got a flea in your bonnet about that place, Mr Dobie. I don't see any way I can go poking around up there again without getting a bee in my ear.'

'Of course you can. We'll go together if you like. Just don't tell Pontin.'

'Tell Pontin?' Jackson giggled hysterically. 'Oh yes, I can see myself telling Pontin. Just been up to the Centre again, sir, with Mr Dobie, not causing any trouble for anyone, mind, just looking for a stolen hockey stick. You know what, Mr Dobie? You're *dangerous*. You should carry a government health warning sticker, you should, This Man Ruins Policemen's Careers. Have a heart, Mr Dobie, *please*. I got a wife and family to consider.'

Dobie was inexorable. 'It's no good, Jacko. You've got to find that hockey stick if you want to prove your case. Or find what's left of it. Just one little blood stain—'

'*My* case? What case? I haven't *got* a case. Have you?'

'Well, no. Not really. Not yet. That's why we need to find the hockey stick, don't you see. Just one little fingerprint—'

A click. Jackson had hung up. Dobie shook his head sadly as he replaced the receiver, not actually on the *cradle*, no, but near enough to make very little difference. It was ever thus, he reflected. They hadn't believed Galileo, either. Just because he'd passed his leisure hours dropping things over the edge of the Leaning Tower of Pisa. Not hockey sticks, of course, but the principle was the same. Also the effect, if you happened to be passing underneath at the time. But *that* hadn't stopped our hero. *Nothing* had. Or, er . . . well, yes, the Inquisition had, come to think of it. But that was different. Or was it? There'd been Pontins around even in those days. *That* was all it proved. . . .

No. It didn't prove anything. In the long run there was only one kind of proof that counted; you didn't need to be a Galileo to see that. Mathematical proof. Mathematics doesn't deal with what *is*; it deals with what *must be*. You can argue about the one, but not about the other. Dobie got up from the chair and went back to his own irreparably untidy but comfortable bed-sitting room, where Eddie was waiting. Eddie, his trusty IBM. 'Now look, Eddie,' Dobie said, 'you better not goof on this one or I'll be cross with you. *Very* cross.' Eddie, who had long ago privately arrived at the conclusion that his lord and master was mad as a hatter, said nothing and went on waiting. He wasn't booted yet. Dobie switched on and repaired this omission and then got to work on the keyboard.

HOLIDAY MARCH 24th TEN DAYS
£2000   £3000 TO FOLLOW

He set for CRYPTO and then for ANAL and watched the letters and numerals begin to spin round each other like demented roulette wheels. They were likely to go on doing this for the next five minutes or so, no doubt enjoying themselves hugely at this release from the irksome restrictions of a man-made construction; to the outward observer, however, the show as such was somewhat lacking in zip and Dobie therefore retired pensively to his armchair, where he lit and started to smoke a cigarette. When he had finished it he looked again towards Eddie; the monitor was now blank except for the single word appearing in the centre of the screen,

NEGATIVE

and that was, of course, to be expected. Dobie stubbed out his dog-end and returned to his labours at the keyboard. He was still so engaged some forty minutes later when Kate walked in, apparently miffed.

'Dobie, you left the telephone off the hook again.'

'Oh, did I? Well, it doesn't matter. I didn't want to make any more calls anyway.'

'As always,' Kate said, 'your logic is irrefutable but contrives somehow to miss the point completely. Which is that someone else might want . . . Oh, never mind. What game are we playing tonight? Space Invaders? Or shouldn't I ask?'

'In a way, yes,' Dobie said, blinking at her as she plumped herself down in the armchair he himself had not long since vacated. The incriminating dog-end was tucked away well out of sight underneath it, but some vestiges of the aroma might still be . . . In any case, this was *his* room and if attacked on the surreptitious-whiffing score he was fully prepared to brazen the

195

matter out. 'I'm invading someone else's space, you might say. Doing a little quiet hacking, as we experts call it.'

'Hacking?' Kate, as he had anticipated, rose sharply to the bait. 'That's *illegal*.'

'Yes, it is.'

'Who have you been hacking into?'

'Oh, just some of the Ministry of Health records at the Welsh Office. Child's play, really. I had the access code to start with, you see, and . . . Yes, but it's all very puzzling. I think I'll have to bring Merrick in on it. He knows their set-up back to front, which is the way some of it seems to be coming out. Which is what I expected, but on the other hand—'

'What do you mean, back to front?'

'Well, not literally back to front, no, but there's been some kind of an erasure. Or correction. To the Rehabilitation Centre file. I've been running through the entries for the last couple of weeks and there's this . . . irregularity come up. On March 24th. Last Saturday.'

'The day of the . . . ?'

'Yes,' Dobie said.

'What *is* the irregularity?'

'It's like I said. There's a demagnetized strip where something's been erased and something else put in. Well, concretely a record fiche for someone called Martin Cooper. Does that name ring a bell with you?'

'No.'

'Nor with me. But according to the fiche, he entered the Centre for treatment on the morning of the 24th. Quite a long history of drug addiction, took a course of treatment in 1989 some place in Bristol but it couldn't have been too successful because here he is back again – voluntarily, apparently. I can't see anything odd about it at all except that he's maybe a little older than the average for the Centre. But then so is Adrian and quite a few others. I can't make it out.'

'Can I see?'

Kate peered for a while at the monitor screen as Dobie scrolled the disc entry. Then shook her head. 'Why does there *have* to be anything odd about it? People arrive at the Centre for treatment two or three times a week. It's on the 24th, well, OK – that's just a coincidence. Surely?'

'Yes. But it's the erasure that interests me, you see. There shouldn't be any erasures on a Central Office fiche. Not ever. Unwanted or inaccurate entries, they get transferred to store. I'm, er . . . intrigued.'

'But what can you do about it?'

'Not much. But maybe Gwyn can. A hard-disc erasure isn't necessarily gone for ever. Sometimes it's possible to restore the original, or at least to piece parts of it together through an enhancement process. Only you've got to know exactly what you're doing. I don't and Gwyn does. And even if he can't get the original text back, he may at least be able to trace the source of the erasure. It doesn't have to have been done through the Central computers – any of the computers with access through the modem link could have set it up. And if he can trace it to the Rehabilitation Centre computer that'll be interesting because that particular link apparently got broken on Saturday and therefore that computer *couldn't* have been the source. I don't know if you're following me.'

'Perfectly. Something's gone wrong and you don't know what.'

'Yes, that *does* put it in a nutshell.' Mournfully, Dobie disconnected the modem and flicked the OFF switch. Relieved of its arduous duties, the computer dropped peaceably into a dreamless sleep, snoring faintly.

'And so you're going to get poor old Gwyn Merrick to sort it all out for you.'

'Exactly. If he can.'

'Dobie, have you no moral conscience *at all*? Or putting it in another way, haven't you got enough enemies already?'

'Me? I haven't an enemy in the world, outside of Cambridge. And anyway, needs must when the devil drives.'

Kate gave it up, as she always did when Dobie started to bring theology into the argument. If he couldn't be stopped, he might, she had found, none the less sometimes be diverted. 'Pork chops,' she remarked cunningly, 'in the oven. But of course, if you're really busy. . . .'

'No, no, pork chops? Really?' Dobie rose from his seat with some alacrity. 'In that case, let the good times roll.'

9

Bad enough, Jackson thought, to be chivvied this way and that by bloody Pontin. Bad enough, but unquestionably part of the policeman's lot; all Detective Inspectors have Detective Superintendents upon their backs to bite them; if it wasn't Pontin, it would be someone else, clearly nothing was to be gained by pricking against the kicks in that respect. But there wasn't any reason he could think of why he should let himself be bullied by Professor Dobie. Or if not bullied, exactly, then obscurely compelled to comply with Dobie's invariably mildly phrased suggestions. 'I don't know,' he complained grumblingly, 'why I'm doing this, I really don't.' It was true. He didn't. He'd never intended to. He still couldn't think why he'd changed his mind. Yet here he was, clumping about like a plain-clothes Babe in the Wood, hoping for Dobie to pull a rabbit out of a hat. Or out of a burrow. Or from somewhere.

All against his better judgement. . . .

He leaned his back for a moment against a convenient tree-trunk and watched Dobie proceed at a curious knock-kneed and camel-like lope, reminiscent of that adopted by Groucho Marx when in pursuit of a fleeing waitress, on a zigzag course through the conifers or whatever they were, peering myopically upwards the while into their clustered and overhanging branches. 'Early days yet,' Dobie babbled incoherently. 'Never despair.'

'All very well, but I'm not going to waste *another* morning. . . .'

He stopped and sighed, observing that Dobie had tripped over his own feet again and fallen into a clump of laurel bushes. Breathing sterterously, Jackson stooped to help extricate him.

'I know,' Dobie said, surveying the damage sustained by his right trouser-leg with some misgivings, 'it's what you might call a long shot. But my reasoning is that no one would want to risk being seen carrying a thing like that around, I mean it'd stick out like a sore thumb, wouldn't it? Except with the one person where it would have the opposite effect, I mean it'd almost establish her identity, if you follow me.'

'Mr Dobie, I'm convinced that nobody would wish to follow you anywhere, other than out of sheer idle curiosity. To see what kind of a . . . What exactly are you *looking* for?'

'Something like *that*,' Dobie said, pointing upwards. 'If you'll observe the configurations of that branch up there, the one stuck in between the . . . You see the one I mean? The one that conforms in outward appearance to the shape of a hockey stick? Well, if we could find a . . . a . . .'

He stopped, with his mouth gaping open. 'It looks,' Jackson said, with some asperity, 'like a hockey stick because it *is* a hockey stick. What a peculiar place to . . .' He, too, stopped abruptly, also with his mouth open. 'A *hockey stick*. Oh my God. Is that what you . . . ? Yes. It is. You said a *hockey stick*, didn't you? Yes. A hockey stick. Well, don't just *stand* there, damn it. Let's get it *down*.'

'It would seem to be, er . . . rather securely lodged. And also, er . . . rather high up. Oh well.' Dobie removed his jacket. 'I used to be renowned for my skill at climbing trees when I was a boy. Doubtless the art of it hasn't altogether deserted me.' He embraced the tree trunk ardently. 'The trick of it, of course, is to secure an adequate foothold before you . . . *Whoops*. Yes. Well, it's no more than another trifling wound. All the same, perhaps you'd better give me a leg-up over the first bit. You see, the initial absence of support . . . Yes, the right shoulder, if you'd be so good. Once I've secured the necessary purchase, you see, I can . . . Yes. That's fine. *Now*. . . .'

'AAAAAAAAAAA!' Jackson said.

Clutching his shoulder, he watched morosely as Dobie disappeared Winnie the Pooh-like up into the wilderness of overlapping branches. By the time Dobie had reappeared some twenty feet above ground level the agony, he thought, had somewhat abated. 'Where is it?' Dobie cried. 'Where? Where?'

'A bit to your right, Mr Dobie. You see that branch sticking out by your right foot? Well—'

'You mean this rather thin one here? AAAAAAAAAAA!' Dobie said.

Jackson ducked involuntarily as there descended upon him with some velocity, (*a*) one hockey stick, (*b*) one rather thin branch (broken), (*c*) Professor Dobie, this last accompanied by a miniature hailstorm of small twigs, leaves, and derelict birds' nests. 'Of course,' Dobie said, massaging his ankle, 'I must have gained considerably in *weight* since the days of my former expertise. It was foolish of me to omit that factor from my calculations.'

'Are you all right, Mr Dobie?'

'Perfectly. Perfectly. All's well that ends well, as the saying has it.' Dobie reached out to grasp the hockey stick and to essay with it an experimental swish. 'Now if only we had a *ball*, Jacko, we could have rather a jolly . . . Or quite a jolly . . . er. . . .'

Jackson turned round to look in the direction of Dobie's glazed-over stare. The three large gentlemen in white jackets looked back at him inimically.

'Now then,' Jackson said, anxious to impress upon them from the outset his official status. 'What's all this?'

But once again it was Dobie who appeared to have excited the newcomers' attention. They gazed at him, fascinated. 'Lord Greystoke, I presume,' the largest of the three gentlemen said. He was, Jackson noted with some alarm, a very large gentleman indeed. 'Answering the call of the wild again, eh, your lordship? Gettin' a bit long in the toof for swingin' from bough to bough, though. Best leave that sort of thing to your chimp 'ere.'

'I'll have you know,' Jackson said, beside himself with ire, 'I'm an infected spectre of the local police farce and I'm engaged in an infestation with this gentleman.'

'I see, sir. Well, in that case I'll 'ave to ask you *both* to cummalongame. Nice goings-on, I *don't* think.'

The two other large gentlemen nodded purposefully.

'*Another* fine mess,' Jackson said, 'you've got me into.'

'Yes. It's unfortunate that my friend Mr Whyburn wasn't among our apprehenders. He'd have remembered me at once, I feel certain.'

'Quite a lot of people remember you, Mr Dobie,' Jackson said meaningfully. 'A lot of people've got good reason to.' He paused in his prowlings around the cell to grasp the bars of the window and peer mournfully out between them. Well, if you looked on the bright side, it was raining out there now. And no doubt it was useful experience for a policeman, on occasion, to see how the other half lived, so to speak. Though Pontin wasn't very likely to see it that way. And the whole thing was *his* fault, as much as Dobie's. If Pontin hadn't kicked up such a shindy the other day, this visit could have been arranged official-like. Instead of. . . . Oh God, Jackson thought, I'm *never* going to live this down. 'I'm *never* going to live this down,' he declared, wailfully.

'Oh, nonsense, Jacko.' Dobie was still fidgeting about with that damned hockey stick, which strangely enough the gentlemen in the white jackets had allowed him to retain – or more probably had feared to confiscate; him Tarzan, lord of the jungle. 'Mistakes will happen in the best regulated. . . . And there *are* blood stains, unless I'm much mistaken.' Peering cautiously at the end with the curve in it. 'At least you've come up with the murder weapon.'

'You're serious? Yes. You are.' Jackson advanced. He, too, peered down at what certainly looked like . . . or feasibly *could* be . . . 'Good God, Mr Dobie. . . . Put it *down*, you'll be leaving your prints all over it.'

'Not on the rubber handle, surely. And of course the murderer's prints won't be there, either. Unfortunate, that.'

'But I don't understand. Why would whoever it was have been going round the place with a hockey stick? Why would he want to *steal* a hockey stick? I suppose we have to assume this is the one that was reported missing—'

'No, no, Jacko, you've got the wrong end of the . . . It was the *girl* who pinched the hockey stick. Beverley Sutro. *She* was the one who was carrying it around.'

Dobie wasn't very good at explanations, as Jackson had noted once before. His air of resigned stupefaction, if anything, increased.

'Whatever for? She didn't even *play* hockey. Leastways, no one ever told me—'

'Elspeth did.'

'Who?'

'Elspeth Mighell. The girl who lives here. She played hockey every Saturday afternoon, and Beverley played hookey at that same time. She came round here. She was *seen* here once, among those trees where we found this stick. Mrs Train saw her there and thought it was Elspeth, mainly because it didn't occur to her that it could have been anyone else. But really all she saw was a tallish dark-haired girl in a short skirt and a parka and . . . carrying a hockey stick. Beverley was a couple of years older than Elspeth, but they were pretty much the same size and they were both dark haired and from a distance they really looked a good deal alike . . . especially when they dressed in exactly the same way. I even came close to making that mistake myself, at one point. And all these dark misty afternoons we've been having. . . . Well, you know how often you see what you *expect* to see. The only girl any of the staff would *expect* to see coming into the Centre is Elspeth and the other kid was clever enough to realize it.'

'But how did she get *in*? The guard at the gate—'

'She walked straight in, of course. And later on she walked straight out again. Knowing that Elspeth would be out of the way for a couple of hours or more playing hockey. The guard would have seen her each time all right and have checked her in and out . . . but again, he'd have checked her as Elspeth, he'd have made the same mistake as Mrs Train. He'd have seen her even less clearly on that black-and-white television screen he has, and of course he's seeing Elspeth going in and out all the time . . . and all the kids in school uniform look alike to him, he told me so himself.'

'She'd be taking a bit of a chance, all the same. Supposing he'd gone out and seen her more closely—'

'*What* chance? She could have said she was calling on her friend Elspeth and all he could do would be turn her away. Of course, then she'd have had to think of some other trick if she wanted to get inside to see the boyfriend . . . but she'd have managed it, I promise you that. A very ingenious young lady, that one.'

Jackson was dubious. 'I dunno. With all this high-tech stuff they've got in here . . . a simple little dodge like that one. . . .'

'But that's what's ingenious about it. The simplicity. It's like flying through a radar screen with an all-wooden aircraft. Or Toad of Toad Hall.'

'*What?*'

'That's how he got out of prison. Disguised as a washerwoman. Beverley got *into* Toad Hall in just the same way. And out again. Quite a few times. But always on a Saturday afternoon, when Elspeth was playing hockey. And always leaving well before six o'clock, when Elspeth would be getting back. It couldn't have been difficult.'

'If you say so, Mr Dobie. Though it seems to me . . . But who was she trying to get in to see, anyway? Who *was* the boyfriend?'

'Ah,' Dobie said. 'As to that, I haven't the faintest idea.'

Jackson sighed. 'Then I can't see that we're tuppence better off. Because it *couldn't* have been anyone here. They've all got alibis, every bloody one of them.'

'Well, there's a time factor involved all right. It would have been far safer to take this stick away and burn it, get rid of it altogether. As I said, your Charley probably wouldn't have wanted to take the risk of being seen with it . . . but it's equally probable there wasn't *time* to dispose of the thing properly. Up there in the trees with the boughs coming into leaf, there'd be every chance of its going undiscovered there at least till the winter, so as a spur of the moment decision it wasn't a bad—'

'You think the girl was *killed* there? Under those trees?'

'Yes, I do. That's how those leaves got knocked off a low branch – when one of the blows was struck – and stuck to the wound. It's a quiet and well-screened spot, after all. Of course she didn't actually *die* till later, but that's beside the point. That's where she got beaten up – with her own hockeystick – and if there was any kind of a fight or struggle, there'd hardly be any traces left of it after all that rain. But most probably there wasn't. A sudden, unexpected, vicious attack . . . that's how I envisage it. And somewhere, Jacko, an alibi that won't stand up. But *whose* alibi . . .' Dobie shook his head. 'No, that I can't tell you. On the face of it, there's only one person here it *could* have been. But that solution makes no kind of sense at all.'

Into Jackson's somewhat befuddled brain there appeared the vision of the huge arrivals indicator board back in the Operations Room, the dozens of chalked symbols and figures, the sheafs and sheafs of statements lying in the wire tray on the desk. There wasn't any way he and his colleagues could go through *that* lot again. Pontin would never allow it. Pontin would . . . 'Can't we narrow it down at *all*, Mr Dobie? Find somewhere to start? Even if it's on a' – looking up hopefully – 'mathematical basis?'

'You mean . . . ?'

'I don't know *what* I mean,' Jackson said. 'I'm just asking myself where to start. That's all.'

Dobie, seemingly, was asking himself the same question. At any rate, he was pacing restlessly up and down, his hands clasped behind his back in approved university lecturer style. Since his head was lowered the while and his gaze fixed on the floor, he appeared to be in imminent danger of walking straight into one of the walls and debraining himself, but . . . Jackson reached out a hand and found reassurance in the thick padding that apparently lined the whole cell. Good. Someone had thought of that already.

'Well,' Dobie said, coming rather abruptly to a halt. 'I don't think it helps very much, but there's someone here who shouldn't be here. Probably under a false name. Which is odd, but doesn't seem to have any real bearing on the situation, because—'

Jackson was nodding. 'Yes, we know about that. And it hasn't. But it's supposed to be . . . How did *you* find out about it, may I ask?'

'One of the medical records in the computer here has been falsified. One of my friends is looking into it now, but it may be a while before he—'

'Records?' Jackson stopped nodding and looked puzzled instead. He was fast becoming extremely good at this. 'There shouldn't have been any need for *that*. The boy's using an assumed name, that's all. You see, his father . . . Well, we won't go into all the details, they're not really reverent, but you can take it from me the police are conservant with them.'

'A boy?'

'Yes. Eighteen or nineteen, maybe. Why?'

'No. It's a *man* I'm talking about. Name of Cooper. Martin Cooper. Forty-four years old, according to the records. It's all a bit puzzling but he didn't arrive here till the Saturday morning, just a few hours before the girl was killed, so obviously *he* couldn't be the fellow the girl was seeing. All the same – you said a starting point, and it's all I can think of.'

'And he's using a false name? I don't quite see how you got *on* to him in that case. . . .'

'I was just checking the entries for that day,' Dobie said, a little tiredly, 'because that was the date the girl wrote down on that sheet of notepaper and when I was running it all through the computer it occurred to me that "Holiday" might conceivably be the name of a person or a private code-name for a person because it's spelt with a capital letter, only the computer couldn't find any—'

'Forty-four?' Jackson said suddenly.

'What?'

'Forty-four years old, you said? Big guy with curly blond hair?'

Height	*6' 2"*
Complexion	*Fair*
Eyes	*Blue*
Hair	*Fair*

said the little computer disc at the back of Dobie's mind. 'Why, yes. In terms of general description. . . . Yes. . . .'

'Oh my God,' Jackson said. 'I've got to get a look at this geezer. *Now.*'

'Well, that shouldn't be —'

'*Halliday*. An A, not an O. The kid was scribbling it down, anyway, it must have been . . . Ivor Halliday. I just hope I'm wrong, that's all, because . . . But she *knew* him. Of course she knew him, he was supposed to be her *father* for Crissake. Her mother was Halliday's bit of crumpet before she . . . Come *on*, Mr Dobie, we got to get *out* of here. . . .'

'But who *is* this chap?'

'Used to run a night club and a chain of girls in those days for Dai Dymond. Then when Dai went into the drug scene, Halliday acted for him. His hard man, right? Did all the shoving around that had to be done and put two or three bodies in the Taff, if only we could prove it.' Jackson was speaking jerkily and rather incoherently, as he was now and simultaneously hammering on the door for all he was worth. 'Why in hell's name doesn't some-one *open*? They can't keep us stuck in here for ever, can they?'

'Last time it was only about half an —'

'Those bloody *imbeciles* in their white jackets, I'll have their guts for garters, you see if I don't.'

'Jacko, what are you getting so worked up about? Even if this chap *is* here, he'll be locked up in a cell in just the same way as we are.'

'I hope so. Because this is making sense in a way I don't like. If this Cooper character's Halliday, then he's here for a reason and I fancy I know what that reason is. Dai's given him the contract.'

'What contract?'

'Tit for tat deal. Heavy stuff. Dai wants to get back on a guy called Tom Haining who grassed on him and knocking off Haining's son is how he plans to do it. We were *warned* about it only last week.' Jackson removed his right shoe and began hammering on the door again with the heel of it. 'Why do I wear rubber heels anyway? Oh *hell*.'

'Ah. I begin,' Dobie said, 'to see the light. This is the boy you were talking about—'

The door opened and the face of Horatio Carter peered cautiously round it. Cautiously, and displaying apparent perturbation. He opened the door further, revealing two more of the ubiquitous white-jacketed gentlemen in close attendance. 'Now looky here,' Jackson said, about to brandish his shoe threateningly and then changing his mind, 'I'm a police officer and I'm here in the dereliction of my duties and I demand to see a responsible official of this establishment immediately. Do I make myself clear?'

'Er, well, no,' Carter said, his eyes darting past Jackson to meet Dobie's placid, indeed ruminative gaze. 'But obviously a mistake, *another* mistake has been made. Professor Dobie, of course, I . . . Yes. Recognize. And you, sir, are *really* a police officer?'

'I keep *telling* you I am. I'll reduce my identical dottyments if you require them.' Jackson was clearly in a state of high excitement.

'No, no, that won't be necessary. In fact your arrival here couldn't be more opportune. We have very urgent need of your services.'

'What? Why?'

'Because someone's just been murdered,' Carter said.

Thursday March 29th
Another really dull day.
Aren't they all?

No news. No letters. Nothing. Tried to work on my novel but no, it wouldn't gel.

Everybody seems to be on edge, somehow. Like in prison when they're leading someone off to the execution chamber. But I can't see any reason for it. Bad vibes, maybe.

Horse has got the sulks and won't talk to me. Charlie Chan won't even let me help him with his bloody crossword puzzles. The paranoid kid down the passage goes

on and on about he thinks his cover's been blown, like
John le fucking Carré or something. And the big guy next
door is the worst of the lot, even worse than the Chicken,
just sits there staring at the newspaper and clenching and
unclenching his fists like he'd like to crumple the thing up
and ram it down someone's throat. How can I ever write
a book about this place? It's like being *in* a crossword
puzzle. With all the clues screwed up.

1 across   Backward horse is in at the death (3,3)

—except they used that one in that Jack Nicholson thing,
didn'tthey? A pretty stupid film that was, too. Going mad,
it isn'tlike that at all. I can say that quite definitely. Going
mad is

He stopped typing.
He listened instead.
Footsteps. Outside. Heavy, purposeful. Clumping along down
the passageway. He knew all the footsteps by now but he didn't
recognize these. Further down the corridor, a door slammed loudly.
Someone shouted.
Something was happening. Seymour wondered what.

'Now listen,' Jackson said, striding vigorously down the passageway. 'There's a prisoner here called Cooper, you know who I mean?
Well, I want someone to get through to whoever's on duty at
the main gate and tell him that Cooper isn't to be allowed through,
under whatever circumstances. He may try to do a bunk. In that
case, he's got to be stopped. Never mind why. I have my reasons.'
'He won't be breaking out,' Carter said. 'You can be quite sure
of that.'
'I don't know that I can. Frankly, the security here—'
'He's the one who's dead.'
'Ah,' Jackson said. 'Is he now.'
Not the wittiest of rejoinders. But then he had yet again been
taken quite seriously aback.

Despite Dobie's increasing familiarity with the characteristic con-
tortions adopted by other people's corpses when sprawled untidily

out over the floor, he was still unable to view them with that degree of professional aplomb achieved, as a matter of course, by Kate, or with that air of faintly proprietorial approval demonstrated by Jackson. He didn't go so far as to avert his gaze while Jackson was examining the body, but he contrived none the less to suggest his own dissociation from all these goings-on, gazing fixedly into the middle distance like a Pekinese owner whose pet has just voluminously vomited over somebody's suede leather shoes. The corpse in question lay almost in the exact centre of a cell room virtually identical to that in which he and Jackson had been until a few moments ago incarcerated; it was that of a large fair-haired man whose features (since it lay face downwards) weren't immediately discernible, though it was apparent that something extremely nasty had happened in that area where the thick blond hair cascaded down over the nape of the neck. There was blood and stuff there. Ugh. Jackson, who had stooped over at a dangerous angle in order to perceive the deader's face more clearly, righted himself and, teetering awkwardly back on his heels, stepped back a couple of paces.

'That's our Ivor all right. Well, I'm blessed.'

'What happened to him?'

'What *happened*? He's been shot. That's the exit wound you can see there, the entry's right in the centre of the forehead. He must have been facing the gun when . . .'

'Or looking out the window.'

'*Or*, I was going to say, looking out of the window when . . .' Jackson circumnavigated the cell floor cautiously and peered, equally cautiously, at the open window space. Behind the bars, green leaves glistened in the raindrops, a grey cloudtorn sky. And on the floor, a corpse. *Our Ivor*. Or Martin Cooper. A name that fitted an entry on a minidisc corresponding, in turn, to an entry in Dobie's memory store . . . that no longer corresponded to anything. . . . There were times when, in their endless pursuit of mathematical paradox, the cells of Dobie's brain seemed themselves to have become locked in an endless circle, as a natural response to the ultimate inconceivable weirdness of life; this was one of them.

'The room was locked, was it?' Jackson, turning back and towards Carter, who also stood by the door leaning slightly forwards like an attentive footman in a very old British B-movie. 'Who *found* him?'

'I did. But just. . . . Only because I was running a routine surveillance check on the monitor screen and there he *was*, lying on the floor. I didn't realize that he'd been . . . I thought he'd fainted or something like that. So I came round at once. And then, of course . . .'

'Did you examine the body?'

'Only in the way that you just did. And he was clearly dead.'

'Not long dead, though.'

'The wound was still bleeding, certainly. And of course he seemed to be perfectly OK at the time of the previous monitor check. Half an hour earlier.'

'And what was he doing then?'

'Standing by the window. Looking out of it.'

'Yes. That's how it happened all right. Someone out there among the trees with a gun. A pistol, by the look of it.'

'But people here aren't *allowed* to have guns.'

'Someone here has got one, all the same.'

Dobie wasn't paying too much attention to all this. He, too, was looking out of the window, but without seeing anything very much; the expression on his face was one of total vacancy, but Kate would have recognized it as being, on the contrary, indicative of intense and probably highly idiosyncratic ratiocination. The little grey cells were back in operation, putting two and two together to make three, as usual. 'All right,' Jackson was saying. 'I'll ask you to lock this room again, if you'll be so good, and let me have the key. My colleagues should be here in fifteen minutes or so and in the mean time I'd best have a word with the Director. He won't be too pleased at this development.'

'Yes, I mean no. Not pleased at all. He'll be in his office. I'll take you there.'

'No need for that. I know the way. I'd like you to return to your own office, if you would, carry on as usual for the time being. Same goes for those two. . . . The warders. Say nothing to anyone. Follow your normal routine, as far as possible. I'll know where you are if I've any further questions to put to you. And if you'll take Mr Dobie along with you, so I know where *he* is, I'll be greatly obliged.'

'Oh. Right. Certainly,' Carter said.

Carter's first action on entering his office was one that Dobie found immensely reassuring. To the left of his desk was a small green metal cabinet. This Carter opened with a key. Inside the cabinet was a bottle of Dimple Haig. This Carter placed on his desk. Inside the neck of the bottle was a cork. This Carter removed. On another shelf of the cabinet were several glass tumblers, two of which Carter also placed on the desk and proceeded forthwith to fill, or very nearly. Dobie nodded sagely. It's well known that in times of great stress and strain one does well to fall back on a comforting and familiar routine and Popeye, though a psychiatrist and a fitness freak to boot, obviously had sound instincts at bottom.

'Well. . . .' Carter said.

'Yes, well. . . .' Dobie said. *Cheers* hardly seemed an appropriate rejoinder. They sat down on opposite sides of the desk and with one accord imbibed the invigorating liquid. Dobie's head in fact was still aching slightly from his over-indulgence of the night before and a hair of the dog, he decided, would do him no harm at all. On the other hand, he didn't intend to get sloshed. Not a good idea. Especially since out of the fog swirling around in his brain some kind of a pattern seemed at last to be emerging. A paradox, taking shape. A picture forming. . . .

'All very well to talk about following normal routine but this sort of thing is *disturbing*. Damned disturbing. Another little snort?'

'Oh. Right. Certainly,' Dobie said.

Carter refilled Dobie's tumbler and added a good three fingers to the content of his own. His hand appeared to be perfectly steady, but there was that in his facial expression which suggested him to be badly shaken up by the morning's events, as well he might be. 'We had a suicide here last year. Someone hanged himself. But we've never had a murder. And it can't be anything else, can it? Someone shot him. Deliberately. But why?'

'I expect Inspector Jackson will soon establish the facts,' Dobie said a little dreamily. 'I understand it may turn out to be a gangland killing.'

'A *what*?'

'As they call it.'

'But that's absurd.'

'Oh, I don't know. This place is full of former drug addicts, after all. People with contacts with what used to be called the underworld – only of course it's the overworld, these days. Finan-

210

cially speaking, anyway. Lots of money to be made from drugs. Everybody says so. At any rate I imagine Jackson's thinking along some such lines.'

'But the whole idea of this place is to keep them *away* from those contacts.'

'Perhaps.' Dobie's voice had become dreamier than ever, to the point of seeming almost somnambulistic. 'But one makes them unexpectedly. One goes out into the country for a gentle jog, a little healthy exercise, and then . . . I take it that *is* how you met her?'

'Met her?'

'Beverley Sutro. In the first place, that's to say.'

'I never . . .'

Carter stopped rather abruptly. His face had become darkly flushed, possibly as a result of his having drunk the whisky in his tumbler rather too quickly and possibly not. Dobie's expression, on the other hand, was as palely vacant as ever. 'Later on, of course,' he said, 'you met her *here*. You're the gentleman she was seeing on Saturday afternoons. I could see how *she* worked it – getting in and out of here, I mean – but I couldn't see how *you* worked it. Not until just now. So I don't suppose Jackson's tumbled to it yet. He'll be a bit annoyed with you when he does, though, I shouldn't wonder.'

'He knows perfectly well where I am on Saturday afternoons. Invariably.' Carter made what was intended to be a gesture of impatience but which somehow lacked sufficient resolution to pass for such. 'So does everybody else. I'm *here* all right. With—'

'With Adrian Seymour. Wednesdays and Saturdays.'

'Exactly. It's all on the treatment schedule.'

'Exactly. And the treatment schedule includes hypnotherapy.'

'But that doesn't mean—'

'It means the inducement of a state of hypnosis,' Dobie said patiently. 'You don't have to be a psychiatrist to know *that*.'

'Look, just because . . .'

Carter stopped again, abruptly as before.

'He remembers her, you see,' Dobie said. 'Not consciously, of course. But in his dreams. And you don't have to be a psychiatrist to see how *that* might happen, too. Of course it was seeing her photograph in the newspaper that triggered off his recollection, so to speak . . . so if Beverley hadn't been killed, everything might have been all right in that respect. Except that you couldn't have hoped to keep up those assignations for very much longer, could you? She'd've been rumbled sooner or later. And so would you. Simple in one way, I grant you . . . but much too complicated in others. Don't you agree?'

'But she *liked* complications. She thought it was . . . I don't know . . . more *fun* doing it like that and fooling everybody. Oh God,' Carter said. 'She was a *weird* kid. You've got to realize that.'

'I do. I also realize you probably have a weakness for weird people. Otherwise, you'd hardly be in your profession.'

The sound of Carter's breathing, Dobie realized, had now become clearly audible. Odd, for a man who liked to keep himself in peak condition. But then the little office was extremely quiet. Very soon Jackson's colleagues would arrive, baying no doubt like foxhounds and trampling round in circles, but meantime the passageways were silent, except for the occasional sounds of hurried footsteps outside the door; minions being summoned, perhaps, to the Director's office. It was also odd that no one, apparently, had heard the sound of a shot that morning. But that had been outside the building . . . and besides, there were silencers, things like that. . . .

'You're right. That's how it started off. But it's not going to be my profession for very much longer. You know,' Carter said, 'I wrote out my resignation last weekend. I've been waiting for an opportunity to hand it in, but what with the police buzzing round the place like bees round a hive and putting everyone in a tizzy . . . Maybe it's just as well you've decided to force my hand, if that's what you're doing. I don't know how the hell you found out about it but I'm almost glad that you have. That *someone* has. Yesterday I was talking to Ram about it and I as near as a toucher came out with the whole thing. But . . . Shit, I don't want to talk to a psychiatrist. I *am* a psychiatrist. That's half of the problem.'

'The other half of the problem is dead,' Dobie said.

'Indeed. Which makes the whole thing seem all the more inexplicable. Even more crazy. Because . . .' Carter threw up his hands again, this time in a rather more convincing gesture of despair – or maybe of futility. 'Crazy about a girl, that's a figure of speech, we just don't *use* the word in that way, and yet the way I was behaving, what else can you *call* it? And now she's

212

dead it's still the same, only a different *kind* of crazy, you know what I mean? I just can't understand now what I thought I was *doing*. What *we* were doing. I mean, there's no way I can make *you* understand this, either, but it wasn't really the sex bit. I don't think she ever enjoyed the sex bit at all and I'm not sure that I did, either. That was just the *excuse*. For all the rest of it.'

'Yes,' Dobie said. 'I can understand that perfectly.'

'You can?'

'Yes. In a place like this, you naturally think in terms of sexual repression, just as you would in that girls' school round the corner. You *are* repressed, and so was she. But not sexually. That's the excuse. The let-out. Just as it is for everyone else. But of course the real trouble isn't sex at all. It's boredom.'

'Oh, my God,' Carter said again. 'You are *so* right.'

'And as sex is obviously just as boring as everything else . . . naturally you have to make it seem exciting somehow. I imagine Beverley would have been good at that. She wasn't any good at hockey, but she was good at other kinds of games. At fooling people. I understand all that because my wife was just the same. And someone killed *her*, too. That's the trouble with games of that kind. They can be dangerous.'

'Is that why you . . . ?'

'Perhaps.'

'Or is it a game for you, too?'

Dobie had to suppose that the habit of asking questions was engrained in those of the psychiatric persuasion. As indeed in his own profession also, where – however – the important thing is to ask the right ones. From Carter's viewpoint, it could hardly matter whether he viewed it as a game or not; the question could only be designed as another means of packing up the board as unobtrusively as possible, of shovelling all those nasty red hotels away out of sight. He sighed, and shook his head.

'Actually,' Dobie said, 'I'm never bored. I don't know why not. Some flaw in my nature, I suppose. It makes it hard for people to understand *me*, sometimes. They think I'm absent-minded, when really I'm thinking about something that interests me more than the things that *they*'re thinking about. Of course I don't *mind* that. Though sometimes I think that maybe I should.'

'I remember reading about your wife,' Carter said, 'in the papers.'

'They gave it quite a splash.'

'When I saw Bev's picture in the papers, my reaction was . . . different. All I wanted to do was to look the other way. I've been doing that ever since. As though the whole thing was really . . . I suppose I was afraid that someone might assume that I . . . *did* it. I mean . . .'

'You had a good enough motive, certainly.'

'And quite a . . . responsibility. You might say that if it weren't for me, she'd still be alive.'

'That's undeniable.'

'But I didn't kill her.'

And that, Dobie thought, had always been obvious. What Carter had done was confuse the issue, which – at least to a mathematical intellect – was considerably worse. Quite unforgiveable, in fact. 'And,' he said, with some severity, 'you don't even know who did.'

'No, I don't. But . . . Do *you*?'

'As a matter of fact, I do,' Dobie said. 'But that isn't to the present point. I mean, that's one of the things that might very well interest other people but doesn't really interest *me*, or not in the way I'm quite certain you mean. After all, it's just another let-out, isn't it? Killing people? Crime is just another sociocultural phenomenon – or at least, that's what you lot seem to be telling all your patients. It's not surprising if now and then one of them believes you.'

Carter stared at him for a few moments before reaching again for his whisky glass. Outside, other footsteps rapped quickly down the corridor; a woman's high heels; Miss Daly, summoned to the presence. 'What we *claim* is that the root causes of any specific crime can be heuristically established. *Can* be. But nobody claims that the whole chain of effective factors in any given case can be elucidated in such a way as to . . . Look, a *let-out*, I don't think that's the right way to look at it. It's hardly instrumentally useful to say . . . In fact it's definitely retrogressive. Crime as the easy way out, that's a typical *policeman*'s view, if you don't mind my saying so.'

'Well, then let's say the *greedy* way out.'

'No, I wouldn't agree to that, either.'

'But *she* was greedy,' Dobie said. 'Wasn't she?'

Kate, also, had had a tiring morning and was inclined to be snappish. Although as a doctor she was hardly in a position to disapprove of death on a point of principle, she didn't like being obliged to deal with its more obvious manifestations at times when she should normally have been running her clinic and when, moreover, that old layabout Paddy Oates should have been at hand to deal with them. 'So where *is* Paddy?'

'Gone to a funeral, I understand,' Foxy Boxy said. 'A relative of his. As I believe.' Kate made a snorting sound through her nostrils and gave the recumbent corpse beside which she knelt a savage Kung Fu prod with her stiffened fingers. 'So what does Jacko expect *me* to tell him? This man's been shot. Cause of death, a bullet. What else?'

'Yes. We've got it. A nine millimetre, we reckon. It's being packed off to ballistics right now.' Foxy, familiar with Kate's little moods, was being conciliatory. 'Death would have been instantaneous, I suppose? Going straight through his head like that?'

'In this case, yes. Of course where *men's* brains are concerned, you can never be sure. But where a fair amount of them have been spattered over the floor —'

'Very nasty weapon, yes, a nine millimetre. Fired at close range, would you say?'

'From outside that window, anyway. No sign of any powder burns. I'm not into ballistics, Foxy. The FS crowd should be able to tell you all you need to know about *that*.' Kate got to her feet and smoothed her skirt. 'For the rest, the guy seems to have been in crude good health. Muscular tissue's in pretty good shape for a man of his age and I don't see any obvious signs of drug dependency. So what was he doing in *here*?'

'We'll be finding that out soon enough, I dare say.'

'They'll have the medical record on file here. I'd like to see it.'

'I'm sure we can dig that out for you. You, er . . . Is there anything *wrong*?'

'Of course there's something wrong. The man's dead.'

'But apart from that, you say he's in pretty good nick?'

'I'd say he'd been *in* the nick. Done time. Does Jacko know about that?'

Foxy shook his head admiringly. 'Oh yes. We know this lad of old. He's on our own formbook and has been for years. One of our pet nasties, in fact. And you're right, we *did* put him away. But not for long enough.'

'Well, he's been put away this time for good and all,' Kate said, stripping off her surgical gloves. 'Get him off to the morgue as soon as you can and I'll do the PM this afternoon, OK? Now I'd better go and see the Director. Jacko's with him now, I take it?'

'I believe so, yes. And Mr Dobie.'

Kate stared at him.

'*Dobie*? What's *Dobie* doing here?'

'Well may you ask,' Foxy said, and shrugged. 'Always in the thick of things, is your Mr Dobie.'

'I don't believe this,' Kate said.

The door of the office next to Carter's stood ajar and Dobie pushed it open and went inside. He wasn't surprised to find the Registry empty; he had already heard the sound of voices coming from the Director's office almost opposite and Kathleen Daly's had been among them, a firm and resonant contralto raised in counter to Jackson's modest tenor and the Director's rather wobbly basso profundo. For a moment he had been reminded of that scene from *Don Giovanni* from which, in a sense, the whole of this present imbroglio had originated, the cassette tape unwinding on the car stereo system, the rain beating mercilessly down against the windscreen; now he, perhaps in the role of Uninvited Guest, made his way past Miss Daly's desk towards the inner sanctum of the computer console and paused there, a little uncertainly. He wasn't good at searching for things and he knew it. Perhaps. . . . He looked for a moment at the telephone but didn't pick it up. Jackson was good at searching for things, if he had someone to tell him what to look for and to show him where to look for it. That was Jackson's job. But Jackson, clearly, was right now very busy. Maybe if . . .

The key of the filing cabinet was in the cabinet lock, on a ring from which other keys, efficiently colour-coded, dangled. Dobie turned the key, pulling open the topmost drawer, and commenced his search. He wasn't good at looking for things but now and again he got lucky. That morning he had found, for instance, a hockey stick. Carter, on the other hand, had found a corpse, a considerably more spectacular achievement. The topmost drawer of the cabinet contained only tape cassettes, neatly stacked and carefully labelled. Not, of course, of Mozartean opera, but of Drs Carter and Ram and Mighell and Hudson, all holding self-consciously cheery converse with their various patients. One such

216

tape had been put consistently to good use on those wet Saturday afternoons, the voices on it – like those of Jackson and Morris Train and Kathleen Daly – audible in the passageway outside the closed office door, while inside the office Adrian Seymour sat peaceably in hypnotic stupor and Carter entertained a naked Beverley Sutro within his own inner sanctum, games, yes, games people play, games of a ludicrousness almost akin to that of grand opera but nevertheless to be taken very seriously by those concerned, their pleasurableness being indeed directly related to their degree of complexity, a board game like Monopoly but being played on a hard-cushioned couch with the stakes getting higher and higher as the greed of the two competitors increased and the rental fees went up and up, the girl had been greedy, yes, but so had Carter, though being a highly trained psychiatrist he naturally hadn't had sense enough to realize it, the implicit threat of the square that said GO DIRECTLY TO JAIL being in itself enough to keep the rental payments rolling in, fifty pounds for each throw of the dice, motivation there all right. . . .

But he hadn't done it, no. He was responsible for what had happened. That was all.

So was she.

Because there'd been another occasion when the door of this office had been ajar and padding on her sneakered feet down the passageway outside, hockey stick in hand, little Greedyguts Sutro had heard another voice speaking on the telephone and had pushed the door gently open and had gone in and the voice on the telephone had gone on speaking, had mentioned a name that Greedyguts had recognized and a seemingly colossal sum of money and the stakes had suddenly gone up again, from fifty a throw to five thousand, because this was still a game, yes, but a game of a different kind with a new player . . . and much more fun. . . .

. . . because a lot more dangerous, she'd have to have realized that, but even so . . . Nothing. Dobie slid open the bottommost drawer and lowered his head to peer inside. More tapes, discs, a few unlabelled files. A box file might. . . . But these weren't box files. No. Just folders.

'Is *this* what you're looking for?'

Dobie raised his head, blinking nervously.

'Ah,' he said. 'Yes. *That's* it.'

217

'It's Ivor's, really. Ivor Halliday's. But he won't be wanting it any more.'

'Yes. I mean, no. I imagine not. It's rather a. . . . It's a bit *heavy* for you, isn't it?'

'I think you'll find it's accurate, all the same. Though you won't be so stupid as to. . . . But you're not a stupid man. Anything but. And now you're going to demonstrate your undoubted intelligence by stepping outside with me. Very quietly.'

'Oh, come now,' Dobie said. 'It's too late for that. You know it is.'

'Maybe. And maybe not. We'll see.'

'Medical records? Yes. Of course. Our Miss Daly will look them out for you. She's in the Registry, right across the passageway.'

'In fact she isn't,' Kate said. 'We've just been in there. The place is empty.'

'But. . . .' The Director peered towards her puzzledly. 'She was here with us until a moment ago. She only just left.'

Box went to the door and summoned Wallace.

'That the blonde lady, sir? The one with the . . . ? Just this minute gone out. With Mr Dobie.'

'Gone *out*?'

And Kate, 'With *Dobie*?'

'Just went off, they did. In Mr Dobie's car.'

'Oh my God,' Kate said. 'They've *eloped*.'

'Didn't ought to have done that,' Foxy said. 'Against the Inspector's orders. Ought to know a whole lot better, Mr Dobie did.'

'He was always a fool,' Kate said, 'for a pretty face.'

'I'll have to tell Mr Jackson about this.'

'And don't waste any time about it, either.'

Dobie didn't doubt that the person sitting next to him in the passenger seat of his car was – whatever Carter and his other colleagues might have to say on the subject – more than slightly bonkers. Madness doesn't after all manifest itself in so conveniently obvious a way as in the case of Captain Scott, who in comparison with Dobie's present companion might well pass as a model of gracefully balanced behaviour. Miss Daly had already killed two people this week and if she felt she had to kill a third clearly wouldn't hesitate to do so. One had to say 'felt' rather

218

than 'thought' because thinking didn't really come into it – that was the trouble.

Dobie had just spent half an hour talking to a pseudo-intellectual nitwit whose brains had, over some considerable spell, been addled by some strange kind of sexual compulsion. If he'd never met Beverley Sutro, Carter might have been all right – whatever that means. Perhaps if she'd never met Ivor Halliday, Miss Daly would have been all right. She and Carter, in other words, would have been enabled to carry on their respective social duties efficiently and effectively, making – as was the common belief – the world a better place. But perhaps there was something fundamentally wrong, either with the way in which they carried out their duties or, much more probably, with the common belief itself. It's dangerous, Dobie thought, to ignore the presence of evil in the world, to play with the gypsies in the wood. Play with people like Big Ivor and Beverley Sutro. Because that way you can end up more dangerous than either.

Miss Daly didn't *look* dangerous, of course. Right now she looked obstinate and sullen, staring out through the rain-splashed windscreen of the car. Seeing – as Dobie already had seen – that the main gate of the Centre had been left open, no doubt to facilitate the recent sudden influx of lamp-flashing police cars. 'Go on driving,' Miss Daly said tightly. 'I wouldn't even *think* about stopping if I were you. Drive straight out and then turn right, there's a good boy.' Dobie was fully prepared to be a good boy. Miss Daly still had the gun and it didn't even *have* to be accurate, the way she was holding it, which was with the end with the hole in it pressed firmly into Dobie's side, just above the hipbone. It was rather a chilly morning, but Dobie's ungloved hands were already leaving slippery sweat marks on the steering-wheel. 'Tell me,' Miss Daly said, showing no perceptible signs of relaxation as Dobie obeyed her instructions and urged the Fiesta onwards down the road, 'I can't get away with it.'

'G-g-get away with what?'

'Getting away with murder, isn't that the cant expression? And on second thoughts, don't tell me anything. Just keep on driving. Rather faster, though, if you please.'

'You won't get away with it,' Dobie said. 'Not in *this* car, you won't. It won't do much over sixty. And anyway we're driving in the wrong direction.' Though possibly they weren't. This wasn't the direction, after all, in which anyone would have expected them to go. 'People *do* get away with it sometimes, I've no doubt. But not often enough to make it a really profitable practice. And certainly not in *your* case. You screwed it up right from the start, if I may say so.'

'I enjoyed it, anyway,' Miss Daly said. 'I enjoyed screwing *her* up. That nasty little bitch. A couple of minutes with that fucking hockey stick of hers, you could say that made the whole thing worth while. It really made my day, as Clint would put it.'

Or Ivor Halliday. Ivor had liked hurting people. And Kathleen Daly had to have caught the habit. Not, Dobie thought, that it's *really* Kathleen Daly who's sitting beside me, the Kathleen Daly they all know at the Centre. It's someone different. The difference is hardly visible, but it's there. Drugs aren't the only things you can get yourself hooked on.

'Yes, but you didn't do it properly. You thought she was dead. But she wasn't.'

'And so,' the different Kathleen Daly said, 'what?'

'A doctor knows when someone's dead and someone isn't. A doctor would have made quite sure she was dead . . . and couldn't tell anyone what had happened when she came to. So it wasn't any of the doctors who duffed her up. But what confused the issue—'

'Just keep driving,' Miss Daly said, 'and shut your trap. I don't want to talk about it, not any more.'

'But we're *supposed* to talk about it.'

'Why?'

'Well . . . It's the tradition.'

'Fuck the tradition,' Miss Daly said.

'Oh yes. By all means. If you say so. By the way, that gun . . .'

'What about it?'

'I don't suppose you could, er . . . You see, the way you're holding it, it could go off by accident.'

'It could also go off on purpose, if I get annoyed with you. And I'm prone to fits of very naughty temper.'

'Oh, right,' Dobie said. 'A little faster, you said?'

'Uh-huh.'

Unquestionably, this was a very awkward situation. But that was the real trouble with murderers, he thought sadly; in the last resort, they're not very reasonable people. They don't seem to be able to follow through, somehow, in matters of cause and effect. 'That's not why you make mistakes, though. It's nothing to do with fits of temper. You kill the wrong people. That's all.'

'Look, they force me into it. They don't give me any choice. *They*'re the ones who make the bloody mistakes.'

'What mistake did Ivor make?'

'Screwing me.'

'What?'

'You heard. Just a business discussion it was supposed to be. Money. That was all I wanted. But then he has to pull me into the bedroom and tear all my clothes off and screw me and show me that I . . . wanted that as well. . . . Damned right I did. How was I to know that bloody kid was his *daughter*? He'd've killed me if he'd found out . . . and he was bound to. I knew he'd kill me . . . after he'd shot that other one . . . so I killed him first, the bastard. Oh my God . . . *what* a bastard . . . and so was that Bev kid, really. That's going to be my mission in life – to kill all the bastards I can find. Starting with the clever ones, like you. I *knew* you'd be a bastard, soon as I saw you. I was right.'

One moment, seemingly almost normal. The next, right over the top. But the tone of her voice still casual, relaxed, unexcited. I've got a right one here, Dobie thought.

'You know,' he said, trying his best to maintain the conversational tone while steering an uneven course past the Dame Margaret School, 'there are things that are called recurring ciphers. Some people are like that. There'll always be girls around like Beverley Sutro. There'll always be men around like whatshis name. His name doesn't matter because there are others in Cardiff exactly like him, and one of those others is going to take his place. Only he won't be looking for a boy in a Rehabilitation Centre. He'll be looking for *you*. Surely you realize that, don't you?'

'He'll have to find me, though,' Miss Daly said.

'Oh, they'll find you. Even if the police don't find you, the other lot will. You let the boys down and they don't like that. There's nothing *personal* about it. From now on, you're a number on a contract. Another recurring cipher. That's all.'

'No. They won't find me. I'm going to Italy. I always wanted to see Italy and now I've got the money. . . . Two thousand he gave me. In advance. I insisted on that as part of the deal. Clever of me, wasn't it?'

'As things have turned out, yes. But even so—'

'How would you fancy going to Italy, Dobie? Don't you ever hanker after a bit of southern romance?'

'Romance? Well, I, I—'

'You're a clever bastard, too. We clever people ought to stick together. And that way I'd stand a better chance of getting through at the airport.' No longer casual and relaxed. Not the least bit. 'Honeymoon couple sort of thing. Weekend returns to Como. Only of course we wouldn't use the returns.' Incredible, Dobie thought. She was quite serious.

'*I* mightn't use the return. That's what worries me.'

Miss Day surprised him again. She giggled.

'You might do better to worry about what's going to happen when I tell you to stop the car. In five minutes' time. My way, you go on worrying a while longer.'

'I see your point,' Dobie said. 'The trouble is I'm not very quick on the uptake. In fact I'm not very clever at all. Not really.' Clever enough, however, to realize that however sick she might be feeling she wasn't about to press that trigger while the car was cavorting along at its best speed of just on seventy miles an hour. They'd *both* be killed if she did that. 'So why—'

'Why not?' Miss Daly giggled again. 'The ship . . . The ship . . .'

'What ship?'

'The ship's gone down . . . And everybody's drowned . . .'

She stopped giggling. Something had happened to her breathing. It had gone all jerky. Dobie didn't like the sound of it. He glanced down towards the speedometer, which . . . yes . . . showed sixty-five. She wouldn't. . . . Surely? At sixty-five? Would she?

'Sunk with all hands . . .'

Dobie had often felt that if called upon to meet his Creator he would like best to be engaged at the time in some rather tricky mental mathematical calculation, so that God could at once tell him where he'd gone wrong. And *something* had gone wrong. That was obvious.

'I didn't need *him*. And I don't need you. Stop the car.'

Dobie did no such thing. Careering downhill at, if anything, a slightly increased velocity he began to work out the equation that would adequately demonstrate the margin of safety factor applicable to a speed of 70 m.p.h. in a dilapidated Ford Fiesta, given a tangential equivalent not in excess of 15 degrees . . . this to an accuracy of within four decimal places, which would surely be sufficient. . . .

Or anyway *would* have been surely sufficient if he hadn't in the stress of the moment very understandably forgotten all about the watersplash still covering the escape road to a depth of just over two feet and seven inches . . . and which of course he failed to see until it was eighty-five hundredths of a second too late. . . .

'It was like this, Your Worship,' Dobie said, sailing inelegantly towards the windscreen.

But Kate merely snorted.
'There you go,' she said. 'Typical, really.'

10

Dobie was really quite comfortable in the Royal Infirmary, though a difference of opinion arose almost at once as to how his condition should be treated. The consultant physician was firmly convinced that his patient was suffering from the after-effects of a nasty concussion, while Dobie no less emphatically maintained that his behaviour and manner of speech were perfectly normal. Kate could see that a great deal could be said for both points of view but agreed that it would certainly be prudent to keep Dobie under observation for a few days, partly to be on the safe side but chiefly to ensure that over that period of time he'd be prevented from scaling (and destroying) valuable trees, driving to the public danger, escaping from the police with generously-proportioned murderesses, and generally making an idiot of himself. Though you could never be completely *sure* of that. Not with Dobie.

As soon as the news of his latest escapade had reached the

general public, the usual fan mail began to arrive. Among the get well cards was a carefully indited missive from Elspeth, bearing a spirited depiction of a pussy-cat with enormous whiskers and with several large X's scrawled on the back. This, and a few others, Kate allowed to stand on Dobie's night table. She gave strict instructions to the ward sister, however, to discourage all female visitors. Especially that Mrs Train.

Here, again, she considered she was being prudent, since – as the police and civic authorities had decided to issue the most determinedly noncommittal of official statements to the media – the gentlemen of the local press had drawn their own conclusions and had treated the whole affair with unusual discretion, the *Sneak* (for instance) merely offering its eager readers the banner headline across three columns:

COLLEGE PROFESSOR'S
WHIRLWIND ROMANCE
ENDS IN TRAGEDY

Cardiff Romeo Survives
Secret Suicide Pact
With Sexy Secretary

'I'll say one thing for Mr Dobie,' Foxy said, tossing the *Sneak* into the receptacle conveniently placed to the right of his office desk. 'No murderers are safe when he's around. He makes a tidy job of it while he's at it.'

'Not many policemen are safe when he's around, either,' Jackson said. With feeling.

However, he toddled round to the Infirmary that evening and, having shown his identicky dottyments to the ward sister, was permitted to enter the inner sanctum where Kate was rearranging Dobie's collection of memorabilia (observing in so doing that not many of the get well cards had emanated from his colleagues, and none at all from the members of the University Senate) and the Man Himself was leaning back on an imposing pile of pillows, looking as pale and interesting as he could with a thick roll of bandages circumscribing his jawline.

'Oh h'ho,' Dobie said, sounding like something recently thrown out of Sandhurst.

'Great,' Kate said. 'Now Jacko's here, maybe someone can tell me what *really* happened.'

'Wouldn't be the first time someone's been croaked in porridge,' Jackson said. 'There's always limits to the amount of protection we can give these people. Even in flowery there'll always be a few hard boys around who're ready to do the Man a favour, especially when there's something in it for them. We reckoned there wouldn't be anyone like that in the Rehabilitation Centre and we were right – there wasn't. So if they wanted to get to the Haining boy they had to put someone in. So they did.'

'Harriday.'

Dobie, determined to make effective contribution. But it wasn't very. Kate shushed him with an impatient flap of her hand.

'Halliday. He took on the contract. Only of course he couldn't have gone in *as* Ivor Halliday, with a record like *he's* got he'd have been rumbled from the start. He had to find another identity for himself. Well, we've traced this Cooper geezer, he's an authentic drug addict with a six-year medical sheet – a genuine case for treatment. But he's only twenty-two years old and physically he hardly resembles Halliday at all. So Halliday had to switch the record sheet to make it agree with his own age and overall appearance. Or more exactly he had to find someone to do that for him.'

Dobie nodded. 'Yes. Kathreen Dary.'

'Kathreen. . . . Yes, *her*. I had your chap Merrick on the blower for all of fifteen minutes explaining how she did it but I must say I still don't . . . But apparently she had to erase the Cooper record sheet and type in a description of Halliday, so that when the doctors checked on the record—'

'Except,' Dobie said, 'she made a mesh of the erasure and cut off part of the accesh code ash well. Thereby incapatitashing—'

'Yes, but then some cluck went and put that right for her. Free of charge. While *she* expected to make five thousand nicker on the deal. Not bad for ten minutes' work on the q.t. And of course Halliday . . . No denying it, he always had a way with the ladies. She had to have been under the influence, so to speak. That's the trouble with working with drug addicts. You make undesirable contacts.'

'*She* was an undeshirable—'

'Mind you, once he'd had his spot of bed fun with her he'd have wanted to keep his contacts with her to a minimum, for obvious reasons. In the end he'd have confirmed the details of the deal over the telephone. A bit of a risk, you might have thought, but safer than arranging any more meetings . . . and in the ordinary way it would have been secure enough, with no one around to overhear the conversation. But,' Jackson said, lowering his voice impressively, 'it just so happened there was someone around who *shouldn't* have been around, who'd just left Carter's office next door, who was nosy enough to listen to what the Daly was saying and clever enough to realize what it was all about. After all she'd heard a name mentioned she knew something about. . . . Well, hell, she must've known that Halliday was reckoned to be her father, she'd only have been a kid when her mother was shacking up with him but she'd have remembered him well enough. Not the sort of character it'd be easy to forget, I can tell you. And she wouldn't have had very tender memories.'

'Sho she shought she'd try a bit of brackmail.'

'Right. Maybe she had the idea of paying off an old score or two on her mum's behalf, maybe she thought she saw a way to some easy pickings. . . . But either way she picked the wrong person. When she showed up for the meeting next week hoping for the pay-off, that's just what she got. And badly beaten up into the bargain, partly because Daly really *was* the wrong sort of person and also because Daly knew what the kid had been up to and reckoned she could make it look like a rapist's killing. Which would naturally divert any suspicion away from *her*. By the same token she didn't want the kid's body to be found in the Centre, so she put what she thought was the corpse in the boot of her car, drove out through the gate, and unloaded it a little way down the road. She had a perfectly good excuse for leaving the Centre at that time as she had to report the computer failure so she drove on into Cardiff and that's what she did. As is a matter of record.'

'Yesh, but—'

'And Halliday of course had already arrived that morning. All he had to do was locate the Haining kid and then she'd slip him the gun and he'd carry out the contract and disappear. Only Daly was beginning to get cold feet. She hadn't expected to find the place seething with police asking awkward questions, she hadn't expected Mr Dobie here to be showing such a lively curiosity into

226

the computer entries, and worst of all Halliday had read about the girl in the newspaper and had to have a pretty good idea of who had done it to her. Of course, it's ironic in a way – Halliday working out this plan for killing someone else's son and finding his own daughter being killed as a direct result. Of course Daly couldn't have *known* the kid was his daughter but he wouldn't be disposed to let her off on that account. An eye for an eye, that was always Ivor's motto. Daly was good as dead once Ivor had got hold of her again, and she knew it.'

'And show. . .' Dobie said. 'And show. . .' He had almost given up, but not quite.

'Yesh, and show she decided to cut her losses and run. Halliday being one of the losses, of course. She had to kill him before he got a chance to kill *her*, was the way she saw it. So she didn't give him the gun, after all. She gave him a bullet instead. Smack between the eyes. There's those around as'd give her a medal but of course we can't *allow* that sort of thing. Not on Her Majesty's property, anyway.'

Kate could barely restrain her admiration. 'Jacko, I think it's simply *brilliant*, the way you've gone and worked it all out.'

'Oh well,' Jackson said modestly. 'Old-fashioned police methods usually come up with the goods, y'know, sooner or later. It don't do to be relying all the time on flushes of constipation.'

'Though perhaps it's just as well the case won't ever come to court.'

'You're right there. But then it seems they don't very often when Mr Dobie's around. He's a dab hand at saving the taxpayers' money.'

'Washn't on purposh,' Dobie said indignantly. 'If a little money was shpent on the proper upkeep of the road shistem—'

'It's not as though she *drowned*, Mr Dobie. Dead before she hit the water, according to Dr Coyle here. Took most of the windscreen with her so it's not surprising. *You* got off pretty lightly, if you ask me. Shame about the face, of course, but then it looked a bit odd to start with. And you can always grow another moustache when those stitches have healed.'

'Over my dead body,' Kate said.

Rather a rash thing to say, perhaps. But then Dobie was such an obviously harmless person. . . .

She sat with him for quite a while after Jacko had gone, in a companionable silence. He wasn't after all in very bad condition. It only hurt him when he laughed, as the old joke had it. Soon a pristine Dobie would be safely returned to her, to go maundering about the place as ineffectually as ever.

He wasn't really in tune with the modern world, that was the trouble. He wasn't into all the contemporary trends. Not in criminology or psychiatry or education or anything else. He had no sense of modern *values*. That had to be the *real* Dobie Paradox. Dobie himself.

There he was, propped up on the pillows, as good as gold. He wasn't *really* going to blow up the known physical universe, was he?

Hadn't he got himself deep enough into the soup already?

Kate sighed. Yes, that was the trouble with Dobie all right. . . .

You never could tell what the bastard would be up to next. . . .